THOMAS GAGE

Thomas Gage

James Fleming

JONATHAN CAPE
LONDON

Published by Jonathan Cape 2003

2 4 6 8 10 9 7 5 3 1

Copyright © James Fleming 2003

James Fleming has asserted his right under the Copyright, Designs
and Patents Act 1988 to be identified as the author of this work

First published in Great Britain in 2003 by
Jonathan Cape
Random House, 20 Vauxhall Bridge Road, London SW1V 2SA

Random House Australia (Pty) Limited
20 Alfred Street, Milsons Point, Sydney,
New South Wales 2061, Australia

Random House New Zealand Limited
18 Poland Road, Glenfield,
Auckland 10, New Zealand

Random House South Africa (Pty) Limited
Endulini, 5A Jubilee Road, Parktown 2193, South Africa

The Random House Group Limited Reg. No. 954009
www.randomhouse.co.uk

A CIP catalogue record for this book is available from the British Library

ISBN 0–224–07119-X

Papers used by Random House are natural,
recyclable products made from wood grown in sustainable forests;
the manufacturing processes conform to the environmental
regulations of the country of origin

Typeset by Deltatype Ltd, Birkenhead, Merseyside
Printed and bound in Great Britain by
Clays Ltd, St Ives PLC

Thomas Gage

One

THE MONEY was newly warm against his ribs. Swinging his cane, his feet turned out like a dancing-master, humming and hatless, he strolled down St Martin's Lane and into Trafalgar Square. His hair, which seemed to burst out of his head and was the first thing anyone noticed about him, rippled in the summery breeze. A woman of a comfortable age came walking towards him, a wicker basket on the crook of her arm. She drew level, and he made her a smiling bow, because he'd done what had been asked of him, the day was glorious and life his to command.

He'd been obstinate, had stood out for every last penny. The sum had been disputed, ledgers unsnapped and entanglements placed in his way – deliveries over, deliveries under, discounts misapplied, the quietness of the season. Oh, it had been a game alright. Roberson had tried to make him feel like a provincial, ignorant and wormy. 'Do what you like up there. Ninety days' credit for London trade, plus the usual forgiveness,' the man had said. 'Sixty if you want to keep our business,' he'd replied. He'd braced his calves and stiffened his jaw. 'Sixty, as it always has been with our firm.' Then he'd insisted he receive the debt in bank-notes and counted them twice, under Roberson's nose, despite the fact that it was indecorous.

And there they were, plumping out his London frock-coat, which had been cut three monarchs ago and was no longer easily buttoned. It was stupendous, when he thought about it, an act of a truly lavish god, that this humble commercial operation that was keeping him and Isabel afloat should still be without competitors. No, it was too small a word. He should call it a miracle and have done with it.

He halted, the church to one side, the raw yellow ashlar of the National Gallery to the other. Hands cupped over the smooth porcelain knob of his cane, he gazed around. Mongrels fighting, the arguments of barrow-boys, a squadron of cavalry jingling down Whitehall, bugles piping from Horse Guards, the squeal of ungreased wagon axles. Noise, everywhere noise and haste.

'It's you who should be doing this,' he'd said to Lutwylch, 'you're the one who's running the show. You know the language. I'm just an artist.' But Isabel had been looking severely upon him, and Lutwylch, fob-watched and obedient at her elbow, lawyerish in his wealthy spectacles, had said, 'Think of the fees if I have to send the duns in. Besides, you're going to town anyway. A few strong words and he'll settle.' They'd left it until the last minute, when there was no time to argue. The horses had been unrugged and backed into the traces. Blissett, burly and leather-gaitered, had checked the buckles; was climbing onto his box. 'Don't forget my coffee beans,' Isabel cried. The groom stood back and the coach rumbled out of the cobbled yard.

No point in being a niggard about it, he'd said to himself later. It's for the good of the family. A man who entrusts the exchequer to his wife must accept the obligations that are thereby entered into their arrangements.

'Well, Thomas, did you get the money?' That was what she'd ask him as soon as he got home and the children had gone to their beds. The question would shin up that measured voice of hers and clamber out of her mouth with a cutlass and a brace of pistols at its belt. She might pretend otherwise but within her careful, managing mind that would be the foremost issue. And now, as of twenty minutes ago, he could answer, 'Yes, by God, I did.'

Therefore his character was in credit and he could set about the real purpose of his trip with an unhampered conscience. He removed Isabel from his thoughts and tucked her into a cubbyhole along with Lutwylch and certain aspects of the modern epoch that disquieted him whenever he travelled to London.

His picture, that was the thing, not Roberson or the coffee beans. It wasn't every day of the week that a man had his work hung at the Royal Academy. How would it look? Would he feel it could have been done better? Would anyone pause for more than a second beneath it? He'd imagined some reviewer selecting his pithiest words: 'The work, however, before which everyone halted was that by an unknown artist from Norfolk. His colouring, the texture of paint, the sheer intensity of expression, by these Mr Thomas Gage has elevated his profession to an altogether superior niveau . . .' But now that he was here, a stone's throw away, he felt his confidence ebb. It would look tawdry, a daub, amongst such a wealth of talent. He began to enumerate all the points of composition on which it was open to criticism. Here – such and such; there – the other, ending with the fact that he'd fussed at it and titivated long after he should have left well alone.

He squinnied up at Lord Nelson. A little fellow in his socks, and by no means faultless. But audacious, and with pluck by the gallon.

A button-hole, a crimped red rose-bud laced into a corset of moss, was twirled in front of him.

'Only a ha'penny, sir.' Her wheedling voice took him by surprise and he started.

'I believe I can afford that,' he said, and wishing to diffuse his nervousness, prattled about the fine spell of weather they were having and Nelson also having been a Norfolk man as he stooped to let her grimy fingers pin the flower.

'Luck live in your hat!' she cackled, stepping back to seek fresh custom. He touched his note-case for reassurance. He had a final whittle at his nose. Then he made swiftly across the street to the Academy rooms, his heart bump-bumpering in its socket.

Two

THE COACH was stationary. They were delayed at the railway crossing beside Whistlefield Halt. It was the Cambridge line and Prince Albert, in the company of Her Majesty, was going to be installed as Chancellor of the University. The horses shuffled in the traces. Their braided tails hung despondently, like sausages on a butcher's hook. One of the leaders rolled back its upper lip, angled its head, and began to chew at the top rail of the barrier gate, its stained teeth grinding into the white-painted wood. Blissett's whip leaned at an angle in its pot. The shadow of its lash swayed to and fro on the pale highway. The man himself was dozing beneath a tree a few yards off.

Ten years ago, when Thoroughgood held the reins, the Norwich *Phenomena* had been a crack flyer. Polished and buffed, resplendent in its livery of yellow and chocolate, it had whirled its passengers over the flat eastern roads without a worry in the world. No longer. The railways had seen to that. Its magnificence was gone; it was dying the seedy and ignominious death of a king in exile.

But Thomas did not care. He had no moral or philosophical objection to the railways, on which he had travelled three or four times. The experience had merely been uncongenial to his soul; strident, rude and lacking in honour. He preferred the curiosities of journeying slowly with Blissett, especially in the summer when he would take an outside berth at half the price, on the roof with the luggage. The views that were unfolded across the countryside, the intimate peeps over garden walls and into bedrooms, these were what he relished. Also the old-fashionedness, the hallowed procedures, and the conversations that were to be had with people ·

who had time to think. He could see no merit in urgency for its own sake. Only men who knew they had five minutes to live could have a reason for hurrying. Speed was a thief when one considered it in the round.

He put aside his newspaper and distributed his slight portliness in a general way along the bench. A snap of wind stirred the bale of his rich hair.

Did it matter that the coach had to wait a few minutes or even half an hour provided that it reached Norwich at a reasonable time? Only because he'd stayed longer in London than he'd intended, in fact by three whole days, and Isabel's nose would be out of joint. 'Think what you will, but this is a capricious world,' he would say with an adequacy of penitence. For he had done the business with Roberson and remembered the coffee beans. And what else! His brown eyes took on the glow of a profoundly satisfied man, in which he had the help of a day whose excellence had overwhelmed him ever since 6 a.m., when he'd clambered puffingly up the ladder and found himself the only passenger on the coach.

What hadn't he done! Of a sudden he wished to be at home with his children, quickly, in a single bound, so that he could tell them his news. He said to Blissett, 'How much longer are they going to keep us here, eh?'

Blissett rose and shook his whip until it rattled in the pot and the gatekeeper on the far side of the track looked up. 'When's she coming, then? Quarter of an hour us have been kept here, Mr Gage and self, and that's a quarter too long in my line of work.'

'Any minute now. Royal train to Cambridge. Down from Tottenham at eleven twenty, up from Cambridge at three on the dot this p.m. Speed never to exceed forty—'

'Why's that? 'Fraid it might blow up?'

'Her Majesty may be carrying, or so people say.'

'Then why don't she be like sensible folk and stay put?' He turned towards Thomas. 'It's all because of the German wifey. If she's ready to drop another of those great bullocks, then she shouldn't be out travelling. Plain as a pikestaff. She should be tucked up at home and the doctor patting her hand.' He raised his voice again. 'You over there, you know something? It's the likes of you who're putting the likes of me out of a job.'

'No call to get humpy. It's not my fault.'

'Never said it was. Only making an observation. Anyway, there's your minute gone. So where is she? Mr Simpkins won't be liking this. He'll nail my skin to the wall unless I make up time on the road. As if I could, with the sort of horses he buys nowadays. Look at us, can't even afford to carry a guard any more.'

'Oh, she won't be far away. May have been a problem getting up steam,' the gatekeeper said comfortably, scratching the top of his back on the knob of an iron railing. 'Something of that nature, p'raps.'

'Then stick your ear to the line and have a listen,' commanded Blissett.

'Can't do that. Says in the rule book that nothing—'

'As surely as God made little apples so he gave us gutless nibcocked prats. You give me headache, you do.' Grinding his teeth and muttering, 'Blooming Germans, nothing to do but breed like rain drops,' Blissett returned to the shade of his bush.

The gatekeeper removed his cap and jiggled it a full circle on the tips of his forefingers. He whistled the opening bars of a popular tune. A caged starling continued it from the window of his cottage. The horses shifted their tufty hooves; the harness creaked; a few mean, dry globes of dung golluped into the dust. Otherwise there was a hot and listless silence, through which a family of magpies swooped gleaming onto the sun-striped track.

Thomas said 'damnation' and spread his arms along the back of the bench.

The trees around and the hawthorns that fringed them were heavy in leaf. How did they do it? How did they achieve all those dancing tints of green? How could the colours of a simple leaf be so elusive when in action? It was the wind. It huffed and it puffed and its myriad slaves twirled their skirts, stood on their heads, lay down, sat up and flashed their bellies. So what was the wind that had such a power? An invisible despot, born in a cauldron to invisible parents. 'Oh Nature, thou art a damned deceiving rascal,' he murmured, and closing his eyes, let all the greens and blacks tumble through his blindness. How could he show people what they weren't capable of seeing for themselves? Whoever would be persuaded if he painted not only the facts but also what floated between them, the dreams, the loveliness, the unsayable shapes that gave them light, air, and character, that made his canvases sing for him? He'd been lucky with Mr Wheaton. He still had difficulty believing that this well-dressed man should have made a beeline for *his* picture, his and no other, at the very moment he was standing beneath it. He was sure his heart had lost a good stone in weight for all its jumping about. But he knew Wheaton hadn't properly understood it. He'd said Yes, how beautifully it was realised, with the storm rearing up in the background and Jammy staring intensely over the boat's gunwale. Such a marvellous composition, he'd said, their shoulders touching; such immediacy, such a fine portrayal of boating. But he'd had no feeling for the *nervousness* of the water, nor had he apprehended that what Jammy was staring at was a vision of watery death. Perhaps he'd come to it. Perhaps he'd hang it at the foot of his bed and one morning his wife would remark, 'I do wish you'd put that thing somewhere else. It quite frightens me.' Then Mr Wheaton might come to an understanding of the picture he'd bought.

He should have started painting earlier. All that piddling around being a soldier – parades, drenchings, rising at dawn, having to march for miles on his flabby ankles. What a waste of the years that had been. And just because his sister Anne, who was crueller than anyone he knew, had told him every month without fail that he'd never get a wife unless he reduced himself, that he'd perish lonely and fat. Their father, who ran his small farm solely with a view to eating prodigiously three times a day, would laugh and tell Anne to hold her tongue. But he, Thomas, became terrified and would retreat to his room and knead his pinkening belly flesh with tears flowing down his cheeks. For he believed his older sister and detested the thought of loneliness, which he could imagine only too easily on the vast bare land of Norfolk. The notion plagued him so horribly that one Sunday morning, after breakfast prayers, he announced that in future he'd walk the three miles to church, there and back.

'You never will,' jeered Anne, poking him in his soggy ribs, 'you'll collapse, even though it's flat the whole way.'

'I shall do so, and then I'll go away and be a soldier,' he said, from a certainty he would become as lean as a bayonet and so never be lonely.

Baggy Gage they called him. 'Here, let me fetch a chair for you,' they sniggered if there was ever a question of his mounting a charger. A pudding was named after him, a clumsy affair made of suet and Sicilian currants. 'Hang on there, men, is this not what we see when we look upon our Mr Gage?' said the Colonel, reddish-haired Mayhew, jovially prodding the mound on his plate. Whereby Thomas had been given to understand that when it came to beauty, valour and virility, he was no competition whatsoever to the whiskered heroes around him.

But all this time their ladies had smiled on him, at his stand of hair, his lined and homely face, into his large brown eyes. On the night of the Regimental Ball, one, Bella Cartwright, had gone further. So Thomas had ceased to protest when Mayhew taunted him for being the least handsome officer in the mad king's army.

A thunder-bug alighted on his wrist. He brushed it away. So blue was the sky! It almost made him ill with joy. He had no idea why it was fixed at blue instead of yellow or cherry. Today its blueness was incomparable, without a cloud anywhere – no, that could never be, not in England. He searched the horizon. Sure enough there they were, a string of small grey eggs, woodlice crawling over an azure carpet.

'You should travel on the railway, sir,' the gatekeeper called over. 'Only four and a half hours from London to Norwich on the fast train. You'll never get better than that. That thing you're on – had it. Pushing up the daisies.'

'Bosh,' he said, his mind splendid with clouds and the colours of leaves and the midsummer yolkiness of the sun above him. He thought, I would like to have a river meeting the ocean here, with trees down to the water's edge and fishermen beaching their catch, the spray from tautening ropes, the tide sucking at the sternpost, meaty arms, salty eyebrows—

Two brindled oxen loomed out of the tunnel of oaks opposite him, drawing a laden hay wagon. A youth, fifteen perhaps, sat coiled and dreaming on the bench, the reins idle in his hand. Round his neck was a scarlet handkerchief, bird's eye pattern. His shirt, limp with sweat, hung from the cross-bar. The gatekeeper stretched out both arms, raised and lowered them with emollience. 'Woa, you brutes, I tell you woa now.' The boy hauled back, a tense slip of sinews and golden skin, his ribcage grooved. A fillet of hay fell onto his head and crowned him in saffron. The wagon frame groaned. A thistle wrapped round one of the spokes resolved itself into a cluster of purple buds that slowed and ceased to turn. The oxen blew out their wide nostrils and looked at each other.

'Don't move an inch,' Thomas whispered, feeling under his seat. With quick fingers he unbuckled his saddlebag and took out his sketchbook. He centred the date, 9th July, 1847, dashed a line beneath it and started to draw.

'. . . I don't care what anyone says, she's German and that's the fact of it. So's that prince of hers,' Blissett was saying.

'Got something against them, have you?' The gatekeeper's voice was devoid of interest.

'You can say! Right the way back to the one who didn't have a word of English between his lugs. How can you have a king who can't even say Good Morning? You might as well sit a paving slab on the throne, that's what I say. What's the matter with us on this island? Run out of the proper sort of spunk, have we, that we need to fetch Germans in to rule us? And here's another thing, cock-o-me-lad—'

The rails trembled. A whistle cried, and the train was upon them, a pilot engine leading the way.

Thomas steadied his eyes and flexed his fingers. The royal banners twittering in their scabbards, the metrical ratchet of pistons, the glowing firebox; the whisked-away faces, the coaches with the hay towering above them, the steam writhing between the rails, the gatekeeper's shins, the scattering magpies – he observed them all in the flashing seconds. The plume of smoke he saw as the breath of a galloping elephant.

At Colchester he finished everything except the sky, which he did when they stopped at Ipswich for another change of horses.

It was evening before they reached Norwich. He had Blissett put him down at the livery stable where he'd left his horse. There, for Isabel's sake, he touched in a stub of flame sprouting from the funnel and, with his smallest brush, the blur of a grey glove inclining fingertips to him with bestowing regality. It was not the truth. It was in every way better, and would give pleasure to a woman.

Three

ISABEL GAGE was a prudent woman, about five foot eight and weighing mediumly. She had a round, quiet face, seldom used rouge and wore no other rings than her wedding band. Her dark hair fell tidily onto her shoulders. She was proud of her hands, and of her waist, to which she liked to draw attention by means of bright panels in her dresses. Otherwise she lacked all ostentation and had long since reached the age of providence. She was forty-three.

Her eyes were more blue than any other colour. When she was really adamant about something – when her children had gone too far, for instance – she would speak with them closed, and her eyelashes would quiver furiously, not with rage, which was alien to her, but with the obstinacy of someone who has firm principles and intends to uphold them.

Because of an injury to her neck as a girl, when she'd been thrown from the governess cart, she carried her head upright and turned it with her body. This, together with the slight arthritis from which she suffered, had led her to adopt a slow and purposeful gait. She was unable to skip upstairs if she'd forgotten something. Consequently she had made it her business not to forget, and would complete each portion of her tasks with calm efficiency. When playing croquet, she never dawdled over the shot, which she had planned while stalking up to the ball. Food she seemed to place in her mouth according to a stratagem; and when she had their groom, Sam Buzzerd, drive her somewhere in the trap, she went there without deviation.

When she was young her father, a self-made industrialist, had been caught cheating, quite blatantly, at whist in a private house.

For a long time they'd been shunned by the county, her father, mother and herself, every single one of the Merediths. She had never forgotten this. She therefore mistrusted society and kept her own counsel.

For this reason and perhaps also because of the stiffness of her movements, matters appeared to flow sedately within her. Strangers very easily made the mistake of assuming that she had lost interest in the world, or that her brain was operated by gravity, as though it were a water-tank at the top of a very steep hill. Only her intimate friends were aware of the labour she put into assisting the poor and uneducated, and only Thomas knew that every pulse of her heart was reserved for her family.

Her first marriage ended on a morning of freezing fog, when her husband's horse slipped and crushed him. She was left with a daughter called Harriet. Soon afterwards Thomas, who was six years her elder, declared himself. She was reckoned lucky to have a second chance. It's for her money, people said spitefully, those who saw nothing but plainness in her, who set little store by constancy and loyalty and had no inkling how much Thomas yearned for domestic ballast in his life.

She had a black pug called Venus, the only dog she would allow in the house. Thomas kept two pointers, Natasha and Verochka, that he and Sam took on occasional forays after partridges. These lived in the kennels behind Sam's cottage. She also had her poultry, a dozen or so bouncing, boyish Black Minorcans who were permitted to desecrate the garden without fear of further rebuke than 'Shoo, off with you, you villains.' She loved them as she did her children.

She was sitting with Harriet on her usual bench so that she could keep an eye out for Thomas on the long straight road from Sparling. Below them the garden sloped gently down to the bridge across the river where in olden times there had been a toll-gate. It was a fine relic, with a recess on either side in which foot travellers could wait until carriages or farm animals had passed. A previous owner had planted a belt of pines to screen it from the house but Thomas had had them cut down. He enjoyed sketching the motley that crossed it, their stoppings and greetings, the gesticulations and palaver (which when the wind was right he could hear quite distinctly), the cattle and donkeys, the carts, the troops of high-headed geese. It was the only bridge for miles in either direction. Isabel believed they possessed some ancient manorial rights to it from the days when the tolls had belonged to the owner of their house. Leonard Lutwylch, their family lawyer, had mentioned it when they came to Fordwell.

A sinuous band of evening mist was starting to form over the river, raised above the surface as though on stilts. Below the bridge by about a hundred yards was the mill-house and its gently dripping wheel. She heard the crack of his mallet as Mr Rodgers tapped down the planks to cut off the millstream for the night. This was the man who had the grazing of their water-meadows on the other side of the river.

A little way above the bridge and masked from it by the boskiness of their pleasure grounds was their boathouse and a deep pool where Thomas and the children swam, fished and in winter skated. There had been occasions when Isabel, after exacting promises of good behaviour, would join them in the boat. But since these invariably seemed to end in one prank or another, she now left them to it.

'What can he be doing all this time?' asked Harriet plaintively. She was eighteen and very like her mother, only a little thicker round the neck.

Isabel took a handful of barley and linseed from her metal scuppet and tossed it into the flower-bed for the Minorcans. She knew Thomas's weaknesses by heart. She didn't think he'd have stayed so long in London for the company of men. He was easily bored by their obsessions and brutish humour; soldiering had given him enough of men. But for women, or rather for a certain type of woman, he was quite helpless. He admitted it, withheld nothing if she landed her question on the button; would roll his nightingale eyes at her, wrinkle his scalp so that his hair moved like a field of corn, and say: 'My dear, that look she gave me – I was lost! Taken by storm! It's Bella Cartwright's fault. She started it all.' She was aware of the significance to him of Bella, who on the night in question had yet to become a widow. Without difficulty she could point a finger at certain of his other loves. She didn't reproach him: frailty she understood. She was inclined to blame her own sex for preying on him; harpies bored with their husbands, and he so defenceless. But the moment of rebellion had come, a few years after Fred and Emily were born, when she deemed it just that her womanliness should no longer be at his beck and call. Affectionately yet firmly, in the pearly glimmer of a May dawn, to the distant rapture of skylarks, she had removed his hand and declined him his hour of plunder. It was not the word she had used: he would have been unbearably mortified. But she had felt it to be plunder that he should enjoy her body while thinking of Bella Cartwright and others she could name. She'd taken refuge in her age, in a drying-up of essential fluids, in the demise of that particular urge now that she'd borne his children. They'd talked it over and agreed it was the best, perhaps the only, solution, seeing as how nature had provided for them in these different ways. He'd become tender and remorseful, pledged himself to her until the day of judgement – laid his head on her shoulder and gone back to sleep.

She said to Harriet, 'Remember that he has a picture hanging in the Academy Summer Show.'

'Is that such an honour? He never really gave me a straight answer. He seemed rather embarrassed about it.'

'Oh yes, it's a terrific feather in his cap. At the first attempt! I expect he'll have popped in to see it, though he was rather dithering when he left. I do hope he has. It'll have done his confidence no end of good.'

'But it can't have taken him five days!'

'There was some business that Mr Lutwylch asked him to attend to, a man who wouldn't pay our bills. Difficulties may have arisen. We all know that dear Thomas is not very apt when the question is of business. He's probably bumped into friends, been asked out to meals, that sort of thing. He'll come home when he's ready.'

The gong rang for dinner. Starched and formidable, Mrs Macbride appeared on the terrace and called down to them – unnecessarily, for they were already on the move, chilled by the evening mist. Arm in arm, like a pair of tall white wading birds, they walked up the slope between Isabel's espaliered roses while behind them the Minorcans noisily stabbed a slug to death.

Four

THOMAS'S BELLY was rattling like a drum. A bowl of soup and the end of a loaf was all he'd had since morning. He should have put aside his painting of the royal train and had a decent meal when they stopped to change horses. But he'd wanted to finish it while the scene was still fresh in his eye so he could give it to Isabel as a peace offering. He'd gone without and now he was hungry.

His mare was going well beneath him, throwing her legs forward in a firm trot that raised blisters of dust from the road. She was an animal that was completely sufficient for him, being neither tall nor haughty nor so narrow that he scraped his feet on her elbows. Sam Buzzerd was resolute in his opinion that a mole had adulterated her horsiness somewhere in the pedigree, both on account of the mare's colour and what he called her 'burrowing' style of going. 'I reckon master mole crept into the stable and slipped its dam a portion when she did sleep,' he once remarked, the closest he dared to venture to rudeness. (He'd had no say in her purchase.)

Thomas was unmoved. He had no wish to terrify himself aboard some rampant foaming stallion. Nor was he out to cut a dash, for which he knew he had the wrong figure. What he sought in a horse was obedience, patience, a short distance to the ground, and a good broad wither on which to rest his sketchbook.

'G'dap, my love, or we'll be late for our supper.' He made a forwarding motion with his wrists and clicked his tongue at her, whereupon she batted her ears, as much as to say, Can't you see, I'm doing my best.

The day was hanging onto its heat. Sweat caked the lines

that slanted down from his temples, and the horizontal wrinkles on his forehead. It had gathered in the corners of his eyes. Everything in his face crackled when he blinked. His cheeks were burning. He was looking forward to the coolness of Fordwell House.

He went by Lutwylch's villa, which he thought more vulgar with every day that passed. The lawyer was taking an after-dinner constitutional across his fields with his wife and son. They looked up on hearing the sound of hooves. 'Tomorrow,' he shouted, raising his top hat, 'no time to talk now.' A couple of straight miles (open road, save for one small grove of elms), and he came in sight of Sparling, a cluster of low houses, thatch over flint, gathered beneath the rising ground on which stood the ancient church of All Souls. The evening sun had goldened the long arched course of its clerestory windows, transforming them into a sheet of flashing bronze. He left the highway; a bend to the right, a dip down into the village, and now the graveyard trees were between him and the windows, splintering the light into spikes of flame, dragons' tongues, jagged portents.

Wombwell was fetching his milk cows in for the night, flicking at their dirtied rumps with a wand of elder. They were still at it in the joiners' yard, Bill Latham standing atop the tree-trunk while his son crouched below him in the pit and the blade of the double-handled saw moved up and down between them with a somnolent rasp. Past the blacksmith's foundry Thomas went, and the almshouses on either side with their small, bright gardens of phlox, into the spreading shadow of the great elm that grew in the centre of the square.

'No—' His saliva was gritty with dust, and he spat. 'No malarky now, lads,' he called forward in case the village urchins were waiting in ambush behind its trunk. At the same time he searched through its boughs. Water-bombs, dead mice, packets of hens' feathers, all had been known to fall on the heads of travellers. He skirted the tree at a safe distance, curling a sideways glance round it as he did so. The ambush was empty; in the background he saw the vicar bending over in his garden, his shirt very pale among the box bushes.

'Good evening to you, Mr Johns, home again.' The other straightened, took his spectacles off the wall, but said nothing, even though he stared after Thomas for a good half minute. Meditating on his sermon, Thomas decided. Last week it had been on The Advantages of Travelling by Foot; the benefits to the soul of contemplation, the flowers the Lord has planted for us, Sunday trains a sacrilege – the day of rest and whatnot.

At his raking trot he rode past the parish pump with its new iron handle, past the pond and its scum and sailing ducks' feathers, checked for a boar that was stumping across the square with sunken reproachful eyes, and came abreast of the coaching inn, once The George and now The Lord Nelson. Why was the place so deserted? There was usually a crowd of men outside it at this time of the day instead of just the two old Button twins, John and Bobby. He forgot about his stomach and went over to where they were playing shove ha'penny.

'Where is everyone then?'

'Why, there's a fair arrived at St Margaret's, what they call a minadgerry. That's where they've all gone, to see camels, a Rooshan wolf, an elephant and a lion that once ate somebody.'

'Don't be forgetting the smallest dwarf ever born,' said the brother. 'And wasn't there talk of a boxing match? Wasn't Albert Rodgers going to take on all-comers?'

'So why haven't you gone with them?'

'Cos it'll all turn out to be hokey-pokey, that's why. John here had a report from our sister, who said only the wolf was halfway interesting, and seemingly that's in a rough way because of the heat. You take my advice, Mr Gage, and keep your tuppence for that boy of yours. Tuppence! Who'd want to spend that to see a freak when you can see Jammy Peach for nothing any day of the week?'

'My Fred's all right then? Not got into a scrape since I was away?'

'Right as rain, Mr Gage, or us'd have heard, wouldn't us, John?'

The butter-smooth coin sped up the board and dropped off the end without striking another. 'Thy brains were in thy feet for a-thinking about friend Jammy. Have another go, brother. I won't mark you for that one.'

Thomas's mare was keen to get home and suddenly launched an array of heraldic capers. He clapped her dusty neck and trotted off. He didn't bother to look into the coaching yard. That fellow at the Whistlefield crossing had been right: the railways were winning hands down. Even the poor could afford to use them, crammed into things like open-air toast racks and charged a penny a mile to shiver their skins off and have their pockets picked. Not a pot in sight for folks with a full bladder. He'd never get Isabel on a train. If she saw what he had, drunken oafs pissing over the side, shaking out their blubbery cocks while their women laughed, she'd never leave the house again. Anyway, at least they didn't have one running past their front door. No money could be made from building a railway in their quiet corner of Norfolk. He turned the corner and was out of sight.

The Buttons wiped the beer off their whiskers, folded their arms and got down to business.

'Jammy says he's been to London town and not returned when he should have. Mrs Gage is most disapproving, he says.'

'Don't you go believing everything Jammy tells you. He's a loaf short of a meal is that one. Any road, Mr Gage is far too fly to get himself walloped. I heard—'

'What's that you heard, brother?'

'Our sister was speaking to a friend of hers from out Gantling way—'

'You mean that Rosie woman?'

'Course I do. Who else could it be, lumpkins? Who else does she know from those parts? Don't be interrupting all the time . . . and what some dicky bird told Rosie is what I'm going to tell you now.'

Their brown felt hats converged across the table. The air grew swollen with gossip. '. . . minding you, I'm not saying as how he did or how he didn't lie with the lady. Only that if it's true, and you know it doesn't take much to set our sister squawking – well, I'm not the one to be blaming him. In fact I'd say more meat on his bone, him being the age he is and not what you'd call a bunch of forget-me-nots so far as looking's concerned. Queer business what ladies see in a man, I always say.' He leaned over and wiped the board down with his crumpled hat. 'You to go, Bob.'

'Where are they? Where's my Fred and Emily?' he demanded, his face poised above the threshold of the dining-room like a crimson moon. He'd meant to look solemn and repentant. But the expectation of seeing his children had got the upper hand; the larky, boisterous, unreformed scamps, the only true Gages.

'You haven't shaved,' Isabel said. She too had wished to assume a different aspect. She was sincerely glad to have her husband back. But distaste for that bristling roughness was what reached her at that moment.

'Haven't shaved? Of course I haven't shaved. I wouldn't be here now if I'd waited for the fellow in front of me to have his beard taken off. Then the coach was held back at Whistlefield while the Queen's train passed. Prince Albert on his way to be made Chancellor. It seems like we hung about for hours. I tell you, I did damned well to get here at all today.'

'Oh, Thomas, don't look so hot and grumpy. Sit down and take the weight off your feet.' She rang the hand bell. 'Mrs Macbride, you can fetch Mr Gage his soup now . . . There, drink your beer and tell us the news from London. Your picture, was it admired? Did you remember to get the coffee beans? Was it as scorching as it has been here? Tell us everything. It's always lonely without you.'

'But the children, what have you done with them? You know I like to have them around me when I get home.'

'You must be reasonable, my dear. How were we to know it would be this evening you returned? They've gone to stay with the Lutwylchs for the night. Leonard and Joan are taking them with some other children to the circus at St Margaret's. You should have seen their faces, they were *so* excited.'

Thomas had spent much of the day planning this scene, how he'd torment his darlings, tease them without mercy until they begged him to say what his surprise was. Emily would pull his hair in vexation, Fred would crawl across the floor and imploringly splash his boots with tears – here! In this very room! Where they weren't, because they'd gone to see an elephant stand on its head with cocksure Mr Lutwylch and his half-baked wife. Harriet's company was simply not the same. He clamped a crust of bread between his teeth and tugged at it until it broke. Moreover he felt belittled by the casualness of Isabel's enquiry. She should have been able to feel his moment of triumph from a distance, like a seer; sense it happening the instant Mr Wheaton strode down the gallery, adjusted his eye-glass and said resoundingly – fortissimo!

Loud enough to flatten Jericho! – 'By Jove! What a cracker, that's the one for me.' Instead all she'd wanted to know about were her coffee beans. He didn't fall into a sulk but he was peeved; sticky, hungry, thirsty and peeved.

Mrs Macbride came in with his soup. He asked would she boil the water for his hip-bath afterwards. She snorted, refrained from spilling soup onto his lap and marched out grumbling, clicking her long red jaws.

Isabel remonstrated with him. Mrs Macbride was cooking a piece of lamb. It would be intolerably hot in the kitchen if she had to boil a lot of pans as well, especially on an evening like this, despite having both windows open. She regarded him steadily down the table, eye-lids going up and down like candle-snuffers, their lashes starting to twitch. 'I think you could make do with a foot-bath just this once,' she said in a way that was more than a suggestion. When Mrs Macbride returned with the saddle of lamb she gave her the new instruction.

He finished his meal and immediately felt tired. Harriet and Isabel left to shut up the Minorcans. He went down the corridor to the kitchen. Mrs Macbride had laid out his slippers and embroidered cotton nightgown. The copper foot-pan was waiting for him in front of the cooking range. He stripped naked and with a scowl started to flannel his white, quivering slopes. He wished, oh how he wished, that Fred and Emily had been there, jumping around on the doorstep as he rode in. Instead it had been Sam he'd met, reporting in tones of the utmost lugubriousness that the dog-cart was in need of a new axle. He reached behind him and pulled up a chair. 'Phooh' – and he fell back wetly onto it, his buttocks lapping the wooden slats, soap in the corner of one eye, towel over his hunched shoulders, a wronged Canute.

Mrs Macbride entered with a tray of dinner things, on her way through to the scullery.

'Bridie,' he said, 'can there be a purpose to it all? You women build up such knowledge of everything. I don't believe there's a single one of you really dies – you know, disappears for good and all. You just go behind a screen, get yourselves looking different and come back wiser than ever. Here, give my neck a rub, will you? I must have got a chill in it somewhere.'

His considerable nakedness did not alarm her. She was used to it. Wherever men rode horses, there were injuries to be repaired. In her own domain she was quite at ease with Thomas.

He and Isabel lay back on their pillows, separated by the sacrosanct corridor of crisp linen. Sometimes, on a cold night, they would warm their feet together. Otherwise she had declared it a no man's land. If Thomas encroached too far into her territory when sleeping, she'd get out of bed and climb back in on his side.

'Does it mean nothing to you that I sold my picture?' he said, still out at the elbows.

'How can you say that? It's an extraordinary thing to have done, without formal teaching or a single friend at the Academy. I can't tell you how proud Harriet and I are. And Fred and Emily, when they hear of it – you can be such a silly. As if we didn't care – of course we do!'

In fact she hadn't properly understood the picture, despite his explanations. She couldn't for the life of her make out why Jammy should have that expression on his face if death was on its way. Why was he sitting staring into the water with that storm coming on? Why wasn't he rowing like mad for the bank? What she liked were scenes of sheep fairs, of fishing vessels, of images that were familiar.

Jammy now having entered her thoughts she said, 'By the way, Jammy told me this morning that he wants to learn reading and writing. He was so shy about it that I wanted to hug him. Can you imagine it, Jammy a scholar? He said it was because everyone laughed at him so. He wants me to teach him so that he can better himself. Of course I agreed.'

'I suppose that means we'll have to find a new back-house lad one of these days. He may be on the simple side but he works his fingers to the bone.'

The day was going from good to bad. Despite his wash, he still felt dirty. The room seemed stifling. He gazed round at the walls which Isabel had had papered in chocolate, with a thin pink stripe of prancing angels. In winter it was cosy enough but now it was suffocating him.

'How that girl of yours can snore,' he said unkindly.

'I expect it's Venus you're hearing,' she replied, for the dog had its bed on the landing outside their room.

'Well, gag it then.'

She rolled onto her side and planted her elbow in the corridor. She was immune to his tantrums now she had achieved a position of equality in their marriage. He was lying with his hands behind his head, wondering whom he could use as a model if Jammy left them.

'The business, Thomas, did it go off alright? Did you get the money?'

He glanced at her, seeing less her lacy nightcap and heavy-lidded eyes than Jammy peering at the reflection of his pimpled, strong-chinned face in the threatening water. 'Yes, it couldn't have gone better.' He swung his legs out of bed and fished around for his slippers. 'I'm going down for a swim.'

'But did he actually give it to you, in full?'

'Didn't I say as much? Of course he did. I'll go into town tomorrow and hand it in to Lutwylch.'

Dogs were barking in the village. There were voices and laughter on the bridge, bursts of song as people walked home from the circus. Layered above the cool breath of the river was the scent of cut clover. Tomorrow the women would troop down from Sparling, toss the swathes of hay and make a picture for him. Cows were snuffling and blowing on the bank opposite, their hooves sucking at the mud as they waded in to drink. Wild roses shone in the undergrowth, winking whitely. Nightbirds called, the poplar leaves rustled, the bullrushes whispered to each other, and three miles away the church clock at St Margaret's struck eleven.

Something plopped into the water as he opened the door to the boathouse. He hung up his gown and spreading his torso upon one of the children's bundles of tied reeds, paddled out into the bathing pool, his slowly moving legs gleaming in the silverlight like immense clumps of celery. The cattle raised their dripping muzzles and watched him as he swam upstream, his round powerful strokes and the prow of the reed mattress disturbing the water and causing it to murmur. He reached the point where he'd had Jammy pose for him and for a while trod water. The river had gouged itself a hole just there. When he was mooring the boat that day, the anchorstone had sunk, fizzing and bubbling, for what seemed an eternity. Even in summer the stream boiled at this point. It was why he'd painted Jammy there. But now it was dark. The dangers were hidden and the current was flowing between his parted thighs, tugging at his blood. Far away the band struck up 'God Save the Queen'. He floated himself back to the boathouse, wondering what Fred would say when he told him about the picture.

Five

THE DOG-CART was too dangerous to use. Harriet had to go into town to consult the library of a friend's father: Isabel was preparing her for local society and had assigned her various intellectual tasks to enlarge her conversation. Accordingly Thomas took her into Norwich the next morning in the one-horse gig. Sam had given him the measurements of the new axle; in his note-case was the money to deliver to Lutwylch.

Harriet was not a confident girl. She stuck close to her mother, suffered terribly from hay fever, and dreaded the prospect of marriage. Her world extended in a radius of about fifteen miles from Fordwell House; even to contemplate more distant regions intimidated her. And she was uncomfortable with Thomas, her stepfather, whom she regarded as a usurper.

She lolled in her seat, gnawing the hem of her shawl and speaking only when it was impossible not to. She viewed with particular disrelish the return journey, when the gig would also have to accommodate Fred and Emily, whom they were collecting towards the top of the day. She felt estranged by the obviousness of their love for Thomas and by the rowdy and possessive way they showed it. Exclusion, a sort of emotional blockade, was what came to her when the conversation swarmed with the gaudy complexities of the Gages.

They came into Norwich on the Spixworth road, past Stump Cross and down Magdalen Street to Fye Bridge, where they stopped so that Thomas could get out to see what goods were being moved on the quay. She had known he would do this. The barges were of no interest to her. She looked stolidly to the front, wondering if she could find an excuse to spend the night with her friend and thus avoid having to witness Fred and Emily clambering all over their father.

Thomas returned, saying he'd seen a drove of lambs being taken aboard. The springs sank as he stepped in. 'A few good dinners for someone down there, eh! You're being very quiet, pet. Had a bad dream last night, did you? Or has your mother set you a real twister of an essay? That's it, I'll bet. Nothing easy was ever born in her mind – and a fine morning to you too, Mr Mundy, Mrs Mundy . . .'

They crossed the river and drove into the centre of town, Thomas hallooing his friends and raising his brass-handled whip to the tradesmen he knew. Meanwhile he persisted humorously with his questioning. They reached her friend's house in Lobster Lane. Thomas said he'd come back for her in a couple of hours. She got out hurriedly, clutching her pencil case.

'Well, what is it she wants you to do? You can't not tell me.'

'I'm required to describe the influence of red-haired men in history and if you don't mind, Father, it's not very amusing at all.' The door opened and a rather pretty maid appeared on the steps.

'Good heavens,' he said to himself, turning it over in his mind as he preened his side-whiskers. He cried, 'The Plantagenets, Harriet! Don't forget the Plantagenets!' But the door had already closed behind her.

Still dwelling on the question about red-haired men, he went to the coachmaker, Mr Belling, and asked him to have the axle ready by the end of the week. Afterwards he drove to the three-storey brick house in St Giles where Lutwylch & Lutwylch had their offices. He turned into the stable yard through the wide blue gates and handed the reins to the groom. Having asked him to cover the seats in case of a shower, he checked that he hadn't forgotten the money and went in, stooping so that his hair wouldn't brush the lintel. He was wearing his everyday clothes: boots, whipcord breeches, and the long faded blue coat that had belonged to his father. It was rather hot for the weather.

The 'business' for which he had to account to his wife and Mr Lutwylch was paint, or, more specifically, a paint known throughout the decorating trade as Meredith's Grey. It had been started by

Thomas's father-in-law, the man who was found sharping at whist.

Mr Meredith had formed the opinion that the white with which everyone painted their best rooms was insipid. He understood that they did this in order to reflect the candlelight and thus make reading easier and their surroundings less mumpish. But he thought it could be done better, more tastefully. After some years of experiment he succeeded in producing a brilliant, translucent whitey-grey with just a hint of blue, a colour very close to a pale aquamarine, that fairly threw the light around. Its drawback lay in the stiffness of the liquid, which made it unsuitable for the finickety work on cornices. When his first clients complained of this, he made up a thinner cornice paint which he sold in a variety of colours, each of them illustrated by hand in a sturdy oblong booklet entitled *Meredith's Gracious Paint Emporium*. However, by its very purpose the cornice paint sold but slowly and it was Meredith's Grey by which his fortune was made and sustained. In due course he constructed a manufactory in Norwich where he employed only persons of the most wholesome integrity, such as Methodists.

Some said his secret lay in an admixture of very finely ground glass similar to that Mr Gainsborough had used in his portraits. Others that he had paid an outlandish sum to a German living in Leipzig to formulate an entirely new chemical. Meredith did nothing to discourage this rumour. Whenever some competitor tried to prise the secret from him by promising every sort of lucrative collaboration, he would allow the chap to dine him royally and afterwards, over the finest bottle of port in town, would reward him with an exact description not only of the district in which this alchemist had lived, but also of his laboratory, his height, his posture ('hump-backed. All that crouching over his retorts, you know'), his apparel, his comical errors with English idiom and even the scent of the tobacco he smoked, never forgetting to mimic the way the man flicked up the metal lid of his pipe, and the movement of his lips ('like a feeding cod') as he persuaded the angled match to draw. 'Alas, Karl is with us no longer and I omitted to write down what he told me,' he would conclude mournfully, thereby drowning the aspirations of his suitor with weights round both ankles. In this manner, and despite many attempts to unseat him, he kept his recipe privy until very nearly the day of his death. Apart from the foreman in the manufactory, only one other person at this time knew the formula to Meredith's Grey, and that was his lawyer, Leonard Lutwylch, who as a youngster had drawn up his standard contract and thereafter handled all his affairs.

Not for one moment had Thomas hankered after admission to the business. What he sought from this brusque and overpowering man was not the fiddle-me-fee of buying and selling, but the hand of his daughter in marriage: stability and a family. His view on life was wholly provisional. After eight years of the army he harboured no certainties, not even a tenuous pattern of likelihood. Several times – the night before the battle of Waterloo, for instance, when the rain had washed him out of his bivouac and prevented sleep – a terrible fear had gripped him, and his mind had sidled over and peered into the crater of existence to see what might be disclosed; truth, a purpose, at any rate something not to be denied. All there had been were chance and the unknowable prowling round the moonlit bowl of mist. He had never glimpsed fame, ambition or money, only a tableau of muddle and accident. 'A mouse has as good an idea of it all as I have,' he would say cheerfully. 'Live for the day.' 'Strike the bell while you can.' When the talk turned to profit margins, discounting bills of exchange, and how many days of grace this customer or the other should have, he looked out of the window.

This was not an attitude that appealed to his future father-in-law, whose belief in hard work and the unerring finger of destiny had accrued at the same pace as his wealth. At first Meredith was suspicious, for his fortune was considerable. Later he began to see that the marriage might, after all, have its advantages, and decided to inveigle Thomas into the business. He would have someone to bully. Isabel had had bad luck being widowed like that; alright, the fellow was green, but anything was better than naught. And when Thomas, prompted by Isabel, laid upon the damask tea-table cloth his Waterloo medal and its crimson, blue-flanked ribbon, he plunged.

'Good man! I can use a fellow who knows how to stand the enemy's fire and give knock for knock. You were in the thick of it, my daughter tells me, held the line together single-handed. Cavalry charging, moustachio'd stalwarts coming straight at you with bared teeth,' – he flattened his lips and made a pumping motion with his arms, as if approaching the last fence in a steeplechase – 'death only yards away, then the order, "Front row, kneel and fire" – bang! "Second row" – bang!' He thumped the table and made the spoons rattle in their saucers. 'God, I wish I'd been there. The most glorious day in our history. Self-discipline, sacrifice, battering the Frogs. Good man, Gage!'

He paused and whispered something in Thomas's direction.

'Frightened?' Thomas exclaimed. 'Of course—'

'Don't waste your breath on an answer! Just seeing if it had made you deaf, all those cannons blasting away in your lug-hole. Deaf men don't sell paint, eh! Now tell me what you remember best about the day. Take your time. Tell me as it comes to you. Then we'll see how to get you fixed up.' He sat back expectantly, gentling his palms on his stomach.

And Thomas, who had returned from France at the age of nineteen to hear of a whole string of barges of the wounded floating forgotten on Regent's Canal, who adored loveliness above all else and who for a time had found it repugnant to speak of the battle to anyone, replied after a long hesitation: 'What the men chose to remember best – the survivors, if the word is not too harsh for you – was a poor bewildered hare that ran up and down in front of the enemy cavalry as they galloped towards us. Whichever way it turned it was trapped. In the end it crouched, shivering, behind a tussock. A dragoon leaned out of his saddle and sabred it in half.'

He could still see it so clearly: the creature's flattened ears, its muddied pelt, its desperate efforts to escape. He could have imitated the terrific arc and flash of the blade. He could have told Meredith how casually it had been done – in passing, much like someone riding along and lopping the head off a thistle. But he didn't like to remind himself of anything more than was necessary. 'Two minutes later we shot that man. I think the hare had the better death,' he said.

In saying this, he rather stumbled over his words. The dragoon had been hit in the stomach and had lain screaming only thirty yards in front of them for the rest of that awful afternoon; until evening, in fact, when the line at last began its advance and Sam

Buzzerd finished him off with a shot in the head. Also something else had occurred that he had absolutely no intention of revealing, even to Isabel, because he would always feel shame for what he'd done in the madness of victory.

Meredith noticed his falter and eyed him more coolly, as much as to say, Is that the best you can do? We smashed the tyrant and all you can remember is how a hare was killed? Thomas, however, was lost in his memory of the carnage and since he was staring at a set of commemorative porcelain on the wall behind the old man's head (George IV's coronation), never saw the spasm of disapproval that wrenched the other's face when he went on to refer to the Duke of Wellington, the saviour of Britain, as His blood-spattered Nibs. He came to the end. His hand shook as he took another cup of tea from Isabel. 'You asked if I was frightened,' he said very quietly. 'I tell you, Mr Meredith, I was as petrified as that hare. I thought, I need protection. Which is why I must have your daughter as my wife.'

Isabel said defensively, 'I'm sure all the other soldiers felt the same. It's not natural to have to stand there and be shot at for hour upon hour. And, Father, he was so young.'

But Meredith had no desire to hear more. Then and there, in front of both of them, he drafted the terms of Isabel's dowry. Thomas was to have one third of the paint business to add to the slender competence he had received from his father, and thus to be made respectable. '*Provided that,*' – Meredith's voice reverberated mightily, the sound of a roll of rugs being thrown out of a window – 'you play no part in its management, now or at any time. Do I make myself clear? Lutwylch will deal with all that. An able man and greedy – what more could you want? He'll do anything for a steady one hundred a year.'

'Is that sufficient?' Isabel said. 'It doesn't seem a great deal for the work involved.'

'Then consider how many wills and conveyances he'd have to do to earn that sort of money. Don't pamper him, Isabel. A hundred is ample. Economy at all points of the compass, that's the thing.'

Six

LEONARD LUTWYLCH was in his early fifties, an arid, sparely built man with a narrow skull and measuring eyes. Some years ago he'd bought eighty acres of land a few miles from the Gages and there had constructed what he called a country villa, a concept quite unknown in Norfolk. Thinking it insufficiently imposing, he'd later had it painted white. It was a constant rumour that he was still dissatisfied with it, that he was planning further embellishments. An orangery, a third floor, wings in the Adam style – no one was certain.

His mother had a distant connection – by marriage alone – with the ancient Norfolk family of L'Estrange. In his hall, above the stick stand and so impossible to miss, hung a framed genealogical chart tracing his ancestry through five centuries of the L'Estranges. Its most prominent names, those of distinguished royalists in the time of Charles I, marcher lords, Griffin prince of Powis, Hugh II, the crusader king of Cyprus, and any number of Anglo-Norman potentates, had been picked out in red ink. The minor branches of the family, which is to say the riff-raff, he'd had blanked off with the note, 'Issue of no importance'. He had been a member of the Corporation of Norwich for many years and was a strong candidate for the Mayorship. Anyone who examined the genealogy closely could see that he had already pencilled in this honour beneath his name. Not so long ago, the political and economic power of the entire country had been controlled by just four hundred great families. It was Lutwylch's dream that these days would return and he could somehow join that number.

He'd made a late marriage to a lady called Joan Pardon. They had one son, Jeremy, who was a year younger than Fred Gage.

Thomas despised Lutwylch for his pretensions. He also disliked being beholden to him for his monthly allowance. 'As if I were a common remittance man,' he would grumble to his friends. 'Treating me like a fellow who's been banished to the colonies – pah!'

'I have some money for Mr Lutwylch,' he said to the clerk who came out from behind his tall desk with much twining of his ink-stained fingers.

'For Mr Lutwylch senior, sir?'

'You know perfectly well that's who I do my business with. Whatever would I want with the other?' He was on the point of saying something dampening about Lutwylch's nephew, whom everyone knew to be an ass, but had second thoughts. Hands behind his back, the bunched skirts of his coat catching on various obtrusions, he paced up and down a red-patterned Turkey carpet, thinking about Fred and Emily and the women who'd soon be tossing the hay in the meadow. He selected in his mind a canvas, his favourite size for that sort of work – 24 inches by 20, just right for a couple of women and a wagon – and primed it vigorously. (Pens scratched. A black-robed clerk climbed up the library ladder. Pinned batlike against the wall of books, he opened a volume of Blackstone's *Commentaries*.) He was just reminding himself to tack some brown paper onto the back of his canvas to prevent the sun shining through it when his eye was taken by a visiting card lying on the tray by the door. He picked it up and tapped it against his thumbnail.

'Who's this fellow, then?' he asked the clerk.

The door opened to the partners' office. Lutwylch came out, settling the folds of his coat and dolling up his neckcloth.

Thomas turned to him. 'Who's this fellow? Gobby, Gooby, the print's too small for me.' He passed it to Lutwylch.

'Never heard of him before. Julius Gooby of the North Norfolk Railway Company. More trumpery, I've no doubt. Every crook in the country has a finger in the railways. You'd think they'd have learned their lesson after the bust on the Exchange last year. Must have dropped it by in the hope of catching a fish.'

'These railways are dangerous affairs,' Thomas said.

'Not a single one of our clients took a knock when they smashed, I'm glad to say. Stick to what you understand, that's always been my advice. Paint, worsteds, cattle, whatever your line happens to be. How can you believe anything railwaymen say when their estimates are always so hopeless? Always under the mark, mind you. You never hear of a new railway costing less than the figure advertised.'

'Curious name that, Gooby,' Thomas said. 'A little bit of the Levant in there somewhere, perhaps?' adding mischievously, 'You never know, he may be a relation of yours. A member of the Cyprus branch.'

Lutwylch declined to be drawn. 'We must have a good chat about the paintworks one day. I was obliged to engage a new foreman last week. I don't believe I mentioned it before. The last one was completely out of his depth. I only had to look at the production figures to know that. You and I and Isabel should make an inspection sometime. There are things an outsider like yourself sees that the rest of us are blind to.'

'Why on earth would anyone want to build a railway in the north of the county?' persisted Thomas. 'What's up there we don't know about?'

'It's probably the section joining us to King's Lynn. Or maybe they're going to build a line to Wells.'

'Fat lot of good that'd do.'

'Nothing to concern us down here, we can be sure of that. Anyway, Thomas, I've got only a few minutes to spare. My sister is arriving on the fast train from Cambridge and I promised to take the trap and meet her. She's bound to be carrying a mountain of luggage.'

'Don't feel you have to hang around on my account,' Thomas said. 'I only came to get a receipt for Roberson's money.'

'So you collared him? I told you he'd settle. He needs our paint as much as the rest of them. Here, Gurlin, disembarrass Mr Gage of his spoils, would you, and write him out a ticket. No hurry about it, he can pick it up later . . . Come along, we can talk as we go to the stable. There's something I need to speak to you about in private. We'll find a corner where my groom can't hear us.'

However, he had scarcely closed the door behind him when he started. 'Your boy Fred . . . Now I'm not the sort of man to lecture another as to how his children should behave. A father can undertake only so much by way of instruction and example. There comes a time when the small people must go it alone. Emily, yes – she was well-mannered enough, but that boy of yours is a proper handful. I don't want to hurt your feelings, Thomas, but I'm afraid you'll have to take the strap to him. A dozen of the best. He'll be grateful to you when he grows older.'

'What can you mean? There's nothing wrong with *my* son, I'll have you know.' Thomas was instantly affronted, and showed it in his face. 'A few high spirits – what young lad doesn't kick over the traces now and again?'

'You call it high-spirited to throw apples at a circus performer? I call it downright bad manners. He was a disgrace to my good name. I dread to think what the other children in the party have been telling their parents. He even tried to get our Jeremy to join in, but of course I soon put a stop to that.'

'Oh, stuff! That's what circuses are for, a bit of fun. So long as he didn't take a shy at the animals themselves – didn't you ever throw apples around when you were a boy?' Thomas measured Lutwylch up and down. 'No, I don't expect you did.'

'You ask Joan when you go to fetch them. She'll give you chapter and verse on the entire incident. Really, I would never have believed it of a child born and raised by Isabel. Harriet now, she's altogether different.'

This altercation was taking place under the arch that gave onto the street, beside the blue wooden gates. It was drawing to a close when a closed gig with a grey pony in the traces clattered down St Giles in the direction of the Market Place. Its paint was peeling and the roof stained with birds' droppings. About twenty yards on it halted. A huge straw sun-bonnet with a cerise band and a dangling swallow-tail poked out.

'Thomas! Thomas Gage!' It was Georgiana Farrant.

Her head withdrew under the canvas cover. A shoe with a trodden-down heel crept out, searched distractedly for the step – and paused. 'Hup now, stand still, will you,' Thomas heard her say to the pony, which was quite stationary. 'Flummox and worry, the daily plagues of womanhood – where can I have put it?' The gig rocked as various movements were undertaken. She leaned out, her plump face anxious in case Thomas should have left during the performance. 'Wait for me, do . . . I'm so disorganised this morning. I know I had my purse when I started. The General will have a seizure if I lose it again.'

'Charming!' Thomas said as he hurried forward. It was a word he used with absolute sincerity towards ladies.

'Indeed so,' murmured Lutwylch, who in the course of his professional career had encountered everything that was possible under the human sun but remained unable to understand how women stopped everything and came running when they saw Thomas.

'So there you are, you little criminal, and there you can stay, quite safe and sound. Thomas dear, I was almost sitting on it, hiding right at the back of my cushion. Who can have put it there? Not I, said the wolf.' She twitched up her cotton dress, baring her ankle and the lower part of her fat creamy calf. Turning herself around, she descended, bottom first, holding tightly to the wooden bracket.

'Thomas Gage, the new Raphael!' She threw her bonnet onto the seat, spread her arms wide, and waited for him, opening and closing her fingers, her cheeks dimpling with the pleasure of this chance encounter. He embraced her completely, and to shock Lutwylch, lifted her until her toes trailed on the ground and she squeaked and patted him on the shoulder to let her down. He kissed her hand. She pinched his cheek roguishly and stood back, flushed. 'My hero!'

'You're in the presence of genius,' she said to Lutwylch, placing herself between the two men. 'How long have I been in town this morning? An hour? At the most, and already four people have stopped me to say, "Have you heard about Thomas and his picture at the Academy?" Of course I knew all about it anyway. My husband, the General, sent a message up on the train yesterday. He'd been passing through Trafalgar Square and thought, I'll just drop in and see – and there it was, with a special label all to itself. Sold! Isn't it the most wonderful thing you can think of, Leonard, when someone like us cocks a snook over all those arty people in London?'

'I'm not entirely *au fait* with what's going on in the capital this season,' said Lutwylch, wishing to thereby convey something about the superiority of Norwich.

'What! You didn't know—'

33

'Of course I knew about Thomas's picture. I just had it in my mind that the Summer Show had already closed.'

'Heavens, you can be a stick-in-the-mud,' Georgiana exclaimed, and turned away. 'Thomas, dear, you are a deep old dog. Fancy having a picture hung at the Academy and keeping mum about it. If it had been me, I'd have sent a card round to every single person I'd ever met. At Home, Fabulous Mrs Farrant at the Royal Academy – you know my style. I'd have got the General to order a detail – incident, whatever they're called – of his men to stand underneath and point at my picture with drawn swords. In complete silence, of course. Silence is so much more impressive.' She slid her arm through Thomas's. 'How did you do it? You paid that man to buy it until the Show's finished – go on, admit it! You can't get away with fibs to me. I know you too well!'

Thomas fluffed himself out. His large eyes wandered over Georgiana's bosom, which rippled as she walked – she was steering them back towards Lutwylch's office, where the street was quieter. His family made fun of her because she was so feather-brained with money. There were times when he too thought her foolish, for different reasons. But her prattle was refreshing, and their friendship long-standing. A long time ago, before he married Isabel, he'd enjoyed a little winter-love with Georgiana's aunt, who was a year younger than her niece. (A late spasm of virility in the collateral branch: all sorts of hoo-ha and complications.) A foot of snow had lain on the ground. Her family house had been large and cold. Georgiana had surprised them snug in a curtained alcove trimmed with streamers and berried leaves and left-overs from a New Year dance, giggled fetchingly and told no one. The memory had rested between them, never far from the surface.

Thomas was grateful to her for rescuing him from Lutwylch. Her flattery was agreeable. He found himself wishing that his lawyer were elsewhere.

As if reading his thoughts, Lutwylch placed his fob-watch on the flat of his palm and studied it intently, with the appearance of someone learning astronomy.

Georgiana said to him, 'Oh dear, I can see I'm keeping you from something. Were the two of you in the middle of a terribly important discussion? I did so want to speak to you, Leonard, though what it was about I really can't remember. I'm too excited about Thomas and his picture. Can you wait? Whatever you have to do, it won't run away.'

'I thought for a moment it had stopped,' Lutwylch said, tucking away his watch. 'I have a train to meet. My sister is on the express from Cambridge.'

'Pooh to your stinking trains. You can always tell her your horse carried you away going down Thorpe Road. It'll come back to me in a minute. It was only a teeny-weeny enquiry. You'd be able to answer it with your eyes closed.'

But Lutwylch was not to be delayed. Trousers flapping round his bony pins, he hurried into the stable yard and a few moments later drove off down the hill to the station.

'You know the General's being sent to one of those horrible islands near America where everyone turns yellow and dies before they've finished breakfast?'

'Isabel told me,' Thomas said, bringing up his wife's name for the sake of decency, seeing as how they were in a public place and Georgiana had a carrying voice that morning.

'She did? Nothing private can happen round here. Though I expect it could if one applied one's mind to it,' she said archly, with a certain pressure on his arm. 'Anyway, that's where he's going. It's a special appointment, so we get more money. I don't know where it all disappears to. It just – vanishes! Over the hill and far away, like chasing rainbows.'

'Wasn't there some talk of mutiny in a native regiment?'

'Oh yes, desperadoes, no-good men, you'd have to ask the General for the details. He says it'll be as easy as snoring. Sail out, string up the ring-leaders and sail back on the next tide. But I'm not a fool. I know what happens when lawyers start arguing.'

'How is it you're not going with him for the voyage?'

'Not you too! That's the sort of thing Leonard would have said. Given me that my-dear-woman look of his and told me my duty lay at the master's side. I ask you, why should I risk getting yellow jack? Would you want me to die with a face like custard?'

'I don't believe Lutwylch would have said anything of the kind. He's far too afraid of losing a client,' laughed Thomas, who refused, as a matter of principle, to call the lawyer by his Christian name.

'So it's off with the General, and the instant he leaves I'm getting all my lady friends round to tea to tell me how I should amuse myself while he's busy at his hanging and thrashing. You will come, won't you? They'll curl up at your feet and simper like mad – you'll adore it, it'll be like having your very own harem. You're the most famous man in the county now that farmer Coke's gone to his maker . . . And while we're on the subject, you will do my portrait, won't you? So I've got something nice to show the General in case he's at death's door when he comes back. I promise to sit still – oh, Thomas, it would be the event of my life.' She stroked his sleeve and looked pleadingly at him with tumbling, moistened lips. 'Say that you will – my hero!'

Lutwylch met his sister as planned and drove her back to his house. In the afternoon he returned to town in order to attend a meeting of the City Council. During the attendant chit-chat, he was surprised to hear the name of Julius Gooby frequently mentioned. However, no one could say exactly what the North Norfolk Railway Company was about. A pot of gold, a barrel of saw-dust – none knew which. He got home rather tired to discover what had earlier been concealed from him, that an expensive Chinese vase had been cracked by Fred Gage, a catapult and a marble.

'Never again!' he roared at his wife. 'He's a monster! The most unmanageable little Turk that I ever did see.'

'But the family pays us good money each year,' she observed cautiously.

'A hundred pounds is not what it was. Prices have risen since old Meredith died. And the work – have you any idea how I slave for them?' He went into his study and shut the door against her firmly.

Seven

I⟨T WAS⟩ agreed. Thomas would come over and take tea with
Georgiana and her friends and consider doing her portrait. 'But
I can't promise it. Time! My family and one thing and another,
you know,' he said, finishing the sentence lamely.

'I suppose you mean I'm not handsome enough,' she pouted,
pushing her chin up with the tip of one finger and showing off her
profile.

'Not at all. I merely haven't tried a sitting portrait before. I don't
know that I could do anything so delicate. I like to work with
tanks of strong thick paint beside me. What if I said yes and you
were disappointed? Our friendship might suffer a reverse.'

'I'd wear my brightest clothes so as to give your thick paint its
chance . . . oh, but whatever you did I'd love it, I know I would.
Then things might go the other way,' she said, trying to be demure
and flirtatious at the same time but looking him so ruthlessly in the
eye that suddenly he was reminded how foolish she could be. Her
aunt, on the other hand, had been a most intelligent woman. He
was sorry it had come to nothing in the end. 'Let me see how
things turn out,' he said amiably and handed her into the gig.

He walked down St Giles, through the Market Place and into
London Street where he bought Isabel a pretty coral-pink brooch
to complement the panel on one of her dresses. She might never
wear it but the act of giving would please him. In the window of
the shop next door was a pair of ladies' woollen gloves, each finger
a different colour. He thought of buying it for Joan Lutwylch as a
thank-you present for taking the children to the circus, but decided
not to in view of her husband's oafishness about Fred. He had
some small conversations and collected Harriet. They set off to get

Fred and Emily. Feeling the heat of the day upon him, he removed his coat and rolled up his sleeves. His linen shirt, chalky with thin blue stripes, billowed like the sail of a Castilian treasure-ship as the pony stepped smartly out on the dusty road. He drove erectly, his back hollowed and elbows well down. He had Harriet hold the reins for him as they turned up the drive to the Lutwylchs' house so that he could tuck his shirt back into his breeches.

'Your money or your life!' It was Fred and young Jeremy Lutwylch, darting out from the bushes with painted wooden pistols, their faces daubed with clay.

'We surrender!' shouted Thomas. He finished stuffing in his shirt and held up his hands. Then with a cry of 'You little devil, you,' he helped Fred scramble into his lap while Harriet looked sullenly in the opposite direction.

'You're getting a bit old for that sort of thing,' Thomas said. 'And what's this I hear about chucking things around in the circus, you rascal.'

'I love you, Papa,' Fred said disarmingly, jigging up the pony.

'Shouldn't we have Jeremy aboard?' asked Thomas, looking back to where the apple of the Lutwylchs' eye was trudging in their wake.

'He can bother off, he's a twerp.'

Emily at this time was eleven and Fred, who was small for his age, a year younger. After a period of unfruitfulness that had made their parents begin to despair, they had arrived in a rush, two mewling, squalling, fractious tyrants. For Isabel, discreet and stoical, the births had been as she expected. For Thomas, waiting below in the drawing-room and frenziedly polishing his boots, the silver, his Waterloo medal, anything he could lay his hands on, they had been nights of the purest terror. He placed candles in all the rooms, surrounded himself with light, prayed, swore and took every pain upon himself. These children, this Emily and then this Fred, had already become so much a part of him, even in the womb, that he felt as if it was his body they were leaving. That was the word he thought of, leaving, and the image of departure distressed him so intolerably that he cried out loud and went on blubbering and polishing until Mrs Macbride brought in the brandy decanter and sat with him until it was over. Then he ran upstairs and on seeing what he was responsible for was transformed instantly into a prince, a giant, the inventor of all glory. Of course Isabel loved her children, but not in the way that Thomas did. For he loved them as if they were gods.

Since one housemaid was ill that day and the other had gone to see a relative, Thomas went up himself to pack his children's things. Joan Lutwylch was both distant and accommodating; offered them a plate of cold meats and invited Fred to come over and play with Jeremy some time soon. She said nothing about the apples.

They drove quickly away, Fred and Emily jammed in the middle of the gig whispering, 'Faster! Faster!' at the pony's flickering ears as Joan waved to them from the portico.

'I've been told to take the strap to you,' Thomas said solemnly.

Harriet, on the outside, snorted her approval.

'How long a strap?' enquired Emily. She had always been a girl who wanted to know the practical aspects of everything.

'But it was Jeremy who said spitting marbles was sissy. I told him we shouldn't use a catapult—' Fred bit his tongue off, remembering that Mrs Lutwylch had said nothing to his father about the cracked vase. 'We had a really good time at the circus last night,' he continued, 'didn't we, Em?'

'Don't change the subject,' Harriet said implacably. 'Father, make him say what they used the catapult on.' Because Emily was between her and Fred, she couldn't pinch him as she wanted to.

And Fred, laying his head on Thomas's shoulder and ogling him sideways with sardonic, mirthful eyes because he knew he'd never get the strap, related the affair with impudent precision: the terms of the competition, the colour of the vase, the distance to it as stepped, the change of weapons, the fatal shot, how nabbed by Mrs L. – every little detail.

'That's rude and horrible,' Harriet said. 'Girls never spit.'

But Thomas only chuckled. 'So what about the apples, eh!'

'That was deserved,' Emily said, wiggling herself more comfortable. 'The wolf had mange, the lion couldn't be got out of its cage it was so sleepy, and the elephant was tiny. I promise you, Papa, no bigger than a large dog. I was so miffed that—'

'Elephants can swim underwater, like you and me,' Fred said

excitedly. 'They screw up their eyes and jump straight in. Jeremy told me that.'

'I tried my best not to, but I couldn't stop yawning and then this white horse came in and galloped round and round on the end of a rope, and a man dressed up as a Red Indian said he was going to perform the greatest feat of bareback riding ever seen outside America and show us all sorts of tricks with lassoes and shoot his gun from under its belly—'

'Gutswill said he was drunk,' Fred said. It was their pet word for Lutwylch on account of the fact that he was so lean.

'You should have seen him, Papa! He couldn't stay on the horse for toffee and ended up by running round after it holding its tail, so Fred and I, you see we'd filled our pockets with the horriblest little green apples we could find—'

'Why? What would you have done with them otherwise?' Harriet said accusingly. 'You see, Father, they were up to mischief all along.'

'Well, it was something we did as we were waiting to go in. You don't need to have a reason, you just do it without thinking. So we started throwing them at him as he ran past, and some boys on the other side of the ring made a game of throwing them back. It was a bit of fun, that's all.'

'And one hit Gutswill,' shouted Fred.

'Slap on the middle of his conk,' giggled Emily. 'So it wasn't our fault, really it wasn't.'

'Then the band started to play, I think they were drunk too, and Gutswill said it was time to go home. What shall we do this afternoon, Papa?'

Thomas took in a mouthful of air and sighed deeply. Oh God, how rich life was! There were occasions when the sheer weight of the pleasure to be had from it was too much for him and he wished he could call it off and somehow become anonymous, or absent himself until all those he loved had vanished and with them any conceivable cause for disappointment. Or that the world would stand still and the future be abolished. The presence of so much happiness was unbearable to him. Its wings beat violently, their tips thrashing at the walls of his heart.

They were halfway down the long slope to the river. The chimneys of the house were clearly visible. He counted them out of habit: six altogether, three in each stack, the brickwork spiralling into the sky in the Jacobean style. They were magical to him, these traditional dark red bricks; weathered, flaking, with courses of different widths, in all ways a delight when set against the nasty modern things they'd started to use in London. Chimneys and house alike were host to a patina of silver-grey lichen. At one time Isabel had proposed planting a wistaria up the front, but he'd talked her out of it. 'Blue dingle-dangles hanging down its face? Why disfigure a couple of centuries for the sake of some piddling novelty? It's not a house down in Surrey or somewhere. This is Norfolk we're in.' So Fordwell had stayed as it had been since 1619, the date in the panel above the front door; a house of boldness and great beauty, warm in spirit and colour, neither too large nor too small, resting on watch over the ancient toll-bridge below.

'How many windows are there in the ground floor?' he asked Emily.

'Two rows of five. Five times two is ten. Potty.'

'How many—' He remembered that Fred and Emily knew nothing about his triumph in London. Changing his tone, he said: 'I do wish you'd been here when I got home last night.'

'Couldn't. Mother had lent us to the Gutswills,' Emily said.

'You'll be for it if she hears you calling them that,' said Harriet, getting bolder now that they were back in familiar territory and wishing to reassert her position as the oldest child.

'Why, did you bring a surprise for us?' Fred said.

'You'll never guess!'

'Please, pretty please and kisses all over.'

'I know what father did,' Harriet said in a superior way.

Thomas was unable to restrain himself. 'I sold it! That's what I was up to in London. I sold my picture!'

'Clever Papa! Clever, clever, clever,' and Fred threw his cap in the air while Emily wanted to know to whom, how much for, and who got the money.

Thomas beamed with joy and would have gone on talking about Mr Wheaton for ever if he hadn't thought it would be unfair to Harriet to keep Fred and Emily on the boil. So to make sure everyone arrived home in good humour, he leaned forward and said to her across the others, 'How did it go, then? Did you find lots of important men with red hair?' His own children looking puzzled, he added, 'Mother's asked her to make a list of all the red-haired men who did anything in history.'

'Colonel Mayhew had red hair,' Fred said. 'You've always told us that.'

'Right you are! He did indeed, the old dictator. He was a fearsome chap, was Arthur Mayhew. I suppose you could say his hair was red. Nearer sandy, but red'll do.'

'Did you call him Arthur?' Emily asked.

'No more than he called me Thomas. It would never have done to be familiar with the senior officers. That's not the way of the army.' He swung the gig rather quicker into the drive than he should have so that they all lurched against him.

'Tell us again how you saved Sam's life,' Fred said contentedly, putting his thumb in his mouth.

'Oh yes do, Papa, just once more,' Emily said. 'Before we reach the house and have to go in.'

But Thomas had only time for the preface, as they drove through the shrubbery. The children never let him start in the thick of it but insisted on hearing about the thunderstorm the night before Waterloo, how the forces were drawn up, how at first the enemy cannonballs wouldn't ricochet as the ground was so sodden. To get us into the right mood, they would say, paying especial attention to the deployment of the troops and the colours of the uniforms and flags, correcting him in a flash if anything differed in the slightest respect from his previous account.

'We'd had an easy time of it until then, but at three twenty exactly we were ordered out of our hollow to take up position on the forward slope—'

'So you could be shot at properly.'

'Of course.' He drove into the stable yard and they got out, except for Emily. Harriet went into the house immediately. Fred took hold of the whip and stood to attention.

'So there we were, in squares of thirty for when the cavalry charged, and their artillery was giving us a fearful pounding, whole files of men being bowled over in front of my eyes.'

'What were you thinking about?' asked Emily.

'The funny thing is that I can't remember. Truly, not a blessed speck! Anyway, we were having a poorish time of it, when suddenly I saw this cannonball coming straight at Sam. About forty yards away, a huge black round lump, with waves of heat shimmering round it so that it was all grizzled and hairy. Don't ask me how I saw it, I just did, in a fraction of an instant. I happened to look that way and there it was, flying steaming and hissing at Sam—'

'You couldn't tell it was *hissing*,' Emily objected, 'not thirty yards away.'

'Of course Papa could. He doesn't mean it was like a kettle under your nose. He means it was out there making a racket and to him it was hissing. Don't spoil the story. You always ruin it for me, Em, you and your questions.'

'And I said the first thing that came into my mind. I shouted at Sam—'

'Duck!' shouted Fred, doing so.

At this moment Sam came limping in from the fields, leading Thomas's horse in case he wanted to ride out in the afternoon. He was wearing heavy boots, corduroy trousers tied with string beneath the knee, and a collarless white shirt, grimy round the neck. As he was fond of telling anyone who enquired, he was 'older than he once were'. One corner of his mouth went down and he twisted his face into a leathery smile as he saw Fred duck.

'Not like that, Master Fred,' he said in his clipped way of speaking. 'It was like this I ducked. Do you mind, sir?' He gave the mare's halter to Thomas and sticking out his gammy leg, ducked swiftly so that his back was horizontal to the ground. 'When a man shouts at you like that in battle, you don't drop your head as if you were saying prayers, you make yourself as near to a beetle as you can.' He retrieved the halter from Thomas and watched Fred practise.

'Then what?' Emily said as Sam made to lead the mare off. 'You can't leave out the best bit.'

Sam and Thomas looked at each other. 'You tell them, Sam. They'll never let us go or else. Anyway I didn't see it. Too busy not getting myself cut to shreds.'

'Now the Duke, old Nosey, had sent round orders saying we were all brave men and as he wanted the Froggies to know it, we were never to duck when they fired. Well, I ducked but the bloke behind me, he didn't, 'cos he was brave as instructed, and the ball went through his throat, right at the blooming root, and took his head clean off. And you know what? Next thing it was bowling down the hill beside me – ear over ear, not lengthways. Oooh, children,' (he knew this was what they'd been waiting for) 'I can see it to this day, that black hair of his going flippety-flop as it rolled over and over – and then it stopped on a flat piece about six yards away and somehow it seemed to be sitting up on its stump and looking at me. His moustaches were bristling, his tongue was licking away like he had a bowl of sugar—'

'Steady on, Sam, no need for every detail,' Thomas said.

'Winks and frowns next,' Fred prompted, paying his father no attention.

'And his face was making these winks and frowns like he was still alive. Very blue eyes he had, that's another thing I'll always remember. Poor fellow getting himself killed when I should have been the one, but that's how luck works. If Mr Gage hadn't shouted like he did, it'd be me you'd be saying poor fellow about . . . Soon afterwards their cavalry charged us and your father got a dent in the chest from a spent bullet, which wasn't much of a reward for having saved me. Luck! That's what it's all about.'

He chuckled coarsely. 'Still tickles me to think about it. When you've seen as much as I have, you say to yourself, "Old fellow, that could have been you" and then, "But it wasn't, so I'll get to draw a dead'un's grog ration tonight", and after a while it doesn't matter any more. See what I mean? Anyhow, that head of his raised a good laugh when I told the lads about it later, which is more than it ever did when he had it on his shoulders. He was the dullest man in the regiment was Charlie Bedingfield, duller than night. Never had a thought of his own, just went round repeating what he'd last been told. I always told him he should have been a parson . . . The moustaches, that was the most comical part. And the way his coconut went rolling past my boots with its tongue sticking out. I had to glance twice to make sure Charlie wasn't attached.

'Queer things happen in battle, Master Fred. You didn't want to be a soldier if you can't abide strangeness. Your father and I, we about got through with strangeness at the same time, didn't we, sir? That's how I come to be here.'

'How many medals do you have, Sam?' asked Fred. But Thomas indicated enough was enough and closed the conversation.

Emily, pale yet excited, scrambled out of the gig. Sam tied the mare to a wall ring and went in to get a bundle of hay. He unharnessed the pony and began to wisp it down. Fred made a few bayonet lunges with the whipstock, got in a tangle when he trod on the lash, and placed it across the gig's seat. Isabel walked into the yard with the pug Venus in her arms. Mrs Macbride was putting the food on the table, she announced.

Eight

THE FAMILY was sitting down at lunch. Thomas, Emily and Fred decided that afterwards they would help Jammy repair the boat. Someone hadn't tied it up properly and in the winter a flood had floated it out of the boathouse and battered it against the central arch of the bridge, springing a number of planks. They'd had one go at mending the damage but it still leaked in several places that Jammy had marked with chalk. Now they were going to re-nail it and put fresh oakum where necessary.

Isabel objected to this. She'd been on the point of asking Jammy if he'd like to come up to the house to get started on his lessons.

'What, Jammy Peach learning his words?' exclaimed Fred, who'd heard nothing about this development in their domestic life.

He and Emily were in many ways similar to their father. They were incapable of dissimulation. The fact of being young never intimidated them for one moment. They couldn't keep a thought in their heads without sharing it, and since they had busy minds, there was rarely a quiet interval in the house. Fred was the more impatient, but they both spoke rapidly and from close range, as if to prevent their parents from escaping. Their faces were rich in expression, always on the move, wrinkling and wriggling and at moments of high mirth, bursting at the seams. Fred's was triangular, with a peaky old man's nose. His chin receded somewhat and had a cleft in it. He had the same floppy brown eyes as Thomas and the same wonderful stand of brisk chestnut hair. His teeth were small and appeared inadequate for the size of his mouth, especially when he laughed. One of his incisors had been chipped when he'd collided with Emily out skating and taken a tumble. Somehow it seemed to suit him, to set a seal of approval on the other irregularities in his features. All things considered, it was a face that on a boy with a more placid temperament might have been described as ugly.

He gripped his knife upside down in his fist and laboriously imitated Jammy trying to write – his head inches from the table, one eye completely closed, his tongue poking from the corner of his mouth and his face knotted with concentration. He held his breath until his cheeks were bright red. 'My . . . name . . . is . . . j-j-j—' But Jammy was a favourite in the house. Sam was always getting at him, trying to make his life a misery. Everyone had sympathy for their back-house lad who got up at five in the morning and fetched in the milk, riddled the grates, saw to the kindling, cleaned the boots and now wanted to raise himself a notch in the world. They longed to help him with his stutter, as it were to reach into his mouth and pull the words out for him.

'How can you be so mean?' cried Harriet, and Fred was assailed from all sides so tartly that he realised he'd overdone it. 'Sorry, I didn't mean to be beastly about him,' he muttered and resumed eating, for the moment subdued. Even Emily and his father had been against him, although Thomas had been cleaning his nails beneath the table most of the time this was taking place.

When they'd finished eating, Thomas sent the children on ahead to the boathouse and took Isabel into their big drawing-room.

Some of the furniture belonged to him: his father's knee-hole bureau with its two brass candle-holders screwed between the drawers, the plain chair that went with it, and a round country table with a striking figure to the grain. Most had come as part of Isabel's inheritance – solid, dark, heavy pieces built to uphold the majesty of an industrialist and weighty conversations about God and profit. The room was anchored in the centre by a long table with bulbous legs. The fireplace was narrow. On the mantel-shelf above it was a seven-day clock that was wound only when they had company, two vases of dried flowers, and a silhouette of Isabel as a girl. To the right was a large portrait of Mr Meredith seated writing at his desk, perhaps doing up an invoice. By his elbow was a stack of books, each at a different angle, entitled on their spines, *Gracious*, *Paint* and *Emporium* in descending order. To the left was a much smaller portrait: Mrs Meredith. There were no other pictures. The rugs were sombre. A mahogany bookcase

47

took up the wall facing the door. The two sofas and the formal chairs were upholstered in a brownish maroon. On one of the former was spread a new antimacassar that Isabel had purchased because a friend had caught her feeling frumpish and persuaded her it was quite the latest thing. Thomas thought it cheapened everything. 'Must we? Why do people have to put all that grease on their hair?' But Isabel, having succumbed in a moment of weakness, would brook no dissent. In point of fact neither of them liked the room. They only kept it that way because Isabel had a sentimental attachment to the furniture she'd grown up with, and they had nowhere else to put it. 'A mausoleum,' was Thomas's opinion. They sat there when they entertained or wished to discuss something in private, for the children avoided it like the plague. As a family they used a small and much cosier room.

'I saw Leonard this morning,' Thomas said, pronouncing the name with disfavour.

'Of course, my dear. You gave him the money Mr Roberson owed us for all that paint he had.'

'It's none of my business – your father's stipulation – I've never once tried to interfere, you know that, Isabel. You know I've always kept well clear of it.'

'Tell me what disturbed you this morning,' she said evenly, her eyes steady on him. Inwardly she acknowledged surprise. She could not recall when he'd last shown an interest in the paint-works.

'As I said, it's nothing to do with me – I'd actually forgotten all about it until we got home – but do you think it's proper that Leonard should have absolute control? I'm sure his heart is in the right place and all that, but the fact is that he's sacked the foreman you thought was so reliable and gone and appointed another off his own bat. It seems excessive. I mean, who is this new man? What sort of character did he come with? How able is he? Isn't this exactly the sort of thing he should consult you about? Unless, of course, he's spoken to you already.'

'No, he hasn't said a word. And I saw him only yesterday morning when I took the children over. That's not like Leonard. He's usually very open about what's going on.'

'He's getting too big for his boots, I'd say.'

'It's what we pay him for. We can scarcely blame him for doing his job.'

'How much is it a year?'

'A hundred, the same as when he started. Don't pamper him, that's what Father said.'

'Well, it's not a king's ransom, by any manner of means. But there are things he simply shouldn't be allowed to do without asking us first. After all, the business is ours, not his. We depend on it for our daily bread. It's all there is between us and the wolf – you know what I mean. What happens if he makes a mistake? That's what I'm really saying. Or – look at it another way – why should we be paying him anything if the new man turns out to be a scoundrel? Speaking of which—' Thomas's face became animated. He re-crossed his legs. 'Some men were saying in the Club that Mr Hudson, you know, the chairman of our railway and many others besides, is no better than a common crook. Hudson! The railway king! Would you believe it!'

'He paid a very handsome dividend to shareholders last year. Nine shillings a share.'

'That's it! Those fellows were saying it must have come out of capital and not profits. What's the difference? I asked. Eggs in the nest, potatoes in the oven – why worry where they come from? Why be pedantic? Pay it out and give everyone a treat, I said. My dear, they looked at me as if I'd just walked off the Ark. Anyway, I thought I should mention it about Leonard. You must decide what's for the best.'

He slapped both knees and stood up. 'Why don't we pop your father's furniture and make something of this room? It's too depressing for words.'

She smiled without parting her lips. 'Perhaps we'll let the children choose a few pieces when they get married. It won't be long. Harriet's nineteen on her next birthday.'

They went out, he to get his paint chest while she promised to look at her copy of the contract with Lutwylch & Lutwylch that her father had signed. This quite put his mind at rest, for he knew that Isabel kept her promises and that by 'look at' she meant 'investigate thoroughly'.

He noticed that he was running low on gamboge yellow and scribbled 'Go to colourman in Pottergate' on a piece of card – he

49

forgot his name for now. And at the very height of the summer, he thought, how irksome, as he walked down the path to the boathouse from which he could hear the tap-tap, tap-tap of Jammy hammering oakum between the new planks, and the muffled sounds of a conversation. Splash, something heavy went into the water. He smiled.

The boat (spinach green, black thwarts and gunwale) had been raised onto trestles. Jammy was squatting on his hams wielding the double-ended oakum mallet. In his left hand was the caulking iron. He frowned as he worked. If the iron rang hollow, the oakum hadn't been forced deep enough between the timbers. He was always listening, the fullness of the chink-chink at the edge of his mind. He moved on a pace, reaching for another handful of the woolly, dirty yellow fibre. A brazier of tar was simmering in a corner; the boathouse was full of its reek. Fred was following behind Jammy with the tar-pot, stubbling the black viscous skeins into the joints to seal the oakum. Having Jammy working so hard beside him filled him with penitence for what he'd said earlier. He made a point of helping him tease the oakum apart, asked him repeatedly if he was applying sufficient tar, and went doggedly about his job, not realising that his tongue was sticking out in exactly the same way as when he'd made fun of Jammy. Emily was brushing some blond curly wood-shavings into a heap. (She'd just found a broken mooring ring. It was this that had gone into the water, Jammy crying out too late that it might be useful.)

Such industry could not last. The heat of the sun, reinforced by the mingled scents rising from the river and the incessant murmur of insects, gradually imposed a sort of companionable indolence on the proceedings. Dragonflies aired themselves on the lily pads or raced over the water, wings clattering, their bodies like bright blue pins. Swallows were nesting in the roof. Now and again a parent swooped in to feed its fledglings, and the children would pause, ever more frequently, to ask Jammy if swallows could swim and such like, questions that were part serious and part in jest and thus in keeping with their half-hearted attempts to keep sloth at bay. It was usually Emily who did the asking. She was trying to make a plait out of the wood-shavings almost underneath the nest and could hear quite clearly the hungry twittering of the young birds.

'Everyone happy?' Thomas stuck his nose in and looked around.

'Corking,' said Fred, hastily applying himself to the tar-pot.

'Ha, ha, ha, very funny I don't think,' Emily said, put out because she hadn't thought of it first.

'Why, what's so funny?' And then he twigged and said it again, with a grin as wide as a cart-wheel. 'Absolutely corking, Papa!'

'Take your belt to them if they get uppity,' Thomas said to Jammy, laughing. 'Whip 'em to ribbons,' at which both children stuck their tongues out at him and Fred said he'd put a lump of tar in his mouth if he didn't go away and let them get on with it.

Emily asked him to leave the door open in case the swallows found it easier. He picked up his paints and went about fifty yards to the bench on what he called his look-out point, a grassy mound halfway between the bridge and the boathouse. The sun had come off its zenith. The light was no longer so stinging. He would make a start – sketch a few figures, let his eye settle to the colours of the horses and the women and all the movements of hay-making. When he was ready to begin painting, the sun would be perfect. He pegged the easel together, tried it in a few positions and rather fussily laid out his brushes.

'Mr Tom . . .' It was Jammy, the only person in England who called him that.

'What is it?' he asked with a trace of irritation.

Jammy Peach was twenty-four. He was short, beefy and ripe with miscellaneous odours. His face was round and pock-marked and his hair cropped squarely across the neck, which was strawberry red from the sun. Everything about him was strong; calves, thighs, forearms, his frank blue eyes. He lived with his mother in Sparling and shaved once a week, in the kitchen at Fordwell on a Saturday.

He wiped the sweat off his forehead. His large hands fiddled uncertainly with the oakum mallet.

'Put it on the ground, for heaven's sake,' Thomas said. 'Well?'

'There was a man on the b-bridge this morning, around sparrow-fart.'

'And?'

'He was a furriner,' Jammy said darkly. 'Looking, p-p-poking about, at an hour honest folks are still a-bed.'

'Could it have been the district surveyor?'

'Not he, I knows he. He doan't need to swilly about in case he's watched. He owns the bridge. This were a furriner in a tall hat, not big, small.'

'You're talking in riddles now.'

'Do I am!' Jammy expostulated, his face fraught with indignation. 'A furriner! Arter suffen, yew can be sure. Us had better watch our tail-ends. Furriners mean trouble.'

Pish-wash, Thomas thought to himself, because just then he heard Rodgers' wagons going empty down the road, bump and jingle, and he was in the mood to be diverted. He was certain he could work up something quite pretty. The river would be in the foreground; he was wondering how much of it to show. The Ark was still in his mind, and water and animals and Abel Rodgers, who was blessed with the bushiest of beards and more sons than anyone could keep track of.

The wagons crossed the bridge and turned left into the meadow beside the grove of poplars in the corner. They drew abreast of him. Rodgers' sons were lined up on the swaying bottoms, hitching their trousers and spitting on their palms as they prepared to receive the first pitches of hay. It had been cut the day before he went to London and was now in that condition of readiness that Rodgers called 'gay', a word Thomas knew would be incomprehensible to anyone who had not smelt for himself the perfume, almost inflammable, that ascended in clouds from dried clover and sweet meadow flowers. He looked across at the women leaning on their long wooden forks, chatting: thick brown legs, faded blue shifts to below the knee, straw bonnets tied beneath the chin.

'Nonsense,' he said. 'I'll wager it was some friend of the parson doing a spot of amateur archaeology. You know what his friends are like.' He slid his thumb up a pencil and took a measure of the women vis-à-vis the poplars, which he had decided to introduce on the right, as a sort of flanking movement.

Nine

TWO YEARS passed. Jammy's prying stranger was forgotten. Nothing further was heard about the North Norfolk Railway. People who were considered to be in the know said it had been a reconnaissance, that Mr Gooby was waiting for more propitious times on the Exchange. Scoffers called it a try-on. Where the deuce was the goods traffic to come from up there that would make it profitable? Speculators who had bought land everywhere kept their mouths shut.

So life continued in this slow, distant province with only a few jolts from the stampede of progress.

A coach driver fell off his box one cold February. The horses trotted on, none of the passengers aware of the loss until they reached their inn. The Norwich *Phenomena* gave up the unequal struggle and was sold for firewood. Blissett entered the Poor House. The Norwich & Newmarket Mail became the last coach in England to deliver the post to London.

Cholera broke out at Rudham with the loss of many lives. The Gages had an outing *en famille* to watch the garrison steeplechases of the 16th Lancers at Stanninghall. A new coin, the florin, was acclaimed by republicans for denying, or at least omitting to claim, that the queen reigned 'by the Grace of God'. General Farrant fractured his leg in the most mundane of circumstances and was unable to proceed to the West Indies. Georgiana therefore did not press Thomas to do her portrait, since nursing had given her a permanent scowl, she said. And Jimmy Rush, a most dreadful bruiser, the murderer of a father and son, was hanged in public from the engine of death that had been erected on the bridge between Castle Hill and Castle Meadow.

Thousands (at least fifty, it was alleged, including very many children) journeyed to Norwich to see Calcraft the Executioner draw the bolt. Extra trains were laid on from London and cheap return tickets sold by the basketful. To the regret of all, especially Sam, who was drunk even before leaving Fordwell, there was no confession from the scaffold, and the prisoner, who was dressed completely in black and behaved without any emotion whatsoever, turned his back on the crowd before the fatal moment.

'Not even a frightened little scamper,' Sam reported to Thomas the next day. 'He should have tried something. What did he think we'd come for? Just stood there like a gatepost – and then plop. A waste of a day, and that's what my friends thought as well. Why, old Dick Turpin, when they strung him up at York, he slapped his leg again and again to stop it twitching' – which he proceeded to do, most realistically – 'and that was honest of him, and it's right he should still be remembered for it after all this time. Anyone would be nervous waiting to be dropped. But Jimmy Rush – most disappointing indeed. Never looked like giving folks a show.'

That was in April. A month later, on a Sunday, Thomas and Isabel celebrated the twentieth anniversary of their wedding by giving a luncheon party for two hundred friends. A five-poler tent was erected in the garden and garnished with a cockled trim of blue bunting along the ridge and down the guy-ropes. The contingent of guests from Norwich came by horse-drawn omnibus, as did the band of the 16th Lancers. Both parties were observed to be in high spirits on arrival. Champagne and sherry were served on the croquet lawn. The first course, gulls' eggs with a twist of salt, was served at one o'clock. The Mayor of Norwich, John Suckling, made his speech at four. The second of the two puddings was consumed shortly after six. While this was being digested, an agitation was got up for a tug-of-war between the soldiers and certain gentlemen farmers, but it started to rain and the party fizzled politely to its close.

Two weeks after this Isabel came home from town with the news that Mr Gooby had been seen entering a house in Thorpe Road, very close to the station, in a most ownerly fashion. It had been Leonard who had told her.

Ten

THERE WERE circumstances in Julius Gooby's early life that he had no wish to recall. A reference to them existed in his unpolished accent, and in a certain hardness in his business dealings that had a far deeper character than simple greed. His face, which was as sallow as that of any Londoner, had about it a hiddenness, as if it were a face he'd borrowed. To have called it calculating or straightforwardly commercial, in the mould, say, of the industrialist Meredith, would have been to understate its gist. These were traits easily guessed at, but there was an additional quality that was unreadable, so that people wondered if a secret password had to be invoked in order to gain entry. Bland was a word that came to them, before they decided it wasn't awkward enough. Gooby was in his thirties, a bachelor, the seventh son of a clerk in the counting department of Mr Gladstone, the merchant prince.

This evening he was angry. It was not like him; he had long since tamped home the stopper on any emotions that might be unprofitable. Nevertheless he felt he had a right to his anger.

On his first visit to Norfolk he'd ridden the course of his railway to satisfy himself it was practicable. He'd scattered some cards around town to sow the seeds and to keep interlopers at bay. Then he'd returned to London to find a backer.

Now he had come to Norwich in earnest. He had taken up residence in one of the new houses in Thorpe Road, which he'd rented by letter for an indefinite period. He'd had his landlady fit a lock to his business room on the ground floor, hung Stanford's large map of the county on the wall, and shelved his small travelling library: a couple of Scott's novels, legal books, a work on geology, Jones's *Instructions for Railway Surveyors*, and a much-thumbed *Tables for the Calculation of Compounded Interest*. He'd tried the three bedrooms in turn, made himself agreeable to the maids, and approved the cooking (he was not discriminating). Out of professional curiosity he checked his watch on hearing the departure of the first up train to London at 7 a.m. and again when the last down train arrived at 9.25 p.m. He'd tuned his ear to the natives' dialect, ingratiated himself with the town notables, and with increasing impatience awaited the arrival of the florid, porky young man whose haunches were now distending to its limits the rush-backed chair opposite him.

He did not care that Walter Harrington had been delayed by the death of his aunt. All he knew was that his surveyor was a week late, and by taking it upon himself to inspect Fordwell bridge in broad daylight as he travelled into town had acted with criminal carelessness.

'Dangle 'em, dangle 'em like ducks, wasn't that to be our policy? Keep 'em guessing. Play one against the other. Stop 'em trying to ramp up the price of their land. So what do you do? Without so much as seeing me first – you thought what? Let's get this straight, young sir. I'm the one who does the thinking and you're the one who does the doing, if I say so and when I say so and how I say so. Not a minute before and not a minute after. Not weather depending, or women or drink or sleep or any damned thing but me. Me!' His light olive eyes were bolted to Walter's face. 'Understood? Yes or no?'

'But the bridge—'

'Is a bridge and under every bridge there's water, and railway engines can't swim, should it have escaped your attention. They can't swim and they can't burrow, jump or levitate. But the water is there and somehow we have to get our trains across it. Therefore bridges are especially interesting to us. What are they? Louder, young sir. Speak up. Treat me as you do your godfather, our esteemed chairman, whom I recall you describing as a moribund old fart-box. Louder, I still can't hear you. Very good. So are we alone in understanding what the function of a bridge is? Are we Archimeeds?'

Walter didn't know if he should correct him. This was his first job. He crossed a thick booted leg over the other and looked penitently at a tear in the knee of his riding breeches.

'I'll tell you who else knows. Only every clodhopper in the county, that's who. So what did you do? Did you *crawl* and *slither* round the bridge like a serpent? Oh no, clever Mr Harrington rides up bold as brass and inspects it from top to bottom so that the whole of Norfolk can see what his game is. Furthermore he does it on a showy great horse that everyone will have paid heed to – as if he was Lochinvar. Furthermore he is proud to have done it. Proud of all things! What do you keep between those ears of yours? Soup? Porridge? Whey?'

'I think you might be happier with another surveyor,' Walter said after a pause. 'Or you could do your own surveying, one or the other.' Now was the time to stand up for himself, now or never at all.

And there, without realising it, he had hit upon Julius Gooby's weak point. For the latter was very far from being an outdoors man, was in fact metropolitan to the core. No easterly winds rushing across the wintry plains of Norfolk had ever bruised his cheeks or made his tears run. No barley stubble had ever scratched his pallid shanks. He had conceived a theoretical and romantic attachment to the countryside from reading the works of Sir Walter Scott; but the practice he detested. Whenever he went to see his old uncle in Dorking he caught a cold. The smell of animals disgusted him. Wasps flew out of apples and stung him. His feet iced over when he went for a walk in his glossy long-toed shoes. Scott was as far as he wished to take it; images of soaring eagles, and the sun setting over misty crags. True contentment came of an evening when he could take *Ivanhoe* off the shelf and race kilted over the moors of Caledon while all the time sitting with a glass of hock by his elbow and a fire roaring in the grate.

This last had additional significance for him since his father, the ever frugal book-keeper, had ruled over a household where pokers and all such instruments were expressly forbidden, in words like gunshot, on the grounds of economy. The coal was obliged to settle under its own momentum, its heat leaching meanly outwards and penetrating with only the faintest blush into the region where a seventh son had to sit. Capital fires were as much a sign of his independence as was his career as a railway promoter.

In this he had started quietly, with six parts of determination to three of fear and one of hope. Fortune smiled on him. He worked hard, saved harder, and acquired sufficient prosperity for his brothers to be jealous. Then, in the summer of 1846, his eye was caught by two pieces of information. One, that Mr Thomas Cook was advertising to the public an 800-mile round tour of Scotland for the remarkable price of a guinea a ticket. The other, that an excursion train had in one day carried six thousand people from Norwich to Yarmouth and back for threepence a child and a shilling an adult. He had little enough idea where Yarmouth was, let alone why such a multitude should want to go there. But he could visualise them with total clarity, each and every person packed like pebbles into those tiny roofless wagons that tuttered and tumpled down the line beneath snowy trails of smoke. He could see the six thousand, he could hear their squeals of joy – and he counted the takings. 'Aaah-ha!' he said, with such an expenditure of breath that a film of moisture formed on the window at which he was standing. If they'd go to Yarmouth, why not to somewhere else? He abandoned *Ivanhoe* for an atlas and settled down to make a list of all the coastal towns in Norfolk without a railway.

After his reconnaissance he began to look for some great person to lend him credence. One night the name of Sir Hector Mountstuart came to him, a profligate, doddery thing reputed throughout the City of London for his unblushing availability as a figurehead.

An introduction was procured through his father's connection with Mr Gladstone's trading house. He tried to get him for ten years and ended up with five. On the other hand the imposing name on his letterhead cost rather less than he'd expected. Only at the final bend, when he had his fingers round the door handle and was wondering with whom he could celebrate, did this threadbare grandee, this leaky old cockerel whom he'd thought seven-eighths addled, start fanning the fire with their contract and say slyly, 'My godson Walter, you'll have to employ him, of course. You'll need a surveyor. Did I forget to mention that before?'

So there it was. If he allowed Walter to leave, he'd lose Sir Hector as well, and the writing-paper of the North Norfolk Railway Company would be shorn of the only title to which he had access. Who else could he find at short notice? He bunched the wings of his underlip into a pair of dwarfish buttocks and weighed Walter up afresh. He hoped he hadn't been foisted with an idiot. Dear God, how he hoped that his surveyor wouldn't sink him. The scheme was so pure; the territory undefended; the capital lined up and waiting. It was a plum on a plate, as juicy as could be and calling out to be skinned.

'You've only got to say the word,' Walter said.

Gooby regarded him bleakly. He had made his point. His anger had shrunk to a small knob of disappointment. Already he was regretting having spoken so harshly. But the fact was that the man had blundered. When he himself had looked at the bridge two years ago, he had done so at dawn. No one could possibly have seen him. Yes, Walter had behaved stupidly. He would have to be controlled. But was he too well-bred to take orders? And now he had thought of this, other anxieties presented themselves to Gooby. Was there a hard enough grain to the man, any pounce, any claw? On the question of truth – lax or rigid? Attitude to expenses – cheese-paring or giddy like Sir Hector? He searched through the other's guileless blue eyes and the word simpleton flitted across his mind. It was sufficient. He felt safe in his judgement when someone drew a strong reaction from him. Good or bad, he could live with either so long as there was a tug. It was the mealy in-between man he distrusted. He nodded across the table. Walter would do.

'Slow but sure, that's how I work,' he said with a wan smile of encouragement. 'No need to charge at it like a buffalo. An inch at a time, keeping our wits about us, and it'll all drop into place. Remember, the North Norfolk Railway will be no concern of ours once it's up and running. We're just the promoters. It won't be us who have to make it pay. Of course we must act responsibly,' – his mouth twisted sarcastically. He was about to say 'up to a point' but Walter looked too honest to take it – 'we'll get a poor name for ourselves if solid is found to be bog when they come to lay the track.'

'Like at the Bow marshes,' Walter said. 'That'll have cost someone a pretty penny.'

Gooby looked at him with more interest. He passed his tongue round his lips, a flicker of pinkish grey in the darkening room. 'In the final analysis, where we make our money is by the sale of an idea. We make our dream convincing, we propose a price. Discussions, a handshake, the usual formalities, and thereafter our good friend caveat emptor takes over. You know what I mean by this?'

Walter smiled. 'Of course.'

'What matters is that handshake. So next time you go out with your rods and pegs, be tactful. Do it by night, or when people are at church. Keep clear of trouble at all costs. If a gent comes up to you, goes a queer colour and starts using legal terms, don't argue. Run away as fast as you can. I assure you, it saves a lot of bother in the end.'

Walter had never actually met a surveyor whose head had been broken in a fight, but he knew it happened. 'I don't see them as trouble-makers in these parts. Too dozy. It'll be like tapping a bluebottle on its casing.'

Gooby liked that. He pinged the nail of his forefinger against the brass lamp stand. Like tapping flies. That was a good one.

'At least going by what I heard in the inn at Sparling. I said I was after some partridge shooting this autumn, what were the prospects locally and so on. The two parties I spoke to were most forthcoming. Twins I'd say, the right old sort of blabberers. Stuffed with gossip from head to heel.'

'That's more like it, Walter, that's more in my style.' Gooby struck the lamp again. The boy wasn't such a noddy by any means. It was where he'd have started himself. He turned the oil tap on the lamp and lit the wick.

He wondered if Walter's connections might not actually turn out to be useful. (The distinctions between the various layers of the aristocracy were a mystery to him. They intrigued his mercantilist nature, for he was certain that buying and selling were at the heart of the system. Where and how it took place, he was at a loss. But it occurred to him that the class of person they'd have to deal with up here, the owning type, would talk more readily to Walter than to the son of a clerk.) He smiled to himself. His hollow waxworks face filled out under the lamplight and grew confiding. It had been some days since he'd had a worthwhile conversation. It was a relief to be talking trade again. He launched into an account of the quarrels that were forever occurring between landowners and the railwaymen.

'. . . cattle go dry, don't sleep as they should, lose weight. Foxes can't be chased properly. Trains carry epidemics and animals die. What else? Sparks set fire to the crops. Birds drop dead from the coal fumes. Views – ruined. Trees – butchered. Pleasure grounds – disfigured for eternity. In short, losses will be catastrophic and the noblest families in Britain condemned to penury.

'So we are told. These great squires sit us down beside their agents and stewards and lawyers – Walter, you never did see such a lot of scallywags in your whole life – and they tell us this that and the other about the labours of their ancestors, oh, they spin such tales as would make a stone weep.

'Then they summon Lady Jane and put her up to a story about how her divine angels are sure to be chopped to pieces on the metals. Instead she says, "Ooh, will I really be able to get to London in an hour?" Whereupon her Lord pricks up his ruined ears and thinks, Good God, I'll be able to get my hands on a decent whore quicker than I can a cup of tea – the passages in their mansions, you have to take a ball of string with you or you'd never get out alive. It takes forever to be brought a glass of water.'

'So they come to their senses and a bargain is made?'

'Invariably. When you get to the bottom of it, they're as venal as tinkers. The stuff about sacrifice and principles and the work of centuries is nothing but smoke. Added to which, of course, they're all up to the cornices in debt.'

Gooby set off round the room slapping his paperknife against his palm. 'Debt – vices – the opinions of wives. That's what governs the price of their land. That's what it boils down to when we come to negotiate. Now . . .' He came to the map of Norfolk, unhooked its linen tab and steadied the black wooden roller as it unfurled with the noise of creaking parchment. He put down the knife and took a pencil from his pocket. He'd already shaded in the possible routes from Norwich to the coast while waiting for Walter.

'There are other ways we can drive it besides over the bridge at Fordwell. Here, or here, or even out here, making a loop to the west. They are all possible.'

'But the river, Mr Gooby—'

'Gets smaller. It has to, and then it becomes a brook, exactly where the point of my pencil is. Small river: small bridge: small cost. However, I agree with you. Fordwell is the best. Solid footings, I've seen them for myself. Those old people knew what they were doing.'

He put his hands on his knees and peered closely at the map. 'Who lives in the manor house there?'

'A Mr Gage, I was told. Seemingly an easy-going fellow.'

'What did those twins at the pub have to say about him? Any hint of financial weakness? Gambles, perhaps? A married man, we may assume for now, the bigger fool him.' He straightened, stroking his chin. 'All fish come to the bait eventually. Dangle, dangle, dangle. Dangle 'em till they dance. And if they demand too much, why, we'll tell 'em their neighbour's land is better for a track like ours.'

There was a double tap at the door. Walter went and unlocked it. Their landlady was there, saying dinner was ready.

The meal, their first alone in each other's company, was awkward. Gooby had little conversation outside the railways and Scott's novels; and in Walter's opinion the Laird of Abbotsford was the most boring writer in the world. He hoped he wouldn't be subjected to a bed-time reading – he'd had enough of that as a boy. They shared a bottle of thin claret and Gooby studied Walter's table manners.

Afterwards they returned to the business room and locked themselves in. Walter agreed to exchange his ostentatious chestnut for a humbler mount. 'But for God's sake don't get a skewbald,' Gooby told him. 'People always remember skewbalds. See if you can't get a common palfrey somewhere.' He'd just met the word in Scott and believed it would still be current in a place so benighted as Norfolk. Then Walter was to get on with his survey. Meanwhile he, Mr Gooby, would make himself known to the members of the Council, for, as he remarked, everyone likes to be associated with the coming thing and a little buttering now 'would make it all slip down more smoothly when the day came'.

Then Gooby said something that surprised Walter. 'Believe it or not, there are still people who look on us railwaymen as complete ogres. The ranter Sibthorp, for example. He should have his tongue cut out for all the lies he puts round in Parliament. *We* represent the future, not those pinchbeck aldermen. They can make laws till the cows come home about drainage and street lighting, but it's only us, the pioneers, who can give the country its liberty. Yes, liberty! This is what the railways stand for, the unchallengeable right of the common man to take his family and seek work wherever he desires, and to do so cheaply. The railway system will alter the conditions of life for everyone, including the class of person from whom our rulers are drawn. At their peril will our political dynasties oppose it. What I am speaking of is a revolution caused by price, convenience and speed, which has itself been caused by certain mechanical discoveries. We – you and I, Walter – have been chosen as the midwives of the future. When the good citizens of Norwich go to holiday on the sands, to sport themselves amid the sea breezes and the little cheeping birds, it will be thanks to us. We must never forget that we have a duty to civilisation as well as to our pockets.'

For a moment his sallow face bared itself, his eyes gleaming with evangelical fervour. Then he picked up his paperknife and *Guy Mannering*, which he had started on the train from London. He plumped up his cushions and neatly slit the next sixteen pages, his ration for the day. From time to time he glanced over to where Walter was playing backgammon against himself, rattling the dice-box above his shoulder, ooing, phewing and whacking down the counters like musket-fire as he swept his forces round the board with deft red fingers. There was something obviously mathematical to the game that attracted Gooby. On the other hand he had forsworn all operations of chance from the very earliest age and therefore kept his distance.

Eleven

THE SEPTEMBER equinox passed with its brief season of storms. Night won its annual victory over day. Autumn had arrived, or to be exact, an Indian summer. In the low sunlight of morning, the pastures glistened with spiders' webs as if coated with icing. Maples were brilliant in the blackberried hedgerows; the dangling keys of the ashes like ebony against their persevering green foliage. Bronze-tinged chestnut leaves flopped from one branch to the next towards the waiting earthworms, and through the colossal Norfolk sky a motherly breeze herded flocks of tousled clouds at a leisurely pace.

Thomas spent most of the mornings painting. Of an afternoon he would let himself be chivvied by Sam into shooting partridges for a couple of hours. Jammy laboured at his grammar beneath Isabel's quilted eye. Fred started at the Norfolk Free Grammar School as a day boy. Nelson had been educated there, and Isabel had been much taken by the new headmaster, John Woolley.

He'd hated leaving Fordwell. When the day arrived, he climbed up an apple tree in his new knickerbocker suit – cried – pelted his parents with apples as they stood below remonstrating – told Thomas he was a beast and said unprintable words to his mother. Thomas threatened to cut the tree down upon which Fred stopped his tears for long enough to inform him he hadn't enough puff to cut down a raspberry cane. It was Mrs Macbride who did the trick, hands on her hips, giving as good as she got. 'You say that once more to me, Master Fred, and I'll box your ears so hard they'll meet.'

When he returned in the evening he started to cry all over again because the older boys had taunted him for his size. However, he soon learned to cope with that and would retort to any slight, 'I may be small but I'm not stupid' – or slow or asleep, whatever the circumstances required. It took him only a week to decide that his family were dunderheads and it was he who was king of the castle.

General Farrant received a new posting and departed overseas. Georgiana and her friends began to clamour for Thomas to do their portraits. She sent her groom over to Fordwell with a pound of honeycomb as a reminder that she'd asked him first.

As always at the onset of the Michaelmas quarter, nature was tainted with a beautiful sorrow and mankind grew urgent as it tidied away the going year and considered its mortality.

The day that Fred went to school an important meeting of the City Council took place. Two items were of particular interest to the members. They knew by instinct, by the scent of the phrases on the order paper, that so long as these delectable subjects were debated with befitting attention to detail, they could be made to last well into the winter.

Full-whiskered, deep-voiced, expectant of a good show, by 10 a.m. they were gathering on the steps of the Guildhall. The more ancient held their order papers tight against their noses, scrutinising them with suspicion. Some waved them like flags at arriving friends. Others flicked them up and down behind their backs as they discussed local affairs. To one side stood the Clerk, sober and dutiful in a black tailcoat, and the Mayor, John Suckling, a short, bustling, thick-eared man not known for tolerance. The two of them completed their review. Suckling consulted his watch. As the single bell from the cathedral split the sunshine on the dot of the half-hour, the members trooped through the iron-studded wooden doors. Suckling led the way with a heavy baronial tread, his gold chain of office regal with authority, the ermine ruff of his maroon gown high across his neck and its ermine hem lightly brushing the flagstones, which had just been mopped and were damp.

The upstairs chamber was pleasantly airy beneath its high, timbered ceiling. From the panelled walls a selection of city notables looked down from their gilt-framed portraits upon the table of darkened oak that filled most of the room. Four brass gasoliers hung from the centre beam on adjustable cords. Natural lighting came from the windows overlooking the Market Place and, at one end of the chamber, from an oriel window whose leaded panes were a mixture of clear glass and pallid mauves and blues. Today there was no carpet. Someone had bungled: the scattering of tired old rugs had been thrown out before the new Axminster arrived. Feet echoed from the unevenly coloured boards as the members made for their customary seats.

The zealous, the deaf, and those who were distrustful of the Mayor's crabby governance jostled for a place near him at the table. Lutwylch was on his right. A couple who could not stay for the full session leaned against the fluted pilasters of the fire surround. Some lounged across the seats in the oriel window, arguing good-naturedly amongst themselves as to whether or not it should be opened. Two lucky men had a fold of curtain at their backs to lean against. (The curtains had only one span, and that purely by way of ornament, for it was a principle of these good burghers that the workings of democracy should at all times be visible, especially to the mob, which they still feared.)

Everyone stood while the Clerk rushed through the ritual Latin blessing on the works of man and God. Chairs scraped as they sat down again. Certain old-fashioned parties placed their snuff-boxes in front of them. The deaf inserted their ear-trumpets. John Suckling plucked back the sleeve of his gown and struck the block smartly with his gavel.

'Pursuant to the charter granted to the city – what is it now, Mr Spennylove? No, I will not hear of it. I will not! The correct preposition behind the word pursuant is "to" and not "upon". My legal friend upon my right concurs with me so let that be the end of it now and for always. Every time we meet you drive us insane with your quiddling. Wheretofore, whichsoever, here-sounder, God knows what – who cares? The shorter the better. The word is "to" and I shall not put it to the vote. Mr Clerk, what can you be thinking of? Delete Spennylove's nonsense this instant.' He leaned upon the Clerk's shoulder, said, 'There, and the next line as well,' gave the block a couple of sharp taps, and continued: 'Pursuant to the charter granted by his puissant majesty King Henry II and renewed on divers occasions since, and by the powers vested in me, I declare this session opened.

'Apologies received – Mr Clerk has the list – the usual malingerers. Next: matters arising from the last meeting . . . '

Within minutes Suckling had glowered and bullied his way through all that would normally have occupied the entire day. The police had their powers renewed for another year, the coopers' apprentices had their conditions improved, the river was dredged, daffodils planted, clocks re-gilded, and Spennylove again routed, this time with such vehemence that he got up and left. No one was sorry to see him go. He interrupted constantly, he knew what every word of the Latin meant, he was an awful fellow.

'Now,' said Suckling, eyes gleaming like polished pewter, his bullfrog cheeks already colouring up, 'now, gentlemen,' rubbing his hands so ferociously as to be almost flaying them, 'to the business of the day – the refurbishment of the Palace Theatre and how we are to celebrate it. The date, the scheme of colours, the allocation of the boxes – ah! I knew your ears would shake when I mentioned the boxes. We shall get there by and by. First: I intend no sacrilege – your gods are as good as mine – however, the Palace Theatre is not a church and anyone who believes that we are speaking of a species of Harvest Festival should follow the example of Mr Spennylove and go home and stay there until the day is past. No clergy and no blessings, that's what I'm getting at. If I have my way—'

'When did you not have your way, John?' asked a voice from the window.

'Every pack of dogs needs a leader. So, in this wise we shall have no holiness, no cant, none of our wormy local saints – you all know who I mean – getting onto the stage to pray for our souls. What I say is thank you, but they're very fine as it is. This is to be a gala, *our* gala. We shall enjoy ourselves up to the hilt, I am determined of it. What do I see? Clowns, trapezes, jugglers, acrobats, and our children laughing their lovely topknots off. A choir. The band of the Volunteer Guard done up to the nines. I hear drums, fifes, cornets – the big drum, the biggest they can lay their hands on, going bonga-bonga-bong' – he thrashed the air with his gavel – 'as though it was the Queen's birthday and they were marching up the Mall. Afterwards we'll have a feast for the city, roast fowl, hams, stewed celery, plum puddings, custard by the pint, and acres of apricot jam tart. At midnight the Volunteers will play us to our homes with Britannia and all the stars will rejoice and exclaim one to each other, Thus do the men of Norfolk make good cheer.

'We have the money, we have the resolve. Our deliberations must be thorough. We must plan like generals. The spark, gentlemen, is what we must find among ourselves today, the spark of genius that flashes only once in every century.' He sat down.

Lutwylch thought the last an unhappy reference since it was by the operation of a spark that the Palace Theatre came to be on their order papers. In any case the celebrations were of little interest to him unless he and Joan could have a box. Whereas the next item to be discussed . . . He waited quietly, staring up at the wooden vaulting as he reviewed the components of a particularly awkward conveyance that had been brought to him yesterday.

It was not known how, on the frost-still night of 19 February, 1845, the theatre had been burned to a shell. At the time there were few who cared if some old pikes, Elizabethan doublets and sweat-stale taffeta gowns had gone up in flames. What was this compared to the fact that a waiter at The Swan Inn – a waiter! – had just made a fortune from dabbling in railway shares? But when, six months later, two speculators appeared with a proposal to rebuild the theatre as a hotel, everyone suddenly remembered the Christmas shows of their youth, their Congreve and their Sheridan, and it became the critical redoubt in the battle between civilisation and commerce. John Suckling was overcome by the certainty that he'd never played a finer Macbeth than on the Palace's pokey stage. Mrs Suckling went round reminding her friends how as girls they'd chanted,

> Eeny, weeny, winey, wo
> Where do all the Frenchmen go?

when it came to the scene where Bonaparte Butters, their favourite pantomine villain, had to choose between one of three trap-doors for his mortal shrieking. plunge. 'Three of them, my dears! We were so spoiled! We can't stand aside and do nothing. No theatre in town? Whatever will our children think of us?'

A committee was formed. Subscriptions were raised, the Council chipped in the balance, and the speculators were vanquished.

Among the five scalps that Lutwylch had been told to bring in was that of Isabel Gage. In fact she topped the subscription list, for which she was rewarded by having her name printed in bold in the *Norwich Mercury*. She was aghast at this, regarding it as a form of trespass on her quiet and withdrawing character, and wrote a firm letter to Mr Marley, the editor. She left it to Leonard Lutwylch to ensure that at least she wasn't mentioned on the commemorative tablet that Suckling planned to affix under a bust of Shakespeare, on the wall between the two staircases leading to the upper circle. Nor did she think she had done anything to deserve having a box on the gala night. She let it be known that in her opinion it should be given to unfortunates from the Poor House.

However, hers was the only name on which the Council found itself able to agree. To all other proposals there was an objection. The deaf became whole and started to shout, old rivalries were resurrected and new ones discovered. John Suckling, who considered his claim the purest, was told he couldn't possibly run the show and speechify from a box. Lutwylch, who thought his wife's pedigree entitled him to the very best treatment, was reminded that he detested music. A public lottery was suggested. When someone asked if that meant his gardener or a family of gypsies could end up having a box, a wholly different stratum of argument was exposed. 'Am I to sit beneath the man whom I pay to trim my beard?' 'He'll lean over and spit on us, that sort of person is always spitting.' 'Now, gentlemen, let us try and be more tolerant. Lotteries stand for equality, and we all know that equality is the mother of justice' – but this mild observation went unheeded. With the exception of the last speaker, no one was interested in justice or equality. Each wanted a box for himself; was already reviewing his social obligations; raking through family quarrels; designing an invitation card. The only person who had an incontestable right to one of the four boxes was Isabel Gage. This and this only was the common ground between the councillors.

'I suppose that means Thomas as well,' grumbled someone. 'You'd think he knew all the numbers at the lucky dip.'

'They say he's going to hold an exhibition of his paintings at Mr Batt's hotel,' his neighbour remarked.

'The women will buy, we can be sure of that. At least my wife will. She calls him the new Rembrandt.'

'Did you see the picture he sold at the Academy? One person said it held the wall very well, which is a low form of praise. Another that he couldn't make head or tail of it.'

'Queer set-up, being a painter. Books – I can fathom those. You fill the inkwell, scratch your head, and once you get to the bottom of the page you turn it over and off you go again. It's like speaking only you write the words down. But pictures – where do you start, in the centre, in a corner? How do you choose what to paint? Well enough if it's there in front of you and can't get away, like a horse your groom is holding. But what if you're doing a parable from the Bible? You can't tell me that a painter knows any better than we do how big the loaves were, or what sort of fish they shared. Were they trout? Were they grayling?'

The gavel sounded. 'Number eight on the order paper and then we shall have lunch. The North Norfolk Railway Company, of 312 Fenchurch Street—'

'Tricky job that, painting. Of course children love it, sloshing—'

'A very becoming address, I don't need to tell you gentlemen that. Chairman Sir Hector Mountstuart, the well-known financier, General Manager, Mr Julius Gooby. I've made my enquiries and I'm completely satisfied you won't find more experienced people in the railway business than these two. Very fine men, both of them. This is an enterprise that can only increase the prosperity of the county. It is in our interests that it succeeds. I hope fervently that we shall see eye to eye on the North Norfolk and be able to give it our blessing.'

A degree of pleading had entered Suckling's usual take-it-or-leave-it form of delivery and people noticed this. Fresh rumours had been circulating about the North Norfolk. Several members had been overtured by Gooby. The impression he'd made was that of a very commercial man. 'Where's the harm in that? He hasn't got to where he is by driving a train up the river,' remarked one of his defenders. Yet still none could say precisely what was afoot, which redoubled their curiosity. Why in the north? What was so splendid up there besides Houghton and Holkham? Why should the Council be involved and why was the Mayor nervous? The odour of money reached them. They were inquisitive and stared greedily at Suckling, as hawks will wait for a tasty titbit to pop out of a bush.

'It'll be a first-class operation, I've received assurances on this,' he said.

'You mean it'll be for swells only?' The speaker was the same man who'd proposed a lottery for the theatre boxes. 'No cheap fares, no Parliamentary trains, is that what you're saying?'

'By first-class I intended top notch. Of course there will be Parliamentary fares on certain trains. A penny a mile is all the common man can afford. A penny a mile makes him tick. No one is more in favour of the system of Parliamentary fares than Mr Gooby.'

'Will they run at decent hours? Without undue stoppages and bullocking about? One hears daily of the law being made a monkey of for the sake of shareholders and their dividends. Parliamentary trains starting at four in the morning. Taking sixteen hours from London to Liverpool. So what's in the North Norfolk for the common man, eh, Mayor, eh?'

'Hold hard there, don't go biting my head off. This is a railway that hasn't even got to a House of Commons Committee yet—'

'Then why are we talking about it?' said another.

'Because they're playing fair with us, that's why. They've come to us at the outset, placed their cards on the table and said, "Let's put our heads together and make this work for the good of everyone." Railways increase trade. I have the figures before me; they are indisputable. Norwich is not the city that it used to be. Our population has declined since the last census. We have to be modern. We have to encourage the new type of manufacturing into town. Transport is the key to everything. We must act now, not sit on our backsides and dither. The North Norfolk—'

'Norwich to where?' demanded a man from the oriel window.

'If we cannot attract the manufacturing classes, we shall have to look elsewhere for new sources of wealth. Are we to allow this great city of ours to become moribund?'

'Norwich to where, I said.'

'Think how many people took the excursion to Yarmouth three years ago. Six thousand of our citizens. This is the future, I say—'

There was a general outcry of 'Where? Tell us where?'

John Suckling swelled himself out, glared truculently down the table. Gooby had been very persuasive.

71

'Cromer,' he said clearly, pitching his voice at the far end of the council chamber.

'Cromer!'

'I say, Cromer! That's a laugh!'

'Crabs from Cromer,' said another derisively.

Lutwylch fingered the curve of his nose. So that was the idea. He knew the map as well as anyone. There could be only one route a railway to Cromer would take. He waited until the hubbub had abated and said very audibly, 'An excellent scheme. For every person who went to Yarmouth, two will want to go to Cromer. The purity of air is astounding. Nowhere has a better view of the German Sea. Give it a pump-room and pavilions, a lending library, billiard hall, botanical garden *and* a railway, and we'll have another Brighton on our door-step, I am quite confident.'

His neighbour tapped him on the wrist with the stalk of his ear-trumpet and winked. 'They say crabs from Cromer but if this railway goes through it'll be clover that some people will get to harvest. Clover, Leonard! That farm of yours will turn out to have been a pretty speculation.' His voice carried down the table. Lutwylch found he had a tickle in his throat and quickly started coughing.

'Exactly! A second Brighton! Perfectly expressed, Leonard.' Suckling nodded his gratitude to Lutwylch and continued. 'And here's something else you doubters can put in your pipes and smoke. Us locals may think we know best but others, Miss Austen now – quiet! Quiet for a moment! – no less a writer than our own immortal Miss Austen has declared in one of her books that Cromer is the best of all the sea-bathing places in the country. Everyone has heard of Miss Austen. Everyone knows her to have been a woman dedicated to the truth. With judicious promotion – and I believe I could play a strong part in that – Cromer can become the leading sanatorium in England. People go to Bath for its waters. To Cheltenham. To Matlock. To Brighton. So I say, why not to Cromer also? And when they do, they must pass through Norwich. They cannot do otherwise. Geography is against them if they try.'

He made some neat movements with his fingers, as if positioning the pieces on a chess board. 'They buy a hat here, a dress or two there. Gloves, a cane, some perfume for a friend. They spend a few nights in a hotel, attend a performance at the theatre, admire the cathedral. They fall ill – the doctor. Want a tooth drawn – the dentist. They eat, they drink, they are human. Gentlemen! Be more temperate, I beg of you. I am speaking of trade, which we are all in love with. What shall I say to Mr Gooby if you do nothing but jeer at me? That we already have enough buying and selling? That we turn our backs on railway money? Shall I say to him that we are too proud?'

'Gooby is a strange name,' said a man from the oriel window in a thoughtful voice.

'Something of the sable in him, I don't doubt,' said his friend.

'More like one of Isaac's lot, if you ask me,' muttered a third, unpleasantly. 'Do we want to give the business to a Jew? Turf him out, I say, and let one of our own have it if it's so profitable.'

Everyone looked at this pampered young man (the son of John Gostlin, the city's wealthiest cheesemonger) and back to Suckling.

'You try me too far, Master Gostlin,' he said in an ominous voice, the one he used when playing the part of Macbeth. 'Now listen and do so carefully. This Julius Gooby – I have spoken often with him. The railway cause is like the Holy Grail to him. He talks of little else but how it will benefit civilisation. He is a rare combination, a merchant and a man of principle. As for the other, he is as English as you or I or your father, and the next one of you to say otherwise, I will unseam him from the navel to the chops. From his breakfast' – with both hands he thrust an imaginary dagger into the stomach of the air and hoicked it upwards, jumping as he did so – 'to his gizzard and Heaven help me if I don't.' He repeated the movement. 'From here – to here.' Breathing deeply, he stared pugnaciously at Gostlin.

The Clerk asked him if the last exchange was to be minuted. Suckling said yes, by God it was. When this had been done they left the chamber together.

The cathedral clock struck one. For a moment the members sat in silence, dwelling upon the liveliness of that slitting, rending motion. The Mayor had always been an impassioned man, leading from the front, never shy with his words. But this was well beyond his usual range. They saw the blade go in, they heard the gas escape, they rehearsed the little jump in their minds, and they believed every part of it. But why such emotion over someone like

Julius Gooby? Then one man said reflectively, 'If I didn't know John better, I'd say he's taken the Jew's shilling,' and another turned to him with large eyes and said, 'Do you think they're in it together? Well, if one looks at it like that . . .' Suddenly it became apparent to everyone that this was both the easiest solution, and in fact the only one.

In small groups they sauntered off to consider the North Norfolk Railway and what they'd find on their plates for lunch. But Lutwylch left quickly and by himself, for he was afraid that his customary table at the Union Club might have been given away, and he disliked eating amongst a crowd when he had a full mind.

Twelve

THOMAS WAS persuaded by Sam Buzzerd to have one last go at the partridges. He was not a good shot, partly because he was too slow on his feet, but mainly because his heart wasn't in it. He loved the small birds for the soft greys and russet of their plumage (which he would sometimes paint, on board), for their intelligence, and for their soulful cries of alarm in the nesting season. When the snows arrived and he saw a covey huddled beak to beak on the white field, like buns on a tablecloth, he vowed he would never raise his gun to them again. But he loved eating them as well, roasted, with Mrs Macbride's bread sauce and good brown gravy, mushrooms from the horse pasture, and a pint of Burgundy in front of him. And since his father had shot partridges, and his grandfather before that, he felt he had a duty to shoot them, as a means of preserving some of the connective tissue between the generations. It was in the same spirit that he wore his father's long blue coat, despite its open seams and faded nap, and clung to other inherited totems. He hoped that when he died, Fred would preserve some of his own belongings. It all came quite naturally to him. Tramping the stubbles every autumn was like having a monarchy: it reassured some unrequited part of him that what had been done for centuries would continue and that nothing would ever change too much.

Jammy had done his lessons in the morning and was to handle the pointers, Natasha and Verochka, and a borrowed spaniel they used for retrieving. Sam was in charge of the muzzle-loader and strategy.

The day started dull following a night of rain. In case the weather should come on again, Sam fitted on the dog-cart a sort of light wooden shed that he'd built. It had a makeshift door hinged with strips of leather, and two rectangular openings, one towards the front for Thomas and one at the back so the pointers could see out. Beside the door he'd nailed a pannier of netting to hold the dead birds.

Emily was practising the piano. Harriet was doing something with her mother – Thomas wasn't sure what. They all knew where he was going so he laced up his boots, put on a hat, and went into the yard where the men were waiting.

'Six,' Emily had said, 'you can't come back with less than six. Two for you, one for each of us, and one for Fred.'

'Oh but he eats for two these days,' Isabel said, 'that school of his – we can't be starving the child.'

'Seven's what we must get,' Thomas said to Sam, looking around to see what the sun was up to. (It had come out as soon as Sam fitted on his shed.) 'My ladies won't let me back until we've got seven.'

'That's not very many when they're as plentiful as they are this year,' Sam said reproachfully. He lived for his sport, the type of man who'd shoot the tassels off a hearse. 'Why, there's you and the family and Bridie, and me and the missus and old Jammy here what'd scoff half a dozen if he could—'

'My mum, you shan't miss her out if you're making a list. They're easier on her gums than turnips,' Jammy said and immediately looked embarrassed.

'So that's Mother Peach as well, which makes, let me see, eight – twelve that makes so far. And then there's your gifts, Mr Gage. It'll never do to be forgetting them what expect to be remembered. The vicar has to have his brace – and minding you, they've got to be young birds or he'll kick up again – and the blacksmith and Mr Lutchamabob up the road . . .'

Sighing, Thomas lowered his head and clambered into Sam's contraption. 'Push over,' he said to the dogs. Natasha, who was the nearest, sniffed his coat, licked his cheek and panted adoring, rancid breath at him. 'Go on, push over, I said,' he repeated, jerking his cushion from beneath her.

'Best we go to Dix's, then,' Sam said, inclining his mouth to the window. This was a field of some thirty acres of which they had the shooting from their neighbour in that direction, the widow

Dix. 'There's still a lot of birds on it . . . tck, tck, up and along with you,' he said to the pony. Then to Jammy, 'Now don't go pointing the gun at its backside, you great lummox. Hold it up straight, between your knees. And if you drop the ramrod over the side and it breaks, I'll pull your silly lights out and wave them in your gob.'

They set out up the rutted track, the dogs shivering with excitement, making mewling noises (Natasha had a habit of clacking her teeth like an angry old woman when sport was in the offing) and poking their long white-patched noses through the back window to see what was on the move.

The spaniel jumped onto Thomas's lap. He thought, At least you're not a pug, not that bare-arsed tart Venus, and began to scratch the small pits behind its ears. This took his mind off the list of gifts, which he had indeed forgotten about completely. What was it about pugs? Mrs Mayhew, the Colonel's wife, had had one. It had been a weekly joke of Bella Cartwright's husband – now dead, but when not so, the lewdest man in the regiment – that Tansy, as it was named, had got its squashed-up face from the number of times it was called on to pleasure Mrs Mayhew. Remembering this made Thomas chuckle.

Feeling the mirth vibrate through the wooden partition at his back, Sam cleaned off the scowl that Jammy had induced and half-turned in his seat in order to share the jest.

'Nothing, nothing at all,' Thomas said, for he had finished with Captain Cartwright and was thinking about Bella and the night of the Regimental Ball: Bella declaring magnificently that a woman should give of her body without being squeamish or grumbly because it was her greatest gift to the world; the shell of her ball-gown spread-eagled on the sofa, the plump sleeves still expiring, the humid air still withdrawing as blowsy, generous Bella stepped away and – he found he could no longer recall the exact order in which it had all happened, only that her flesh had been like milk in full flood and that in the distance the band had been playing. What tune? He could not remember that either, for it had been over thirty years ago and he was growing old. A sadness entered him, for he dated his life from Bella, and if his memory could no longer snare that upon which it had previously fed, how was he ever to be complete again? Were pieces to drop off him like slates from the roof of a ruined mansion? Was he becoming derelict? Was this why he detested Gooby's railway, which everyone was joking would pass through his kitchen? He'd shrugged it away. Said he and the family would pocket the cash and up sticks and off. Said it light-heartedly to his friend John Suckling, over his shoulder, as the two of them were walking in the garden and he had his back turned while having a piss so that he felt it didn't count. John had been delighted, told him how sensible he was, and rattled off all the family houses in the county that were for sale. Somehow the conversation had veered away from the North Norfolk and he'd never had the opportunity to retrieve the lie, to tell John that the idea of a railway running anywhere near Fordwell was so repellent that no amount of money would win him over.

He continued to scratch the spaniel's ears. Yes, he would hold out against Gooby as a matter of principle. He believed himself a modern man. Yet at the same time he was aware of his strong relationship with the past. To concede the point to the railwaymen would be an unforgivable breach of faith. 'It's an instinct I have,' he said to Isabel one evening.

He wished he hadn't hit upon the subject of Bella Cartwright and thus the railway. It had disturbed too much sediment; made him cross and perplexed. The afternoon was turning into a scorcher. He threw open the door to give everything a good airing.

They reached the field and the dogs spilled out eagerly, the spaniel getting itself knocked over by the pointers in their haste to get to work. Jammy caught it and Verochka and snapped their collars onto the leash. As if to say, I knew I'd be chosen first, Natasha rolled and squirmed luxuriously in the stubble in front of them, her dugs very pink against her strong liver-and-white markings. Sam put a straw hat on the pony, which he'd tied to the gatepost. He pulled its ears through the holes, fastened on its nose-bag, and began to load Thomas's gun, all the while keeping his eye on Natasha in case she took it into her head to start without them. He primed it, put the powder flask in his canvas satchel, strapped the ramrod across his back, and they set out up the side of the tall thick hedgerow that surrounded Dix's. It was his intention to work the field outside in, moving the birds always into the centre so as to keep them out of the hedge. He was looking forward to his roast dinner. He had no objection to seeing the birds shot on the ground if Thomas could be prevailed upon.

The stubble was no longer golden but the colour of earthenware. It had become waterlogged in the rain and ejected tiny spurts of water as they walked through it. Normally Thomas enjoyed watching Natasha work, to and fro, to and fro, as she quartered the wind, always at the same raking pace, ears flopping, tail lank and her huge dark nostrils assaying the air – air, nothing more! – from which, he thought by a miracle, this princely yet otherwise rather stupid creature could map the whereabouts of every living species within fifty yards. Thrush, lark, corncrake, she would say to herself, and pass on. Even, it might be, slugs and snails. And then suddenly, right in the middle of one of those galloping strides, she would hit off a different scent. Something unknowable to him or Sam or any living person – a spore, a germ, he could not begin to visualise how it would look to a human – would shout 'Partridge!' to Natasha; and mid-bound, almost so as to snap her spine, she'd spin round and crouch to the point, rigid as a board, tail stiff as a poker, nostrils brooding and her eyes intense.

But today the spectacle held no pleasure for him. Lutwylch had proposed himself for a cup of tea and he knew the conversation would only add to his sense of unease. More complaints about Fred, the paint business, it was bound to be something troublesome.

Natasha ranged before them in her long, free, floating stride. She overran a barren pair of partridges that flipped over the hedge with a shrill piping cry, and looked penitently back at Sam with one paw raised. 'Damned buggers,' he growled, but made no attempt to bring up Jammy with the other pointer. Natasha saw she was reprieved and galloped joyously off again, the sun glinting on her collar buckle.

Thomas walked several paces behind Sam. He had no wish to encourage his chatter. He put Lutwylch out of his mind and thought about the flowers he was treading on, the tiny scarlet pimpernels and the white clusters of shepherd's purse. Dawdling, he gradually fell further and further behind. They came to turn at the end of the field and now it occurred to him that the swathe of stubble he was following was perhaps two or three inches taller on the left than the right. He stopped to consider this. As he did so there was a shout from Sam: Natasha was on point, just where the stubble ran into a patch of nettles in the corner. He ambled forward reluctantly, hoping the birds would fly away before he got there. He took the gun from Sam, who snapped a leash onto Natasha's collar and coaxed her forward, leaning over her and stroking her ribs. Whirr! The partridges exploded over the hedge, and Thomas let them go.

'Bit quick for you, were they, sir?' Sam said, unclipping the leash. But in his expression Thomas read, What's wrong with you, you silly buffer? Getting too old for the job? He was sure he was correct, and for the first time in his life he decided that he didn't really care for Sam as a person. He said he hadn't fired in case there was someone the other side of the hedge, and went back to thinking about the strange brush to the stubble.

A few minutes later another covey rose and by a fluke he killed two with one shot. Jammy rushed up with the spaniel, the birds were gathered, and in a flash Sam had forgotten all about the covey that had escaped and was full of a hunter's primitive glee. He made a great fuss of the dogs, including Verochka, although she'd done nothing but try to pull Jammy's arms from their sockets. He admired the dead birds, gloated over the quantity of meat on their breasts, and gazed upon the rest of the field with lustful, half-closed eyes.

'I think we should try Vroshkie now,' he said, and told Jammy to catch up Natasha.

'You know, Sam, I'm not feeling myself today. I think I'll go and wait for you at the cart. Shoot as many as we need.'

'I'll knock their little blocks off like they were a bunch of Frenchies,' Sam said with relish, grabbing the gun from Thomas. Then, thinking that he'd been too forward, he added: 'You do look like as how you've got a bit of an upset, sir. It's sure to pass if you have a sit-down in the shade.'

'P-painting's not easy on a man,' Jammy said suddenly. Thomas looked at him with surprise, and he flushed. 'I mean . . .' His lips trembled as he rehearsed the words to go with his thoughts. He was holding a dead partridge, rippling its neck feathers with his thumb. '. . . it takes so much thinking about.'

'That's enough of that, Master Peach. Mr Gage couldn't give a brass farthing what you mean.' Sam unclipped Verochka himself, put the gun under his arm, and waved the pointer forward.

The two men set off downhill. Gradually they were diminished by the slope of the field; their braces and collarless shirts, their red necks, the sideways straw in Sam's mouth, and last of all, like the funnels of a sinking ship, their black stove-pipe hats. Thomas took his coat off and sat on it with his back to the hedge. He was sure Sam would want to get into a covey on the ground if he could. Line them up and kill four at one go so that he and his missus could fill their bellies and the vicar'd get his brace and the honour of the Gages and Sam Buzzerd would remain intact. Well, he supposed it was as good a way as any if the job had to be done. He closed his eyes and listened to the faint rustlings in the hedge: voles stocking up for winter, tattered hawthorn leaves moving in the slight breeze.

Presently there was a gun-shot, hugely loud in the stillness, and he got up and strolled towards the dog-cart. The tilt of the stubble was certainly a puzzle. He imagined that he was holding a reaping hook and made a few passes with it, bent well forward, his left arm curled to receive the truss of corn. It became clear to him that the man had been lifting his shoulder at the end of the stroke instead of making a flat sweep with the blade. But why should it be higher on the right? He tapped his nose – ah, because the reaper had been left-handed. The discovery pleased him, and sitting beside the dog-cart he wondered what people would say if he put a left-handed reaper into one of his pictures. Farmers would shout, 'Break his bloody arm so he has to use the other. Who wants a bollock-handed reaper in the line? It'll get the whole operation in a tangle.' Sam would be the same. The army had been cruel to misfits.

> 'Who's sitting up there on the big white horse?
> The bugger giving orders, of course, of course.
> Who's the carbuncle on the wrong bloody hill?
>   Brains made of mutton, feet made of clay,
> Who's gone to fight on the wrong bloody day?
> [Chorus] I'm Bollocky Bill, I'm Bollocky Bill,
> I've never thought straight and I never will . . .'

It had been one of his men's carousing songs. No two versions were ever identical but the theme was always the same: the comically inglorious disasters that befell a half-wit who mistook the recruiting sergeant for God and vowed to follow him everywhere, from inn to brothel to battlefield.

'How did it go, that song about Bollocky Bill?' he asked Sam when the latter returned. But Sam professed to have forgotten it entirely, since a whole section of the ballad, a good three or four minutes worth, concerned the adventures of his employer's private parts. He lined up the dead birds on the ground, counted them brace by brace with the ramrod, and singled out a couple of young ones for 'the old amen-wallah'. Jammy tried to draw Thomas to one side, but Sam told him off for being a shirker; had him stow the partridges in the net and pick the burrs out of the spaniel's coat. Then Sam jumped onto his seat.

'Oh no you don't, you were trying to get out of something back there. You can walk home, Master Peach, you can, on those big flat feet of yours,' he muttered from the corner of his mouth so that Thomas wouldn't hear. 'Jammy thinks he'll get himself a girl if he loses weight. He's decided to foot it,' he called back to Thomas, who was shovelling Natasha along the seat.

They set off down the track. Thomas latched open the door. He took a bird out of the net and started to pluck it.

Stolidly Jammy hitched up his trousers and followed. Mrs Gage is a good woman. She doesn't treat me like muck. Mr Tom is a gentleman. Mum's my mum and I love her. But Sam Buzzerd is a pig, he was thinking. 'Pig-pig-pig,' he said to himself, in time with his footsteps. (He was walking on the even ground between the ruts, in the pony's hoof prints.) 'But one day, quite soon now, I'll know more than he does. Then I'll escape and better myself.' His lips moving, he repeated this several times quite fiercely, for Isabel had drummed into him at his very first lesson that to better himself must be the whole object of his life. 'Do better, do better,' he said, his round face bent and staring at the soil.

He looked up. Thomas had hung his coat on the outside hook. Framed in the back window of the wooden shed was Natasha's brown-and-white head and neck, swaying to the lurches of the cart. She's thinking about the gruel I must mash for her, he thought ungrudgingly. Then she and the other one – like Sam, he could never master Verochka's name and was too unconfident to try it – will exchange stories about their day's shooting. He hoped she could still hear properly. It was terrible to see a dog going deaf. Sam had had that shot very close to her head, when he was crawling up to the covey. He shouldn't have done it. Even he knew you shouldn't let a gun off so close to a dog. You could ruin it forever. And Natasha had cost a pretty penny, so he'd heard Sam boasting to one of his friends.

Again and again Thomas's fingers appeared through the doorway and the tufts of feathers floated back past Jammy. He desperately wanted to ask Thomas the question that Sam had prevented him from asking. Now I'll do it – now! – now! – but he was afraid Sam would look round and catch him out, and each time he held back. Natasha lolled on the seat, the fingers came out, the grey and red-brown curls drifted past him, and still he hadn't done it. At last he saw a rough stretch of track approaching. Sam'd have to have his wits about him there. He took off his hat and scuttled crouching up to the window. He slid his hand in past Natasha's neck – she licked it dreamily – and flapped it at Thomas.

He spoke very softly: 'Please, Mr Tom, sir, not to let Sam know I'm here but is it true I need a written character afore I can travel on the railway? Sam says how I does and how I'll never get anyone to speak for me 'cos I'm simple.'

Thomas turned. He saw the hand, he heard the question, he understood everything. For a moment Jammy's face disappeared as he stumbled and recovered his footing. 'Please, Mr Tom, please say it isn't how Sam says it is.' The hand seemed to grope for Thomas, as if it were a continuation of the scene he'd painted in his Academy picture. He caught it across the broad coarse knuckles and held it. 'No,' he said sadly, 'you don't need a character to go on a train. Just let us know before you leave.'

He thought he heard a sigh; the face dropped away. Sam started to peer round the corner of the shed to see where Jammy had got to. Quickly Thomas shouted at him, 'Get a move on there, you know very well we've got someone coming for tea.'

Thirteen

IN THE event it was not Lutwylch's cosmopolitan equipage but the shabby one-horse gig of Georgiana Farrant that came spinning up the drive through the dappled rays of the late afternoon sun, scattering the chickens into the dogwood and mock orange. She had on a flat brown hat, somewhat in the fashion of Sir Thomas More the martyr, and the thick old coat of a dark burled material that she wore round the stables. Beneath it was a plain black dress of her mother's. She had chosen this costume with care, from a wish not to excite Isabel's jealousy, and had made no attempt to sponge the mud off her coat. A clot of straw had lodged itself among the pleats in the small of her back.

'Who is it?' Isabel asked Mrs Macbride. They were preparing the 'polite' drawing-room for Mr Lutwylch. Isabel was drawing the fire up with a copy of last week's *Mercury*. It was some way off roaring and she didn't want to leave it. She didn't think Mrs Macbride had quite the same knack as she did. 'I wonder what she's after. Go and tell Mr Gage he must deal with her himself. What a nuisance, today of all days. Doesn't she have anything useful to do?'

'I expect it's because the General's sailed and she's got time on her hands,' Mrs Macbride said, picking up the kindling box.

'That's no excuse. Now go and find Mr Gage. I heard them all coming into the stable yard. We don't want Mrs Farrant getting herself comfortable just as Mr Lutwylch arrives. You don't know her as well as I do.'

Thomas had his boot wedged in the bootjack. He'd heard the bell-pull go, and believing it to be Lutwylch, was taking his time with the laces. In any case the knots were caked with mud. His face brightened immediately. 'Oh really, Mrs Farrant? That'll liven things up. You know, Bridie, I can't stand Lutwylch. He's so damned pompous I want to hit him on the nose. What's for tea? Some of your almond macaroons? I could eat a whole plate of them by myself.' The bell sounded again. 'Alright, alright, I'm coming ... Hang on, I'd better wash this muck off my hands first ... How do I look, Bridie? No feathers sticking to me anywhere?'

Harriet was in the corridor. For some reason Mrs Macbride had left the kindling box on one of the hall chairs, and she was carrying it through to the boot-room.

'Well done,' he said, at a loss for words with his stepdaughter as usual.

In the vestibule Emily was helping their visitor with her coat. She caught Thomas's eye and made a gesture of wrinkling her nose behind Georgiana's back.

'Here, let me give you a hand,' Thomas said, closing the door into the hall.

Georgiana was having a contest with the sleeves, which were rather tight. She had her arms behind her and now strained towards him with the jutting tilt of a ship's figurehead.

'Allow me to say, dear Georgiana, that you appear to be in the quandary of almost every woman I've known. To go forward or to go back, that is the question. Help her, Emily dear. Give the cuffs a good pull.'

'Oh, Thomas, you're so harsh on us. Why must we always choose one way or the other, why not just go along with things in a general way? Doesn't it all come to the same in the end? Anyway, you know why I'm here. You will do my picture before anyone else's, won't you? These arms of mine, they've grown quite monstrous from all the work I have to do at home. Almost there, one more pull—' She glanced back to check that Emily had a proper hold on the coat.

'Nonsense, it's the fault of the coat. You've washed it and it's shrunk.'

'Pooh, you great flatterer. There!'

Of a sudden her arms were free. Emily staggered beneath the weight of the coat, took two steps backwards and exclaimed, 'Like a whole shop!' She sorted it out but couldn't quite reach the curved wooden hook of the coat-stand. Thomas and Georgiana each took a shoulder and did it together, making little grunts and getting a bit of fun out of it. Thomas gave the sleeves a tug to straighten out their ruckles, dislodging the lump of dried straw, which tumbled down and broke on the floor.

Georgiana clapped her fingers across her mouth. 'My goodness, wherever did that come from? Quick, Emily, have I got any more on me?' Emily walking gravely round her, she continued, 'How perfectly dreadful! Do I smell of the stables? Child, tell me if I smell. Your father will never want to paint me if I stink like an old billy. That's what comes of not having a man round the place. Mind you, the General's not much of a help. No sense of smell at all – no taste – nothing! He eats virtually everything I put in front of him. Thomas, do be a sweet man and lend me your handkerchief. These shoes of mine – perhaps I should have put on something smarter.'

Meanwhile Emily had knelt down and swept up the fragments of dried mud and straw with her hands. She went to the front door and threw them into the hollyhocks, calling, 'Chicky-wickies, time for supper.' As she was dusting off her palms and the Minorcans came scrabbling across the gravel, their scaly yellow legs going for all they were worth, a carriage entered off the road. She rushed back in.

'I really must teach Albert to clean inside the gig as well as out,' Georgiana was saying. 'The trouble is he's so temperamental. He says what he likes to *me*, but the instant I make even a suggestion to *him*, the most inoffensive proposal you could imagine, he rears up like a dragon. What can a woman do?'

'Papa, it's Mr Lutwylch, I think.' Emily never dared call him Gutswill unless Fred was beside her. In any case it wouldn't have been proper with a guest there.

'Pop in and call your mother,' Thomas said.

But Isabel had been keeping a look-out – actually to see if Georgiana had been got rid of – and was already in the hall with her hand on the vestibule door.

'Show Mrs Farrant into the drawing-room, would you mind?' Thomas said to Emily. Then he and Isabel went out together onto the terrace. The afternoon was on the brink of dusk, the air clean and hard.

The coachman climbed off his box and folded down the steps.

Lutwylch, Suckling, Gooby – Thomas watched as the carriage rocked on its springs and disgorged, one after the other, the silent and, as he thought, sinister deputation. He murmured to Isabel, 'The Assyrians came down like a wolf on the fold, what,' and squared back his shoulders.

'Leonard . . . John Suckling too, this is a surprise,' Isabel said. In the manner of some courtly ritual, the two men stood aside to form an avenue down which the slight figure of Julius Gooby advanced, diffidently at first. He halted at the foot of the steps.

'Ah, Mr Gage, the Mr Thomas Gage of whom one hears so much in the county . . .' Though he was standing beneath Thomas and was about four inches shorter, so that the action must have seemed ridiculous to everyone, he extended his hand and carried it rigidly up the steps in front of him, as though it were an object of the greatest rarity that might drop and be shattered. He took Thomas's hand, observing as he did so the faintest twinge in his expression of what he read as alarm, and said, 'So much that redounds to the credit of a gentleman and his wife. Mr and Mrs Gage! The very pillars of all that is civilised,' words that he pronounced syllable by syllable, soothingly, with a falling cadence. His palm hung softly in Thomas's, his olive eyes wandering over his face and taking in everything that was on display. Turning to Isabel, he bowed. 'I count it a great honour to be received in a house such as Fordwell.'

'Come along in then, come along,' Thomas said, wishing to get the whole thing over as quickly as possible. 'Tea'll be on the table by now, I expect.'

'I trust so many of us are not inconvenient, Isabel?' Lutwylch said with a sideways glance at Georgiana's gig.

'It's Mrs Farrant,' Thomas said. 'The General's had his posting and gone abroad – did you know that? She wants me to do her portrait. I believe it's to be a gift on his return.'

'No good hoping for payment from that quarter,' snorted John Suckling. 'I really don't know what the two of them do with their money.'

'But his salary is nothing!' Thomas said. 'The army's as mean as church mice in peacetime. He told me once what he received. You and your good lady wouldn't last a week on it.'

'It's not so much the money as Thomas's time that I worry

about,' Isabel said, 'what with getting everything ready for his exhibition.'

'We can't stand here forever. Come and get into the warmth.' Making a paddling movement with his arm, Thomas swished everybody into the house and towards the drawing-room.

Lutwylch and Suckling had been inside Fordwell so often that they took its décor for granted. For Gooby, however, it was his first visit. He was inquisitive to see the effect of Meredith's Grey on its home ground. When Thomas returned to find where he'd got to, he was prowling round the hall like a connoisseur.

'Making an inventory are we, Mr Gooby?'

'I've been inside a few noblemen's houses in my time, I can tell you – Leicester Castle, Ware Priory, His Grace the Duke of Arlington's mansion, to name only three – but this colour, Mr Gage – it's magnificent the way it shimmers at you. It quite takes my breath away.'

'Oh, the paint, you mean. That's a little secret belonging to our family business. Interesting you should mention it. One grows so accustomed to things the way they are – anyway, Isabel will be pouring so we'd better not dally.'

But Gooby was now peering into Isabel's china cupboard and was by no means disposed to hurry. 'Delightful, such perfect taste ... Not that I'm at all learned about the arts: far too occupied with my affairs. But I always appreciate good things when I see them ... Secret, eh, Mr Gage! No business can go astray with a first-class secret under its belt, isn't that just so!'

He put away his spectacles and trotted down the corridor behind Thomas, looking keenly around him, especially at the skirting boards, which in his experience were always the first place to signal an emptying pocket. Rot, vermin, long in dust and short in staff, there's nothing you can't tell from skirting boards, he thought.

Even with a fire in the grate and the healthy bustle of people, the drawing-room was not welcoming. Georgiana felt this most strongly. It was like a fever-ward awaiting patients. The flowers didn't come off – they were too few and a frost had tipped the petals. The long oak table had been waxed only that afternoon; by putting her head at an angle she could see the smears on it, a succession of oily rosettes. One had to make allowances, of course one did. They couldn't make everywhere comfy in the house. Nevertheless – she accepted a cup of tea from Isabel – she couldn't understand how anyone, unless they'd had every sense cauterised at birth, could regard this as a room in which guests would be honoured to find themselves. She had only to close her eyes and imagine it at night for rats, worms and toads to slither out of their nests in the sofa stuffing and congregate in the moonlight, as if in some revolting fable from Aesop. Why not some homely clutter, scrapbooks and toys, crumbs on the floor? Why not pink and blue covers, or better yet, a raw red carpet to hit one in the eye? Why did it have to look as though Isabel had patented brown? And the antimacassar – well, what the General hadn't had to say about that when it appeared could have been written on the tip of a billiard cue.

She helped herself to a macaroon. She saw she wasn't going to get one from Isabel. A cup of tea for politeness' sake and then off with the woman, that was what she read in the pale blue eyes opposite her. No need to be catty, she admonished herself, merely because she is Thomas's keeper and you are not. Still, the fact was that Thomas was the most delicious man she knew, and other women thought so too, and Isabel should be more compliant upstairs if she wanted to keep him at anchor.

While they waited for Thomas, Lutwylch and Suckling began to discuss the arrangements for the boxes on the gala night. Dissent had been crushed. It was to be a lottery after all, but with this difference: the Mayor had the right to reject anybody that in his sole discretion he thought unsuitable.

'So it's not really a lottery,' Georgiana said. 'It can't be if you're choosing the winners yourself.'

'Oh I wouldn't go as far as that,' Suckling said cheerfully. 'It's just a special sort of lottery, to make sure the right class of person gets a box. Nothing'll be said in public, of course. But that's how it'll work. People will still have to pay to enter it. Except Isabel, of course.'

Isabel rose to refill the teapot from the trivet kettle by the fire.

'Oh, let me help you, do,' Georgiana said, wishing to have Isabel think warmly of her. Over her shoulder she said to John Suckling, 'Now don't be greedy when you decide on the price of a ticket. You men are always the same. You shouldn't be thinking how much you can charge but how little. Be Christian. Have pity on the needy.' She placed the teapot in front of Isabel and sat down. 'On me, for instance, a lonely grass widow who can scarcely afford the seed for her canary.' She put on her most alluring smile, one that caused her eyes almost to disappear between the overlap of eyebrow and cheek. 'Venus, come and sit with me, and look prettily at the gentlemen until their hearts soften and they intercede with the lottery god on behalf of poor Mrs Farrant. I would so enjoy having a box.'

But the pug was resolute it preferred Isabel, and Suckling was giving nothing further away about the lottery. Silence fell. They could hear Thomas and Gooby talking in the hall.

'How big would the portrait be?' Isabel demanded abruptly.

The blood rushed to Georgiana's head. 'Huge,' she said, with a swing of her arms.

'Then he's far too busy. I've enquired in town and they all say the same. He must have at least forty pictures to make a respectable hang. Wouldn't you agree, Leonard? Forty pictures in a room like this? For Thomas to have to paint an older lady would take up too much of his time.'

'On account of her face having progressed from simplicity to wisdom. The weight of profundity to be painted, that's what Isabel means,' Lutwylch said smoothly, to keep the peace between two clients.

'But I meant the frame would be huge,' Georgiana said. 'As for the portrait itself, whatever would please the General – head, shoulders, perhaps an indication of the *poitrine* since he admires me so much in that area . . . ah, the railwayman at last. What is your opinion, Mr Gooby?'

His eyes were sizing up the quality of the furniture and the carpets, the newness of the candles, the patches on the upholstery. His ears were telling him he had fallen into a conversation that offered no profit to the North Norfolk. 'Concerning what, madam?' he answered negligently.

'Why, my bosom, Mr Gooby,' Georgiana said, having marked him for a prig the moment she saw him. Thomas looked startled, which amused her.

'Very, er, fine, Mrs—'

'Farrant.'

'Very fine indeed, I am sure, Mrs Farrant. I don't know what else to say. Um – very fine, very expressive for the purposes of portraiture, very robust, very . . .' Georgiana would gladly have left him treading in his discomfiture; she couldn't stand prigs. John Suckling, wanting to egg her on, said, 'Surely you're not going to stand for that, Georgiana. Robust? I would hardly have thought that a compliment,' but was allowed to go no further by Isabel, who wished that Georgiana would leave so they could get the business of the railway over. She said firmly, 'I'm sure you've come away without any lights on your gig. You really must go home before it gets completely dark. I won't hear of you taking any risks. The General would never forgive me.'

'But my portrait,' wailed Georgiana.

'Head and neck down to the shoulder blades would be the very most he could do.' Pugged and reginal, her rectangular jaw unswerving, Isabel delivered her verdict. 'I don't think you have any idea how busy he is. Nobody is busier these days than my husband,' she said, softening her tone. 'I have to protect him. Don't I, my dear?' she said to Thomas, who was munching the last macaroon.

Georgiana saw there was nothing further to be gained. She gathered up her skirts and rose. Thomas swallowed his mouthful and also rose. He shook the crumbs from his napkin into the fire, wiped his lips and walked after her.

'I behaved rather naughtily,' she said as they went down the corridor.

He skimmed his palm down her rump. 'You're irrepressible. Gooby hardly knew which way to turn.'

She backed into her coat, flapping a hand at him for guidance into an armhole. 'I know what they want to talk about without me. It's the railway, isn't it?'

'I fear so. Lutwylch never told us he was bringing the other two with him.'

'You will be alright, won't you?' Her collar was up round her ears. She settled her flat-topped hat and placed her hands on his shoulders. Her wide grey eyes were full upon him. 'You weren't born for this century, did you know that? Plotting to make money, all this frantic rushing about – it was never for you.'

'All the more reason why I should learn.'

'Then you must go back in quickly and discover what they're up to. Perhaps Fordwell has already been designated a railway station. How I wish Mr Gooby would decide it is through *our* fields his railway must go. We'd have him for ketchup, the General and I would, and then decamp to Venice, where we'd live like doges until we died within a week of each other. He's such a nice, safe, boring man – the General, I mean. Tell me, when can you start on my portrait? I'll tidy up my sitting-room. But you mustn't look at the ceiling. The rain's been coming through in the corner.'

'As soon as term finishes. I do think it would be apter if Fred came with me. He can carry my paints and learn how to mix.'

'Splendid! I shall make my shoulder blades extraordinarily attractive for him. Young men need to get a notion of the geography as early as possible.'

'You should burn this coat of yours,' Thomas said. 'Your figure deserves better. *Poitrine!* What a word to use in front of Isabel! No wonder she looked at you like that.'

They went outside. Lutwylch's coachman had gone in to have his tea with Mrs Macbride. Thomas took the lamps off his own gig and hooked them onto Georgiana's. He oiled up the wicks with his fingers, and lit them. Having closed the glass doors, he watched the yellow buds swell and grow bright. 'Not quite the same as Christmas, but at least they'll be something.'

There was no moon yet, and the night had cold black lips.

'You're the one who should have his coat burned, I don't care how many fathers it belonged to,' she said, offering her face to him.

'My fingers are greasy,' he said, kissing but not touching her.

'Bring enough turpentine with you, Thomas,' she said softly.

He helped her in, stuffed the rug round her knees, and stood listening until he heard the ring of hooves on the road as she turned north to cross Fordwell bridge.

'How do you see it, then?' asked Gooby, when Thomas returned with a second plate of macaroons.

'See what?'

'Don't be dense, Thomas, no need to pretend with us,' Suckling said impatiently. 'The North Norfolk, the new railway.'

Thomas offered the macaroons around, took one himself and

sat down. 'I count myself a modern enough man,' he said, because that was the phrase that had come to him in the afternoon and he believed it to be just. He had intended to continue by telling them that nevertheless he was no friend of speed for the sake of it, that they should look elsewhere to build their railway. He got as far as saying, 'However,' when he noticed how Gooby was staring at him. He saw arguments and confrontation in the watchful face. On glancing at Lutwylch he saw much the same, a devouring intensity of expression. Even his friend John Suckling was looking at him in the same way. He felt the full weight of their purpose bearing down on him, and stopped in his tracks. Opposite him Isabel was sitting quite calmly, stroking Venus's head. Her eyelids were unmoving, which meant she was content. Reassured, he chewed the macaroon until it was finished. Only then did he say, 'I think it's obvious what we think about the North Norfolk. I'm sorry to have to disappoint you, gentlemen. You must find another way to Cromer.'

'Of course, nothing is certain yet,' Gooby said, turning from Thomas to Isabel. 'My surveyor is still working on the levels. It'll be some time before we know which is the best route.'

Isabel said, 'Can you tell me the legal position, Leonard? Can Mr Gooby's surveyor enter onto our land if we do not wish it?'

'You'd be quite within your rights to refuse him. Any such entry would constitute a trespass until such time as the North Norfolk receives Parliamentary consent. Am I fair to you, Mr Gooby?'

'Entirely so. And may I say, Mrs Gage, that I would regard any such action as wholly improper. I would dismiss the person concerned the moment it was brought to my notice. We are no criminals.'

Mightily, involuntarily, Thomas yawned. Their overture had been rebuffed. He could relax now. 'An afternoon at the partridges – all that fresh air and exercise – don't go, don't go! No need to leave because a fellow yawns.'

'I think we've taken it as far as we can for one evening,' Gooby said. 'No point going into details unless we have to. What I always say is, the better you know people in advance, the easier the business goes later. Like marriage, you might say,' and he tried a pleasant sophisticated laugh.

'Yourself? A wife and family in London perhaps?' ventured Isabel.

'I fear not. I have made a pledge not to offer myself to a woman until my economy can withstand superfluities. But I have six older brothers.'

Isabel looked at him with interest. 'I'd like to discuss that with you one day, Mr Gooby. Your upbringing must have been very competitive. You see, I am an only child.'

Again Thomas yawned. The jaw, the entire apparatus round his mouth, quivered, tensed and completed the displacement. His teeth snapped, his eyes filled, and he blinked owlishly at Gooby as he considered the status of the word superfluity in the context of women.

Without further ado the three men made their farewells and left.

Thomas stoked up the fire. He was arranging the cushions at the end of the sofa to make it comfortable for a nap when he heard Sam drive up in the dog-cart. The front-door bell jangled lengthily; school books went plunk onto the hall table; boyish footsteps came skipping down the corridor. 'In 1492, Columbus sailed the ocean blue – grub up, Bridie, I'm starving.' Seeing the light in the drawing-room, Fred put on the brakes – arms outstretched like wings, gleefully watching the carpet rumple. Not bothering to straighten it, he burst in, mud all over the knees of his knicker-bocker suit, a fresh cut over one eye, his lips purple with ink. He ran over and started bouncing up and down on the sofa.

'Listen, Papa, I'll only give you one chance. Bet you don't know the rest of this –

"Smelly Caesar did a fart
Alas he couldn't catch it –"

Bet you! Bet you!'

Pretending to rack his brains, Thomas frowned and stabbed his fingers against his temple, though of course it was the hoariest chestnut to have come out of Latin class. After about five seconds, Fred, still jumping around on the sofa, could wait no longer.

'Brutus hid behind the door
And slew it with a hatchet.'

94

Laughing, Thomas tried to pull him down, but Fred was too nimble. 'I'm going to catch you, you little devil, and give you a good trouncing for getting your clothes dirty.'

They raced and feinted round the sofa, faces warm with merriment, their brown eyes on guard as they waited crouching for the other to make a move. In due course the sofa slid into a side-table and knocked it over. While his father put everything back as it had been, Fred dashed out of the room to tell his brand-new joke to Emily.

Fourteen

CHRISTMAS APPROACHED; Thomas and Emily got themselves ready to drive into Norwich. Having run short of money, he'd arranged with Lutwylch to collect his allowance a week in advance. Preparing for his exhibition was proving more expensive than he'd expected. Paint, canvases, brushes, framing, it was surprising how the costs added up. The price of ultramarine in particular had been a scandal throughout the year.

Furthermore, he wanted to buy for Fred the very latest panoramascope, which had been a temptation to him ever since Hebden had displayed it in his shop window. It depicted the Battle of the Nile from a viewpoint on the low line of hills beneath which the French ships rode smugly at anchor. The introductory scenes of Nelson scouring the Mediterranean for them were a bit boring. It only really came to life with the picture of Admiral Brueys and his officers tucking into their dinner, splendidly oblivious to the danger bearing down on them under a full press of canvas. Then one saw a lone frigate on the horizon signalling back to Nelson that the enemy had been found. At last! A crank on the wheel, and now the British fleet came sneaking through the mauve Egyptian dusk into the narrow strip of shoal water, gunports open, decks cleared for action, catching the French on their blind side – oh, it was magnificent! And the way they showed the L'Orient exploding in the middle of the night, a terrific swoosh of flame and sparks and flying debris – he just had to have it. A spectacle? He'd say, by God he'd say!

After he'd been to Lutwylch and taken the cheque over to his bank, Gurney, Birkbeck & Co in Bank Plain, they were going to fetch Fred home for the holiday.

96

For Emily it couldn't be soon enough. She'd had Jammy polish her brown ankle boots until they shone as brightly as her eyes. She was wearing her best blue woollen coat, the collar tight around her chin, and a baggy yellow tartan tam-o'-shanter. She was quite unlike Harriet to drive with, being vivacious and always alert for a novelty.

Sam brought the gig round to the front door; they climbed in. My darling Gages, Thomas thought to himself. Standing upright he shouted, 'Gdyap, you old mawkins,' and cracked the whip resoundingly over the pony's head, as Blissett had done in the stagecoach when foozled with drink. The pony broke into a stumpy canter. As they jolted down the drive, Thomas leaned out and with the handle of his whip rattled a brilliant spray of hoarfrost off the shrubs.

They came to the highway. 'All clear my side,' cried Emily, hanging onto the strap, her cheeks already flushed a lovely pink.

'Good girl,' he said, and they swung right-handed up the slope to Sparling.

Sam had put newspapers on the seats so they wouldn't get chilled bottoms. Thomas glanced round to check his hadn't slipped off, and plumped himself down. He buttoned the chinstrap of his fur cap, shortened the reins, and took possession of his half of the rug. The pony slowed to a trot and then an amble. Its fat smoky breath hung in the air. Puddle-ice splintered beneath the wheels. The sun was melting the frost except, on one side of the road, for a strip beneath the hedge that it would never reach. They drove through the spinney of elms – the air was suddenly freezing, and the knobbly twigs were coated in a white rind that gave Thomas the impression of thousands upon thousands of emaciated fingers in dance gloves.

He was still thinking about this when they passed the entrance to the Lutwylchs' villa. A few months ago it had been exalted with a triumphal archway, on the keystone of which the escutcheon of the L'Estranges glittered in the icy sunshine.

'I can't believe they want to move if they've built a thing like that. They must be very wealthy,' Emily said indistinctly. She'd tied her scarf over her mouth so that her teeth wouldn't ache in the cold.

'Not from us they aren't. Your mother pays him the smallest

97

possible amount for what he does. Old man Meredith laid it all out in his will and she won't budge.'

'But they must have got the money from somewhere.'

'It's in the nature of lawyers to be rich. If there were no liars in the world, or no money, or everyone behaved as their parents told them to, or children never behaved like their parents did, they'd be as poor as the rest of us.'

'As poor as Jammy?'

'Well, not quite as poor as that.'

Emily considered this. 'Mother's given him a book on steam engines. He showed it to me when I got my shoes this morning. Pistons and condensers were all he could talk about. His eyes were out on stalks a mile long.'

'One of these days he's going to leave us,' Thomas said. 'When we were out shooting, he asked me if he needed a reference to go on a train. Sam had been filling his head with nonsense.'

'How horrible of him! I hope you put Jammy right.'

'Of course, what do you expect? I think we should give him a handsome present when he goes.'

'Me too. Could you do a little picture of him for us to keep? Fred likes Sam 'cos he tells him about battles but I like Jammy much better. Sam's cruel. Should we give him money, or what?'

This occupied them until they reached Norwich. Thomas's nose grew a fine winter mottle. The air was motionless. Chimney smoke from the cottages and homesteads ascended in columns into the beautifully pale sky, wavered and vanished. Farmers were ploughing their stubbles under, hands swaddled in rags, trusses of straw sticking out of their leather boots. Diligently they tramped behind the oxen, straddle-legged, shoulders well back, the foot in the furrow a little lower than that on the ploughing. What were they thinking about? He suspected it would be nothing exciting, probably no more than a calculation of the number of furlongs to be walked before nightfall. In any case he didn't care. Emily was beside him and they were going to fetch Fred. Happiness was flowing through him in a stream that was pure, gentle and so limpid that he felt everything else had been emptied out, that there existed within him only the sweetness of good fortune.

'Luck live in your hat!' he cried out, the feeling was so strong on him, and he tried to describe to Emily the precise sensation as Mr

Wheaton strode down the gallery, as if he'd been tied to the picture by a string.

They made a detour so that Emily could see the panoramascope in Hebden's window. The streets were a-bustle with people in furs and boots doing their shopping. A group of musicians was playing in the Market Place. They had a monkey, which at the end of every tune hopped round the listeners holding out a cap. It was wearing a purple waistcoat with gold buttons and braid. Emily thought it did its job with great dignity, but had no wish to own one.

Lutwylch was expecting them, so they had to wait only a few minutes before being shown into the partners' business room. This morning Leonard had it to himself. A coal fire was burning in the grate. Emily sat on her hands in front of the desk, swinging her legs while the men talked. The desk was double-sided. She would have liked to peep into the drawers facing her, but she'd been afraid of Mr Lutwylch ever since he'd shouted at her and Fred at the circus. Instead she fixed in her mind a picture of their bathing pool at home and wondered when the ice would be thick enough to go skating. Somehow they'd have to keep Thomas out of the way until it would support his weight. 'Hang on,' he'd say, 'I'll just test it first,' and when it began to creak, which it always did because he was so heavy, he'd refuse to let them anywhere near it. Whereas – she found she was staring straight into Mr Lutwylch's face, and that he was speaking to her:

'You can't expect Meredith's Grey to go on making money forever. To do so is folly, and hard behind folly rides perdition. I always think children cannot hear this too often. I give Master Lutwylch a regular lesson on the subject of economy. He is perfectly apprised of my policy by now.'

Emily nodded. She didn't think it any concern of hers what the Lutwylchs spoke about amongst themselves. She returned to the skates, and where they could hide Thomas's.

'And you, Thomas, you're in the same position. A prudent man would look more favourably on Mr Gooby's railway. The permanent way has been the salvation of many a hard-pressed family. Take that Scotchman, the one who made a fortune from coppering the navy's bottoms in Napoleon's war, Lord Glenfender. Did I tell you about him before? Well, let it be a lesson to you. It's as droll a piece of humbug as has happened for many a long year. The story goes like this. His Lordship has an estate outside London that was valued at £30,000 for the whole. No one disputes this figure. When he bought it, he had the best men in London come out and do an inspection. £30,000, they said, *nemine contradicente*. Then a certain railway company found a sliver of his land was quite indispensable to its operations. Lord Glenfender was agreeable at £15,000. A year passed and lo and behold, a second railway company found it was unable to proceed without a sliver on the opposite side of the estate. Glenfender was again agreeable at £15,000 – plus a railway station. The consequence of all this? The fellow's put £30,000 in his pocket, has a station only a mile away and an estate that is now valued at £40,000 on account of the rapidity with which London can be reached. Which is why I advise you to think kindly of Mr Gooby. Opportunities like this are rare.'

'I expect there was a catch in it somewhere,' Thomas said.

'I assure you not. Shareholders were climbing all over each other to subscribe to these railways. They knew the value of the bargain as well as the companies.'

'And see where it got them! Dividends cut, share price crucified, ruination on all sides.'

'But meanwhile Glenfender had filled his pockets, which from your point of view is what matters.'

'Where else would the North Norfolk run?' Emily asked in her sensible way. 'Would it go through your farm as well, Mr Lutwylch? Papa, I like the idea of our own station. Whizz, I could be in London in no time when I grow up. Fred too, and Mother and Harriet. We could have friends to stay from all over the place.' She turned back to the lawyer. 'Do you think Mr Gooby would give *us* a station?'

'Perhaps, if you ask him nicely, dear child,' Lutwylch said.

'Now stop leading the witness. Go on like that and I'll have Emily against me, and then Fred and then – my goodness, look at the time.' Thomas got to his feet. 'We must be on our way. We'll never hear the end of it if we keep the lad waiting.'

He took his cheque from the lawyer and they left. After dropping in at his bank and having a few words with old Mr Gurney, they hurried to the toyshop where Thomas paid for the panoramascope. 'Here, have a look at the French ship blowing up, Em. Isn't it just the bunch? Fred'll be excited as anything, I know he will.' He made a great fuss about how it should be removed from the window and kept somewhere warmer until Sam could collect it. Secretly Emily thought it boring, typical of men's gadgets, but she refrained from saying so.

Fifteen

A SMALL BUILDING adjoining the Palace Theatre came onto the market. 'Too good a chance to miss,' proclaimed John Suckling, and set about raising the funds for its purchase. As a result the gala night had to be postponed. People had to find other subjects for conversation.

Soon it became an open season for rumours. Some were no more than rouged-up gossip and lasted no time at all. Some (that Thomas had been engaged to do a portrait of Queen Victoria) had been so obviously confused with existing events that they rose scarcely a foot from the ground. A third variety, those connected with the North Norfolk, had longer moments of fame.

For instance, whenever Mr Gooby was seen enjoying a confidential luncheon in a secluded corner of the Union Club, the opinion invariably took flight that the route for the railway had been irrevocably settled, and that tomorrow – or at any rate first thing next week – the details were to be laid before Parliament. This was an especially attractive rumour to the burghers of Norwich, since the sound of its wing-beat as it circled amid the cigar smoke and the fumes of the Union Club brandy was agreed to resemble exactly the noise that is produced by a man riffling an inch of fifty-pound notes with his thumb. Also: that the vastest hotel ever was to be built at Cromer; that Mr Gooby was buying a controlling share in Meredith's Paint Emporium; and that Lutwylch & Lutwylch's first invoice for their services to the North Norfolk had run to over 120 folios before a single acre of land had been purchased.

In due course there was added to the list the matter of the gala night, which after a delay of many months drew within range of a long shout. This was an occasion that touched the hearts of all classes.

John Suckling had been heard to say that the arrangements he had in hand would *upside-down* the entire city. What could he possibly mean? Isabel and Harriet stated flatly that if by upside-down he meant plain vulgar, they would have nothing to do with it, box or no box. The Gages secretly hoped that was what he meant. Next it was reported that Suckling and his wife, whose passion for amateur dramatics and the Scotch play were famous, were going to perform Macbeth, sharing the parts between them. Then someone popped up with a really good one: he had a cousin in London, an impresario, who'd been requested by Suckling to provide the services of a snake-charmer, a fire-eater and a *proper* sword-swallower, payment to be at premium rates, plus all *reasonable* expenses, whatever might be meant by that. Explosions had been heard within the theatre at all hours; the jackdaws had been frightened off their nests in the chimney, from which, by some, a greenish vapour had been seen issuing. The porters and door-keepers had had to take vows of silence, their hands on the Bible and with a vicar present, would you believe! There was also the question of the so-called lottery for the boxes. Mrs Farrant was alleged to have made an improper trade with Mr Suckling in return for a winning ticket; and Mr Marley, editor of the *Mercury*, had threatened to withhold coverage of the gala unless he had the prime position in the house. So it went on. And in all these reports there was just enough that was credible to keep the lungs of rumour pumping their frothy, invigorating blood.

'For the life of me I don't know what to make of it,' Isabel said. She and Harriet had spent the day in town collecting for the Irish Famine Relief Fund. They were exhausted and in low spirits. 'All anyone said was, "What's this I hear about . . . ?" If it wasn't Mr Gooby and the railway it was the paint business and if it wasn't that it was some other tomfoolery. The city's gone as mad as gnats. As for giving money to these poor starving people, why, the very idea – how much did we get in the end, Harriet?'

Harriet finished sorting out the coins on the tea-table. She laid a ruler across the stacks of pennies to ensure they were of equal value and counted the oddses into her palm. 'One pound, four shillings and sixpence ha'penny. Oh, everyone's so tight! We'd have got twice, three times as much if we'd been collecting for hurt animals.'

'Tell Thomas about Mr Gostlin senior. Thomas, listen to what he said to my Harriet. It's perfectly scandalous.'

'He came up to me looking quite beamy and I thought, At last, here's a charitable man – Father, you're not paying attention.' (This was true. One of the lenses in the panoramascope had gone blank. He and Fred had the machine in pieces on the table and were attempting to put them back in the correct order.)

'Try that bit now, the smaller of the cog wheels, and let's see what happens . . . Carry on, Harriet, I can do two things at once.'

'Well, he dropped in a penny – one of the richest tradesmen in the city put a measly penny in the box, and when I shook it at him as if to say, Is that all? he laughed at me and said, "If it had landed with a thump, I'd have given you a bank-note too. But it was only a jingle I heard, so a jingle's all you're going to get." Wasn't that horrid of him?'

'How were you standing?' Emily asked.

'What do you mean, how were we standing? What's that to do with it?'

'Was it like this?' Emily jumped to her feet and waved the box around with a lively, encouraging expression. 'Or was it like this, as if you were collecting for leprosy?' She crossed herself, hung her head, and moved her lips prayerfully.

'That's it, I bet that was the trouble,' exclaimed Thomas, looking up. 'If I was going out to beg—'

'We were *not* begging, Father, we were collecting.'

'Very well, raising money, then – I'd cavort around a bit, put on a show and try to make people feel cheerful about the whole thing. So that they get a fine warmth of sentiment in their hearts. No good—'

'Being a gloomy-guts about it,' Emily said with enjoyment. 'Fred, why don't you and I get Sam to take us into town tomorrow and show them how to do it? No one would bother *us* about the railway. We could make up some Irish songs. That'd buck everyone up . . . Mother, how do they decide how much each person will get? Why is there a famine in Ireland and not here?'

'Can't do it tomorrow, Em. Papa and I are going to Mrs Farrant's in the morning. I expect she'll give us lunch afterwards.'

There was a pause, slight but appreciable, as the conversation changed tack.

'I was speaking to my friend Dolly Baunt this morning,' Isabel said, her eyelids going up and down as she gazed at Thomas over the rim of her teacup. 'Seemingly the portrait you are doing is not confined to Georgiana's head and shoulders. Seemingly it is of her entire sweep. Dolly says that by all accounts she has made herself appear extremely glamorous. It will look well in your exhibition, Thomas. We must plan how to hang it for the best effect.'

She spoke carefully. She did not know if Thomas was having an adventure with Georgiana. But the possibility made her curious. He had been so docile of late that it had made her wonder if he still *could* – it was as far as she wished to take the idea. It was so distasteful; the pestering, being pinned down, that whole lunging business. She hoped he couldn't: she wouldn't any longer feel those nasty spikes of insecurity. But she'd seen how he still looked at women, and she feared not. Nevertheless, it could be worse. She knew of other wives who were being duped all ends up by their husbands and who lived in constant fear of being moved out into a cottage. At least Thomas would never do that to her. He owed her too much. She'd borne his children, made a household for him. He needed the cohesion of their domestic arrangements. They were content with each other's company. People envied them. Furthermore, they had reached this understanding about his weakness in a mature and sensible way. If anything, it had made them even more united. So what he did with Georgiana was not unduly a cause for worry, provided that he was discreet and their familiness undisturbed.

She rehearsed all this in her mind and felt the stronger for it. No, Georgiana was not a threat. She looked across at Fred tinkering with the panoramascope. Did he have his father's impulses? She didn't think so. She couldn't believe that anyone could be so vulnerable to women as her husband.

Thomas was growing restless. She knew all the signs – the way he uncrossed his legs, played a few scales on the table, stared out of the window. Really, he was as transparent as glass to her. But she wasn't going to let him escape too easily. It was right that he should be made to realise how accommodating she was, to be reminded of those unflinching lines in the wedding service.

So she said, 'No more portraits after this one. I'm putting my foot down. Your talents are being wasted.'

'Oh I agree. It's turning out to be the most terrible fag. I was a fool to give in to her.'

'I hope she's paying you the proper rate for it. People who complain about being hard-up always have money hidden away somewhere.'

The children pricked up their ears. An expression that was meant as cunning slid across Thomas's face. 'Well now, let me see . . .'

'How much, Papa! Don't be a tease!' shouted Emily.

'As a matter of fact, fifteen when I finish and a further fifteen if the General likes it. Georgiana has stipulated that if he doesn't swoon when he sees it, she won't pay the second lot. So how's that then, children?' He whacked the table with his palm. 'How's that for your old father!'

'Pounds or guineas?' Emily's eyes sparkled with excitement. She went up on tiptoes and pressed her thumb knuckles against her teeth.

'But what do you think? Guineas, naturally, and Fred's to get the shillings in them for carrying my paints and mixing.'

'I swoon!' cried Emily. 'Look at me, everybody! I'm General Farrant, I get off my ship, come racing clatter-bang home, hurl open the door, see the portrait which Mrs F. has propped specially on a chair – and I swoon, medals and all.' So saying, she threw herself backwards onto the sofa. Her slender girlish legs went up in the air showing a flash of long flannel drawers. She went limp, fluttering her closed eyelashes.

'Don't be a fool,' said Fred, joining in for the first time. 'You should have had him pitch you the second fifteen guineas before swooning. He might have hit his head on the floor and killed himself. Besides, some of it belongs to me . . . Thirty shillings for eating Mrs Farrant's cream buns – thirty shillings!' He whistled and rolled his eyes. Turning to his parents, he said: 'Can I have a friend to stay next holidays? It was the famine that made me remember him. His father's a soldier over there – I think they have a house or something. You'd like James Mallen. He tells really funny stories. You see, he went into this hen-house—'

'Where? In Ireland or here?' asked Emily.

'Ireland of course – to collect the eggs, and his brother sneaked up and locked the door on him. So he had to climb out of the window, only he's bigger than I am – actually, he's sort of fat – and he could only get a bit of one shoulder through. Well, there he was, as stuck as stuck could be, and this tinker walks past leading a horse. So James, who's puce in the face by now and has an enormous spider crawling across the back of his neck, calls out for the tinker to help him. And you know? The tinker takes one look at James, says, "Who's the dropsical bhoy, then," and walks on.'

'What colour was the horse?' asked Emily.

'Emily Gage, are you soft in the head? The horse doesn't have anything to do with it. It's what the tinker said that's funny. Anyway, bet you can't say "bhoy" properly. Go on. Bet you a penny.'

Isabel's heart tingled. It was a charming family scene, the five of them in their cosy everyday drawing-room with books and cushions and Fred's school work all over the place. A feeling of contentment stole up on her, shouldering aside her worries. Glancing around she saw that her children had also been infected by this communal happiness. Even Harriet was joining in the fun, her lower lip growing firm and rising towards her parted white teeth. Thomas had ceased his fidgeting; was smiling on her as of old, with quiet enjoyment. Her cheeks flushed and she clapped her hands above her head, not caring about Venus who was chewing something under the table. Swoon! The dropsical bhoy! Thirty guineas for a picture! There was no doubt about it, the Gages were a caution.

Sixteen

AMIDST ALL the chatter about the fee for Georgiana's picture and Fred's new friend, Thomas clean forgot that the next day Jammy was leaving them to live in London. He and Isabel had been plotting for months and now he'd landed a job at Shoreditch Station, the terminus for the Norwich trains.

It wasn't until the morning, when Thomas was shaving, that he remembered. There was nothing for it but to put Georgiana off until later. Jammy came first at a moment like this. He and Fred could go to Norwich, see Jammy onto the train, and then make a dog's leg across country to Georgiana. It would be a long drive. She'd resent being subordinate to his back-house lad. And she'd make a face, a very private signal to him, when she saw he'd brought Fred again. The picture was getting along. They were running short of opportunities. Unless – but what more did she want of him? Delight in the day, he'd always told her, and go home when the clouds roll in. He thought she'd understood this. She'd said she had. No maiden was Georgiana Farrant.

He took a fresh grip on the curved bone of the razor handle, made accessible the bristles under his nose, and sighed. What pickles Bella Cartwright had got him into, one after the other.

He washed the lather off his face, put on his house slippers and his green-and-red-striped dressing robe, and went down to the stable yard to tell Sam he must go and inform Mrs Farrant of the change of plan.

The engine was taking on water when he and Fred arrived at Thorpe Road station. A man was standing on the cowling gripping a swollen, jerking hose while at the same time another was filling up the overhead tank. One foot was braced against the

108

stop in front of him. He was in his shirtsleeves. He drew the pump-handle in towards his stomach with long steady strokes, as if he was rowing a boat. The stationmaster at the end of the platform raised his arm; with a roar and a billow of black dust, like a swarm of bees, the hopper chute delivered a stream of coke into the tender. A small goods engine puffed breezily down the line and shunted eight carriages of mixed classes into position. Passengers appeared from the waiting-room and spread across the platform. Porters staggered behind those in first class laden with rugs, hat-boxes, luncheon baskets covered in white drapes, umbrellas and parasols, shawls and knitted woollen bags. Nursery maids soothed the infants in their arms and worried about the smuts. Single men of a commercial disposition grouped themselves outside the second class.

At the cheapest end of the train a man with a parrot in a cage was drinking beer out of a bottle, his surly eye on two youths who were baiting the parrot. In the ticket office an impassioned argument was taking place as to the surcharge applicable to a Bramah cockerel. The sun shone mildly. Everyone listened.

Dramatically, a strong bare white forearm shot out of the doorway. 'What's that bloody thing over there, then? Is it a parrot or am I the king of Spain? . . . Alright, so we've settled that. Now tell me the difference between his bird and mine. He didn't pay a bloody surcharge and nor will I. What's that? You call that creature domestic? You call a *parrot* domestic? You try sticking your cock through the bars and then tell me if it's domestic.'

The arm withdrew, and the torrent of words continued unabated. The porters sniggered. The youths laughed, said something coarse to the parrot's owner. A lady from first class sauntered down the platform and inspected the width of the bars.

'We should try a train journey some time,' Fred said, touching his father on the sleeve. 'All of us together, the whole family. I'd really like that. Lots of the boys at school have been on a train.'

'Stand away!' shouted the stationmaster. 'Wait till the carriages are ready.' Hands clasped behind his back, he peered down as a ganger looped the engine coupling onto its hook.

'There he is,' Fred said, and they walked down the platform to where Jammy was observing operations a few feet away from the stationmaster.

He was wearing a fresh brown suit and waistcoat and a brown billycock hat that Thomas had never seen before. His boots were polished to the nines. This was a Jammy they'd never suspected could exist. Sandwiched between his legs was a broad leather hold-all that Isabel had given him. It was secured by a new brass padlock. His mother was with him, also in her best clothes. Though Jammy was by no means tall, the top of her bonnet came only a little above his shoulder. She clung to his arm, pressing herself against him. He patted her hand while he described to Fred and Thomas the purpose of the various procedures.

'And here I am, Jammy Peach, going out into the world, a thing marvellouser than I ever thought to see. My ticket' – he removed his bowler and showed Thomas the piece of cardboard tucked under the hat-band – 'and down there my case: two pairs of everything, pens, paper and the dictionary I had from Mrs Gage. And see here, Mr Tom, isn't it like a mother to take care of her boy?' He unbuttoned his coat and opened it a fraction so that Thomas could see the stitching in the lining where he kept his money reserve.

'Will you walk from the station to your digs?' Thomas asked.

'I s'pose. Can't be more than twice as far as from the village to Fordwell. There'll be all sorts to look at as I go along. I've read ever so much about London. And when I come back I'll be able to tell Sam just what I think of him. Look, Mum, the porters are beginning to strap the gentlemen's cases on the roof. I'm a passenger porter. I won't have anything to do with that sort of work . . . One, two and up's a daisy – now don't start carrying on, Mum. You'll be seeing me twelve Sundays a year and we'll have our boiled ham together just like we always have. There, steam's up now, I'd best be getting aboard. Down to the other end for third class. Come on, Mum, this is no place for grieving.' He set off quickly, his mother's feet fairly dancing to keep up.

'Two minutes!' The stationmaster unfurled his flag and marched along the platform. 'Two minutes! Take your seats now!'

The strappers unhooked their ladders and stood back. Jammy twisted half-round, one foot on the carriage step. His face was bold and shining, it seemed to Thomas, with some great spirit of purpose.

'Thank you, Mr Tom, thank you for everything. I'll never forget it, never. Shall I walk down and see you one Sunday?' He wriggled his hand into Thomas's and shook it firmly.

'You must. I insist on it.'

'Goodbye Mum, goodbye Master Fred. Back in a month—'

A porter pushed Jammy in and closed the door on him. The three of them followed him down the carriage as he negotiated a fearful jumble of baskets and packages until he found a gap on a bench. He greeted his neighbours as if they lived in the house next door – interestedly, eyes bright, country written all over him. He put his case on his lap, planted the brown billycock on top of it, and smiled resolutely at his mother.

'Stand well clear!' The stationmaster raised the whistle to his mouth.

Suddenly Mrs Peach darted forward and beat against the window with her fists. 'Don't let them trick you. Don't let them get away with anything—'

'Stand back there!'

The whistle sounded. The train shuddered and started to pull away. Jammy struggled to the window, clambering and kicking and fighting with his elbows, and pressed his shining face against it.

'I'll be alright, Mum, I'll be right as rain. Go warm to bed—'

'Be an honour to me—'

'Proud . . . uniform tomorrow . . . gold buttons . . .'

Now she was running, her old bent legs crabbing along the platform, running and waving as volleys of smoke bombarded the sky, the wheels ticker-tacked and the carriages slid intransigently past. For a long time she watched, and even when the train was out of sight she continued to stare down the lines. Drooping, she sat herself on a barrow and buried her head in her hands.

'Papa, I think we should take her home before we go to Mrs Farrant,' Fred said. His own eyes were moist.

'She has people in town. She and Jammy spent last night with them. We'll ask her. Either way I don't feel up to doing any painting today.' He put his arm round Fred and clasped his small muscular body to him. 'I couldn't stand Georgiana's prattle. Not today, not after this. He was so – honest. Telling him a lie would have been like feeding him poison. That is, for you and I it would.

But Sam, he hasn't a scruple to his name. That's why he always got the better of Jammy.'

'Until now.'

'Yes, until now. Our Jammy's off to make a go of it, and good luck to him ... So what shall we do instead?'

'Take the boat out? Get Bridie to make us a picnic? Look, Papa, she's gone already. We must ask her if she wants to come with us. Hurry up and we'll catch her in the road. Didn't she just vanish! James Mallen couldn't have brought off a thing like that. There'd have been oohs and aahs and all sort of giddy-up noises from him. He couldn't vanish even if the earth opened beneath him. You'll like him so much, I know you will ... I wonder how Jammy's getting on. Was the man with the parrot in his carriage? Did you see at all? Everything happened in such a rush at the end.'

They overtook Mrs Peach fifty yards down Thorpe Road, as she was scuttling past Julius Gooby's house. No, no thank you, she would rather walk. It was only a mile or two to her brother's house. She needed to keep her own company a-whiles. 'You know how it is, sir, when one's had a shock to one's system. A bit at a time and I'll get there.'

Thomas clicked his tongue at the pony and they returned to Fordwell.

'One day he's painting the likeness of a lady whose husband is most conveniently absent and is observed leaving later than that man would have approved, and the next he accosts a woman in the street. Mr Gage is indeed a great admirer of the ladies.'

Gooby was standing at his curtained window, as he often did at train times. He thought it advantageous to form an opinion about people's railway habits. 'It's important to us that Thomas Gage thinks favourably of the North Norfolk. His price may not be reduced but matters will be settled more easily. So it is interesting that he does not hate the railway so much as to avoid it altogether. Evidently he is not a horse,' he added after a pause.

'She looks a bit on the gamey side,' said Walter Harrington.

'And she's refused him. So that's that. Better luck elsewhere, Thomas, old cock.' He let the curtain fall and turned to face Walter. 'I received a letter from Sir Hector this morning. The fish are already nibbling. The notion of Cromer as a second Brighton is catching on, he says. He asks when we'll be able to come forward with a definite proposal.'

'The river is our only obstacle.'

'And Fordwell our only possibility?'

'I've taken cores upstream and down. It's Fordwell or nothing. A good hard footing on both banks.'

'Much as we feared. It would give Mr Gage the edge on us if he knew of it.'

'People say she is the shrewder.'

'I agree with people. He did nothing but yawn when we met.'

'What makes their position all the more secure,' Walter said, 'is that they own the fields on both sides of the bridge. They've got us over a barrel. Could take the ramrod to us *per anum*, if you follow me, until we sick up enough money.'

'Well yes, and there again no.' Gooby sat down. A situation requiring great fineness of calculation was the warp and weft of life to him. The possible twists and turns of his quarry, their vices, their Achilles' heels, the incidental alliances that might have to be forged, from all these considerations he derived pleasure. He wrapped and unwrapped his fingers, inspected his nails with his head on one side, and said casually, 'You see, Walter, there is a man in this city who will do anything to oblige us. Oh yes, the chap is completely in the bag. I've crammed him in as deeply as can be. If reason fails . . . but you are right in your way. In the first instance it is the Gages who hold the key to the railway. Next week we shall propose ourselves for another cup of their tea and let us see whether Thomas Gage is yawning when we leave this time.'

Seventeen

S AM LIKED carrying messages to Mrs Farrant. He could have
wished for a more swaggery horse than Thomas's slow,
unanxious mare, but taking one thing with another, it was a small
price to pay for the chance to drop in on friends, put Mrs Farrant's
groom right on stable matters and in general loaf around. Didn't
he have as much right to enjoy himself as the next person? For the
truth was that Sam had reigned for so long at Fordwell that he
now regarded himself as being on an equal footing with his
master. He'd even been heard to declare in the Lord Nelson that
actually it was him and not Thomas who'd shouted 'Duck!' at that
moment of peril.

'Do you want me to go there or don't you?' He tapped his whip
against the side of his boot and eyed Thomas sulkily. 'You should
make your mind up, or one day it'll fall out of your head and
you'll be left like Jammy Peach.'

In fact Thomas had only been dithering about whether he
should give advance notice of Emily being in the party so that
Georgiana could have enough lunch prepared. (Emily, being the
most reliable in this line of work, was being sent to get the
measurements of the portrait.) Sam had misinterpreted this as an
order. He had been on the point of riding off and was aggrieved.

Thomas told him instead to put the pony to the gig. Since the
children weren't ready, he went to his painting-room to fiddle with
the last picture he was doing for his exhibition. It concerned the
tragedy of Daedalus and his son Icarus. He wished to portray not
their flight, which had been done often enough, but their
preparations for it in the labyrinth. This he saw as a gloomy
echoing catacomb, penetrated from a distance by strokes of dusty

Mediterranean sunlight that picked out feebly their work-bench and the pinioned carcass of the owl they were using for a model. He'd read that Daedalus had been a notorious inventor and had made statues that could move of their own accord. It was upon these that he was now concentrating. He knew the subject matter was not such as would appeal in Norwich, but was unworried. At the back of his mind was the notion that it was really an Academy picture. It would be better suited to someone whose taste had been exposed to the classical tradition at the highest level.

He sat down in his stout canvas-backed thinking chair, which he'd had off a ship.

The light, mealy and speckled as it strained into the chamber through the high, louvred casement; the owl, stripped of its wing feathers; gaunt Daedalus at his bench, surrounded by diagrams – they were good to his eye. But what of this statue, the first he'd attempted? He peered at it intently. What's on your mind, old fellow? Why are you leaning over Daedalus like that? Some useful suggestions about the strap-work for the wings? A brisk lecture regarding the melting point of wax? Friend or foe, eh? An idea came to him, and he scumbled in an arm of alabaster which he had lie across Daedalus's shoulder in a position of excessive familiarity. Now the runty head, the cock sparrow eyes, the twattering mouth . . . He lay back, teeth combing his lower lip. What else was there about Sam he could ridicule?

He heard Fred calling for him, the rush of feet down the corridor. Perhaps the whole composition was too murky. Funerals and the like were never a catch with the public, no more than peacocks. He'd think of something to shake it up – make the sun's rays more brilliant, give the labyrinth a door, let the air gust in and have Daedalus laugh as he tried to stop his papers flying around.

'Coming, coming,' he shouted, dropping the brush into a pot of turpentine.

The three of them were bouncing along in the gig.

'All that remains are Mrs Farrant's feet,' Thomas said.

'Has the rest of her been eaten?' asked Fred, quick as a flash.

'By lions. Nothing left but the skeleton and her shoes,' Emily said. 'Her reticule is in a crack between the rocks. Also her necklace is still round her neck because the lion didn't think it would taste well. I can see it quite plainly.' She had a biblical scene in mind. They'd stumbled on the bones in the desert, only a mile from an oasis, where palm trees were growing and a solitary Ishmaelite, shrouded in a hairy brown robe, was grinding corn in a hand-mill. A he-lion was roaring above them, from a cave on the hill-side that was hidden in a grove of wild olive trees. 'Give me one of your sweeties, dearest brother. Let's talk about something else. What size are her feet, Papa – normal? How long will it take to do them?'

But Thomas didn't answer. Sam had annoyed him; he was fretting about the composition of Daedalus and the statues; there was a slight pain in his temples. He would have liked to spend the day resting, alone in a room where the household noises reached him at a distance. Not total silence, he was too sociable for that. A few rumbles and squeaks, the pitter-patter of domestic economy that someone else was dealing with.

It surprised him that he should be feeling so apathetic about finishing Georgiana's picture. He adored women, the entire species, almost on principle. They were living proof of the value that God placed on loveliness. It was not to do with usefulness or being different or the properties that enabled them to bear children. It was to do with this one word, *loveliness*, by which he meant their softness, their beauty, and the gauzy, arresting thoughts that sprang, he felt, from the existence within them of innumerable particles of sorrow that enabled them to reconcile man to his condition. There was something to be gained from a woman that a man was incapable of giving. And when there was not, there remained the panoply of colour with which she surrounded herself. He had yet to meet a woman who was unremittingly drab. Even in mourning, there would be a dash of tinsel somewhere – in the sparkle of a brooch, mother-of-pearl buttons, the peeping corner of a lace handkerchief, on shoe-buckles and rings. Isabel was the quietest dresser he knew, yet each of her costumes had a bright panel at the waist. Her friend Dolly Baunt could look like the floral competition at the County Show when she set her mind to it. And Georgiana, even though she made her clothes out of inherited left-overs – well, the wardrobe she'd put together for the portrait was a cracker. Blinding! Outrageous! No one but a woman proud of her body could have occupied that dress with such sultry magnificence. Starting at the top, below the waves of gleaming hair that she'd grown down to her shoulders in the fashion of Rupert of the Rhine; swags of shimmering oystered silk that poured over her bosom like a waterfall; a cummerbund of peridot green gripped in the centre by a tortoiseshell buckle; and finally, her greatest triumph, a billowing skirt of the most gallant scarlet imaginable that spread so widely that he thought parliament could have been convened beneath its rustling pleats. In this she would sit for a while, parade gesticulating, or recline languidly on the chaise longue. When the weather was hot, she would unlace, coquettishly, the upper structure and taking a pinch of the silk between her scrubbed fingers, hold it away from her as she fanned a muggy zephyr into her loose, white breasts. His brushes had turned away in embarrassment. But he had not, because everything he saw, and would presently see, filled him with admiration.

And now only her shoes and their silver buckles were left to be done. Yet his eagerness had gone. The bargain had been corrupted. She was spinning the picture out, since she had no idea how else to pass the day and he was a fine entertainment. She had told him this, not in so many words but near enough. So he was glad the children were there to guard him. He hoped there'd be sufficient time to finish the portrait for good and all. It was almost a relief that Gooby was coming again for tea.

'The Lord doth not speak?' Emily said enquiringly. 'You'll have to say something to us sooner or later.'

'He's wondering what the General will think,' Fred said. 'Wait till you see it. The paint's that thick you could drown in it. And the colours! They'll knock you flat, Em . . . I don't think our mother would lend herself to a caper like that,' he added judiciously, screwing up his small face as he considered the matter roundly. 'Not in a month of Sundays she wouldn't.'

Thomas took one of Fred's caramel sweets. It was true what the boy had said. He didn't think Isabel would look at all kindly on the portrait when she saw how bold it was. The virtuous citizens of Norwich would gibber with excitement the moment it went on show; gossip till the cows came home. 'Us artists . . .' He started to compose a speech in his defence and in so doing reanimated his enthusiasm.

Her shoes – their colour was so delicious. Dark green and brown streaks, like the skin of a ripe fig. Had she contrived the dye herself? And there were her insteps. Of course he couldn't paint them if she was wearing the shoes, and the General would throw up his hands in horror if he had her going around barefoot like a gypsy. But it would be a shame not to make a few sketches of her naked feet. Ah, such insteps she had, and such pleasure they'd given him, both in the looking and the doing. Such pleasure! Of all a woman's parts the instep was the most exquisite. Fancy God having hidden away such beauty down there! The arching, the tiny blue veins, the satiny firmness of flesh . . . He took off a glove and suppled his fingers. Poor blind people, who were denied the sight of miracles. He closed his eyes to imagine how his senses would respond if their only guidance came from his lips.

Eighteen

THIS TIME Gooby did not linger in the hall. His whole bearing said, I know my way well enough, and after the courtesies he set off down the corridor to the drawing-room in front of Thomas.

A message had come that Mrs Peach was feeling poorly, and Isabel had taken the dog-cart to the village to see her. That had been in the middle of the afternoon; she was expected back at any moment. In the meantime Harriet was in charge of the tea-table, an office that to her surprise she was enjoying. She placed Walter Harrington on her right, sat her father opposite with Mr Gooby, and rang the bell to inform Mrs Macbride they were ready for the macaroons. There was an amusing exchange when she realised the napkins hadn't been warmed. Walter said he'd sit on them, that'd soon do the trick, but Thomas knew that Isabel would be horrified and insisted on taking them back to the kitchen.

While he was out of the room, Harriet drew Gooby's attention to the different teapots. She pointed out that the one with the knob on its lid shaped like a coolie in his hat contained China tea, and the one with a bare-headed figure in a robe held Indian. 'In this house we never take boiled milk in our tea,' she continued, 'but you may be sure it's perfectly wholesome. The sugar—'

'Comes from the palm trees that grow at Cromer. I've heard it's the best in the world,' put in Walter, wishing to liven things up.

In her inexperience Harriet did not know how to reply. A blush broke out on the crest of her cheeks. Gooby started a sniggering sort of laugh, for which she disliked him immediately. She poured him a cup of their Twankay tea, which she was certain he would find too bitter, and declined to hear his protestations. Conversation turned dull, but she still had a colour in her face when

Thomas returned, shoving his children in front of him. Emily had the plate of macaroons and Fred the napkins, which he held in front of him, balanced on his palm like a stack of plates.

'Why, thank you, little man,' Gooby said, which made Fred scowl.

Harriet finished pouring; the children fidgeted; Thomas had his first macaroon. Gooby was prevented from getting off the mark by Walter, whose instincts told him it would be useless to discuss the North Norfolk without Isabel present. After searching round for a bit, he alighted upon the subject of the gala evening at the Palace Theatre. This kept everyone talking until Isabel returned.

'Now, Mr Gooby, please tell us exactly what your plans are for the railway,' she said without preamble as Walter slid her chair in beneath her. 'The rumours are as thick as sea-mist, and we find ourselves in the midst of them. You already know the opinion of my husband and myself. But the children want to hear your views at first hand ... My usual, please, Harriet. Fred, offer Mr Harrington another cake.'

'To be quite blunt about it, Mrs Gage –'

Sharp is always better, Fred thought. He longed to disfigure Gooby with a really cutting remark and was practising.

'– a new railway is a most awkward business. There are so many interests to be reconciled, such a multitude of appetites to be gratified. Shareholders who've dipped for the capital, landowners like yourselves, bankers, lawyers, contractors, city corporations, honourable Members of Parliament, so many people and so many opinions that a man in my position—'

'Which you would describe as . . . ? Tell us about your position, Mr Gooby,' Isabel said.

He took a sip of his tea, which was more revolting than he could have believed possible. 'I think of myself as a cook labouring among princes. I prepare, combine, taste and hope to please everyone. It is far from simple. I risk losing my head should I fail. You see, the railway is my only source of provision. But I do not complain. We live in an era of change from which everyone will benefit. You, your children, Walter over there, down to the ordinary labourer and his wife. No one will be forgotten in the coming order of affairs. To be in the vanguard of these extraordinary times is a challenge I enjoy.' He looked at Isabel with pride. 'More than enjoy. It's a cause I consider myself honoured to lead. But to go back to your question … A new railway is in a constant state of flux. One never knows how it will turn out from one minute to the next. Then suddenly, one fine day, it transpires that everyone is in agreement and pop! There you have it.' He smiled at Isabel. 'Truly – pop! Like the proverbial cork. You would scarcely credit it could be so.'

'But it is,' Isabel added to his sentence, for the sake of neatness. 'Are we close to what you call "pop" in the present case?'

'If you mean, has our survey been completed, the answer is yes. The gradients are satisfactory the entire way to Cromer. There exists not one obstacle that is insurmountable.'

'And if I meant something else, Mr Gooby?'

'What are you thinking of? Don't hesitate to say, I beg you. I always admire candour in a woman.'

'Quite simply, we wish to learn whether you propose to pass your railway through our property. We are growing weary of the tittle-tattle flying about town. Yes or no, so that we can prepare ourselves accordingly.'

'I understand completely. But for your part you must understand that until all the negotiations are complete, none is complete.'

'Yes or no, Mr Gooby. It's no good shilly-shallying with me. I refuse to believe you don't have a firm opinion.'

'Alas, it's impossible. It would be quite wrong of me to give you the impression that the route is fixed, that the metals must run in this place or that and nowhere else. I must tell you outright that there is no unique value to your property. So far as we at the North Norfolk are concerned, the ground is equally favourable on either side of you.'

'And the river? Where else could you cross it?' Thomas asked weightily. Georgiana had put him up to it. The moment he'd told her Gooby was coming to see them a second time, she'd been unable to think of anything but the tactics he should pursue. He'd scarcely done more than lay out his paints. She'd been up and down and all over the place, never sitting still for more than five seconds. 'He might offer you a fortune. Now don't be so silly, Thomas Gage. There are plenty of other nice houses in the county. Think of your children. Who knows what the future may hold?'

'Almost anything is possible thanks to our iron-founders. Consider the swing-bridge at Trowse. 107 feet long. Ample for anywhere along your river,' Gooby said, leaning back.

'Then why have you spent so much time surveying at Fordwell? Someone was scrambling around it at dawn a couple of years ago. He was seen. He thought not, but he was. And a few months ago my back-house lad told me we'd had another visit of the same nature. A fellow riding a damned great chestnut.'

'I fear you've deceived yourself, Mr Gage. Believe you me, there are any number of places above and below Fordwell that would take a bridge.'

'I don't believe you. I know every inch of our river. There is only one place to put a bridge and a bridge is there already.'

Gooby allowed himself a moment of theatre, threw up his hands and exclaimed, ' "Yes it is, no it isn't!" Come, Mr Gage, we're in danger of behaving like children!' Then, with great earnestness, 'I didn't pay this call in order to steal the ground from beneath you. I'm not one of those scoundrels you read about in the newspapers. If I was interested in your land, I'd say so and the terms of my proposal would be flat on the table between us.'

'So why have you come here?' Thomas persisted.

'Why? Because I don't like it when people are hostile to the railways for no good reason. You're a highly respected man, Mr Gage, and it'll harm me if you go round talking down the North Norfolk. How shall I put it? Can I say that Walter and I have come here as missionaries?'

'How do you propose to convert us?' Isabel said. She liked the reference to missionaries and gave him a smile.

Gooby drew himself up in his chair and pushed away his teacup. 'What do you do with a dog that won't run? You let go a rabbit in front of it, that's what. So I thought, Why don't we treat Mr and Mrs Gage and their family to a round trip on the railway so they can see for themselves what it's all about? What do you say to that? The entire family,' – he twinkled his eyes round the table to recruit support – 'all expenses found – a carriage for yourselves and another for the servants – no need to spend a night away from home – vehicles laid on to make the connections – the bees' knees the whole day long. Think of it, an outing, Mr Gage, a family adventure!'

Thomas had not expected the offer. He saw Fred and Emily shuffle uncomfortably. Their faces had grown lively at the prospect of such a tour.

Gooby also noticed this. He continued quickly: 'You know my views. It's progress or revolution. Look at that trouble in Europe in '48, armed insurrection from one end of the continent to the other. Kings went down like ninepins simply because they couldn't keep up with the pace of history. They didn't understand, couldn't get it into their heads how everything has changed. Do we want the same to happen here? Why take chances we don't have to? We must be helpful to the future. What I say is this, a man with a railway ticket in one hand and his belongings in the other can't be holding a gun. Doesn't that sum it up fairly?'

He found he had got rather carried away. Leaning towards Isabel, he tickled Venus under the throat. 'Take the dog with you too. There's nothing dogs love more than staring out of the window of a railway carriage.'

'There's got to be a tunnel,' Fred said sturdily. 'I'm not going unless there's a really frightening tunnel.'

'As the little man commands. Not too many tunnels in these parts, but I'll find you something. You leave that to me.'

'Will Venus need a ticket?' asked Emily.

'What about the smuts?' demanded Harriet. 'I refuse to get myself dirtied all over just so that Father can look at Trowse bridge. One bridge must be very like another.'

Thomas had been mulling over Gooby's remarks about revolution. He was uncertain if they were intended thus, but they smacked of a threat and this had put his back up. 'No matter what you may say, I dislike the railways,' he said. 'I've been on them – and detested it. They stink. They've fouled the country. They are an ignoble form of transport. People say they promote our national trade. I say, what of it? Is trade our god? People say they are faster than a horse. I cannot deny it. But I reply, when did anything happen differently because someone got there faster?'

He could have said a great deal more about speed, which he saw as uncivilising, injurious to the arts and harmful to the whole scheme of human intercourse. It was obvious to him that happiness was a dozy, lumbering affair and that only mischief wanted to travel as fast as possible. In his opinion, speed was a disaster as an idea. With a schoolmasterly air, he said: 'One can be progressive, as you call it, and still believe that some matters were arranged better in olden times. One can be discriminating. It's not axiomatic that everything new-fangled brings a benefit. I – well, no railway will ever be built across my land. That's all!' He had not intended to speak so forwardly. But now that he had done so, he knew it for a just measure of his feelings.

'I think you're wrong, Papa,' Emily said. 'I don't want to take a whole day getting to London. Anyway, your silly old coaches have all been chopped up for firewood. I want to be able to go to town – ssshew! – like an arrow!'

'Em's right. Say you wake up wondering if a picture's been sold, what are you going to do, walk there?' demanded Fred.

Thomas smiled benignly. 'I expect I'll go by train like everyone else. I won't enjoy it, but I expect that's what I'll do.'

'Papa, you great hypocrite!' cried Fred. 'Don't say things like you just did. He'll never give us our day on the train if you go on telling him they're horrible.'

'I respect a man who speaks his mind,' Gooby said. 'We may not agree, but at least I'll know why. There again – you never can tell – you may come back from your trip and say, "Mr Gooby, I have erred and strayed from thy ways like a lost sheep. Just give me my own station and you can build your railway anywhere you want." And that would be something we would consider most carefully, wouldn't we, Walter?'

Obeying orders, Walter had taken himself off to observe proceedings from one of the ugly brown sofas. Harriet, who was convinced the railways were filthy, and was in any case unhappy at the idea of going so far from home, was trying to interest him in her album of pressed plants. He was uncertain exactly how Gooby wished him to reply, and asked him to repeat the question.

But Emily got there first. 'Our own station!' she said, jumping up and clapping her hands. 'You mean I could walk to the village and the train would stop, just for me? I wouldn't have to put out my hand – or lift my skirt?' She twitched its hem at the knee, waggled her eyebrows, and conjured up such a delightfully novice leer that Thomas burst out laughing.

Isabel was furious. 'Emily! That's a disgusting thing to say. And in front of a guest. Go to your room this instant!'

But Thomas whish-whished and flapped his turpentine-smelling hands until peace had been made between mother and daughter. Turning to Gooby, he said, 'My philosophy remains unchanged – but I'll do it. For the children's sake I'll do it, even though they can be amazingly uncivilised at times. Do you think I should leave them behind and go by myself?'

'Oh no you don't,' shouted Fred. 'I'll never speak to you again if you don't take me with you. I mean it. Never again in my whole life.'

Gooby narrowed his olive eyes. The evening was drawing in, and they glinted in the light of the branched candle-holder that stood on the table. The hollows in his face were immeasurable. 'So it's settled then. Send me word of the date once you've had a chance to talk it over. Thirty-eight Thorpe Road will always find me. An astonishing improvement, this new postal system, don't you think? Birds have their wings, horses their feet, but only man has brains worthy of the name. After Mr Suckling's gala, shall we say? Just give me a week or two's warning, that's all I ask. Why don't I leave you with my copy of Bradshaw? It'll be knocking around somewhere in the vehicle. Then you can have a proper family discussion about train times and where to go. Let me see – the eleven o'clock to Wymondham crosses the bridge I want you to see. You dismount there and inspect the curiosities in town, take the country train up to Fakenham – invariably a most pleasant run – have lunch and come back a different way in the afternoon. Something like that. You can work out the details with my Bradshaw. Oh, you'll have a nailing good day, I guarantee it.'

Nineteen

ISABEL HAD arranged for Thomas's exhibition to be hung in the drawing-room of the Three Crowns Hotel, which had lately been refurbished at great expense. All the pictures except Daedalus and Georgiana's portrait were to be offered for sale. She had persuaded Mr Batt, the hotel's check-trousered and mettlesome owner, to delay his grand opening until the day of the gala. In this way people's appetite for novelty could be satisfied on three fronts simultaneously.

Everything looked set fair. Thomas's reputation in the county could stand no higher. John Suckling had had handbills posted all over town promising an entertainment such as no man or woman had ever seen before. And Mr Batt was boasting he had customers to fill his rooms twice over. The servants' quarters were to be pressed into action and the chambermaids sent into lodgings. There was talk of putting mattresses in the cupboards beneath the stairs and even of introducing a rota for bed-sharing, the details of which Mr Batt laboured at in his glass-fronted cubicle, scratching the curly strips of his side-whiskers as he studied a complicated grid of sleeping schedules and wondered which of his guests were night birds.

The morning before all this was to take place, Thomas went downstairs as usual. He stepped out of the back door to examine the weather – and went skating across the slabs as his foot descended upon the conical chalky residue of a Black Minorcan's dinner. He put out his hand to grasp a rail that wasn't there and fell awkwardly. He picked himself up, washed the dirt off his skinned wrist at the stable yard pump, and went in to tell his family he was cancelling his show.

It was a bad omen, he said to Isabel. The gods were telling him what in his heart he knew to be the case: the two biggest pictures, the eye-catchers, were not ready to be viewed in public. The statues crowding round Daedalus were imperfectly observed – in any event he fancied it for the Academy. As for Georgiana – the paint was too fresh; it had yet to harden off properly.

She stared at him in disbelief.

'If I could have had it out in the sun for a day or two, well and good. But the General insists he won't risk it – a whirlwind – jackdaws pecking the eyes out, I don't know. It's so cool in their house, the paint doesn't stand an earthly of being dry by tomorrow.'

Emily and Fred entered the room and were instantly all ears. They were aghast. They'd been bragging to their friends for months about the genius they had for a father. 'You just wait and see,' and so on.

Thomas was resolved. He told them about his fall, showed off his wrist, and said anything to do with chicken entrails was an especially bad omen – Fred should know, he was the classics scholar. When they laughed at him, he became angry, called them insensitive and trotted out the same excuses as he had to Isabel plus a few more for good measure, all the time growing more choleric. 'The seas will part before Batt sees an inch of my work,' he declared at last, 'not one inch, I tell you,' and throwing down his napkin, he stamped out. In his painting-room, he turned the faces of his lesser pictures to the wall, chalked 'Abandoned 1851' on their wooden stretchers, and said 'Damn the Farrants' several times.

What had happened was this.

It had required a further two and a half days to finish Georgiana's feet. Though he said so himself, the portrait was gorgeous, of Byzantine magnificence. He'd caught her as if she were some voluminous, hedonistic Empress, reclining on her throne amidst shimmering swathes of cream and scarlet raiment. He'd slathered on the paint without a thought to the cost. There was no mystery in any part of it. It was a portrait of voluptuous-ness, of a woman true to her desires from top to bottom, from the emerald green turban she'd lately taken to wearing, through the flounces and ripples and the indolent camber of her bosom, through the shadowy dimples and valleys, all the way down to her crossed ankles and those green slippers, the greeny-brown of Smyrna figs, in whose viperous tongues lived the devil. What he could have done in an hour had taken him twenty. He should have dashed it off and set his face against her repertoire of curling sensual gestures. But she'd purred, entreatied, and posed with her lips parted, even though it had been upon her feet he was working. She'd squirmed and stretched so that the movement of light on those banks of oystered silk could not fail to distract his eye. She'd said that ugly men had always excited her, why else would she have married the General. She'd told him of her disappointment on the dawn that her rose had been plucked; by a pudgy youth, in a brace of shakes, in a dewy meadow beneath an apple tree, to the sound of a cow roaring for its calf not twenty yards away. She would always remember it, she'd said, because she'd been too rushed to take off her dancing shoes, which were pink and had six sets of lace-holes, and she'd thought, even as she lay there, that she should have, that her mother would have disapproved. Both of them had glanced at her feet, and he'd pictured those dainty pink slippers poking through the hushed grasses, like a pair of immense orchids, rigid as she steeled herself. Then she'd said how stuffy the room was and flapped the air between her breasts until his hand trembled and the necessity to slide his fingers down her ankle and kiss the veined smoothness of her instep could no longer be opposed. There were a dozen things he could have said – and bid her good day. The words had queued up in his mouth. He'd had only to give a puff and they'd have flowed gracefully out. But he'd been weak, as he knew he always had been, from the moment that Bella Cartwright had sworn to him that her husband, his fellow officer, had long since ceased to mind what she did.

Thus the painting of the shoes had continued, through two long and humid afternoons while the thunder rumbled, the lightning cracked, and in the darkened bedroom she'd straddled him, easefully and at her leisure, not caring that he might leave two full sets of green fingerprints on her riding underthighs because it was what she liked best, to be in command and watch his brown eyes start to beg.

At a certain point, when the shoes had actually been finished, the General had arrived home unexpectedly – out of the blue, one would have said, had it not been through a summer's drizzle that he'd galloped like a madman straight to the front door without pausing to enquire, as a prudent soldier would have done after so lengthy an absence, if there was a gig in the stable yard that was not his wife's. From out of his saddlebag peeped the nervous head of a spaniel pup that he was bringing Georgiana. This lumpy, bearded man, who could scarcely walk he was so crippled by lust, this warrior who'd had mutineers hanged by the dozen, kicked open the front door, loosened the band of his dark green regimental trousers, hollered for his woman and was halfway into the house before—

Thank God for the puppy and a lucky stroke of wit, Thomas thought later. It had been as close as anything; but he believed no damage had been done. If the General had been suspicious, he hadn't shown it. They'd admired the picture together, and he'd taken himself off when a decent interval had elapsed.

Therefore, seeing as how these had been the circumstances, he had decided it would have been indelicate – more than that, provocative – to exhibit the picture. Isabel would have known immediately, and felt herself humiliated in public. And without Georgiana as a centrepiece . . . Well, to be frank he didn't care greatly for the smaller works. So that was that, and the hotelier would learn that artists were unreliable.

Mr Batt was indeed furious. He had sent out specially engraved cards announcing Thomas's exhibition, and faced losses as a result of its withdrawal, both as to expenses and deprivation of his commission. Many others declared themselves upset and expressed a wish to treat with Thomas privately. By and large, however, the anticipation roused by Suckling's gala far outweighed the absence of some pictures from The Three Crowns.

The appointed day was glorious, too hot perhaps. The air hung heavily over the city as the hired showmen urged people towards the theatre. 'Walk up! Walk up! The greatest show ever held in Norwich! Only a few seats left – none at a bob – a sovereign still wins – walk up! Keep going in front!' There were bowler-hatted merchants secured to their solid wives, ladies of the dowager hue in dresses half a century old, nervous spinsters armed with parasols, troops of dapper young cocks out for the night, parties of gentry yodelling to each other, louts, tarts, sharpers, Julius Gooby and Walter Harrington, Mrs Peach with her brother and a bevy of nieces and nephews, two discreet parsons, some tourists from London – oh, John Suckling had done his business alright.

At 6.30 – half an hour before the off – word spread to those outside that the last ticket had been sold. As they watched, a few unfortunates were ejected from the hall, the wedges were kicked from under the doors, and the showmen ominously linked arms to form a barrier. For a while there was a rustling, quarrelsome silence as the import of this was digested. Then 'Knock their bleeding tops off!' yelled one. 'Forward the 51st!' cried another, a military man. And the unhappy, vituperative crowd was about to battle it out when John Suckling, triumphant, genial and wholly preposterous in a pink silk tunic, stepped out onto the small balcony overlooking the street. 'Let them in, d'ye hear me,' he shouted down. 'Room for everyone somewhere, sitting, standing, kneeling, who gives a damn. Let them in, fellows, and may the best man win.' He raised his arms as if about to declaim – and was pulled inside by Mrs Suckling.

'I do believe John is drunk already,' Isabel said with distaste. The Gages had had to leave their carriage some distance away on account of the press of vehicles in town and were therefore later than they'd intended. They were walking quickly towards the theatre, Fred with an exaggerated stride to keep pace.

'Ugh! What on earth has he got that pink thing on for?' Harriet said.

They passed the main doors and went up a side street to the entrance that led to the boxes.

The noise and heat in the theatre hit them the instant the footman flung open the door to their box. The children stopped and gasped. Thomas coddled them forward, and they took their seats according to the lots they'd drawn beforehand: Thomas and Fred in the front row (a projecting wall allowed for only two chairs in the space), the women in the back. The footman hung up Isabel's mantle. Thomas rested his arms on the balcony and called down to his friends. The ladies fluffed out their skirts, made themselves comfortable, and looked around to see who had the other three boxes.

As neighbours they had Leonard and Joan and young Jeremy

Lutwylch, with a couple Isabel didn't know. On the far side of the stage, the long woolly beard, a trifle soiled at the corners of the mouth, and the splendid muttonchop whiskers of Mr Marley, editor of the *Mercury*, were the most prominent occupants of one box. The Farrants had the other. In the front the General sat composedly in his evening regimentals, stroking his dark, clipped beard. Isabel thought his cheek-bones hollower than she remembered and wondered if he'd had a fever. Georgiana was in a chair a little behind him and to one side. She was picking at a thread in her dress, which was a dirty lilac shade. Isabel considered it dowdy for the occasion. She'd expected something more showy, Georgiana being the person she was and the accounts of her portrait costume having been so lurid.

She watched as Thomas's head bore round on the Farrants. The General raised his hand amiably and spoke over his shoulder to Georgiana, who smiled in their direction. Thomas made no gesture that she could see. Satisfied, she exchanged greetings with Leonard and his family. Maybe she'd been wrong. Maybe Thomas was too old after all.

Wanting to say something to Leonard about how well the furbishment had come off, for she knew the paint had come from her manufactory, and also to suggest that it was time for another of their business meetings, she caught his eye, and leaning across Emily, said, 'I believe we should have one of our little talks soon.' He nodded and was on the point of speaking when the cathedral bell boomed seven. He smiled wryly at Isabel and took out his spectacle case. His penetrating nose bent to consult the programme; she turned away.

The chatter faded. The audience had a last cough and fell into an expectant hush. A squad of footmen appeared. Two worked the cords that unlatched the windows high above the stage. Others went around turning off the gaslights, including those in the boxes. Section by section the theatre darkened until it was perfectly black. From a gallery somewhere near the roof could be heard the sound of creaking machinery, something like a windlass being rotated.

Footsteps padded stealthily across the boards. Silence. Fred gripped Thomas's arm. 'A battle scene,' he whispered. 'Or Roman gladiators—'

Whoosh! A flare path of intense greeny-white light sprang down the stage, illuminating the front rows in a frightful pall, as if they were corpses sitting upright. A growl of approval spread through the hall. Shapeless figures scampered back into the wings. Again there was silence. Then from nowhere, it seemed, a trumpeter emerged, blond-haired and immensely tall, wearing a medieval tabard and harlequin thigh-tight hose and pouch. He took up position in the centre of the flares, filled his cheeks and squirted a short fanfare over the audience. The notes died and he retired, without bowing. A few people clapped but mostly they were quiet, sensing that a huger spectacle was in store.

The pots fizzled gently. 'That's limelight,' Thomas said to his family. 'It's what they use to guide ships into harbour in a storm.'

The smoke curled up to the ceiling and, quickening, was sucked out of the windows. Now people understood why the footmen had opened them. Now too, as they stared upwards, they learned what the sound like a windlass had concerned, but scarcely had they time to wonder why a thick net should be suspended from the roof when bang! The back of the stage exploded. Hot red light blazed as if a furnace door had suddenly been thrown open, and airborne through the writhing vapour soared a pink spherical body, arms arrowed in front of it, tunic streaming – like a meteorite! Like a colossal radish! Like nothing seen before in the ancient city of Norwich.

'Bravo! Bravo!' As one the crowd roared and stamped. Something like a scuffle seemed to be happening up there in the darkness. Then the gas was re-lit, the net began its descent, and the Mayor, the squabby, irascible John Suckling, was swayed down onto the stage like a gigantic flamingo-pink fish, or some newly captured divinity. He stepped out jubilantly.

'It wasn't him at all, Papa! He changed places up there, where no one could see. It wasn't him, I swear it,' objected Fred.

'We'll pull his leg about this, won't we just,' Thomas said.

'He *must* be drunk,' murmured Isabel as Suckling tossed aside his tunic, showing himself clad in a suit of black knee breeches and white stockings.

He brushed himself down. 'Old mawkins, the wife, she sez to I, "John bor, there hain't nivver nobody nowhere what'll not think et common to git yisself popped out of a gun." And I sez to her,

"Ma bor, do yew not stop thy yowling, I'll give yew sitch a ding athwart the lug as'll make et cum orf. Think yew I be some dwandly Londoner? There hain't nothin' doesn't do in Norridge." Which for the benefit of all the furriners who are with us tonight, means – Welcome to the new Palace Theatre!'

A stage hand came out and garlanded him with his chain of office. He raised his little arms to accept the acclaim of the audience, and Harriet said to her mother, 'He'll never stop. You know what he's like. We'll be here all night.'

'You wait,' Thomas said, turning in his seat. 'He's a terrible chatterbox is John. But he'll get there eventually and then we'll see some fun.'

It was as he promised. First the Volunteer band marched on and played a rousing selection of old favourites that had everyone's feet tapping. The effect was rather loud but as Suckling said afterwards, 'What can you expect? The enemy have to be frightened somehow.' Then jugglers, acrobats, a sword-swallower and magicians took over and showed good sport: extracted the Mayor's note-case from his inside pocket, discovered a daisy chain in it, filched his gold regalia, had the tubby fellow attempt a handstand, and in general ripened the audience towards the point where refreshment was imperative if lives were not to be lost.

When the last of them had gone, Suckling, who was having as much fun as anyone, stepped forward and in tones of the utmost gravity, announced that the climax of the evening had been reached. After this it would be downhill all the way. 'Mawkins and I are now going to perform for you Act 3, Scene 1 from Macbeth. I shall be doing himself, Banquo and—'

'Boo! Boo to Banquo!' shouted everyone.

'What? No Macbeth? Then in that case we shall have . . .' And two ladies, who all along had been itching to exchange the hottest gossip in town and hadn't the slightest wish to see another fire-eater, looked at each other and slipped out into the street.

'The General should never have ridden in without sending word in advance. Fancy doing that to a woman. I mean, Diana, really!'

'According to Georgiana, he all but fractured his sitting-bones on the saddle he was that keen to get at her.'

'Men! Isn't that just like them! But that's no excuse, he still should have warned her he was back. She might have been doing anything.'

'Or she might have been doing something.'

'No! That wasn't the impression she gave me.'

'Well, even Georgiana isn't that bold. But the portrait Thomas has been doing – it's taken an extraordinarily long time, don't you think? I don't know about him, but she's certainly not a chess-player.'

'And he has a weakness . . .'

'Quite so, poor dear Thomas has a weakness. I pray it doesn't get him into real trouble. It's not as if he's a satyr, or the kind of man who goes around aggravating marriages for the sake of it. It's just that when someone like Georgiana pushes herself at him, he's incapable of resisting.'

'So the General rides up – and then? Had they really been . . . ? You must have an inkling. You can't leave me on tenterhooks.'

'I don't *think* so, not that time. But even so – you can imagine the scene, my dear. There are always traces, however careful a lady is.'

'I wonder . . . do you think he ever actually *does*? He's always struck me as rather womanish, as one of those men who have a pat and a stroke and run away. Perhaps it's because I'm not his type, not round enough where it matters,' she laughed.

'Oh no, not Thomas. A certain someone we both know said she tingled for days afterwards.'

'But she's frightfully vain. She'd say anything to make herself appear desired. Anyway, the General gets home – then what? If I've heard one story I've heard ten.'

'And who does he find in occupation but Thomas, feet on the fireguard, drink in hand, looking very comfortable thank you.'

'You're exaggerating.'

'Of course I am, but you know what I mean. So he and the General look each other over and Georgiana becomes very busy with the cushions and no one knows quite what to say. Then this puppy the General's brought her lifts its leg on a column in the hall and do you know what Thomas said? "Doric, Ionic, Corinthian, all the same to a dog." He came out with it just like that, like snapping his fingers, so they had a bit of a laugh and that was the end of what could have been very unpleasant for everyone.'

'The end? The absolute end? Dick Farrant must be purblind.'

'Not him! The next morning – this is what she told me – they were having breakfast and halfway through his coffee he put down his cup and said, "Georgie, you know why I don't mind about Thomas? He doesn't count, that's why. He's a nothing to a man." That's what she said, the exact words.'

'She is remarkably indiscreet, I must say. What did the General mean?'

'I suppose that he doesn't count as a threat. That he's harmless. Large, white and harmless.'

'And not particularly attractive so far as a man is concerned? Not the Achilles type? That must be important to a husband.'

'Poor Thomas. I don't expect he's ever *really* been in love – struck by lightning, a bolt from the skies. He's like that character of Buckingham's, Prince something or other, who only has to sit down and pull his boots on to be certain he's in love. That's Thomas for you. I'm afraid he'll come a cropper one day – and then what? There's a triste side to him as well, you know.'

'He's always got Isabel to pick up the pieces. She'll stand by him through thick and thin. Look, they're coming out for the interval. There's that queer little man, Gooby, or whatever his name is. He's no Thomas Gage, that one. We'll be quite safe with him! Let's go and be nice to him and see if we can discover where he's putting his railway. Incidentally, the latest *on dit* is that he made an approach to the Gages and Thomas sent him packing. Wouldn't hear of it. And so pompous Leonard Lutwylch is incandescent with rage because if it can't run through Thomas's land, it can't run through his, and he won't make another fortune by selling to Mr Gooby. Lawyers, Hermione! Aren't they repulsive!'

'It'd have been different if Thomas and Isabel were as poor as we are. Without that paint business, they'd have gobbled down Mr Gooby and his money till only his heels were showing.'

'My dear, that's wonderfully expressive, if a trifle vulgar.'

'The truth is often vulgar.'

They strolled off to find Gooby, who was himself searching for the Gages in order to tell them he'd found a railway tunnel for Fred. It wasn't a proper tunnel with pediments and a coat of arms, like the one at Audley End. In fact it was no more than a cutting that had been temporarily timbered and roofed while a spring was led under the track into a new culvert. But it was dark and exciting. It was just the job for the little man.

Twenty

THE FARRANTS didn't return after the interval, which pleased Isabel. It had disquieted her to see Georgiana every time she looked across, even though she'd been dressed so poorly.

The gala evening drew to a close. The entertainments had been showered on them so rapidly that Thomas's ladies felt bruised by the unremitting jollity of it all. To make matters worse, John Suckling now took it upon himself to deliver a speech which was not only far too long but which also referred specifically to Isabel's donation to the theatre and her other charitable works. He pointed her out to the audience; obliged her to stand up and expose herself to a ringing chorus of cheers.

She sat down, pink with embarrassment, and fanned herself vigorously. 'I really do think we could leave,' she said to Thomas. 'Who knows what other nonsense he may dream up before the night's out. And it's as hot as an oven in here.'

The instant she'd spoken, Suckling announced that as was customary on these occasions, which were, he said, incomplete without the shedding of at least a little real blood, a brave and beautiful lass would be enclosed in a steamer trunk and sawn in half. He handed the lady in – someone recognised her and shouted, 'Good luck, Lisa, cry out if it hurts,' which drew a laugh – fingered the teeth of the huge double-handled saw, swore it affected him too much to watch and only uncovered his eyes when Lisa's spine cracked and he was invited to open the trunk, which was of course empty.

Fred was spell-bound. 'Just one more, please,' he said to his mother. His urchin face was so filled with enjoyment and his eyes so bright that she couldn't refuse him. In any case, just at that moment the lights were turned out for 'A Scene from Salome's Boudoir', and so an orderly exit from their box became impossible.

'I think there's only one left after this,' Thomas said to placate Isabel. 'Here, why don't you take my seat? You'll get a much better view.'

But she thought he should have made the offer long ago, and besides, had no wish to see Salome any closer than she had to. She declined stiffly, as did Harriet after her. Emily had already nodded off it was so warm in the theatre.

Slowly from out of the darkness floated the haunting, decadent notes of an alto flute. Feet sounded on the stage and halted. A costume, which no one could have failed to visualise as a wispy slip of a thing, rustled; and from out of nothingness sprang ten glowing green fingertips, which looped and curved through the heavy black air, caressing it with unmistakably sensuous gestures. The flute moaned, an Indian drum joining in with a soft pattering that made the hair tingle.

'Ooh,' breathed Fred, thinking what a scare he could give Emily in the tunnel if he could get hold of some green stuff like that.

The fingers swooped and twined, stroked and glided so rapidly that people became giddy and then started to shuffle in their seats, whether out of boredom or embarrassment it was impossible to say.

A light came on over the centre of the stage and was quickly dulled. Into its glow Salome slithered, black-eyebrowed, cherry-mouthed and expressionless, casting off her veils until all that remained was a sand-coloured shift reaching down to her ankles. The music sank to a whisper. Arms wrapped round her body, she spun in a blur to the edge of the stage. A toss of her head, a final twirl, and she arched over backwards and spraddled away into the darkness on her palms and soles, loins very prominent and her long dark hair trailing across the boards.

'Look at her, Papa, she can't have any backbone at all,' gasped Fred.

'John'll get a talking-to for putting on a number like that,' Thomas said to Isabel.

'I call it outrageous. The committee should have put a stop to it. No ifs and buts, just a straightforward No. She was a harlot, that's all she was, a dyed-in-the-wool harlot.'

'But she wasn't indecent. A little suggestive, I grant you that.'

'Don't you go making excuses for her, Thomas Gage. We don't need any of that in front of the children.'

'But it was nothing,' Emily said, stretching. 'It happened in the dark.'

'Can you get me some of that green ointment, Papa?' asked Fred innocently.

'Do let's go home now,' pleaded Harriet, 'so we won't get caught up with all the other carriages.'

They had actually got as far as standing up, the entire family, when Suckling returned to the stage, not a hint of reticence on his shining face. 'Well, old mawkins said I'd never get away with a Salome like that—'

'We can't go now,' Thomas said in a low voice. 'Everyone will notice us. It's just not *comme il faut* when John's speaking. Be patient' – and they subsided into their seats.

'—but the business with the fingers, it was very cleverly done, you must at least admit that.' Suckling dibbled his own fingers around, as if he was playing the piano at shoulder height, and made a comical swaying movement with his squat hips. Someone called out that he was better than Salome any day, which restored the audience's humour.

'That's more like it! We've had a grand evening, no need to be grudging, let's give Salome a proper Norfolk cheer – there! And now, before the Volunteers play us out to dinner, my last, absolutely my last words to you tonight, give or take a few concluding remarks concerning the importance of the theatre in all our lives and in those of our children, whether born or not . . .' He droned on blissfully, the sweat running down his cheeks, and Isabel was on the point of taking her mantle from the hook, etiquette notwithstanding, when the words suddenly popped out: 'The Queen of Melody! The Pearl of Australia! Ladies and gentlemen, our finale, the grandest any man could hope for – as youthful as she is beautiful – Miss Nina O'Reilly!'

'A medal should be struck for John for his work tonight,' Thomas said over his shoulder. 'Who else could have carried the evening off like he has?' and he turned back as the Mayor withdrew, clapping, into the wings and Nina O'Reilly, the discovery of the season, the sensation of all London, stepped forward with a becoming bow, flattened her stomach, inflated her white, corseted bosom and in a husky voice that instantly reminded Thomas of gooseberries, took the audience in her arms and cradled them through 'The Soldier Bridegroom' until eyes grew moist. She held the last note for what seemed an eternity, raising her robed arms like an angel's wings, her upper lip quivering. She finished, and lowered her golden head. For seconds, as long as it took for Thomas to find his breath again, there was silence. Then pandemonium broke out. Thomas was not alone in jumping to his feet. Everyone except the most elderly of the ladies was up, waving their programmes, cheering and huzzahing. She bowed again, twice to the front and once, left and right, to the boxes. She saw Thomas – it was impossible to miss him, standing there so hugely – and smiled up at him.

The applause tailed off. Thomas sat down, the last person to do so.

'Capital!' he exclaimed to Fred. 'Capital!' he said to his family behind him. Impulsively he leaned across the partition and tapped Lutwylch on the elbow. 'Did you ever hear anything to beat it, Leonard? Capital! First rate! Absolutely top notch!'

Without waiting for a response, he put up his opera glasses and studied Nina: the fairness of her skin, the strong shoulders, the beribboned parapet of her bosom, the bowl of her hips, the movement of her friendly, unaffected face as in that same entrancing voice she told the audience something about her childhood (he judged her to be about thirty) and the jobs she'd had to take in order to pay for her passage to Europe. Wonderful, he said to himself, so fresh, so honest, such softness of manner. Folding his arms across the rail, he buried his chin in them, from time to time raising the glasses to examine some feature that was newly revealed.

'I'd say it must have taken a large oyster to produce the Pearl,' observed Fred.

But Thomas was not listening. He had ears only for Nina, who was singing again:

> 'For he's bound to come in at the window
>   If you don't let him in at the door;
> Or through the skylight, in the dead of the night,

Or make his way up through the floor.
By the lightning flash or the water-spout –
  There's no use trying to keep him out;
For Cupid's a dodger beyond any doubt,
    He's love, love, love.'

Every note he saw as a bubble of enchantment rising from her lips and floating up to him personally, as love, as warmth, as companionship, as a dream that would be in all ways perfect. This feeling arose from nowhere and was quite dramatic in its completeness. At first it terrified him, and he tried to smother it. But at each verse the notes burst afresh from her glorious mouth and spread outwards from his heart to pollenate his entire being, and the longer he listened the more they became, not frightening, but like some delicious and soothing balm that promised to cure him of the ailment which, in the flick of one stupendous moment, he recognised to be his wife.

The notes, these exquisite messages of love, soared up to him as Nina turned, mid-song, beneath their box.

'Strewth! Like cannonballs, great white cannonballs!' murmured Fred, but not so quietly that Isabel was unable to hear him. She could not see Nina at that instant; unlike her menfolk she wasn't hanging over the edge of the box. But she knew very well what he was referring to, what he and Thomas were thinking about. She had heard – who hadn't? – all those exclamations of 'Capital!' and quailed at their force. She saw the opera glasses wedged against Thomas's eyeballs, saw them as steady as his pointer on Nina, the flush creeping up his neck and pinkening his ears, the nervous scuffling of his feet. Every instinct shrieked within her. There was much she could forgive him, for as a wife she was imperfect and acknowledged it. But in public – to a colonial – a fat chantéuse—

She gathered her skirts decisively. This time they would go. She would take her family and get them safely away before people started to notice. She glanced purposefully at Harriet and Emily on either side of her and nudged Fred in the back.

Suddenly Thomas leapt from his seat. His opera glasses fell with a clatter onto the stage. Everyone looked up at him. His face was aflame, all its odd, torn angles working against each other as if in torment. 'I must go – John has just signalled to me – there must have been an accident somewhere.' He barged through his family, who were halfway to their feet, and rushed out of the door.

Isabel tried to call out, but only a grunt emerged. She snatched despairingly at the tails of Thomas's evening coat, stumbled and struck her shoulder on the seat. The Lutwylchs looked across sharply. Nina smoothly continued her song.

'Mother, they're all watching us,' Emily said urgently.

Lutwylch, prodded by his wife, came round with a glass of water. 'Only a dizzy spell,' Isabel said. 'It's the heat, nothing more serious, I assure you.'

It was not until Nina was finishing her act that Thomas returned. He entered the box quietly and kissed Isabel and Harriet on the cheek. 'My dears, I'm so very sorry. Such clumsiness, do forgive me. In fact John had no need for me anyway. It was a complete waste of time.' Fred gave his seat a pat. 'Come and sit down again, Papa.' But Thomas remained standing at the back of the box, even though the gaslight was hot against his neck, while Nina sang an encore, then another, and at last indicated enough was enough.

A footman trotted up the aisle with a bouquet of flowers, their stalks laced with curlicues of sky-blue ribbon. He passed it tenderly, as if it were a sleeping child, up to John Suckling who held it behind his back while he made his valedictory speech. For the first time Nina looked awkward as she watched his fingers crushing the stems and wondered how the transfer was to be completed with dignity.

'Sadly, it only remains for me—' Suckling halted. A second footman was approaching him; young, slick-haired, grinning widely, a whole bale of flowers heaped loosely in his arms. 'Competition, eh! Then I must do the deed and do it quickly: 'twere well it were done quickly,' and whipping the bouquet out from behind his back, he pressed it into Nina's grasp. He closed his hands over hers and remained like that, laughing, so that she was unable to accept the rival blooms. 'Ha! Now what will you do, my friend?' he called down to the footman.

The footman glanced at Nina and John Suckling above him on the stage, and back to the flowers, which he'd gone to a great deal of trouble to procure at short notice. His face reddened as the audience started to cheer him on. He looked up at the Gages' box for instructions – and now Isabel understood what Thomas had been doing. 'Hussy! Minx!' she burst out, and continued, almost hysterically, with these hissing sounds until Thomas placed the mantle round her shoulders and led her from the box.

Twenty-one

Two DAYS later Isabel took herself off to stay with her friend
Dolly Baunt. The visit did not bring the relief she'd hoped for.
She'd lived for too long within her own walls; had drawn up most
of the ladders; had forgotten how to parley. It embarrassed her
even to mention Nina, and to admit that she herself was a reason
for Thomas's meandering eye was an outright impossibility. The
week passed slowly.

On the Saturday, which was printing day for the *Mercury*, there
appeared Mr Marley's report on the gala evening. Dolly insisted
they put aside their jam-making and read it together, by which she
meant that she would do the reading so that she could admire the
accompanying woodcuts. Thus Isabel had no choice but to listen
as Dolly lingered, with infuriating fascination, over the details of
the one person whose name she never wished to hear again: Nina
O'Reilly, the Pearl of Australia. She was, Dolly reported, unmar-
ried, twenty-nine years of age, and had one brother, who was a
waterman in Sydney. A Miss Corfield had taught her music. After
her triumph at the gala, she had returned immediately to London
where she was to spend the remainder of the season. Thereafter
she had an indefinite booking at the Metropole in Brighton. Her
fee for this was said to be the highest ever commanded by a
performer in the country. At even double the price it would be
cheap, concluded Dolly, if what Mr Marley had heard was
anything to go by.

Dolly swivelled the paper round to show Isabel the woodcut,
which was simply captioned 'The Pearl'. 'How good was she
really?' she asked. Isabel replied that she couldn't properly say, it
was so stuffy in the hall by then. 'But Thomas was very taken by

her,' she said, with an effort, a plea in her voice that was well nigh inaudible. 'Then the evening wasn't a complete waste of time, was it,' said Dolly, rising to attend to the jam.

While Isabel was away, Lutwylch called to enquire after her health, and Gooby with a list of possible dates for the railway excursion. Also General Farrant sent the entire sum for Georgiana's portrait; a cheque by itself, without any note, which struck only the children as odd.

On her return Isabel arranged a meeting with Leonard, after he'd taken his family on a tour of the Lake District, so they could have a thorough discussion of the paint business. She asked Thomas if he would like to attend, not expecting for a moment that he would, and was very agreeably surprised when he accepted. He looked her in the eye, repeated his apologies for the incident in the theatre, and though rather subdued, seemed to be his old self again. They resumed their evening walks in the garden, which he'd broken off when he started to paint Georgiana. They talked about new plantings, took strolls along the river bank, and shooed the chickens out of the roadside hedge, in the coolness of which worms were readily found even at the height of summer. He suggested they grow a wistaria up the front of the house, something he'd long resisted. When it grew dark, they lit the candles, gathered the children around and with the aid of a map and Gooby's copy of Bradshaw's timetable, plotted their journey on the railway.

This gave rise to much argument of the sort common to all families organising a joint expedition, and the matter might never have been agreed had not Gooby sent word that it was only on one specific day that he'd been able to engage for them the coupé carriage that belonged to the Eastern Union Railway.

Emily had been invited to a birthday party on the day in question – it was August 25th, a Monday – and naturally wished to know how a coupé was superior to a normal first-class carriage, in which, as she pointed out, they could travel on any date they wished. Gooby was summoned. Isabel was in town when he arrived – he couldn't think how he hadn't passed her on the road – but four was declared a quorum in her absence. He explained that the coupé had a special compartment at one end that was luxuriously outfitted, totally private, and usually at the disposal only of the directors of the Eastern Union. He tapped his nose. He couldn't possibly divulge any details of the negotiation that had secured its use. But it was there for the taking – on a plate – the finest carriage in the kingdom. He couldn't recommend it too highly.

'What of it then, Mr Gage?' He'd seen and comprehended everything that had happened in the theatre during Nina's act. He foresaw a rupture between man and wife. He had to hurry matters along. There were sufficient complications as it was. 'What I'm saying is that it's now or never from a practical point of view.'

'Well, in for a penny, in for a pound,' Thomas said resignedly.

Emily, however, demurred. She had nothing against being secluded in the coupé with her family. She just preferred travelling more sociably – and Olive Thompson, whose birthday party it was, happened to be her closest friend.

'And the little man?' queried Gooby, drilling Fred with his look. Fred was afraid that if there were strangers around he'd never have the nerve to play the really cracking joke on Emily that he'd been working on, and plumped without hesitation for the coupé. Harriet also wished to have as little to do with strangers as possible. So Emily was voted down, and Thomas said to Gooby, 'I shall make a voyage with my family like an ancient pasha with his seraglio. They'll feed me with sweetmeats, tickle my feet with peacocks' feathers, chant lullabies – and I'll fall asleep.' As he was showing him to the door he added, 'But you'd be foolish to believe that this trip will alter my opinion an iota. Very foolish indeed, sir.'

When Isabel got home she discovered that in a fortnight's time she was to do exactly as Gooby had suggested when he came to tea: go to Wymondham so that Thomas could see the extent of the Trowse bridge; change trains and go to Fakenham for lunch; then back to Wymondham to get into a horse-carriage to take them to Forncett for a first-class dinner at the inn. Afterwards they would catch the stopping train to Norwich, to arrive back at Fordwell at about 9 p.m.

She immediately started to concern herself with the details. (They were having a family game of croquet, parents versus the three children; Thomas had painted the extra ball white with blue stripes.) 'That's very well, banquets and the directors' coupé and so forth. It's easy for all of you to rattle off times and stations as if you did this every day, but there's the in-between arrangements we have to think about. What class of clothes shall we wear? Do the windows open? Has anyone considered that? Will it be dirty? Shall we take soap and towels? Where do we leave our bits and pieces when we get off to eat? Should we take some food with us?' She was talking as they played, holding the game up for everybody. 'What about some books and games? Flowers – that'd be pretty, especially if I put lots of honeysuckle among them. The upholstery may smell. Which of you can tell me whether gentlemen are allowed to smoke in the carriages? There, you don't know everything after all . . . What else? Shall we need Sam? Would we have to have him in the coupé with us? Has anyone told Mr Gooby to buy him a ticket?'

The mention of Sam was the last straw for her children. 'Never!' shouted Emily, miscueing her ball frightfully. 'If he goes, I'm not, and that's flat. He'll try to come the high-and-mighty over us and end up by spoiling everything. Don't get so het up about it, Mother. It'll sort itself out by itself. Frederick Gage, take your foot off your ball this instant. He's trying to cheat, Papa, look at him.'

But now that the idea of this great campaign had formed itself in Isabel's mind, together with lists and rosters and things to be ticked off, she wasn't to be stopped. Mrs Macbride was to pack a hamper for them. It was to contain this and this and this, not forgetting the salt for the radishes and pepper for the strawberries. Then, 'Flies, supposing the carriage is full of flies. It's summer, after all. So I come back to what I was saying earlier – do the windows open? Goodness gracious, there's no end to it. Here, let's get a piece of paper and write everything down.'

The children groaned. There was no knowing what chores might be demanded of them when Isabel was in one of her managing moods.

'Steady on now, Mother, one thing at a time,' Thomas said off-handedly, as he planned the shot to follow the one that would send Fred's ball into the shrubbery. 'Only two hoops to go. We can deal with the railway later. I'm damned if I'll let a carriage full of flies come between me and my winnings.'

He was referring to the column of six pennies balanced on top of the winning-post. For a while they'd flirted with a five-penny regime, each of them contributing a copper. But five was not a number amenable to division between three children. By Emily's reckoning, Fred had owed her an impossible fraction for over two years. So these days Thomas added a further penny to the stake, from his own pocket. It had made him much keener to win.

The only thing no one remembered to investigate, until they were driving up to the station and it was too late, was whether Venus would be allowed onto the train without being shut in a dog basket.

Thomas and the children were a little tetchy on account of Isabel's bossiness. She'd had them up from an early hour checking the cases and provisions.

'We're not going on a sea-voyage, you know,' Thomas grumbled as he searched for the napkins. 'It's not as if we need to fill in a manifest detailing every scrap of cargo.'

'You want us to enjoy ourselves, don't you?'

'But napkins! That's taking it too far. What next, finger-bowls and the silver?'

'It doesn't matter. You never know how things'll turn out. Drinking glasses, has anyone seen them? Ginger-beer, the lemonade? Was that meant to be a yes, Fred? Take that apple out of your mouth. You'll get plenty to eat in due course.'

All this had unsettled Thomas. When the question of Venus and her basket arose, he shut his ears to the new bout of squabbling, tied up the horse and went to meet Walter Harrington who was walking across Thorpe Road and into the station concourse.

'No Mr Gooby?'

'Most apologetic, most apologetic indeed, sir. A meeting in London – the chairman – Sir Hector. I'm sure you know how it is in business.'

'Well, it is rather off, I must say, especially after the way he's been badgering us to do this. I've been up practically since dawn, I'm exhausted already. Anyway, the thing is, does this damned dog of Isabel's need to be kept in a basket or not? They're getting in a frightful stew about it.' He nodded towards the carriage where Isabel was supervising the unloading of the baggage. 'Look at it. Impedimenta, pure and simple. All completely unnecessary. Anyone would think we were leaving the country for good.'

Walter smiled as conspiratorially as his honest face would allow. Not feeling bold enough for 'What we do for our women, eh!' he said, 'Oh, you don't need to worry about the dog. So long as it has a ticket, the guard won't care.' He handed Thomas an envelope. 'I've sorted out the tickets for each section of the journey. The booking clerk's dated them. Labels – I've got a bunch handy in case . . .' He glanced at the growing mound of baskets and hampers. 'No, nothing there that won't go as personal. Insurance against loss of life or limb? Mr Gooby said I was to ask your opinion before doing anything . . . I agree. Once you take out an insurance, you're asking for trouble. And besides, then the ladies get to thinking that accidents are two-a-penny. Why else would anyone insure themselves? they say. Oh yes, no logic to them at times. I believe that's about everything.' He looked at the time on the severe, classical clock-tower that rose above the entrance to the station. 'The Yarmouth train'll be here in a minute or two. No reason why it shouldn't be punctual. Ten minutes for boarding and you'll be on your way, happy as titlarks, Mr Gage!'

A porter loaded their things onto a barrow and wheeled it away round the side. Walter led them through the elegant hallway, pointing out to the children all the various offices where lost luggage could be reclaimed, baggage collected by the town carriers, or payment made for over-weight items. They reached the platform. The train arrived, whistling morosely. Walter started to search frantically through his pockets. 'I had it a moment ago. Hang on, it's here somewhere.' At last he found a piece of North Norfolk business paper, folded very small, and gave it to Thomas. 'The names of the stationmasters where you break your journey – if you have any difficulty, or something's been forgotten – one can't think of everything, can one? They all know you're on the train and are to get absolutely top-guinea treatment. Guests of Mr Gooby, that's the password!' He saw them onto the train and stood back.

Isabel and Harriet were wearing loose grey muslin dresses, appropriate for the weather. Isabel's was the more decorative, having a crimson waist and a ruche of crimson lace round the upper part of the arm. Emily's dress was closer to marzipan than cream, with a Cambridge-blue sash tied in butterfly fashion. She'd tucked the ends back into the sash so they wouldn't get caught in the doors. Thomas's trousers were of whitish uncreased madras cotton, rather baggy, and his black shoes had a high polish. He'd decided that in order to convey to everyone his regard for all that was old-fashioned, for the dilatory mail-coach and the spirit of his forefathers, he would make no concessions to the summer heat but sport his ancient thick blue coat. Fred, who at the age of fourteen was just starting to fill out, had on dark green trousers latched beneath the shoe, an open-necked white shirt and a light plaid coat. The yellow in its narrow check was the most dominant colour. It was belted at the back, with two brown buttons at each end of the belt.

'What a charming young man that Walter is,' Isabel said, taking Venus onto her lap. They'd stowed their things away, arranged the flowers, fiddled around with the leather window strap until it was at the right height, and made themselves at home.

The morning was like champagne. An easterly breeze tempered the growing heat of the day. Slivers of cloud, like old men's eyebrows, ambled through the pure blue sky. The ripening barley whispered down the fields, the feathered sails of the windmills revolved eight times a minute, cattle coloured the shadows beneath the parkland trees, and the dusty lanes seemed to stretch forever. Leaving in its wake the husks of assorted whistles and snorts, clankings and rattles, the country train put-puttered to Wymond-ham. According to Fred, who'd spent his thirty shillings commis-sion from Georgiana on buying a leather-cased compass, it was heading twenty-two degrees west of south.

They crossed the bridge at Trowse, an enormous affair that could be raised to let ships up the river. Thomas paid it scant attention. He had declined Gooby's proposal: how bridges were built was no concern of his. Isabel, however, observed it with interest. She had no particular views on the good sense or otherwise of building a railway to Cromer, but it struck her immediately that so ponderous a construction would be a foolish use of capital. A sensible man would want to cross the river at Fordwell at a fraction of the cost. She leaned back in her seat to consider the implications.

Everything went according to plan. The trains were punctual and the railway officials helpful. They played games, picked through Mrs Macbride's hamper, and debated why the train going south from Fakenham to Wymondham should be five minutes faster than the one going north. (The discovery had been made by Emily.) It was somewhat of a disappointment to them all when in the middle of the afternoon they had to leave the train and get into a horse-carriage to take them across to Forncett St Peter, where they were to board the coupé.

'Quite civilised actually, these railways,' Thomas said. 'Not half as bad as I remember. Fast too, when you reflect that their movement is really only a large number of small jerks. Well, that's what it feels like anyway. Now that Blissett has packed it in with the London coach, I'm not sure I won't use them more often. It's something we can talk about when we get home.' He closed his eyes and slept, snoring gently, his head on Isabel's shoulder.

'Have I missed anything?' he said, rubbing his eyes. 'I say, at Forncett already, that was quick.' He yawned. 'Dinner—'

'And then home,' Harriet said.

'Not before we go through the tunnel,' Fred said. 'You'll hate the tunnel, Em. Bats live in it – they'll come in the window and get their claws tangled in your hair. You'll scream.'

'I won't. I like bats.'

'Bet you will. All girls are scared of bats. James Mallen's sister—'

'That's enough from you two,' Isabel said. 'Emily, help me with the bags while your father gets a porter. Fred, you can take Venus for a walk. It's high time she did something.'

'Oh, alright. Come on, Venus, come with master and have a good blow. You've been very smelly today, you know, and if Papa hadn't been asleep he'd have thrown you out of the window.'

'Frederick!' expostulated Isabel, but without severity. The day was going so well. They'd be home by 9. She and Thomas could take a turn round the garden before it grew dark.

They had time on their hands before the train arrived. Though only Thomas was at all hungry, they decided Mr Gooby's money shouldn't be allowed to sit around idly, and walked up the lane to the Rose and Button for an early dinner. By way of a treat, Thomas ordered a bottle of wine – to get the children into training, as he put it. He was rather over-generous with his tip to the waiter, at which Isabel frowned.

They returned to the platform with about thirty minutes to

spare. Williams, the stationmaster, had already hung out the flag for the train to stop. While his parents sat on a bench and digested their meal, Fred quizzed Williams about the tunnel. He had hidden in his bag the pot of green paste that Thomas had obtained from the people at the theatre. It was the phosphorus in it that made it glow, they'd said, so he must be sure to wear a pair of thin gloves like Salome's or his skin might get burnt. Thomas had the gloves in his pocket. They were in it together, father and son. Fred couldn't wait to get into the tunnel.

'Just before you reach Flordon, the next stop,' Williams said. 'Tunnel goes to within a couple of feet of the platform – sort of awkward, actually, the way the blighters have built it. And they've put their shoring timbers that close to the metals – don't you go sticking your head out, son, or you'll have it knocked off.'

'How will I know when we're getting close?' asked Fred anxiously, thinking about the gloves and how he was to get the lid off the pot in the dark.

'Cos the train'll slow right down, on account of all their bloomin' works,' Williams said. 'You won't miss it, not a thing like that, you won't.'

The train arrived, and they piled into the directors' coupé, which was the last of the carriages. Someone had affixed a piece of cardboard to the inside of the window: 'For use by Mr and Mrs Thomas Gage and family ONLY.' They spread their things round carelessly, seasoned travellers by now.

'The last stretch,' Harriet exclaimed, throwing herself into a soft green leather seat. 'What a relief to have the place to ourselves.'

'You can't say we've been exactly jammed in with a mob of people,' Emily said. 'Only two – no, only three other passengers in our carriage the whole day long.'

'It was the *idea* of a crowd getting in,' Harriet replied. 'It made me nervous every time we stopped.'

The train pulled out. Williams snapped off a salute to Fred as the coupé slid past. Escorted by its evening shadow, which cast onto the banks and fields a duplicate profile of wheels, bogies, smoke-balls, ladies' bonnets, Isabel's vase of flowers and the energetic figure of the stoker, the train headed north to Flordon. Two and a half miles, six minutes give or take, Williams had told him. Fred began to count them off. He'd thought of asking his father if he could borrow his watch but had decided it might alert Emily. He had his bag ready on his knees. He sat touching Thomas so he had only to dip into his father's pocket to get the gloves. His eyes, as bright as farthings, were fastened beadily upon Emily, who was sitting opposite.

'Pooh! Venus!' Harriet suddenly cried. 'What can Sam have given her to eat this morning?'

'Three,' intoned Fred, though he hadn't meant to say it out loud, and he stared across at Emily so rascally, with such obvious mischief, that she instantly became suspicious.

'Bats won't worry me the tiniest bit and it's no good your thinking they will. I've always liked bats.'

But still Fred wore his gloating expression and she knew it couldn't be bats he had in mind.

'Venus, you're disgusting,' Harriet said. 'Father, can we let her out at the next station for a walk? I'm sure they'll wait for us if you tell them who we are.'

Emily looked carefully at her brother, saw his knuckles white round the handles of his bag. As quick as a fox, she leaned forward and snatched it away from him.

'Here—'

'Oh no you don't, you little monkey, you were going to play a trick on me.' In a trice she had the bag open and was rootling through it while Fred said 'Five' to himself and tugged furiously at its woven bottom. The bag came abruptly away in his hands as Emily found what she was after. His legs went up in the air and he hit the back of the seat with a thump.

'What's this then,' cried Emily jubilantly, 'what's someone doing with the property of the Palace Theatre? Who's been a wicked thieving boy?'

'Don't open it, Em! You need gloves! It'll burn you.' Thomas grabbed the paste-pot from her. The train slowed, and they entered the Flordon tunnel, which had lost all interest now for Fred.

'Thomas, there's the stationmaster,' Isabel said as the train came to a halt. 'I'm sure he'll oblige us if you explain about Venus. After all, the directors won't be very happy if she makes a mess in their carriage. Quick as you can, Fred, and this time wait until she's done her business properly.'

She shooed them both out and went herself to speak to the guard. Emily looked at the pot, which was still lying on the seat. Green paste on his fingers! Like Salome! As if that would have frightened her!

Harriet opened her book and started to read. After a moment or two she heard an engine whistle at the far end of the platform, two short, exasperated blasts. A second one chipped in by way of reply, altogether different in pitch, less piercing and in some way apologetic. Now what was happening? She slipped a marker between the pages and got out.

Thomas left off his conversation with the stationmaster and walked towards her. 'Seems they can use only one line on account of the works in the tunnel. The London express has to squeeze in, we have to squeeze out – the trains have to pass each other somehow – we're a carriage longer than usual – some sort of complicated manoeuvre. Blissett never had any problems like this. But a bit of luck for us, eh Harriet! Gives the boy enough time – well, we won't have to be stunk out any more, that's the way I look at it. Hop in. Shouldn't take them more than a minute or two to sort it out . . . Isabel! Isabel!'

Clouds of steam and smoke rose at the other end of the platform where the two trains had halted, nose to nose. Whistles blew. Men shouted and argued. The pointsman crouching over his lever waited for the impasse to be resolved. Heads craned out of the windows. The stationmaster, portly and flustered, bobbed in and out of the smoke.

Isabel and Harriet climbed back into the coupé and sat down. Thomas stood in the doorway, Emily at his elbow.

'Get a move on, Fred, or you'll be left behind,' she shouted.

The stationmaster raised his flag. The heads at the front of the train disappeared. The guard strode towards Thomas, checking the doors. He called to him, 'Hold hard a moment, my boy's still to come.'

'He won't be a tick, sir. He's just on his way,' and out of the smoke Fred came running on his short legs, triumphant, his mouth brimming with laughter, Venus smirking in his arms.

'Hurry, Fred, hurry,' cried Emily, twisting herself about in an agony of apprehension, 'we're about to go.'

Thomas pushed the door wide open and lowered his arms to receive Venus.

'Whoppers, all over the place – catch, Papa – one, two, three,' and Fred swung Venus up and into his father's arms. Thomas recoiled half a pace, collided with Emily. The coupling clanked and tightened. Fred weighed everything up in a flash. 'Budge over, you two,' he said, and with a hop and a skip, he placed his foot where the step would be a second later.

But it was not forward that the train moved. To allow the London express into the station it had to go back, and Fred's small foot, hastened by the downward momentum of his body and that impish and unnecessary flourish, slipped off the edge of the step. He gasped, flung up his arm. Too late was Thomas, off balance and impeded by Emily. His fingers touched Fred's. For an instant they held, the same instant that their eyes met. Then the breastwork of the tunnel caught the door and slammed it against Fred's shoulder. He screamed, and their fingers parted.

The sun vanished. Very slowly, very patiently, the train rumbled back into the tunnel and the coupé began to fill with smoke.

'Pull the cord, Father,' shrieked Emily. 'Outside – above the window.'

But Thomas was powerless to move. He could still feel the tug of Fred's fingers, could still see the helplessness in his beautiful eyes and the white arch of his throat as the door came flying at him and he jerked his head back. He saw it all, in large and in miniature, and his mind was unable to encompass it. It was a dream, an impossibility. He stood rooted to the spot in the grey murk.

'Do it for him. Do it, I tell you.' Isabel rose swiftly and went to Emily's side.

At that moment the train stopped, jolted and began to move, back into the station.

'I can't find it – it's not there—'

'Put your whole arm out, girl – higher—'

'I am, as far as I can reach – it's no good—'

A projection from the scaffolding struck Emily on the elbow; she fell back sobbing. Puffing gently, the train crept along the rails and they were forced, impotent within the directors' carriage, to hear once again that noise, the scraping, the rending, and the gurgles, so close it seemed they could touch it. They looked at each other in silence, trying to close their ears as the train emerged from the tunnel and the evening sun flooded their stricken faces with its bright false light.

The London locomotive drew alongside, its ironwork gleaming green, the same green that Fred had intended for his fingers. Hissing, it blotted out the window on that side. The stoker resting on his shovel stared into the coupé. Thomas stared back, his mouth working, his face as grey as pumice stone, a terrible anger now in his eyes. He clenched his fists. 'Gooby!' – and turning, he threw the women aside and hurled himself, scrabbling, at the door.

The guard was already on the platform. People were running all over the place. Thomas's head was spinning, the whole world was spinning and tilting, and every sheep and cow and all the churches, windmills and houses of Norfolk and all the murderers around him and the money-suckers, harlots and sodomites were sliding into the sea at a place he saw to be Cromer. He charged through the crowd, the skirts of his long coat flapping, blinded by rage, saying over and over to himself the one word, 'Gooby.' A braided cap, a fateful green uniform, a pair of hoggish jowls loomed in front of him. He reached forward, his hands like talons. 'Gooby, I shall kill you,' he whispered, and pressing his thumbs deep into the fat throat, he started to throttle the stationmaster.

Twenty-two

DISASTER SWIRLS. Arrows darken the sky. The devil settles to his work. These are the circumstances in which the exceptional man steps forward from the shadows where fate has providentially placed him. The newspapers later identified him as Captain Oliver Wattson of the Punjab Frontier Force, returning from India on furlough. His name that evening was simply Wattson.

He was dressed in mufti – wrinkled, straw-coloured trousers, a tired violet waistcoat and a jacket made of dun native material, also rather crumpled. He was tall, he stooped, and between the sandy tufts of his remaining hair, his scalp was discoloured by brown stains the size of halfpennies. His eyes were blue; his nose was beaked; a vigorous ginger moustache covered the grooves beneath his nostrils. It twitched as with his hands behind his back he strolled down the platform.

He observed the porters prising a demented man in an absurd blue-green coat off the stationmaster. He saw a boy lying beside the rails, a few yards away from the mouth of the tunnel, horribly injured but still living. A tall woman and two girls were bent over him. He lit a cheroot, retired into the seclusion of a crab-apple tree, and waited for order to be established. Smoke trickled from between his half-closed lips.

The squawking rose to new heights. More people spilled out of the carriages, flapped their wings, gobbled and did nothing. The tall woman fainted. 'Morale disintegrating,' he said to himself. Procedures formed in his mind.

He ground out his cheroot, pulled down his waistcoat, and walked over to the porters. He removed Thomas from their grasp and sat him firmly on a bench. The stationmaster starting to yap, he gave him a volley with his thin blue eyes. 'Wattson here. Shut up and do as I say.'

The guard ran past, blowing his whistle. He stretched out an arm and collared him. 'Wattson here. I'm putting you in charge of the hospital. One: go up and down both trains and find me a doctor. Two: failing a doctor, find me a bottle of opium tincture. Someone will have one. Don't come back without one or the other. Report to me in person.

'Porter – take a mate and keep everyone who isn't family away from the boy. Use force if necessary. Put an umbrella over him.

'Stationmaster – what's your name? Very well, Jack. One: have the points set for the London train. Two: despatch it when I tell you. Three: keep the Norwich train here. Four: have the booking-clerk find a stretcher. A farm hurdle, a door, anything flat will do.' He paused, the sun glinting on his scalp as he looked around. 'Whose cottage is that? Then before the clerk does anything he must run over and obtain all the bedding from your wife that he can . . . Good man, Jack. Don't panic. We'll get it straight between us. Wattson's the name for your records. Two 't's.'

Stooping, chewing at his moustache, he surveyed the scene. The girls were helping the woman to her feet. One of them, the youngest, had blood down the front of her dress. Nothing more could be done about the boy till he had the materials to hand.

The old man's shoulder was shaking when he touched it. Huge tears were gliding unattended down his cheeks. Wattson sat down beside him. It could only be the father.

'You shouldn't be alone, sir. I'll have one of your family sit with you. A doctor is being fetched.'

'He always wanted to be a soldier,' Thomas said simply.

'And so he may be. It'll go hard with him, I fear, but he lives.'

'He lives?'

'He lives.'

'Praise be to God.' Thomas lifted his wet, shining face to the other, his eyes now as soft as feathers. 'Say it again, tell me again that he lives . . . a miracle, oh, a miracle.' And of a sudden he was up, making a hop and a skip, a hop and a skip. 'See that, it's what he did. The train moved. He put up his arm – we touched – I could have saved him. That cur of Isabel's – it was the two of us that did it. The pug and I, between us we killed my son.'

'But he lives. And it was an accident. No good can come of it if you blame yourself.'

'Ah yes, so you said, he lives. I must go to my child. He'll be asking for me.'

Wattson said nothing to this and nursed him down the platform, this large tear-stained man in his coat from the Napoleonic age, at whom everybody was staring. He had thought the sights of India stranger than any that could exist, but to be doing this, on a perfect summer's day, in his mother country, in Norfolk where nothing had happened for centuries . . . The guard approached, a lanky fellow, his boots showing to above the ankle. His expression boded no good; he was holding something behind his back.

Wattson said to Thomas, 'Excuse me for a moment, sir. I find myself in charge here.'

He allowed the guard to lead him a few paces away. He shook the bottle and held it up to the sun. It was enough, provided he could get it down the lad's throat. It would dull the worst of the pain while he straightened the leg and splinted it. Perhaps the other leg was broken too. Water, that was something he'd forgotten. He was on the point of sending the guard off when the booking-clerk came trundling a barrow down the platform. A door was balanced cross-ways on it; underneath were two sacks of sheets already torn into strips, thin boarding for splints, luggage straps and hot-water pans. Beside the barrow marched a hefty woman.

'Mrs Jack? Wattson here. Glad you've come.'

He returned to Thomas. 'Do you trust me with your son?'

'I do.'

'Then I want you to go to the ticket office and remain there with your family until Mrs Jack and I are finished. Here, look after my coat for me. You'll find a smoke in the left inside pocket if you need one. What's your son's name? Fred – is he brave? Be like him. It's my only advice. Afterwards we'll see what's for the best.'

He had the London train despatched and the Norwich train, together with all its passengers, taken a hundred yards down the line. Emily had refused to sit with her parents and Harriet; she now offered herself as his helper. He was doubtful. He was a soldier, he said, not a surgeon. He had experience of wounds, he knew what had to be done – but he was no magician. It would cause her great hurt. She would see and hear all that took place every night for the rest of her life. It would hurt her more if she did nothing, she replied. 'Brave girl,' Wattson said. He jumped onto the track, gave Emily a hand down, and then Mrs Jack, who was less limber.

Fred was lying on his side, his broken body huddled between the platform and the inside rail. From time to time he raised his head a few inches and let it fall. His eyes were open, staring into the brickwork of the platform. Froth was round his lips, and he moaned continuously. Wattson considered the angles.

The Norwich train waited, panting laconically. A knot of people, villagers, had collected outside the ticket office. Vast crenellated banks of clouds were massed on the horizon. Rising, they effaced the livid sun and became fringed with purple. A hot breeze eddied along the platform and made the dust whirl. He repositioned the umbrella and told Mrs Jack to keep it steady.

The booking-clerk set down his barrow. The metal struts scraped harshly against the stone. He didn't want him there. 'Take that door back and have some handles nailed to it. I'll call you when I'm ready.' He took out his watch. A little over five minutes had elapsed since the accident. He removed his waistcoat and passed it to Emily together with the watch. 'Have a care with them, neither is very young,' he said, smiling on her for he also had children and wished her to have confidence in him. It was not a smile she saw so much as a squinching movement of his nose and some rabbity twitches of his moustache. But she understood his meaning and was grateful. 'Don't worry, I won't faint,' she said in a low voice. Wattson rolled up his sleeves. He soaped his arms and hands; told Emily to have the bottle of laudanum ready. Then he knelt in the cinders. 'Hullo, Fred.'

Thomas would have none of it. He would neither travel to Norwich on the train himself nor allow Fred to do so. First he'd been paralysed by fear. Then anger had overwhelmed him. Finally he'd broken down and wept when he believed his son to be dead. Lumps of each of these emotions remained within him, as unyielding as gristle, but overlaying them now was an iron determination to get Fred home by any means other than the railway and never to be separated from him again.

'So you say. I understand your reasons. Of course you want the best for him. But I refuse. My son and I will travel together, by road.'

'But Father, the quickest way to the hospital is on the train. You've only to say the word and it can leave. Half an hour at the most, and we'll be there.' They were crammed into the ticket office, Harriet nearest the door. She turned the handle. 'Just say and we can be gone. It'll take hours to find a wagon.'

'The clerk knows one we can use. He's gone to get it.'

'But across country, down all the lanes ... Thirty minutes, Father. I beg of you to say yes. Please – please say yes.'

'Then what? The man we need is the surgeon, Rouch. He'll be out. He's always out. How is Fred to be got into our carriage – have you thought of that? Is he then to be shaken from house to house, all round the county, until we find Rouch? Do you want to leave him with strangers for the night? And the next day, how is he to get to Fordwell if not down lanes?'

'We don't have to find Mr Rouch tonight. The hospital will care for Fred in the meantime.'

'This is no time to be arguing, Thomas. I agree with Harriet. We'll put him on the train,' Isabel said.

'Hospital!' burst out Thomas. 'Never! Cholera, typhus, scarlet fever, the place is nothing but a charnel-house. He'll be dead by morning. No, you go on the train and find Rouch and bring him to Fordwell. Pay what you have to but get him there. Nothing will shake me. I am not going on the train and nor is Fred. There's nothing more to be discussed.'

'Emily?'

'I shall stay with my brother.' She was exhausted, her face as white as chalk. She didn't know who was in the right. But in her heart she believed more in her father. 'However Fred goes, I go with him,' she said.

'I'll ask Mr Wattson. He at least has common sense, thank God.' Isabel squeezed past Harriet and went out.

But Wattson, who was having difficulty lighting a cheroot his hand was trembling so much, was disinclined to voice an opinion.

He had done all he could. The Gages had got their nerve back; now it was up to them.

'I'm not a medico, just an ordinary soldier. If it were my son—' At that moment the booking-clerk appeared with a four-wheeled country wagon, a strong bay pony in the traces. 'I'd say that's the answer to your question. Fate. Someone means you to use it. Good luck, Mrs Gage. He's a tough lad.'

Isabel returned to the ticket office. Wattson flicked the ash off his cheroot and went off to have a word with the stationmaster.

Evening turned into dusk and dusk into a warm and milky night. An indefeasible sense of purpose gripped Thomas. He could keep going forever, drive across the sea to Holland, to Constantinople, to the Cilician Gates if that was where home was. Tirelessly he cossetted the wagon round pot-holes and down one lane and the next, between thick night-smelling hedges, past farms and barking dogs.

He dwelt on the slaughter at Waterloo and Charlie Bedingfield's head bowling down the slope. Death had been a rude and familiar visitor in those days. In peacetime he thought it should be politer – tap on the door before entering, send a warning message. But Fred had sent him no message. He was certain that he would have felt some transfer of spirit, a knocking or plucking, or would have heard him call out if he'd intended to die. His son was a part of him: there would have been a signal. He was solid on this point. Therefore Fred would live.

On he drove. The moon broke through, lighting the clouds with satin. It striped the lanes with shadows, and dappled the jogging rump of the pony.

Six or seven times they stopped at streams so that Emily could bathe Fred's face. At the same time they checked the buckles that held him to the door and the fastenings round his splints. Occasionally Emily would say a prayer, slowly to start with, to give her father time to summon up the words. Once, when she believed he was nodding off, she sang for him a song of such plaintive beauty that as he listened to her girlish voice curling into the night, he wept, and from renewed anger at the arbitrary, mocking cruelty with which his boy had been felled, shouted at the pony and beat it. Thereafter she sang no more. Sometimes they spoke about the accident, but only haltingly, for it was too near. Rouch's name was never mentioned.

They reached Fordwell a little after midnight. Sam was waiting for them on the road with a lantern, Isabel, cloaked, beside him. Rouch's gig was at the front door.

The fire had been lit in the big drawing-room. Standing with his back to it, Rouch was sipping at a glass of water. (He had refused the offer of brandy.) Death, which had been his constant companion for the last thirty years, had made him kindly. He had brought souls into the world and done his best to keep them there. He had long since concluded that if God did indeed have a scheme that no one could thwart, it was one that involved abominable pain and suffering. He had witnessed such agonies as only a saint could endure, both at sea, as a surgeon on a man-of-war, and round the farms of Norfolk. Where others of his profession had become hardened and sliced and lopped like woodmen eager to get home, Rouch had grown softer with the passage of time. Ever more frequently it occurred to him that soon he too would be called to account in another place, and he wished to be able to testify to his Maker without shame.

Short, fussy, with a pottle belly and small brown teeth, he waddled beside the makeshift stretcher as Thomas, Sam and the two girls carried it in. 'Dear me, how young.' He laid his palm on the brow, observed the dilated pupils and felt Fred's pulse. 'Gently now, gently, steady as he goes.' They were lifting Fred onto the table.

'Do you think . . . ? Mr Wattson wouldn't commit himself.' Isabel was at his shoulder, her round face sunken and horribly distressed. Three hours she and Harriet had had to wait. Her heart had fallen until it could go no lower. Yet she spoke with control. Nothing that Rouch said to her now could be more abominable than her imaginings.

'As Scotsmen say, worse happened at Culloden.' And to give her hope, which he knew to be more precious even than water, he told her how things always looked more dire to a layman than they actually were.

He measured himself against the height of the table. 'As I feared, either I must rise or it must fall. Were it my rain gauge, I would beg it to fall, for I cannot abide the pluvious character of these islands. But since we do not wish to ruin your table, it is I who must do the rising – the carpets, Thomas, is it possible to have them slapped up narrow? It is the best expedient in these circumstances, for then I can travel the length of the table and know my footing is secure.'

While the carpets were being moved, Rouch pottered round looking at the books, continuing to talk to the family over his shoulder, at large and in a confiding way so they shouldn't take alarm when he opened his mahogany instrument chest. 'Tall people rarely influence history, this is what I deduce from my studies. The frame is too copious. What we call genius has too much distance to cover. It gets weary, becomes dissipated and loses its way, with the result that nothing of any consequence lands up in the noddle, which of course is the seat of the spark. Fat men or thin, genius is even-handed in such cases. It is only the giants I am talking about, the six-footers and the Peter the Greats. Don't you think so, Thomas, Isabel? On the whole, I have found it an advantage in my profession to be small. A short surgeon is invariably more adept than a long one, simply because he has less far to bend . . . ah, now that looks more fitting to my height.'

The chatter, the unhurried movements round the room, the composed face and air of experience, these gave everyone confidence. He had Thomas fetch another coal-scuttle. Isabel was sent for hot water and more dressings. Harriet was told to clump up the candles on the table, and to Emily he said, 'And you, my dear, will you help me with your brother while I have a little peep?' Together they undressed him.

'See, he feels almost nothing, the opium is still active . . . now, the deep gash between the ribs and the sternum: it will heal, being cartilaginous in a young man. We need not worry ourselves on that score . . . Severe abrasions on the left upper thigh, sinistral as we were taught, proximate to a nice break of the femur, which we can also pass over without comment. Your Mr Wattson has done well. A soldier, I knew it the moment I saw the dressings – soldiers have a particular way about these matters. Yes, he has done what he could and left to me what he could not, for here' – he worried out some grit with his probe – 'on the right fibia and also, I judge, the tibia, matters will go less easily. A great force has impacted on these two bones so that they have grated against each other and caused splintering. How extensive the damage is I cannot say without an examination.'

'Tonight?' It was Isabel, her arms full of bandaging.

'It would be better.' Rouch took a sheet from her and covered Fred. He stepped down from the carpet and peered at Thomas and Isabel over his steel-rimmed spectacles, switching his glance between them. 'Time has been lost. Had I been on the train myself, I would have addressed the splintering then and there, *in loco*. It is central to the issue. It is in this area that I see the greatest danger. So yes, tonight would be better and now, this instant, would be best of all. We must not, we cannot, take a risk with infection. He is young, he is strong, but even so . . .'

'Will he feel it?' asked Thomas.

'Opium dulls everything.'

'Only dulls? You mean he will have feeling?'

'The poppy sedates. It cannot obliterate every sensation.'

'Is it not true there is a new substance that removes all pain? That woman in the hospital last year—'

'Ether? Yes, and in another case I would heartily recommend it. But I could not hold myself responsible for moving the boy again. Nor would anything be achieved by arriving at the hospital in the middle of the night. There would be no one to administer the gas. We had to apply for an expert from London for the woman you spoke of.'

'Must we decide immediately?' asked Emily.

'In my opinion it is imperative. Would you like me to withdraw while you consider?'

They looked at each other, Thomas, Isabel and the two girls, as they stood in the middle of the room on the now bare boards. Around them was the ugly brown furniture. On the table lay Fred. If only *he* could tell us, thought Emily.

'You'll need an assistant,' Isabel said at last, summing up what they were all thinking but were loath to admit.

'I'll do it. It's my right,' Thomas said, and more forcefully, 'my *right*. The boy is mine.'

Twenty-three

H OW COULD he still live? How could he have survived such a mauling for even an hour? Those huge flanged wheels, the dragging and scraping, into the tunnel and out . . . So people said one to another, and they forbore to visit the Gages out of fear they would arrive at the moment of death. They pressed around Sam and begged him for news when he went into town. They marvelled to see Rouch's yellow gig continue to ply the road to Fordwell. They wrote letters of sympathy. Their stomachs knotted with horror as they relived the scene. They suffered as if Fred were their own child. But they kept their distance. Only one person called at Fordwell: Mrs Peach, Jammy's mother, who stumped up to the front door on her bowed legs and tearfully handed Emily a bunch of white sweet peas from her tiny flower garden. Otherwise the house lay brooding and neglected its appearance, a soul in abeyance.

It was in the small hours that Rouch finished, the time when night is at its most lonely. The fire had gone out and the room, more odious to Thomas than ever before, was in darkness except for the narrow stalks of candlelight, repeated in the long wall-mirror, between which Rouch moved his blood-stained hands and Fred screamed and jerked against his bonds.

At last the splinters were drawn and the bones set. Rouch drew his shirtsleeve across his brow, wiped his instruments one by one and passed them through the candle flame. He folded away his spectacles and knuckled his aching eyes. Children, there was nothing more awful. Their guileless flesh, their ignorance of sin, the terror in their eyes, the straps, the buckles – and then his knife.

He looked across the table at Thomas. It was almost twenty-four hours since either of them had slept.

'You know, there are times when I hate myself,' Rouch said.

'I understand.'

'Yet there have been other times when I was greeted like the saviour of all humanity. It confused me when I was younger. Tell me what you think: which counts for more in the balance, success or failure? A life saved or a life lost?' He peered through the shadows at Thomas standing beside the sombre curtains. 'Of course it is failure. A man who walks away whole does so at three miles to the hour while I rinse my hands and clap myself on the back – I speak figuratively, you realise. Tonight he's at home, in a week he's gone to London and a year later he's made his fortune. He points the scar out, to his mistress let us say. "Some old sawbones did that. Not such a bad cove. His hand was steady. I bit the bullet and there it was . . . Can't recall his name offhand." You see, goodness is gone in a flash. But a death – I never forgive myself and I never forget. Nor does anyone else.'

Thomas drew back the curtains and pinched out the candles. Dawn was beginning to show. He looked down at Fred, quiet now after the last dose of opium. 'Is there worse to come? You can tell me.'

'I cannot say. And if I could – you're a painter, Thomas, so I am especially sorry for you. What you've witnessed tonight will be a curse on your mind. Harsh colours and harsh sounds – there are no pretty daubs on a surgeon's palette. Perhaps,' – he started to pack away his instruments, wiping them mechanically as he slotted them into the green velvet trays – 'it occurs to me that perhaps the image would heal more quickly if you were to make a picture of it. To draw the poison, to assuage, to purify . . . You must excuse me, it's late and I don't know what I'm talking about. But for a man burdened with imagination – well, it's an idea . . . May I leave you to empty the slops? You should do it before the ladies rise. It never does to leave blood in the scuppers before an inspection, if you'll pardon the naval turn of phrase.'

At some stage – they'd heard nothing – Sam had removed Rouch's gig into the yard and stabled his horse. They put it to; Thomas walked beside him down to the road. There had been no dew and the air, though pleasantly cool, was bland and without perfume, disappointing. It offered neither consolation nor hope. His shoulders slumped, and a part of him, the part that had carried him through the ghastly ordeal, shrivelled. Was it now that Fred was sending him a message?

Birds were shuffling in the hedgerow. In a few minutes they'd be out and about, chirping their heads off, worrying the worms and eyeing his raspberries. No trains for them, no mangling and ripping. Good times only, then an unthinking death on a winter's night. To a bird its trifling, to parents their sorrows.

The sky was thinning in the east. At Cromer the sun would be mounting towards the horizon, stretching, preening itself, making ready. A new day, as if the old one had not been enough.

Rouch was saying, 'Be sure and have the dressings changed four times daily. Don't spare the laudanum. Mix it well, as many grains of opium as you want. When he recovers, we shall have to wean him from it, but that's a little way off.'

Thomas said, 'Gooby, he's the one who should have been on the table. He was the cause of it. He made us go on the train.'

Rouch looked at him curiously in the half-light. 'I believe a little laudanum would do you no harm either. Tonight – I mean, today – at any rate. Sleep is the great redeemer. You cannot persecute Mr Gooby for what happened. It was not he who made Venus loose or the train go backwards. You must forget him. You will go mad or else, and where will that get you?'

Pondering over these words, Thomas returned to the house. He emptied the slops down the stable-yard drain. He stroked Fred's damp hair, kissed him on the forehead. They'd have to get a mattress beneath him somehow. Rouch had said nothing of that. With weary footsteps he climbed the stairs, not caring how much noise he made. Venus was snoring throatily in her featherbed on the landing. But madness brings relief, he thought, trudging into his dressing-room. A different ordering of the mind prevails. The actuality of events becomes distorted. Perhaps, if a man is lucky, it sinks into some sort of underground tank where the past is totally annulled, without leaving a single scratch on the memory – he hung his coat on the nail and kicked off his shoes.

Isabel called through to him.

'He's better. He couldn't be worse, therefore he's better.'

'I heard his screams.'

He padded into their bedroom. The chocolate wallpaper with its stripe of lovelorn roses and cretinous angels, her mountainous wardrobe, the glum carpet, they pressed in on him. He sat down to remove his socks. 'What do you expect? Of course he screamed. You'd have screamed. It was the most horrible thing I ever saw. Horrible, do you hear me? I refuse to speak about it. I refuse, I refuse.'

The odour of the snuffed candle drifted across him as he lay staring at the pallid light of dawn.

But no sooner had he closed his eyes than what Rouch had foretold came true. Magnified a hundred times, in the sharpest possible focus, he saw every incision, every welling seam of blood, the splinters white as fish-bones falling into the basin of collops, Fred's waxy writhing face. Every tiny detail returned to him, from the fold in Rouch's belly as he leaned against the table edge, to the candlelight glinting on his spectacles. He did all that he knew to put himself to sleep. He counted the napkins as he placed them in the hamper, the telegraph poles as they flashed past the carriage window, the coins he'd given to the waiter at the Rose and Button. He held his breath and counted backwards from a hundred, first in English and a little later in French. It was unavailing. Relentlessly and without mercy his brain hunted down all that had happened, pausing only to offer taunting suggestions as to how the accident could have been avoided, and all the while Fred's screams drove like nails through his skull. No incident of the vile day was concealed from him.

An hour passed, of craving for oblivion, for the past to be cancelled. At length he could stand it no longer. What had Rouch said? That a couple of spoonfuls could do him no harm? He gathered himself and went swiftly downstairs.

Twenty-four

AT NO point was Fred completely unconscious. He was forever swimming through oceans, the same limitless, incomprehensible oceans, sometimes at a great depth, unable to breathe, crushed by the water above him, his legs being flayed by rocks as sharp as knives; at other times close to the surface, through ripples that were refracted and shimmering, as if he was dizzy from looking into the sun. Sometimes he was aware that vague figures hovered over him, reaching down with what he perceived as boat hooks or grappling irons to pluck at his flesh. Then he would recoil in terror, fight against his straps and begin to scream.

On the fourth day, when on Rouch's instructions the dosage of laudanum was reduced by a small amount, he understood, in his increasing moments of lucidity, that the boat hooks were arms and the shapes to which they were attached were his parents and sisters. Fear still entered his eyes, mingling there with pain and resentment, but so long as his body remained numb, he came to realise, by infinite degrees of slowness, that these smooth and gentle movements, which he saw opaquely, were not intended to hurt him. He ceased to cower. Voices became less jumbled. In particular he found he could distinguish between those of Emily and his father, which he longed to hear, and those of Isabel, Harriet, Rouch and Mrs Macbride. He discovered he could tell the difference between their tread; the ways they had of closing the door; their smell as they bent over him. Even before anyone spoke, he would know who it was.

That evening, as Emily was standing beside him, on the point of raising his head to administer his dose for the night, he lifted his right arm, the only limb he was free to use, and with the back of his fingers stroked the soft curve of her cheek.

'There were never any bats in the tunnel, Em.' A shaft of agony pierced him. He went rigid, sweat drenched his face, and he gulped down the sticky red liquid, his hand like a clamp round Emily's wrist. She wiped his mouth and kissed him as he swam slanting back into his ocean.

But it was an advance. 'If we just keep faith with him, he'll come back to us. I know it, I can feel it. Faith!' Emily said. She and Isabel went out and cut sweet peas, hollyhocks and green fronds from the rockery, which they placed in vases round the room, especially where Fred might see them when he awoke.

Night was the worst, however much they dosed him. In his fevered voyages he now assumed a shape, part fish part animal, part slime part fur, that slithered through veils of dense, clammy weed that either reached out to choke him or wrapped around him thongs that he could clearly see were strips of his own skin. He would creep down and conceal himself in the forest of their roots. No sooner was he feeling secure and ready for sleep than the mud would boil, become pustulous, and a whirling vortex would suck him into a tunnel, always the same tunnel, pitch black, water slapping the roof, boulders grinding in the current. A glimmering eye would loom through the darkness. He'd fight; call out – and be spewed into a chamber lit only by two long lines of candles.

It was then that his screams would start, and Thomas rise from his mattress beneath the window to comfort him.

Isabel found it hard to get any broth into him. He seemed to become gaunter with every tock of the pendulum in the hall. His once rosy cheeks lost their sheen and turned a custardy grey, like the underside of a leaf that is rotting in the autumn mists. His eyes, wide open, flickered as he wandered the oceans. He fouled himself. It was impossible, even with the five of them, to change him without angering his wounds. His nose, mouth, cheek-bones, the whole structure of his face was caving in. Everything grew smaller and fainter as the spirit within him diminished, daily and hourly.

And yet, by some marvel, his power of speech became enhanced. He could still recognise only Emily and his father. He would wait, rationing his strength, until a familiar footstep approached: Emily's gliding like a fairy, he thought; Thomas's gruff and heavy, as if the carpet were a field he was ploughing. Voices and odours, he sifted them carefully before committing himself. He'd turn his head so that his cheek was flat upon the sheet, frowning terribly as he parted the waters of his dungeon. Then his pupils would grow even larger and his eyes glow like those of someone on the brink of an enormous truth.

'What day is it, Em?' Or: 'Tell Papa I want to be an officer in the—.' He would name a regiment, but it was never the same. There was an occasion when he said to Emily, with what she could have sworn was a wink, 'Gutswill has far too much money. He's painted Jeremy yellow, did you know that? Yellow, like that canary we used to have, the one we called Butterball.' He smiled at her, and she saw it had not been a wink but a movement to control a tear which now rolled slowly out of the corner of his eye, across the slope of his nose, and fell, glistening like a pearl shirt-stud, onto the rumpled linen.

'Oh darling Fred, how it sang for us!' Quickly she raised him up, tilted the spoon to his mouth, and ran crying to her room, her slippered feet going pat-a-pat up the sunny staircase that had never, not once in their lives, cocked its ear to a canary called Butterball.

One night – it was the sixth – Thomas was dozing on his mattress. The weather had turned thundery. He had declared a fire excessive, and in fact had opened a second window, partly to feel the breeze on his face as he waited for sleep and partly to dispel the smell of Fred's incontinence, which neither the repeated changes of bedding nor the mass of flowers and the pomanders of dried lavender was able to obscure. That night Fred never once screamed.

Mulling it over, he told Emily in the morning they should try having only a couple of candles in the room, and those behind a screen round his mattress so that he could read when he felt like it. (He'd been looking for Isabel but Emily was first down for breakfast.)

'We've been such fools,' he said. 'The firelight, candles, Rouch, the pain – it's all he associates with the dark, don't you see?'

'Anything, anything that'll help him,' and she rushed away to the sick-room to stand her watch.

Isabel and Harriet now appeared and he told them his idea.

When Mrs Macbride came in with their eggs, he told her also. After his best sleep for days, he was full of optimism. 'Didn't Rouch say the first few days were the most dangerous? And hasn't he come through them with flying colours? I tell you, Fred's on the mend. Not in the clear yet, not by any manner of means, oh no, we can't be raising any flags for the moment, but I just feel . . . Well, for the first time I feel there's hope.' He spoke with such confidence compared with other mornings that it infected the others, and when Emily ran in to say she'd just had a little conversation with Fred, it seemed to them that Thomas was right to be looking more cheerful. The only doubting voice was that of Isabel. Despite being the boy's mother, she'd been somewhat displaced by the possessiveness of Thomas and Emily. She knew they didn't mean it, that it was the Gage clannishness coming to the fore; but she wished they would let her take her rightful place and not put her in the position of having to insist.

So the screaming stopped, and Fred became calmer and more rested. Two nights after his discovery, Thomas was lying as usual beneath the window, the air fanning him with its fresh, earthy scent. He was considering what Rouch had said about exorcising his imagination by painting. He was wondering what inner force drove Isabel that she could control her emotions so tightly. He was listening to the thump of his heart.

To his right, from the centre of the darkness, he heard Fred stir.

'Papa? I know you're over there. I can feel you.'

Thomas blew out the candle and groped his way through the furniture. He lowered himself into the nursing chair. Fred tipped his face towards him, so pale, so dear, so remembered. Thomas raised his hand and one by one kissed the hot knuckles.

'I may be small but I'm brave. Aren't I brave? Aren't I, Papa?'

'The bravest I shall ever know.'

'Were you *really* brave? I mean, like a whale? Was Sam brave? I'm going to be a sailor when I grow up, like you and him. It'll make me as tall as you – only—' He gasped. His body tensed. He dug his fingernails into Thomas's palm. 'The heat, it's roasting . . . my legs feel so heavy tonight. I don't think I'll be able to climb the masts like a proper sailor. I've been trying . . . Do sailors have to run? They want me to run at school tomorrow . . . Did you ever run away from anything, Papa?'

Thomas bowed his head and rested it on the bare, bony chest. He wove his fingers through Fred's and pressed them against his cheek. Roar, little life, run roaring with me forever. He began to sob.

'No snivelling, Papa. You always told me that. Chin up, shoulders back . . .' The small voice started to hurry, drifting and fading as it strove against the waters. 'No rats, tell Em no rats, only green . . . good little Venus . . . catch . . . I'm going, Papa, I'm going back . . .'

His breathing became laboured; his hand went limp. After a while Thomas folded it across his breast and returned to the mattress.

At first light he saddled his mare and rode into Norwich. Watercarts were out laying the dust. A plumber, his lead-ladle threaded through the loops of his canvas knapsack, tramped to his work. Lutwylch drove into his yard. Thomas spoke to neither of them. He went straight to the shop and beat on the door and shouted until the man opened up and in his nightgown and slippers consented to sell him an oval of ivory, for which Thomas had to leave a bank-note since neither of them had any change. He arrived back at Fordwell as Isabel was letting out the chickens. Mrs Macbride had the range stoked and the kettle simmering. He drank two full cups of coffee, fetched his paints into the drawing-room and closed the door. Deft, delicate strokes: no fumbling, no second thoughts, the brushwork noiseless on the slick smooth grain. Half inch by half, the mischievous face began to fill the ivory – the cleft in the chin, the chipped tooth, the fairy-tale eyes—

'Do you want to poison the child with that smell?' It was Isabel, blocking the door with her summery gingham.

'My dear, they're only water-colours. He talked to me again last night, bright as a button . . .' He picked up the scissors and began to shape his brush to a point. The eyes, and their specks of dancing white light.

'But the smell—' She entered the room fully, nostrils questing.

'The usual, I expect. He doesn't do it on purpose, you know. You're not to hold it against him when he's back on his feet.' He fiddled in the eyebrows. How thick they were when one looked closely. And that tiny mole nestling in the outer wing of the hairs, he'd never thought twice about it before.

174

She walked quickly past him, not stopping to look at the portrait. She raised the sheet and bent her nose to the puckered flesh, the bursting sutures. 'Have Sam go into town and find Rouch. He's to tell him it's urgent, and to bring an assistant.'

'We must cut, Mr Rouch?'

'You cannot! You'll kill him.'

'Use your reason, Thomas. Look for yourself. Smell it. Feel the heat in it. We're being merciful.'

'Merciful! Is torture a mercy? How can you say that? How can you grind a child's leg in two and call it mercy?'

'Mr Rouch?' The gingham whirled and bore down on the surgeon. 'Repeat your opinion to my husband. He appears to think we'd be acting unnecessarily.'

'He will feel nothing this time. I have brought the ether. Tomkins is trained in its use. What will happen is that I score the flesh down to the bone, then three quick strokes, backwards and forwards. That's all, the work of a minute. Afterwards – a good flap makes for a healthy stump, I've learned in my time. It's true he'll never run again. But we must look on the bright side – Cervantes had only one arm, as did Lord Nelson, and Candide learned to dance on one leg—'

'Don't joke with me. You're a brutal man, Rouch, who pretended to be kind. You've deceived me.'

The other, coat and waistcoat off and already tying the bands of his leather apron, looked sadly at Thomas. It was the worst part, except for the deed itself. 'No, Thomas, I am not brutal. He will die unless I act. The flesh will putrefy, the poison will enter his blood, and your boy will die. If I was humorous, it was for my own sake. I have seen too much. Humour is the only defence against life.' He raised his arms forlornly and collapsed them. 'It is our only hope. If I do it, you will hate me. If I don't . . . We have no choice. The fault is no one's. We simply have no choice.'

The sky was at its peak as Thomas trudged alone up the dusty slope to Sparling. The cornfields were beaded with the bloody gouts of poppies. The reapers' sickles flashed. Their cruel line advanced. The barley swayed and fell, crippled, done for.

The church door groaned as he pushed it open. Erect, expressionless, his arms dangling between his splayed thighs, he sat facing the great east window and watched the tree-shadows fumble at the broken body of Christ. It wasn't true that the fault was no one's. It was he who'd taken the dog into his arms, stumbled and been too slow. The fault was his, and that of Gooby and the pug . . . The sunlight edged along the wall, across draped urns, from one brass tablet to the next; memorials to the fecund and the feckless, to the paltry squire and his vain relict, to those someone had loved. Occasionally the bell flickered, tipped by the wings of careless swallows. Harvest wagons lumbered past outside. Men shouted to each other. Children were playing in the square, scrambling around in the elm tree, contriving new games, quarrelling.

His feet grew chilled by the slabs, and he knelt. It was at twenty past five that Emily came for him, kneeling at his side and saying that Fred had died.

Twenty-five

NATURALLY GOOBY was sorry for the family. To have a son struck down in circumstances that were so disgustingly remarkable could not be other than dreadful. It taxed his imagination even to begin to think about it. The feelings that a parent must have – how could a bachelor attempt to understand them? And his sister Emily – was it possible to have any idea what was going through the minds of a Gage without being a Gage oneself? He struggled to picture the scene at Fordwell. 'Terrible,' he said to himself several times, shaking his head in disbelief.

'It made me sick in my stomach just to hear them talking about it at the station,' he said to Walter when he got home, only a little delayed, on the night of the accident. 'And to think that out of all the people on that train, luck should have picked on the Gages. It's a calamity for them and a calamity for the railways. It only takes something like this for people to start saying they're the spawn of the devil.'

'Words were spoken on the platform. You may not have heard.' Walter repeated the threat that Thomas had uttered to the stationmaster.

'You can't blame him. The heat of the moment and so on. That's the least of our worries. I might as well say so now and have done with it, this tragedy is most inconvenient for us.'

Indeed Gooby was unconcerned about what Thomas had said, for he knew it was not a positive statement of intent. The worst was that it would stick. 'Gooby, I shall kill you,' was bound to crop up at the coroner's inquest and again when the Committee of Enquiry sat. The words were irresistible. They were exactly the sort of thing a witness would love to declaim in the dramatic hush of a court room, to aggrandise his status and thus become a principal in the macabre fame. Yes, that would be the danger, that he and the North Norfolk would be tainted by this one sentence of a deranged father.

He followed Fred's progress closely. He could not understand why Rouch had taken out the splinters using laudanum when a far more effective anaesthetic was available. Everyone in London was talking about amputations and dentistry under ether that were completely painless. The newspapers were full of it. The thought of the boy's agony affected him so much that he wrote to Thomas mentioning the new style of surgery. He underlined the word painless, and offered, at his own expense, to find a surgeon who had the equipment, should another operation be necessary. When he received no reply, he tried to waylay Rouch, but succeeded only when it was too late, the evening that Fred died.

So now a new question arose for Gooby: would it be wise, in view of what had been said, for him to attend the funeral? He had no wish to be trapped by Thomas's terrible eye, or risk being chased through the tombstones, perhaps stumbling into Fred's pit in the process. No advantage would come from being vilified in public again. Obsolete Thomas might be in these progressive days, but locally he was a figure that counted, and a remark like 'Gooby, I shall kill you' was all too easily remembered. On the other hand it was imperative that he remain in contact with the family. He walked over to St Giles to consult his friend Leonard.

'I tell you one thing, Fred or no Fred, we need to do business with the Gages. Of course it's unspeakable about the boy – what he went through, what they all suffered. I dream about it almost every night. But the fact is—'

'Life must go on, eh?'

'In a word. And the truth of the matter is, despite what I told them, that our scheme would never stand the cost of a bridge like the one at Trowse. It would stick out in the schedule of costs like nobody's business. Buyers will run a mile when they see it. It's Fordwell or nothing.'

'So the problem for you is how to treat with them and not offend the rules of common decency. I suppose that's what you want my advice about.'

'The problem for us, Leonard, for us. Let's be clear about this.

No Fordwell equals no railway equals no nice little plum for you. Buttercups were all your land was good for until I came on the scene. Buttercups and your son's pony.'

Mr Lutwylch, senior partner of Lutwylch & Luwylch, whose mother had married into the L'Estranges who shared the blood of Hugh II, king of Cyprus and regent of the Crusader kingdom of Jerusalem, tilted his narrow skull, supported his cheek on arid fingers and eyed the face before him with all the superiority of his borrowed lineage. A Jew? He had heard it said. But a Jew offering such a plank of money for what was worthless – and the fees he had yet to bill him, 68 folios for this month alone – he was not proud. Straightening, he smoothed away his contempt.

'Of course you're right, it is in both our interests to reach an accommodation with these hapless people. Let us consider it dispassionately. If you go to the funeral, certain unfortunate things may occur which we can both imagine. If you don't . . . No, Julius, on balance I think it better you keep away. The risk is too great that Thomas may say something untoward when he sees you. No sooner does a thought enter his head than it must leave. He's been a blurter for as long as I've known him.'

'But they need to be reminded that we exist.'

'What about that personable young surveyor of yours, Mr – your henchman?'

'Walter Harrington. Good idea. They've got nothing against him. He'll nudge their memories in the right direction.' Gooby reflected for a moment. 'Yes, Walter's the fellow for a county funeral.'

The conversation would have ended then and there had not Lutwylch been struck by a financial nicety.

'Say – let us just suppose it, now we're on the subject – that the Gages' expectations can only be met by building a station for them. It's no good shaking your head like that, it's possible. I know I act for them – to be blunt, there's very little they can do without asking me first – and of course they'll follow my advice, but supposing a station is their absolute demand. In what way would this affect our own agreement?'

Gooby pouched his eyes. 'Not at all. I do my business straight up and down, like a staircase.'

'It would be a cost born *in toto* by the purchaser of the North Norfolk?'

'Who else?'

'Good. My enquiry was for the avoidance of doubt, you understand. Nothing is more precious to me than clarity. In fact I believe that when I have a spare moment I'll draft something reflecting the terms between us. The point at which your company will pay for my land, the default conditions – all the trivia that obsess us lawyers.' He tittered, drawing up his lip and showing a sliver of teeth. 'Nothing long-winded. A simple back-letter, private to you and me. After all, how would Joan know the position between us if I was so ill-advised as to fall under a train like that boy of Isabel's?'

Gooby regarded him long and hard. It was interesting that he should have thought it necessary to formalise what had already been agreed. Did he not trust him?

Walter's face was drained of colour when he returned.

'Funeral? More like the end of the world. Where do you think they buried the lad? Oh no, not in the graveyard, not out in the open air where the vicar can whistle through the bad bits with his head down and no one can quite hear him, lord no. They'd had the bally hole dug slap under the family pew, and it was there that they put him. I'm telling you, Mr Gooby, that part of it fairly made my skin creep. It was like – I can't rightly say what it was like. Nothing you've ever met before, that much I'll warrant. Mrs Gage, she was composure itself from start to finish. I don't know how she did it. She must be made of steel, that one.'

'So you could see her face throughout, could you?' Gooby said.

'Not actually – but one could sense it from the way she was standing. The Farrants were beside me. "Cold, cold," I heard her say to the General, and I agree with her. It was how Mrs Gage held herself. One couldn't help thinking that.'

'A mother buries her son and feels nothing? Rubbish. It's the quiet types who suffer most. Go on.'

'But Mr Gage – well, there was the undertaker and his men, all in their best white gloves seeing as how it was a child being buried, hovering around and looking as solemn as owls, and everything was going alright until . . . This was the worst part. They came to the bit where they sink the coffin – ever so small it was: the old boy had got hold of a regimental battle flag from somewhere, don't ask me how, and it was draped over the coffin with a single wreath of roses on top – and they were carrying it down the chancel when he stepped out and sort of grabbed it and threw himself over it and started to holler and bellow and wouldn't let go for all the tea in China. Horrible it was! Ghastly! Everyone crying like billy-ho, me too, I don't mind admitting it. But what was to be done now? The thing had to be finished off properly. We couldn't just go away and leave him at it. Mrs Gage and that girl of his, not the boring one – Emily, that's her name – came out and said something to him. But he would not let go, he would not. You could see it was going to be a job to get him off. Well, eventually the vicar joined Mrs Gage and Emily and they pulled him away, very decently of course, but it was a tussle whatever anyone might say. So they got the coffin to the hole, and then the people right at the front began to shuffle, and Mr Gage was shouting something, and it seems they'd forgotten to bring along his Waterloo sword that Fred was to be buried with. So off runs that surly groom of his and we all wait around most unhappily not knowing which way to look – can you imagine it? The church packed to the gunwales, no room for even an ant, and the ladies blubbering like mad and Mr Gage beating on the little 'un's coffin. Anyway, after about ten minutes the groom comes back with the sword, Mr Gage snaps it across his knee and only then could the vicar say all the ghastliest words that he saves up for the end and we could begin to leave. Mrs Gage led the old boy out. I don't think he'd have made it without her. Most affecting, Mr Gooby, most affecting. You'd have cried your heart to pieces if you'd been there.

'They were offering drinks and cakes at the house afterwards, but I couldn't bring myself to go and I don't believe I was the only one. I expect some went from a sense of duty, but wild horses wouldn't have got me there.

'Was I seen? Did I make my mark? Oh yes, I was seen alright. Quite a number of people came up and said as how it wasn't our fault and we mustn't blame ourselves. Very civil they were, too. But that was before the service started. Whether they'll want to remember me now, after what we all went through, is a different matter. I don't know how we're to take the matter forward. We can't pretend nothing's happened. It'd be most unseemly to sit them down and talk about money when we've just killed their son, if you know what I mean. Poor old Gage, I'd say the shock's put him clean out of his mind. Maimed him for life.'

Gooby considered this, brushing his middle fingers against each other as if removing an obdurate crumb. 'But not her, you said. I don't know that I believe it. But let us assume for the moment you are correct.' He paused and then said, 'Did I ever tell you that Fordwell belongs not to him but to the two of them together? According to Leonard, it was settled on them by her father, as part of her marriage jointure. Do you get my drift? As affairs stand at present, the head of the household – the nominal head, that is – can't think farther than tomorrow, if that far. Meanwhile the neck that turns the head, as the proverb goes, appears to have her grey matter perfectly intact.'

'You're saying, persuade her to sell while he's mad with grief?'

'I'm thinking aloud . . . We'd probably need to visit the courts to obtain a variation of the jointure. But what's Leonard for if not that?'

'Could he do it without Gage knowing?'

'Would he care in his present frame of mind?'

'He's not as stupid as that, Mr Gooby.'

'No one's saying he is. But she's the one who wields the power in that house. What she commands, happens. Sitting across the table from her would be quite different from trying to do business with him, the old slipper.'

Indignation set fire to Walter's cheeks. He pushed his face forward. 'I'll have nothing to do with a great barging in and no decorum. You Londoners have no idea what's proper. You can't just trample over people who've lost one of their children.'

'Feeling qualmish, Walter? But who knows, they may decide not to stay at Fordwell. After all, the boy did die on their drawing-room table. That'd be enough to get me out.'

Twenty-six

THOMAS STOOD apart at the tops of the steps. Within the doorway and thus out of the sun were Isabel, Harriet and Emily, in that order. Attached to them as if by elastic, drifting between the hall and the vestibule, was Sam Buzzerd. His wild gallop from the church to fetch Thomas's sword had by no means reduced his opinion of himself.

'That's Sir Jack starting up the steps now. Been bothered by gout this past month. Could be a bit on the crabby side, painful business that gout,' he said to Emily as he wormed into the family line. Then to Harriet, 'Very fine man on his day, Sir Jack. He's been the making of her ladyship.' A few minutes later he appended himself to Isabel's elbow and commenced a more discreet murmuring. 'It's the brandy they're going for, madam. Hardly a drop of sherry's been taken, just so as you know.'

Thomas was conscious of this babbling but was too depleted to stop it. He'd been wandering since Fred's death in a distant region, searching for answers to a question that had a hundred forms but not one with substance, not one at which he could halt and say, 'Yes, this is the key and this the lock and this the casket that contains Knowledge.' He'd lain unsleeping, poking his finger into the crannies of the night; seen for the umpteenth time the door hurtle through its fatal arc; felt the tug of that small sweet hand as freshly as if it was happening at that very instant. The questions had multiplied until they littered his brain. To say simply that Fred had been struck down by the brisk treachery of fate was unsatisfying to him. There had to be a greater why. He was owed the truth. And the question to which all others deferred, time and again, bore no solution that was accessible to him: why had he been permitted to march whole from the field of Waterloo while Fred, an innocent stripling, a bystander, had been led away and killed for no other reason than Isabel's dog had been fed a dish of rotten tripe by the man whose life he had once saved? No amount of the poppy had been able to answer that for him.

His mind had fastened onto two or three greetings that he used in turn on the mourners. He had a terrible fear of the moment when they would depart and the house be emptied. A forgotten hat, the uneaten cakes, a glass lying on its side – silence. Then what? Emily would get married. Harriet – he supposed someone would take her eventually. And he'd be alone, with no other company to the end than Isabel and a dismal cortège of memories. Yet at the same time he wished only that they'd go as soon as possible and leave him to himself. Of the two he found he wanted solitude more. As he mouthed his leaden phrases and unhanded one person after another, his despondency increased and he grew impatient for the moment when he could lock the door and shut out the day.

Dark-veiled, oppressed by their heavy-falling funeral weeds and the spectre of death, the women he'd loved took a pinch of their skirts and ascended the steps, two paces to each, their bulky shadows shuffling up the mossy flagstones and dimming the stridency of the bowls of geraniums that Sam had decided would give the occasion a lift. Released by their husbands, they adjusted their expressions and halted in front of him. They looked into his long, torn face, into the brown wells of misery. Lips parted, speaking and yet not speaking, for the truest words were coming from eyes that still loved him, would always love him, and yearned to draw off his troubles and share them.

The sun was fierce on the back of his neck. His expression was fixed. Hope was lying a mile away, cold beneath the family pew. He had nothing to say to any of them.

'Go away, go away,' the stiffness of his manner proclaimed. They had no right to bother him like this, as if some debt remained outstanding from those long ago moments of folly. Wasn't it enough they'd watched him bury his son? All along he'd told Isabel they should have the service in private, that he might lose control of himself. So he'd given them their spectacle. They could prattle about him at their winter tea-parties. 'Ooh, and didn't he make a fool of himself? I bid three red ones, Jane, I can never remember which is which – the caterwauling he sent up, did you ever hear the like? I suppose it was his only son. Still . . . more tea, anyone?' They should wait until their turn came. What were they after, creeping up at him with those artful looks, another display?

Of a sudden he hated them. They were witnesses. By coming to the funeral, they were implicated in Fred's death. So that was that. He'd bury them too while he was at it, wash his hands of the lot of them.

Gone, and good riddance to them. Especially to Georgiana Farrant, who was now simpering in front of him, as silly a tart as ever existed. What if he told the General how things had been between them? Right here, where he couldn't answer back. That'd knock the graveside unction off his face, so it would, quicker than a woman running away from a mouse. Fancy a man not putting a note in with it when he sent you thirty guineas, what sort of rudeness was that? Had he wanted her painted in the nude? He could do it from memory if that was what he was after. Here you are, General, thighs like porpoises, negligible waist, tits to smother a man. Anything soft will do, eh Dick, old chap. Shake on it. My motto too. Can't stand a woman with too many bones in the wrong places. Actually, Dick, they've been my ruin, from Bella onwards . . . Of course he must have wanted her done in the nude. The only explanation. So first he'd check on that and then he'd take Dick's hand, kiss it to show there was no ill will, and tell him, looking bang into the flogger's glinting optic, of his wife's concupiscence, which was a favourite word of the Prayer Book and therefore should be intelligible even to a soldier. 'However, the father of the deceased bucked up visibly when in mixed company he informed General Farrant he was a cuckold.' Marley would print it. Good sense of humour behind those whiskers. Always on the look-out for a gracious literary style. And here he was, puffing and plodding up the steps like Father Christmas, the last of the ghouls . . .

Thomas felt himself swaying. The terrace was rocking beneath his feet like a vessel in a heavy sea. Sweat was pouring off him. In the corner of his vision was a face, the dearest face he knew, that he could never bring into focus. He leaned against the gritty column of the door-pillar and dropped his head onto his sleeve.

'Are you alright, Papa? You shouldn't be out there in the sun. Here, put your arm round my shoulder,' said Emily, coming out to stand beside him.

'It'll take more than that,' said Marley. 'A day like this – your brother – the multitude of folks. A shot of brandy would be the place to start. Easy does it now, Thomas.' He caught Sam's eye, tipped an imaginary glass to his lips.

Thomas waved it away and walked unsteadily into the hall. He could see no one distinctly. What were they doing here, all these strangers?

'Who's that over there? I don't know any soldiers any more,' he said to Emily.

'Where?'

'In a uniform at the foot of the stairs. Talking to your sister.'

'Him! You don't want to pay any attention to him, the little jump-up,' butted in Sam.

'You mean Jammy Peach?' Emily said.

'I never saw him come in,' Thomas said.

'Course I didn't let him in at the front,' Sam said with disgust. 'Let Master Peach in with the ladies and gents? I'd see myself dead first. And he would've if he could, but I saw his game and round the back he went pretty smartish, where he belongs. In fact, I should have had him stay in the kitchen, that's what I oughter've done.'

'And stayed there with him, Master Buzzerd. You sicken me. Get out of my way.' Thomas left him. He brushed between the Farrants and Tobias Rouch, displacing their conversation by the force of his passage, and went over to Jammy who'd just been deserted by Harriet and was standing alone, toying with the metal buttons of his railway uniform. His puddingy face brightened a little as Thomas approached.

'So, they let you out,' Thomas said.

'They didn't care for it. They thought they knew their minds,' Jammy shrugged, more resolute and with a sharper look about him than Thomas remembered, 'but I knew mine better. I said, "It was Mr Gage who gave me what I have, will I do nothing for him when he needs me, bor?" So Mr Abbs let me off for the day.'

'How did you know, Jammy?'

'Mum sent a note down the line. The parson wrote it for her.

She said for me to say sorry if I was speaking to you. She couldn't be doing both with the church and coming here, the way she's taken it.'

'Were you – were you at the church yourself?' Thomas prayed for the answer no.

'I couldn't have, and that's the fact of it. It'd have kippered me. The boy, he was my life.'

Thomas sighed profoundly. They must have speech together, he and this good and simple man. There was so much in his heart that he wished to release, such a crushing weight impounded behind those weak walls. He drew him away from the crowd and with his hand in the centre of Jammy's back, began to steer him down the corridor to his painting-room. But Jammy resisted. He stiffened, dug his heels in, and came to a halt.

Turning he said, 'I can't stay. Mr Abbs has put me on the mails tonight, both of them, the up train and the down. He said if I wasn't back on the dot I'd lose my job.'

'But it's so early—'

'It's a fair walk back into town. There may be delays on the line. I can't serve two masters at once, and it's Mr Abbs who has the shout these days. If you saw how they do things down there . . . Life's not like it used to be, Mr Tom.'

Thomas was disbelieving. It was essential that he pour everything out to Jammy. There was no one else. He couldn't bare himself before Rouch, Lutwylch or his family. They'd helped bury Fred. They were party to his death. Only Jammy was untainted. Was he going to forsake him, just so that he could be thought well of by some foreman in Shoreditch? Was common decency a thing of the past, had it come to that?

'You're not catching me, Mr Tom. The old ways have gone. Speed is all people care about nowadays, and chop him off at the knees if he don't toe the line.'

'You can't do this to me. Be unfaithful, would you, when I'm desperate?'

'It's more like this, you're going in one direction and I'm going in another, and if you say not, well, I'm sorry for you, what with the boy and all. Truly sorry, or I wouldn't have crossed Mr Abbs by coming here, would I?'

Without another word, Thomas turned and left him. He went

back into the hall and had Emily tap a glass for him. The conversation stilled. 'Go away, all of you. It's over. You've done your duty. You've buried him. It's the end. You too,' he said to Rouch who was at his elbow and trying to say something. With an urgent movement of his arms he shovelled everyone out into the sunshine and stood obstinately in the doorway until the last carriage had departed.

Twenty-seven

As soon as the mourners had gone, Thomas instructed Mrs Macbride to put a regular tray of food on the ledge outside his painting-room, went inside and bolted the door. When Isabel knocked and asked what he intended, he told her to leave him in peace.

That night Emily, for the first time in very many years, climbed into her parents' broad oak bed. She drew comfort from the presence of her mother's body beside her, from its warmth and largeness. They were both light sleepers and early risers so none of the usual arguments arose.

It was two nights later that they were awakened, almost simultaneously, by the noise of Thomas moving around in the attics above them. The timbers creaked. Something heavy was being dragged across the floor.

'What time is it, Mother?'

Isabel lit their night candle. 'Long past midnight.'

'What can he be doing up there? Listen, I swear I heard him singing just then.' Instinctively she crept close to her mother. Isabel stroked her hair. 'Sons – fathers and sons – theirs was a terrible affection.'

'More than you or I will ever understand? Oh Papa, Papa . . . Do you think we should go up and see what he's doing?'

The flame started to gutter, making an unpleasant smell. Isabel trimmed and re-lit the wick. Autumn was showing its teeth, although it was only the first week in September. She dreaded the onset of her arthritis, but less than she dreaded their first winter when Thomas would be without Fred. From the moment she'd heard his cry and seen his face snatched from the coupé window, she had known he would die. She had prayed privately and fervently, from the depths of her womanhood, that he would not. When she'd ordered Rouch to get on with it, to cut the flesh she'd created, she'd wished only that she could take Fred's place and suffer every single one of those backwards-forwards wounds for him. Yet throughout the awful days, she'd stood firmly by her conviction that life and death, pain and pleasure, all the curiosities of the human adventure, flowed solely from the agency of God's will. It had been dinned into her so thoroughly by her father that they were beholden to God alone for their wealth that she saw the wagging finger of destiny in every corner of their existence. The unexpected movement of the train, the position of the coupé as the last carriage, the tunnel so tight against the line, this was a conspiracy that only God could have woven. There was no greater force than His. She had been diligent as a mother and given freely of her fortune. But He had looked unfavourably on her son. He must have had a purpose, far huger than she could understand, to which she, as His subject, must bow. Thy kingdom come, Thy will be done. Thus it was written and thus it would always be.

She had reached the conclusion that it could only be through some insufficiency on her part that her family had been punished. In some manner unbeknown to her she had been dilatory or selfish. Therefore she must redouble her efforts. There was a perfect way to do everything.

But Thomas – she knew him very well. He had no faith. It wouldn't matter what she said to so shifting a man. It would be pointless to try and teach him that true calamity, that which tore the purpose out of living, was beyond human explanation. She loved him, now more than ever. She would do anything within her power to give him succour. But only when he was ready. There were certain things that he simply had to discover for himself.

She replied to Emily, 'Man has no mechanism for dealing with sorrow. He needs loneliness before he can come to terms with it. We shall see in the morning what your father's been up to.'

'Read me a prayer,' Emily said. 'One for us, one for Papa, and one for my brother.'

There was a great bumping as something was thrown down the stairs. Then the house grew silent again.

The opium made Thomas euphoric. Time lost its meaning. The days rose and fell, crude and disordered, and blindly he followed their course, searching, always searching.

He had no recollection of what he'd been dreaming in the moments before he encountered the all-important Question. All at once it had been there, a hunch-backed leviathan marching towards him out of a vast and lavender-coloured airiness, leaping from cloud to cloud, whistling and jiggling one hand so that the coins in its pocket rang like church bells (he'd heard them). He'd felt no surprise, for he'd known he'd meet it in the end, as surely as he'd known that in the wrinkled pouch dangling from its belt was a duck-green egg containing the Answer, the only true philosophy of the universe, the only philosophy that was tenable, complete with proofs and never to be denied. Also within the egg, dozing on a bed of lambs' wool, had been the Answer's guardian, a cheery little fellow with cheeks of fox-hunter pink and eyes of deepest Atlantis blue who'd said, 'Take these words of mine, Thomas, take them and use them, you alone are fitted to be my disciple.' And he had. Everything entrusted to him had been intelligible without a moment's reflection. On the instant he had devised a plan to explain to the world this vital, seamless philosophy that had been borne to him in a zone of clouds five and a half miles above the earth. He'd estimated that a total of twenty-seven volumes plus an index, a glossary, and an Appendix of Dishonest Theories would cover it adequately. The first volume had three million sentences, all of which were there in his head, strung out like ropes of toads' spawn and waiting only for a warm day to hatch into pages of irrefutable wisdom. It would take half an hour to write, at the most. He knew it to be infallible. But for the present he could remember nothing more than the passage directing him to burn Fred's clothes and unite heaven and earth with a pillar of smoke.

Not only the clothes and the crude leather hat that had arrived at Fordwell from heavens knew where and that Fred always wore skating, hissing across the ice of the bathing pool like a figure from a wintry Dutch landscape, but also his Latin dictionary, prayer book, hymnal, pencils, toys and bowling hoops; the panorama-scope, the hobby horse with its threadbare mane whose scraping wheel had driven two generations of parents insane, the cricket bat that had been a present on Fred's last birthday, the tin of green ointment – everything he could think of, down to the initialled napkin that Emily wished to preserve in a frame.

Unshaven, his face already starting to grow puffy, from midnight on he ransacked the house, throwing everything into the wicker clothes hamper that he hauled up and down the stairs. His eyes glittered in the pools of candlelight. He bared his teeth as he dipped his shoulder and took the strain on the rope.

'Shssh!' he whispered, and crept cautiously to the front door, finger to his lips, peering round the edge as if in fear of a burglar. He entered the night and padded down the steps. 'Ho! Ho there!' Footsteps sounded on the gravel, and he discovered them to be his own. Soon he was on the croquet lawn, on hands and knees, feeling for the hot pulse from the centre of the earth where the fire should be lit in accordance with the instructions. His head struck the winning-post on which he and Fred had stacked their wagers. 'Eureka!' and he jumped to his feet. 'Halt! Who goes there? . . . Tis me, Gooby . . . Password? . . . Two o'clock and all is well.' He capered back across the gravel, stripping off his clothes, grinning idiotically and shouting 'Ho! Ho-ho!' to the stars. He harnessed himself naked to the hamper, dragged it outside and began to build the pyre round the winning-post.

A ruddy dawn flickered at her eyelids. But how could it be so soon? She rolled away from Emily and pulled the covers up to her chin. Red in the morning, shepherd's warning. Mrs Macbride should have done the washing yesterday, as she'd asked her to. She snuggled down, making badgery noises in her throat.

But that smell – her eyes sprang open. 'Emily, wake up! He's burning the house down. Wake up, girl!'

In a second Isabel had her robe and slippers on. She went to the window. She had her fingers under the sash; the words were poised on her lips, What on earth do you suppose you're doing? – but the sight was too horrible. The jagged flames, the blazing scalp of the hobby horse, the tossing wisps of sparks, the stink and the roar as round and round it the hairy figure of Thomas scampered. He had the napkin that Emily had wished to keep on the end of a pole; was dangling it; was flapping it up and down and taunting the flames and shouting something about Gooby. Now Emily was beside her.

'Don't look! Cover your eyes!'

But Emily, shivering, clung to her mother and together they watched, their white faces pressed against the window pane in awful fascination.

'What's that trickling from the corner of his mouth? Wait till he turns. There! There, Mama! Like a red sort of slug. Is it blood?'

'Blood is brighter. It's something else. There's nothing we can do for him until he learns how to help himself.'

'Is it the same medicine you gave my brother?'

'Shush, Emily. I don't want to talk about that.'

'Is he drunk?'

'I believe Mr Rouch said it had alcohol in it as well.'

'As well as what?'

But Isabel's feet had got cold and she went to bed without answering. Emily stayed at the window as the fire died down. She knew well enough what else was in those black flasks besides alcohol. It was what everyone around gave their children to make them sleep, or when they had gripe. Whenever she went to the pharmacist with her mother it seemed he was never doing anything other than stoppering the different sizes of bottles or counting the gaps on his shelf. No, what she'd been after was whether there was an ingredient she didn't know about, something very powerful that Thomas was drinking, something that might harm him.

Suddenly he was running back into the house, immediately below her. She closed her eyes; it wasn't proper to see his nakedness so closely.

He came out holding the tin of green powder. Whoosh! 'Ho!' shouted Thomas. For an instant the steeple of greenish flame was taller than the house. It blinded her. She cried out, and ran sobbing to her mother's arms.

Three days later they were having breakfast. Thomas was still in his painting-room. Harriet, further estranged by his behaviour, had gone to stay with her friend in Norwich. Isabel was at the end of the table, Emily in her usual place beside her.

Mrs Macbride came in with the teapot and toast and boiled eggs wearing woollen tricolor hats. The butter-pats were already in their dish, grated yellow curls on which the moisture stood out in tiny beads.

'My husband – has he been taking more food recently? What do you think?'

It was on the tip of Mrs Macbride's tongue to say, As if you cared, but instead, as she handed Isabel the set of tongs that made such a good job of circumcising an egg (she had heard the remark from Mr Rouch and marvelled at his forwardness, despite that he was a doctor), she said in a matter-of-fact way, 'I just leave a tray on the shelf so the dog can't get at it, and he eats or not, as the mood takes him. Mostly it's no more than a peck that's gone. But he drinks all the water I put out.'

'His apparel?'

'He changed his under-linen yesterday. The old ones were far from particular, ma'am.'

Isabel flexed her lips. 'Thank you, Mrs Macbride, that will be all for now . . . I was meaning to ask her – it doesn't matter, her mind was on the other thing.'

'What were you going to ask?'

'Whether he ever spoke to her. It's not healthy that your father lives in there by himself.'

'She'd have told us by now if he had.'

'You're right. Of course she would have . . . Emily dear, I've been thinking about what we should do.'

'I love him so desperately,' Emily poked the top of her egg down into the empty shell, and wiped her mouth, 'that it doesn't seem right to be saying this. But do you think we could go away somewhere until Papa gets better? He frightened me the other night. It was terrible seeing him dance round the fire, worse than any nightmare. I'll never be able to sleep properly in this house until we get him back as he used to be.'

'Do you know, that was the very thing I was going to suggest? Leonard said to me only yesterday, why don't you and I spend a week with them in the Lake District. Wasn't that thoughtful of him? They've put back their holiday to suit us. Whenever you want, he said.'

'But you don't really like her, do you – I mean Mrs Lutwylch? Doesn't she have a thing about small dogs?'

'Oh, I wouldn't say that. We may hold different opinions but that's not to say I dislike her. I'm sure if I saw more of her, we'd get quite used to each other. It'd certainly stop us brooding about everything if we were amongst other people. Shall we do it, Em? We can always leave Venus with Sam if needs be.'

Emily wept a little. She could only remember how she and Fred had started an apple-fight at the circus, that one had hit Leonard and made him batey. She didn't know that she'd be able to last a whole week cooped up with the Lutwylchs. And what if Thomas suddenly needed her?

Isabel was also anxious about this, torn between the wish to comfort him and certainty of her powerlessness. They talked about it as they tidied the plates together for Mrs Macbride and put the cruets away in the cupboard. After a while, dawdling in a most uncharacteristic manner over one thing and another, it became firm in their minds that the best plan for all concerned was for Harriet to remain in town, for them to go on holiday with the Lutwylchs (especially as Jeremy was to be back at school), and for Mr Rouch to be set in motion to find a cure for Thomas.

'He'll be more receptive to the conversation of a man,' Isabel said. 'If anyone can reach him, it's Tobias Rouch. I'll send him a note explaining how things stand.'

Putting on gloves and coats, they went into the garden with Venus. Isabel was carrying an egg-tray. One of the hens was laying in a hidey-hole somewhere, and they were determined to find it.

Everything was brilliant with tiny flashing dewdrops in the early rays of the sun. The grass shimmered; the shrubs were strung with necklaces of winking blues and greens. Their feet left a trail of prints across the lawn, and from the tips of their boots an arch of spray rose at every step. Venus flushed the Minorcan out of its lair beneath a berberis. Emily braved the prickles on hands and knees, but there was only one egg. Its warmth stole through her gloves as they walked to Thomas's bench. Not a soul was abroad. The breastwork and bevelled parapet of the old bridge were a marvellous russet. The reflection of the ripples spreading from the neck of the bathing pool was repeated on the underside of the yellowing poplar leaves, an unceasing pulse of shadows. Silently they stood and gazed. A sort of harmony settled on their scored hearts.

Twenty-eight

H<small>E COULDN'T</small> sleep. He felt nauseous. His teeth chattered; he had to wear blankets during the day to keep warm. Yet he was forever coated with sweat, and his skin was on fire, as though millions of molten ants were dancing on it. Any harsh sound was unendurable, even the distant striking of the hall clock. A fluttering bird clawed at the window pane; he buried his head beneath the pillow and screamed for it to stop. He couldn't read, he couldn't write, he couldn't paint. Monstrous visions paraded before his wakeful eyes. His sins multiplied and consumed him. He was a failure, a murderer, the lowliest worm in humanity. He was certain he was going mad.

But worst, far worse than all these punishments, was how slowly time passed. Rouch had warned him of this. He had scoffed at the surgeon's words. Yet it was true. An hour lasted a month. During the nights he thought time must have died, or that it had shoved dawn into a hole and blocked the exit with a boulder.

Three days he had spent like this, since Rouch had smashed the bottles and left him. Like a prisoner in his cell, he marked the hours with chalk strokes on the wooden transom of the door and counted them frequently and with fear, lest the number should have somehow diminished. Lying on the mattress in his studio, watch open on his lap, he pleaded with time, and would shout at the chalk marks things like, 'I'll teach you to go slow on me, you devils. I'll make you pick your heels up. Left, right, at the double there.' Or slyly, 'You watch out or I'll pour hot oil down your breeches and then you'll skip a bit faster.' He would imagine there were some with deformities – too scrawny, or with parts missing – leap up and furiously scrub them out with his painting cloth. Five minutes later he would be seized by a terrible panic, tell them he hadn't meant it and restore them, scrunching the chalk into the wood so they wouldn't escape again. In the night these hour marks assumed wings and he saw them as white crows. They would swoop down and claw the film off his eyeballs while they chatted among themselves using long scientific words, as if he were already a corpse. He dreaded them equally, the crows, his unsleeping nights and the funeral march of time as the opium worked its way out of him.

At regular intervals Mrs Macbride left him a new tray of food. On hearing her footsteps he would shrink into a corner. He covered his ears in case she knocked, and ate almost nothing.

One morning he was overwhelmed by a desire to drink coffee, and left a note out for her. It came, and he tasted paradise, spinning it out as he lay on the sofa under the blankets. He stared at the ceiling. The peeling blisters of paint grew to be starfish stranded on a beach, his eyes widened and he was seized by a sudden inspiration. He jumped up. 'That's it,' he shouted, 'I've beaten the bastard!'

In this way commenced his obsession with hiding the key to his watch, so that it would stop and time pass faster. At first he did it like a child, scratching his head and saying out loud, 'Now where can it be?' though all along he knew he'd put it under the loose brick in the fireplace, for example. Occasionally some portion of his mind would inform him it was pointless, that time was incapable of altering its pace. But he knew otherwise. Time could race away with itself once you stopped tampering with it. So he continued and was ecstatic to be proved right. Fifty-eight hours on the door transom accelerated to sixty-four with wondrous speed, and he marvelled at his ingenuity. By the time dusk fell on that day he had introduced a number of refinements to the rules. He stopped his ears with rag before flinging the key over his shoulder. He would pledge himself to 'no looking for ten minutes' (though counting the seconds was an excruciating torture); or say, 'No looking until the shower passes,' and then have to wait in agony until the panes were dry. He also started searching for the key with his eyes closed.

This brought an unexpected profit since he discovered that the action of physically touching the objects in the room (which turned out to have rather different contours and textures to those his eyes had always perceived) drew the sting from the cruel visions that had haunted him. Moreover, the key was tiny and to hit it off amidst the clutter of his painting-room demanded every ounce of his concentration.

Sixty-four became seventy. He lit the candle. 'You swine! You thought you could get the better of me. I'll teach you to kick a dog that's down. I'll show you the metal Thomas Gage is made of.' He would sleep tonight, he couldn't think how he could fail to.

However . . . (Rarely does even a modest benefit follow this, the most baleful word in the language, Thomas was to decide later, in other circumstances.) In the middle of the night, which was dark for the season and full of gusty rain, when the chalk marks were growing like mushrooms on the transom, he made one last throw before chancing his mattress. He plugged his ears, knotted his blindfold, and flicked the key off his thumb, something he hadn't tried before.

After a bit he took off the blindfold, though he knew it was breaking the rules. He shook out his paint rags. He felt along the top of the beams. Standing on a chair, he inspected the contents of a gigantic nest of cobwebs that was pulsating in the draught. 'Oh come now, you have to be somewhere.' On hands and knees, pushing the brass candle-holder in front of him, hearing nothing but the snickering of his teeth, the scornful titters of the mice and the rain thrashing at the roof, he scoured every inch of the floor. He sat back on his heels, eyes glinting in the firelight. 'I may be small but I'm very precious to you.' The voice was behind his shoulder, low and supercilious. How dare it mimic his boy! And in such a common London whine, so very like Gooby. 'Have you looked in the ashes?' Feverishly Thomas raked out the fire. 'What about your paints? I could have sworn it fell somewhere round there.' How could anyone be so silly, as if a key could have crawled into a tube of paint – but he looked, and there it was, lying on the ledge of his easel.

He pressed it joyfully to his lips. 'Home again, my darling,' and raising his voice, 'Thank you, Gooby, thank you very much.'

It was colder than ever without the fire. He ran to the mattress and heaped the blankets over him. He looked at the watch: a quarter to three. Another hour gone. He'd mark it up in the morning, after he'd slept. He gave the watch a good strong wind, as far as it would go, and settled down for the night.

But when he looked at it after a while, the time was still a quarter to three. He sat up angrily. 'How can you do this to me?' He warmed the watch in his armpit, threatened it with the poker. At last he held it against his ear and when the spring rattled he knew he'd lost. It would a quarter to three for all eternity. He rolled onto his side. The white crows gathered jeering above his eyeballs. What else could he blame himself for? Staring into the dingy candlelight, he began to turn the scroll of his sins. 'Never again,' he whispered, 'never again will I be so deluded.'

'How many drops per diem?' Rouch had asked, having thrust his foot into the doorway when Thomas stretched out his arm for the water jug. 'I offer the question in a general spirit of enquiry. You may answer as you please.'

'Thirty,' Thomas replied, and when Rouch raised his eyebrows he increased it by five, for the miles he'd been above the earth when he met the Answer. 'Or forty.'

Rouch pottered around the room. He aligned a pair of shoes with his foot; threw up the window sash; took Thomas's pulse. 'Well, that's something.' He bared an eyeball with thumb and forefinger. '"How are we today?" I once asked a patient. "Fair to bloodshot," returned the old toper. Truth is somewhat rare and so delightful when one hears it, wouldn't you agree?' Poured some laudanum into a glass and held it to the light. 'Might as well be port from the colour of it. No no no, not good at all. He's killing you, Thomas, is that Sam of yours. What I see in this glass is not forty drops but four hundred, which makes sixteen grains of opium daily by my reckoning. Dear oh dear, what an escapade,' all of which he spoke in the same reflective, wandering voice.

He sat himself on the cracked leather sofa and stretched his arms along the back. He looked at the dust on his fingertips, crossed his ankles.

'Yes, he'll kill you before anything else does. I assume it's Sam who's acting as your porter? I don't see any of your ladies as the culprits. So off he rides into town, like all his type stopping here and there for a gossip, and says to Mr Hopkins the pharmacist, "The master's usual, if you please. Red as a ruby is how he likes it." Then on the way home he'll sell a few drops here and a lick of the spoon there and have you know there was a tiny spillage – the cork came out and his horse shied at an apparition, or someone jogged his elbow. Fee-fi-fo-fum, it's how the world turns, and who are we to say otherwise? And all these poor dupes of Sam's, up to their Maker they'll go. For some it may take years, but once they get habituated . . . Oh yes, Sam's killing you alright.'

He toed a crust away. 'Mrs Macbride could spend a profitable few hours in here. Has she made you a rice pudding recently? With nutmeg and a good crust to it? Forgive me, I was forgetting, you haven't felt too hungry of late . . . "I met a man at thirty who led a bonny life, I met him again at fifty" – how does the rhyme go? Do you remember it? I fear it wasn't very cheerful. Come and sit down beside me, Thomas, I do feel forlorn on this great sofa. Oh very well, you're thinking why doesn't the brute clear out and leave me to my dreams. Why doesn't he let me enjoy a happy death if that's what I want? But it won't be a happy, still less a quick death,' he said, more quietly than ever. 'Isabel will never be able to tell her friends, "He made a good death, did my dearest Thomas." Unless you throw away those dark damned bottles, you'll live out your life in misery and die ignobly, probably alone. I give you my word. I've seen it happen a hundred times. In some instances I have myself been its cause. Thomas, these are burdens on my soul that I would lighten. Help me. Two words, one purpose.'

They walked into the garden, though the sunlight was painful to Thomas, and found themselves on the path to the boathouse.

Resting on the oars, his pottle belly sagging, braces straining at their buttons, Rouch said to him, 'Is this not more perfect than any of your dreams? People tell me of the wondrous journeyings they've made on just a teaspoonful of poppy. Their eyes melt and they go quite silly as they try to pass off Utopia on me. But I'm a simple fellow and always I ask myself, what could be better than what we already have? Every day and every season contains a mystery, more splendid than any we could contrive by ourselves. They are issued gratis at birth to whatever Tom, Dick or Harry wishes to explore them. There are the minute peculiarities of nature above, below and around us. Look . . .' He took a single stroke, tilted the blades upwards, and in so doing leaned forwards from the waist and approached his button face to Thomas, who was seated like an emperor on the after thwart. 'I cannot see them because I'm watching your thoughts, but you can see the beads of water chasing each other helter-skelter down these nice green oars. Is that not a beautiful sight? Incline your head and you can see your reflection and that of the poplars, and behind the poplars that of the sky. Is that not beautiful also? Can it really be possible that your dreams are lovelier than what we have around us, than the whole scheme of God's furnishings?'

He took another stroke, digging the oars into the water with great vigour, as if to wipe away the argument so far. Again he paused. 'Of course you have suffered, no one knows that better than I. But it's given to very few to suffer for ever, and I do not believe you are one of that unfortunate tribe. If you are a painter, then paint. If you are a man, live. That's all I have come here to say.'

Now laughing at himself as he made a messing of turning the boat, he checked the course over his shoulder and started for home. The river gurgled sweetly, gently smacking the counter as he rowed across the current. A painted lady, perhaps out on its maiden venture, alighted on the gunwale, its dappled wings quivering, as pretty as could be. Thomas stood up and plucked at his trousers; the thwart had got wet when they were emptying the bilge.

'Now keep the boat balanced, Thomas, or we'll sink and then where'll we be, eh?'

Thomas looked down at the surgeon, at his bracered chest and the backwards-forwards movement of his rowing. Perhaps the memory that it aroused was not insuperable, he thought. And if he were to be more specific, the idea of dying alone was quite hateful.

Rouch took a last and beefy stroke, shipped the oars on the strength of it, and murmured, 'But this is so civilised,' as they glided out of the sunlight and into the humid shadows of the boathouse. He laid them neatly alongside the stone landing-place. The scent of the river was exchanged for the flatulence of disturbed mud. He made a landsman's knot which Thomas retied. Rouch lifted the oars into their brackets on the wall, put on his coat, tugged down the cuffs. They stood against each other, Rouch, the shorter by inches, near the door at the back of the boathouse; Thomas, partially in the sun, working wet trousers out of his crack, pinching and airing them; thinking it over, his mind on the latch.

'Well?' Rouch asked softly. 'What of it then, Thomas? Have I said enough?'

Only later, when the bottles had been broken and Sam informed as to the exact nature of his duties in future, and Rouch, settling himself in his gig of canary yellow, had drawn on his gloves, did he tell Thomas, as he picked hemming and hawing at his nose, that he had a week of purgatory ahead. 'You'll hate me for this,' he said, 'but eventually you'll sleep like a pudding and then you may thank me.'

Sam became worried. Isabel had been stern enough, giving him a list of do's and don't's for when she was away like he was a slave boy. Not that he'd paid her any attention. But Rouch – there was a different kettle of fish. 'Any more of these black bottles getting into the house and your head will roll, so help me God,' the dumpy bugger had said, getting him alone in a corner and assuming a very ugly tone. 'All those lies, skinning your old master to line your pocket, I've half a mind to tell the authorities. In fact . . .'

Maybe he would snitch on him. Doctors and the like were as thick as thieves with the quality. And in fact what? He shouldn't have said that, left the threat hanging like a noose and walked off. Didn't he know it was the sort of remark that could play havoc with a man's appetite?

Sam had brooded upon this. He considered it unjust. He'd only been obeying orders. Nevertheless he thought he'd better mend his fences. He put on a clean shirt, scrubbed his face and went over to the house.

Thomas was in a vile temper. He hadn't had a proper sleep for four days now. He needed a jeweller's tool to get into his watch and didn't have one. He felt as though he'd drunk a case of port, lees and all. His gums were sore, his bowels obstinate, and his hands trembled like leaves. Outside the morning fog was as grey as boiled mutton. He wished he'd never made that promise to Rouch.

Sam's face pressed against the window, filling the pane with contrition and brown curly teeth.

'Who asked you here? I told you, I don't want to see the stuff again.'

'It's Vroshkie, sir, she's come over poorish and I'm by way of thinking it could be distemper.'

'Then shoot it. It'll die anyway.'

'But shouldn't you have a look first, sir? You've got ever such a way with dogs.'

'Stop soaping me. You've no idea how unnatural it looks on you. I'm glad there's a window between us. You've probably got distemper all over your clothes.'

'But—'

'I'm ill enough as it is, can't you see? Do you want to kill me? Kill the dog if you must kill something.'

'I've never heard how it's catching, sir . . . Sir, I'm not hearing you too well. If you'd only—' Sam made a motion of raising the sash.

Huddled in a double thickness of blanket, Thomas peered back, haggard and unshaven. His balled hands were clamped in his armpits. He leaned forward. When his forehead was an inch from the window, he poked a finger out of the blankets and crooked it at Sam and went on crooking it until the other's stomach was touching the sill and only the thickness of the glass separated their bristled chins. 'You're making me crazy. Shoot the dog and go away. Go to London, go to America, I don't care.'

Seeing his master's face dissolving behind the mist of his breath, Sam moved to a fresh pane. 'Oh but I could never do that, not Vroshkie, she's nothing but a youngster. I'm too soft inside me. I'd as soon as shoot madam's pug.'

Shoot Venus! An eye for an eye, a tooth for a tooth, her life for Fred's – but that would be equity flying flags from every mast-head. He said to Sam, 'Get the gun loaded and wait for me at the kennels.'

He stepped out of the blankets, unlocked the door and staggered down the corridor, fending himself off the pink-and-green-striped wallpaper with his hands. The kitchen door was open; he smelt frying bacon. Having done this, he could not resist forming a picture of it. Planks of meat, dimpled red and spliced with fat, rushed into his mind and were transformed into sizzling, umber-crusted morsels on the end of his fork. Of a sudden he felt ravenous. He could eat an old woman. Meat and then sleep, but first . . . 'Don't let a soul touch it, keep it all for me,' he shouted to Mrs Macbride. 'I'm going to shoot Venus. Come and watch if you like. I'm going to finish her off good and proper, Bridie.' He weaved on down the passage – God, it was so endless, but he'd get there, he'd make it somehow and then he'd put the gun in the brute's mouth, stick it right in and squeeze the trigger and blow every fart clean out, send them bowling to kingdom come. This he would do in the name of equity and render the world pure. Pure! What an astonishing thought! 'And stoke the range as well, Bridie,' he called back. 'Afterwards I shall bathe myself. And shave, you know.'

He stopped in the hall to recover his strength, stroking the layers of soft white hair that had started to creep round his throat. He looked at the poodle staring out at him from Isabel's china cupboard. An eye for an eye. Exactly so. He went out, round the corner of the house and up to the kennels.

Venus had no liking for the fog. Flicking her paws, she had completed one fastidious tour of the stable yard, performed her duty and was waiting for Sam to bring in her breakfast. She wasn't born to kennel hardships. Her pelt was losing its shine. She found the existence lonely. Often she would scratch at the dark pineboard partition, wishing to make friends with the pointers on the other side. But at this moment she wanted her boiled tripe and lay patiently in the straw, ears alert, her brow ploughed with furrows and eyes unblinking on the door.

'It's not the pug, it's Vroshkie that's poorly, sir. The pointer next door.'

'Venus will do very well for me, thank you. Here or outside? Which'll be easier for you afterwards?'

'You can't, sir.'

'Look, its nose is running. It's got distemper alright.'

'That's not distemper, it's the foggy morning that's made her nose run. You can't – you can't shoot that sort of a dog. Pets are different, sir.'

'Who says they are?'

'Mrs Gage would.'

Thomas looked at him. A corporal and yet so soppy. A man who'd kill a dozen Frenchmen and whistle as he did it. 'Wait in the yard, then. Hand me the gun and get out. I know distemper when I see it.'

He raised the gun, not to his shoulder but waist-high. Venus sat up, fluffed the straw with her tail and barked at him, as much as to say, Hurry up with my meal, you. The pink slip of her tongue darted round her mouth.

'Shooting the dog won't bring him back,' Sam said. 'The boy's gone for ever and it's high time you knew it.'

Thomas fitted the gun to his shoulder. It was appallingly heavy, holding it like that. He trained his eye along the barrel and found it wavering around the patch of white hairs on the pug's elbow. Behind the partition Verochka coughed, and retched violently. Venus looked towards the noise and looked back. She stood on her hind legs and did a stupid little dance, showing him her teats. He couldn't miss that, even though the fog was pouring into the kennel in packets, like cannon smoke. He shifted his feet and took aim again.

'If that's what you're going to do, you'd best cock it first,' Sam said mockingly.

'You're getting . . . above your station,' Thomas said indistinctly; and very slowly, snoring before he even reached it, he crumpled into the pure and golden straw.

Twenty-nine

H E ADDED the finishing touches to his miniature of Fred. As an afterthought he introduced into the top left-hand corner his own likeness, a restored and newly cheerful Thomas, murmuring as he squinted down the brush, 'Just so you don't feel lonely, little fellow.' He spent a couple of hours fiddling around with Daedalus and the statues and concluded it was not the masterpiece that he'd believed. He resolved to plan it properly and start afresh. He took Venus for a walk by the river. In the evening he wrote to Tobias Rouch and invited him to a tip-top lunch at the Union Club to say thank you.

On his way through town he dropped off the miniature to have it framed. Sidling, slippered, unctuous Mr Rembers thought so distinguished ('and if I may be allowed, aristocratic') a creation merited gold, and taking Thomas into the street showed him five or six ornate pieces, bouncing the sun off them as he tilted them this way and that. Thomas objected that the tips of the acanthus leaves would tear his pocket linings. He chose instead a smooth, dished frame of solid silver. Rembers said he could have it ready the following morning.

Seeing Lutwylch's gig being polished in his stable yard, he went in to ask the lawyer when he might expect his ladies home. He sank uninvited into the chair, gave the arms a wallop, and said jovially, 'Well, moneybags, pitch you out of the love nest, did they? Or is it some bubbling pot of lucre that brings you back ahead of them? . . . Another week? My goodness, how poor Joan will suffer without you. No, no, carry on with those maps of yours, don't worry about me. Just saw you were here and thought I'd make my number . . . Ah, the dear ladies, I can see them so clearly, tramping the dales in the footsteps of the bard, chanting pentameters to each other, snatching at dactyls and spondees, oh the glories of the Lake District, the poets, the peaks, the clotted cream . . .' He looked more closely at Lutwylch. His skin was rather grey for a man just back from a walking tour. 'Another week, did you say? It'll go in a flash. I'm that busy – painting, luncheon with the sawbones. He's not such a bad sort, you know. It wasn't his fault, it really wasn't. Well, good morning to you. Mustn't stop you earning your crust.'

In the entrance hall he found Gooby hobnobbing with the clerks. His back was turned so he passed him by and rode down St Giles to the Club. The stable boy confused him with another member. 'That makes a change. Usually it's me who gets everything in a muddle,' he said, tipping him sixpence.

Before going in, he and Rouch had a glass of brown sherry each. Their table (Thomas had arranged everything beforehand) was in one of the window alcoves looking over the street. John Suckling, who thought he owned it, scowled at them as they sat down.

To start they had lobsters seasoned with cayenne and a bechamel made without meat. To follow: a cutlet of boiled turbot in its skin with a border of smelts fried in butter, the whole sprinkled with grated parsley. Rouch observed that the fins had been cut off his turbot, which he declared would ruin its taste. Bantering, they swapped plates. Amends were made by a delicious bottle of Constantia. ('This *is* a jolly do,' said Rouch.) To follow: a partridge apiece, the first of the season, coated in breadcrumbs and broiled for twenty-five minutes. Rouch declared the mushroom sauce the best ever. A bottle of Hochheim Riesling was uncorked. Georgiana Farrant walked down the street without seeing them; they drank a toast to her. To follow: vol-au-vent à la crème, crowned with a tiara of green fruit jelly. The concluding act: a syllabub each, light as dew, the sherry and lemon in perfect proportions, so exquisite that they called for seconds.

Tobias Rouch wiped the froth off his lips and unbuttoned his waistcoat. 'What now?'

'A peaceful old age. The fates have hardened me off. Nothing remains that can terrify me. I'm as tough as an old goat. Nothing!'

'I was meaning, should we not take something to settle our stomachs?'

'Of course we should! Hey—' Thomas stuck his hand up and beckoned the waiter with a twirl of his fingers. 'Seriously though, I've quite run out of puff what with one trouble and another. I don't think my balls will ever fill up as quickly as they used to. Grapes, a couple of seedless grapes, that's all they are these days. Isabel will be relieved. Ah, there we are.' He paused while the waiter retreated. Leaning across the table he said confidingly, 'You know, Toby, I haven't been exactly a copybook husband.'

'A bit larger than grapes, I'd suppose,' Rouch said professionally. 'Apricots? The size of apricot they grow in Italy?'

'Oh, but the colour gives altogether the wrong impression,' laughed Thomas. 'Shall we go and sit somewhere more comfortable? At our age we owe it to ourselves to take things easy. Can't dash off as we used to. Cows have the right idea, I've always thought. Snakes too. Ever seen a snake after a heavy meal? Can't budge to save its life. There goes Suckling and his party. Quick, let's grab their chairs before anyone else gets them.'

By and by Rouch left – on foot, for he lived in town. Thomas had a nap. Afterwards he read the paper. Mr and Mrs Smith of Wood Ditton had died within four hours of each other. The Salmonds *père et fils*, from Waterfoot in Cumberland, had failed in their night assault on Mont Blanc, by lantern. Wheat prices were steady. And Nina O'Reilly, 'whose commanding performance we recall so avidly', had opened the autumn season at the Metropole in Brighton.

He rode thoughtfully home where he made much of Natasha, gave Bridie the evening off, and retired. How much would Emily understand? Might she die ignorant of the heart's mess? He begged her forgiveness; he declared his eternal love for her; he said nothing that was false, sanded the letter and sealed it. But it was well into the small hours before he finished with Isabel. He would be away a little time, he wrote. It had the nature of a temporary leave of absence, of a necessity – of a journey in search of one last truth, perhaps the greatest.

The next afternoon, with the first departing swallows of 1851, he left Norwich and headed south.

Thirty

IT WAS not her upbringing in the Irish quarter of Sydney that had laid down the scrolls of pink rich fat on Nina O'Reilly's hips. It was not the receipt of an inheritance, for the O'Reillys were more often destitute than otherwise. It wasn't by the operation of chance (in which she disbelieved). Nor was it from the slothfulness that goes with slippers and a teapot beside the stove: in the whole history of moonbeams fewer had ever been counted than by Nina. No, none of these, singly or in combination, could account for the affluent accumulations around her person and in her purse, her handkerchief drawer, sundry hidden pockets, four per cent Consols and the branch on Macquarie Street of the National Savings Bank.

Passion, that was what had taken her to the top. Packing quarts into pint jars, charging her fences and whacking the stuff out of life.

No one could linger more hauntingly over a Connemara lullaby, or with thrusting bosom and martial chin and a stamp-stamp-stamp of her oddly delicate feet hammer out 'Men of Harlech' quite like the Pearl of Australia. Her vitality, her quenchless exuberance, and her sharp and fruity repartee carried all before her. She adored her audiences and they her. No one could remember when she hadn't given full measure plus a guinea. The ropes of her pinned yellow hair – lustrous, unimproved, half as long as her spine – might come unwoven; she would laugh, gorgeously and without artifice, a stretch below Middle C. Her eyes – flashing with blue fire when at the gallop, a dusky violet for a sweetheart's lament – could make the sap boil in the greatest curmudgeon. If she had new shoes that were a bit tight, she'd kick them off and to hell with the splinters. Instead of one encore she'd give three, four or five, from the sheer love of being twenty-nine and acclaimed. She was as unlike Isabel Gage as was possible.

'She's a spunker alright, a trouper if ever I saw one,' men would say as they drifted tingling into the night.

Or knowingly, 'I bet she's a handful and a half. One flip of that lot and you'd be paste on the ceiling, young fellow. Looking at her from the point of view of the natural offices of man, I'd say there was a bit of the animal in there somewhere.'

Together with this ebullience, and as much a part of her as curtains are of a room, went an almost limitless stupidity in matters of the intellect. Her schooling had been negligible. Nothing she had seen or heard since then had persuaded her she'd missed much. What use was Latin to a singer? What was the point of reading books about history or politics? Let them slumber on the shelf. Let the dome-heads dust and stroke and go blind over them, they were not for her. The nest-egg was what counted, and making a splash. Therefore she was far from being ashamed of her ignorance. In fact she would promote it as one of her attractions and tell her neighbours at dinner straight out, almost before they'd got their chairs properly up to the table, that they were sitting next to the most brainless creature in the room; and when they gallantly pooh-poohed the notion, would proceed to corroborate it disarmingly as she tucked away a good square meal. Yet there was always something about her observations that struck the bone: a verve, a worldliness, and a knack of reducing matters to their flint that convinced every man within earshot that education as they understood it was a waste of time.

The two gaslights projected their bluish stems of flames on either side of her dressing-room mirror. A coal fire burned in the grate. There was an easy chair with cushions, the thick new Axminster carpet she'd insisted on, and an ornate metal stand for her collection of parasols. Her gowns, mostly in a range of lavenders to set off her yellow hair and blue eyes, hung with her petticoats behind a curtain decorated with tendrils of twining green ivy. A line of seamed and polished shoe heels poked out beneath them. In a frame on one wall was a heavily signed programme of the entertainments held on board the crack White Star Line clipper

Pontefract Castle to celebrate crossing the Equator on June 2ⁿᵈ, 1849. On the other was a misty watercolour of Sydney harbour. Her name was on the door, to which she alone had the key. She had a six-month contract together with rooms at the New Steine Hotel where the nobility and gentry could enjoy cuisine and wines of the highest character and sometimes gawp at royalty. Management could not do enough for Nina.

Also among her pamperings, behind an Indian papered screen in her dressing-room, was the patentest of water-closets, a step-up and sit-down mahogany throne complete with foot-pedal flush and one of Mr Maple's peerless china basins reachable with only a slight lean to the left. Here she was crouched, drawers rolled down to the knees and her stiff scarlet petticoat sitting up on the floor like a palisade. Speculatively she drew her thumb across the card's embossed lettering.

MR THOMAS GAGE
GENTLEMAN AND ARTIST
Fordwell House,
Sparling, Norfolk

'Just after the interval, did you say, Mary?' she called out to her maid.

'I heard them cheer you as you came on, then knock-knock and there was Alfred, flowers stacked up to the chin. And that was only the start of it, miss. Why, I daresay five minutes didn't go by without a new lot of blooms. We've never had anything like this before, not in all the time we've been doing it. Alfred thinks it's the single gent who's had the plush box these last two days. I took a peek at him. An older man, comfortably built – takes up all of the seat, if you follow me – lovely strong hair but a bit worn in the face – not what you'd call a beauty. Not like that Mr Hercules you see advertising moustache papers,' she said wistfully, kneeling on the floor and trimming the stems of a truss of buttermilk gladioli.

Nina was in no hurry. It was a Saturday, her solo night, and the crowd had been larger than ever, standing room only for latecomers. Two hours on the boards had tired her feet. It was good to be able to take her ease on the throne. Mary was companionship for the moment, but it would be lonely dining by herself at the hotel. She fingered the card again. 'Any orchids among 'em?'

'Oh, this isn't the time for orchids, miss. It's only in winter you get those. Just as well. They give me the creeps, they do.'

The orchestra jangled down the corridor, chaffing each other as they cased up their instruments. A trombone exuded a couple of humorous bleats outside the door and a youthful voice said, 'Good night, Miss Nina.'

'Good night, Olly. Remember what the doctors say, it can make you go blind . . . Shame there's no orchids. Not until winter! Crikey, am I going to have to spin him out until then?'

'What do you want me to do, miss? I expect he'll be waiting around somewhere. Shall I tell Alfred to have him push off or what? Though he must have the wherewithal to have bought this lot.' Mary sat back on her heels, admiring the bowls and vases and buckets of flowers in front of her. 'No shortage of cash in that quarter, I'd say.'

It was the hour Nina liked to have her best meal of the day; a half of Riesling, mussels, and a roundel of under-cooked beef fillet with golden potato fritters. She had a good idea who the man was. Having a pair of opera glasses fall at her feet wasn't easily forgotten, nor the incident with the rival bouquet of flowers. Nothing like Mr Hercules, Mary had been right there. But there had been *something* about him, an aura of power and energy that had risen from him like steam as he stood, towering, to applaud her. She'd had enough of youths with boiling eyes, of being talked down to, and what she thought of as a very English timidity. Whereas this man with his great loaf of hair, with the experienced and strangely tide-marked face; this *artist and gentleman* called Thomas Gage . . .

She hesitated; pulled her drawers up to facilitate the sideways movement of her under-heel towards the brass foot-pedal.

'Management'll be as merry as grigs tonight,' said Mary. 'Couldn't have found room for a sparrow in the hall.'

Her heel went down, a moment of gurgling and decision.

'Tell him I'm having a piss and he'll have to wait. Don't leave it to Alfred, do it yourself. Get a proper squint at him. See if his collar's fresh. Cuffs. Shoes. See what class of hands he's got.' She raised herself, stepped down, and came out from behind the screen, tying a bow in the tape of her drawers. She tossed the scarlet petticoat onto the chair, shook out her hair and stood with her back to the fire, blue-eyed and vigilant. Her corset – the Amazone, elastic lacings down the front, an immense improvement – cosily sustained her bosom as bending, she cursorily surveyed the array of flowers. 'You know what I mean, Mary, is he a real gent or just some confidence bloke.'

'Get the measure of him then, miss.' Mary put on her coat.

'See if he's the proper article, if he's all in one piece. I don't want to go and waste myself on a cripple.'

It was on the corner of Adelaide Crescent, overlooking the Esplanade, that Thomas found it: a furnished ground-floor apartment that was modern, spacious and convenient for the theatre. It had a wine-cellar (the lintel was rather low for him), a longish drawing-room, and two good south-facing bedrooms with a view of the sea. A narrow staircase led to a room by itself on the first floor that he thought would do very well for his studio. The rent was high – twenty-five pounds per calendar month. The minimum period was a year.

'Market's very tight at present,' said Miss Mimms. 'Hardly worth my while doing it for less.' A deposit of ten pounds was payable against breakages. 'This sort of quality doesn't come cheap. The piano alone cost me eighty pounds.'

Thomas, who was leaning on it, looked down contentedly.

'That's a Broadwood, Mr Gage. You can't do better than a Broadwood. Only quality goods in a house of mine.'

'I hardly think you need worry about damage to the furniture. We are both very careful people. Not youngsters, you know.'

'We, meaning you and . . . Mrs Gage?' she said.

He slapped the piano lid, his hand skidding on the Spanish shawl with which it was clothed. A glass flute, engraved with the word BRIGHTON under the rim and containing a posy of marigolds, teetered back and forth. He laid a finger on it. 'Now now, behave yourself . . . Perfection! Exactly what I've been searching for, up and down, down and around the whole town. Happy – oh, this is the place for happiness, Miss Mimms,' and impulsively he caught her wrist and pressed the lizard skin to his lips.

But Miss Mimms was not to be undermined by his gallantry. She had observed the tiny flicker in Thomas's eye a moment earlier and had arrived at the opinion – a process in which she had many years of experience – that the other half of 'we' was not the lady lawfully called Mrs Gage. She had a reputation to maintain. Therefore a supplement was payable, a *bonne bouche* to console her for the reduced esteem of her neighbours. 'Of course the maid, coal and gas are in addition. Annie's her name. Very good at her business. You couldn't wish for better.' She waited, chin up, her bony fingers twiddling the chain of a garnet pendant. Next time she'd start at thirty pounds. The market would bear it. Brighton was full of love-birds nowadays. He's found an actress, she supposed. They all called themselves that. 'I could get double the price during the season,' she said.

'However this is not the season,' Thomas said automatically. And then, knowing the place was ideal, 'Still, as long as Annie will do the cooking for us. Not that we'll be at home that much in the evening, I expect. You see . . .' What he wished desperately to say, even to this greedy crone, was that he'd found a jewel; that he was torrentially in love with Nina O'Reilly, the Nina who was packing them into the Metropole, the glamorous singer – love! At last! After all these years! – and he'd no idea how a man of his age could be so lucky. Yes, Nina, you old bat! The Pearl her very self! And all he wanted every day from now to the end of the hereafter was to give her pleasure and see that pleasure flood her sweet face – blue eyes! Flaxen hair! Feet the size of thimbles! Oh, Miss Mimms, indescribable! – and to lie with her and care for her, only he wasn't certain how tame she would be in the matter of household operations.

All this he yearned to shout to anyone who'd listen. But when Miss Mimms tapped her tortoise-shell lorgnette against her teeth and said cooking would be a further pound excluding gratuities, he realised immediately she was quite the wrong person. Retracting the words, he went off to lay them at the feet of Nina, who was watching some fishermen repair their nets on the shingle.

Afterwards – he'd barely been able to suppress his excitement – he burst out: 'And I've found the perfect place for us, my darling! Would you believe it, paradise in Adelaide Crescent!'

But when they went back and he began to point out to Nina the details of the furnishings, he realised to his dismay that his first impression had been hopelessly at fault. The doors were flimsy and their mouldings too shallow. The bell-pull beside the fireplace that had jangled so manorially in his mind was attached to nothing more than a hook in the ceiling. The two framed samplers, quite authentic from a distance, showed themselves to be the very model of triteness: bluebells and crocuses posing beside 'Home Sweet Home' and 'Forget Me Not When Far Away', childish sayings done by a machine in gaudy gold and silver with not one interesting piece of stitchwork or lettering. The teacups in a display case were ghastly souvenirs from the Great Exhibition – golly, she'd been quick off the mark there. The miniature bellows hanging on the wall, the black china cat with popping fiery eyes, the valance draped in swags over the mantel-shelf, the lamp with a ring-a-rosy of bronze cherubs for a base – what in heaven's name had he been thinking of? 'And my jardineers,' said Miss Mimms, crumpling the word into a handier size, 'are quite the latest fashion.' She'd been dogging their footsteps like a tiresome child and now pressed between them. A slight mustiness rose from her clothes. 'I don't think you'd find better yuccas anywhere, perhaps not even in London. Annie dusts them once a week, I make sure of that. The dwarf palms you're looking at I had from my friend Captain Vincent when he died. *He* was a most respectable man, Mr Gage,' she said. Yuccas! Palm trees! The lace curtains, the tassels, the pom-poms, the milkmaid figurines, the goody-goody Buddha, the unspeakable wallpaper – not one honest, rugged piece of furniture in the place – and on top of everything, that spiteful little aside. He grasped Nina by the elbow.

She was dressed that afternoon in a full stand of blue, a stronger colour than was usual for her. It was to do with the sea, and the greater part of her wardrobe being at the hotel laundry. She tossed her bonnet onto the sofa, shaped both hands beneath her thick coils of hair, and gazed around. 'Adorable!' She flung her arms wide. 'Adorable! Mr Gage, you're the cleverest man I know, I swear it. Miss Mimms, put the contract in front of him, quickly, before he gets cold feet. Where does he sign? Pen, Thomas – ink it so, halfway up the nib will do – your turn, Miss Mimms – I do the blotting – the keys, thank you – voyler! A home to call my own!'

She bundled Miss Mimms out of the door and then, her dress

spinning, twirled round the room among the yuccas and the late Captain Vincent's dwarf palms, both of which recalled to her so vividly the hot climate of Australia.

'And a piano as well – Thomas, you're such a darling man. Just when I needed rescuing – it's so lonely night after night, without any friends or family – there you were, lording it in that box of yours. "Help me!" I sang—'

'And I heard,' Thomas said uxoriously, sinking into the chintz sofa and looking up at her in rapture. 'How could I not? Your memory has been all that stood between me and madness. Ever since I first saw you, I've known. She's mine, I said to myself. Mine!'

'Do you know, I near as a touch refused the chance of Norwich? "Where's that?" I said to Mr Pauntley, that great thief of an agent I have. "All the way up there for a couple of songs? Would you waste your Pearl on a hall full of yokels?" "The money's good," he said, referring of course to the commission he was going to earn for doing nothing but sit on his backside. Agents – but let's leave them out of it. Let's think of angels instead. Oh, Thomas, I can't tell you how enchanting this is after that stuffy hotel. You're my absolute poppet. P-o-p-p-e-t. Thank God I went to Norwich.'

She opened the piano and began to sing, low and soothingly, her voice stilling the discordant vibrations left by Miss Mimms.

That neck, the movement of her throat – the skin so young, unblemished and sumptuous –

'For Greensleeves was my joy and delight,
        Greensleeves was my heart of gold –'

She exhaled the words with lips that pouted and kissed him. The weightiness of her breasts transferred itself to his palms, which he stroked against his pale cotton trousers. Her delicate ankles glimpsed below the piano stool, the languid sway of her blue-pleated hips, the taut satin back of her little mustard-coloured waistcoat, the indistinct ribbing of her corset – his love grew tumid as he reclined on the sofa and through hooded eyes started to dismantle the silk hair-net, the pins, and the hooks.

She paused, holding the chord. 'What are you looking at me like that for?'

217

'I'm waiting for you to finish.'

'And then?'

'But why then? Why not now?'

'Oh yes, Thomas darling, now, now as ever is.'

The sun was dipping towards the horizon. The air in the bedroom was milky warm, the remains of summer's passion. Near and far the sea was engraved with ripples, its shiny pinkness speckled with the tilted sails of the fishing fleet. He unrolled the blinds and threw aside his coat. She kicked off her shoes and took down her hair, smiling as she placed the pins in a white dish on the dressing-table and Thomas's bulk bobbed and jostled in the mirror. Turning, she came to meet him beside the bed, blue dress and yellow hair, eyes of a lesser blue that were confident and ingenious.

'None of your Mary listening at the key-hole this time.'

'And the carpet had grit in it, right in the middle of my back.'

'Where? Show me. How dare it—'

She sloped her shoulders. The dress slid to the floor. She stepped away from it; closed on him with lowered hands; caressed the peak of his trousers with a grooved palm. 'It must have dropped out of the flowers. Everything happened so fast. I should have resisted you, my bearsome love – just a little.' Her breath was as soft as a catkin. Her wrist glided up and down against his belly.

He was uncasing her breasts, hauling impatiently on the black strong lace of the Amazone. She wanted to say be careful, that it had cost her over ten shillings, but remained silent, fondling his ears while the clicking thread flew out and his head descended towards her waist and the tape of her flannel drawers. Straightening, he parted the wings of the Amazone; smoothed his hands up her rib-cage until her flesh spilled over and they could contain no more. She eased his braces off. But collar-studs had always defeated her.

She leaned on her elbow, scrutinising him. The last of the sun angled across the bed from the corner-post and laid faint stripes upon her stomach. Her hair was a fan on the pillows, her breasts a landslide in cream. At last he came to her, in a rush, ungainly and majestic.

She whispered, 'Sweet Jesus, I could sling my saddle over it.'

Dextrously she absorbed him between her marbled thighs and pulled the covers over his back.

As darkness became complete he slept, his greying head cushioned on her bosom, re-strengthening himself like Samson. Quietly she reached out for her rings. She was wondering how to extricate her luggage from the hotel without embarrassment, also what she might sing that night.

Thirty-one

HE BOUGHT her a dark green riding costume: flowing skirts, long enough to cover her ankles when sitting side-saddle; a jacket with silver buttons embossed with hunting horns and having a tittuping, wedge-shaped tail; and a chiffon veil for the jaunty little hat with its white Prince of Wales cockade that clung rakishly to her coiled hair. First thing after breakfast, whenever the weather allowed, they took their hired geldings and promenaded along the seafront with the rest of fashionable society. When they started doing this, the young bucks would rowel their horses and canter over to Nina in a swirl of capes and gravel. One-handed they'd rein back their plunging mounts, which to Thomas seemed to want only crimson nostrils and a rope of skulls rattling at their withers to have galloped five thousand miles from the plains of Mongolia. Cigars would be deferred, hats raised, and compliments lobbed at the Pearl from all sides. As an afterthought they'd extend their monocles and silently quiz plodding Thomas. And Nina, lonely and pragmatic, would disdain to lift so much as a corner of her veil, at which his heart would recover its breath and they'd ride away to resume their conversation about the wonders of new love.

Then she'd bathe, perfume herself and in her lilac day robe try out some new songs that Mr Pauntley had sent her. Upstairs he would listen to the soar and swoop of her divine voice, ponder on the nature of miracles, and at length begin to paint, fleshing out his sketches of her, of the orchestra, of all those trivial yet arresting scenes on the Esplanade – a lady holding a parasol behind her back as she bent over to give a tit-bit to a poodle; the one-legged hurdy-gurdy man; the vociferous hawkers of winkles and crabs.

Sometimes he'd put on his old blue coat and with charcoal and drawing-book at the ready, perch on an iron bollard until lunch-time, his eyes soft with love, with the beauty of autumn, with the pleasure of idling.

She could not easily understand his attachment to this coat, which struck her as no more than the stained relic of a long-departed fashion. 'Just so long as you don't wear it when you're out with *me*,' she'd say tartly, continuing to play the piano as he kissed the slant of her cheek.

For his part he was never able to find precisely the right words that covered his relationship with the coat. 'It's not that,' he would say, 'so much as the fabric that binds me to my forefathers. Something in that area.'

'What, you want to be chained to them in their graves? That's plain silly. Dead's dead. No point in pretending otherwise. Anyway, I don't want to think of you as anything except brimming with life.' Her eyes would grow flirtatious and the matter be put to one side for the moment.

In the end she prevailed. The coat was put into mothballs and with Nina at his side he refurbished himself extravagantly from top to bottom. A natty straw hat with a light blue ribbon made its appearance, together with a family-sized bottle of the same Rowland's Macassar Oil that he'd once ridiculed. He bought an artist's smock in the French style; tight evening trousers of grey cashmere with an elastic strap to go under his glacé ball-room slippers; several pairs of everyday trousers in a small black-and-white check, sponge-bag; lapelled waistcoats in the striking colours that Mr Mullings the outfitter assured him would be all the rage in the season, and boxes, not to say hampers, of handkerchiefs, collars, cuffs and high frothy cravats. Never one but he bought a dozen, telling Nina afterwards, 'Oh, it makes them think I'm a frightful swell. If tradesmen think highly of you, then so does everyone else and life's that much more enjoyable. One must always try to impress tradesmen, I think.'

Fred's portrait he stood on the mantel-shelf in his studio. The better she got to know Thomas, the more Nina felt the tragedy to be part of her life also. She would question him incessantly about Fred, especially, for some reason, when they were out riding. How had he chipped his tooth? Was he clever at school? Could he sing?

His foibles and ambitions, his best joke, his most memorable prank. She would climb up the narrow stairs to his studio and stare at the miniature without speaking. She begged him to bring it down, to put it somewhere they could see it when they were together. But Thomas was firm that inspiration came to him only when Fred was *there*, six feet away, watching him. There was no rational explanation he could offer. It came from deep within him. That was how it had been when the boy was alive and thus it would always be. 'It happens between fathers and sons,' he said to her. 'It happens and no one knows why, so there he will stay.' But Nina also could be insistent, and Fred got into the habit of making several journeys a week between floors.

One night in November a gale roared up the Channel from Ushant and covered their patch of lawn in leaves. The next afternoon, when Nina was over at the theatre, he indented with Miss Mimms for the use of a rake and shaped them into a fluffy heart beside their front door. Throughout the performance that evening his eyes glowed in anticipation of the surprise she'd get, and he grudged every encore she gave. But everything was ruined by a spiteful wind, the sort that is met on turning a street corner. When they got home the leaves were huddled in a drift under the window, pulsating fitfully as if beneath them some morose creature of the night was stirring.

Thomas was undaunted. The following day he went up to Miss Mimms' apartment on the top floor and paid the rent a week early. At the same time – literally as he took the bank-notes out of his wallet – he sued for permission to plant some spring bulbs in their tiny lawn. He bought a ball of green gardeners' twine and a hinged wooden ruler, and pegged out a double heart; the outer perimeter for a single rank of snowdrops and for the inner, filling it entirely, no more than an inch between the corms, the same light mauve crocuses that he and Isabel had planted at Fordwell. 'It's just that I'm very fond of that colour,' he said to himself vexedly as he scrubbed the soil from beneath his fingernails. After an hour or two of reflection, he took a stiff brush from Annie's closet and restored the nap of the grass in case Nina should notice what he'd been up to.

A week later he started a new version of Daedalus. He knew his mistake. He'd become obsessed by the statues, by their power to move of their own accord in and out of that shaft of sunlight as they discussed the old man's diagrams of his leather wings. It was on the relationship of Daedalus and Icarus, that boastful slovenly son of his, that he must concentrate, to point up the fatal conflict between wisdom and conceit.

It became his custom to do his banking on the third Monday of each month. The 8.45 express got him to London Bridge at ten o'clock without a halt. There was a later train that would have suited his purposes equally. But it stopped at Reigate, where lived a brother of John Suckling, and he had no wish to be cornered alone with Lionel in a carriage.

'What would we say to each other? He's bound to have heard,' he said to Nina, who was complaining that the 8.45 gave them no time for their usual ride. 'It'd be as awkward for me as it was for that woman who was trapped—'

'I know, with the man who cut his throat in front of her and the train didn't stop for another hour. Why are you always telling me that revolting story?'

They were at the breakfast table. The night before they'd been at the birthday celebrations for Mr Galley, the theatre manager. 'It was only once,' he said, recoiling from her dyspeptic glare. 'Anyway, it's so human. It's not as if the chap finished his newspaper and thought, I've had about enough of women, damme if I don't scare the living daylights out of this one. He was obviously potty.'

Annie came in with his kipper. He wafted his nose along its length and continued in the same light-hearted vein. 'Of course it could never have happened in a stage-coach, God bless 'em. A clout on the panel and Blissett'd have clumped down from his box, stuck his head in, and said, "So wort yew be up to with that razor then, bor?" Oh yes, we had some times together. I miss those frosty dawns, him sitting up there with the stars, swaddled in his filthy old rugs, coughing and gobbing. Marvellously red face, just like a Rifleman strawberry. The Belle Sauvage, on Ludgate Hill, that's where he coached from at this end. How the place used to hum – still going, as a matter of fact. The to-do when he was horsing up for the road – you should have seen it! Hey, Annie, am I to get any buttered bread with my kipper? And more hot water while you're about it. I've got such a thirst on me this morning. Look, I didn't mean to upset you with that story – wait!'

'You can be such a damned fuddy-duddy. Coaches, the good old days, grandfather's coat—'

'But I'm only trying to explain why I don't want to chance it by stopping at Reigate. And it'll probably be raining tomorrow. It could be too wet to go riding – oh Nina, my pet, don't be angry with me. Here, let me pour you some more coffee. It'll put you right in a flash.'

But Nina was already pushing back her chair, her face quite bilious. 'I can't *stand* the smell of that fish another second. Catch whatever train you like. I'm going back to bed.' She shouted to Annie to bring her a jug of seltzer and went out, slamming the door.

Sighing deeply, Thomas propped his Bradshaw against the cruet. He tucked the napkin in at his throat, spread it carefully over his red-checked waistcoat and opened the kipper along the seam. The 8.45 really was the most convenient. He wasn't going to take a risk with Lionel Suckling and that's all there was to it. The man would have a letter in the post to Norfolk that very night, he could count on it. Besides, he needed the best part of a day if he was to call on Barclay, Bevan in the City and then get across town to see some paintings, have a decent lunch, and do his sundries.

He diddled the backbone onto Nina's plate and asked Annie to bring in the toast. He supposed he could use another bank, Child's or Hoare's, one that was closer to St James's. But they knew nothing about him. It would take time to alter the arrangements he'd had Lutwylch put into place. Questions, papers to be signed, unfamiliar faces – a botheration. And he felt comfortable with Barclay, Bevan. They were Norfolk people too; did business all the time with old man Gurney back in Norwich. Going down Lombard Street and into their premises in Ball Alley was like being at home. It was pleasant to loiter in their hall while the clerk, Mr Adkins, consulted the ledger; pleasant to have a chat with him as he filled in the pass-book, made up a wallet of cheques and crooking his dimpled fingerstall, counted off the large crisp notes; and positively delightful to hear again the nervous, musical speech of Norfolk. Yes, this was a part of the day that he would sorely miss if he took his business elsewhere. Reeves, the colourman, was close by in Cheapside. And the coffee-house two doors from the bank was both quaint and civil. Therefore, on this one day a month, he would travel up to London on the 8.45, return on the 5.00 (also non-stop), have an agreeable outing and not be embarrassed by Lionel Suckling. Nina would have to live with it in the same way as other women did.

Thirty-two

THOMAS BECAME unsettled as Christmas approached. The German tone at court had made the season fashionable. On almost every window-sill potted fir trees were appearing, with cheery ribbons and tinsel and plump angelic Rhinemaidens. He remembered all the games he'd played with Fred and Emily, and a sadness took root within him. He had put himself beyond the pale, and this he accepted. But he wished he could have them both, Nina and Emily. There was an emptiness in his life without her scampery, pertness and careful way of thinking. As the snow fell silently through the yellow glow of the street lamps and he trudged past the rows of sparkling windows to an evening of Christmas jollity at the theatre, he was bewildered to realise how incomplete he was without Emily.

The immediate question was what he should give her. He confided in Nina. Galley had just offered her what she would refer to only as an 'inducement' if she put on an extra show on Christmas Eve. She was afraid she'd catch cold and lose her voice if she went with him to London to choose Emily's presents. But she understood, and said she admired his honesty. 'Only don't start talking about sacrifice, that drags everything down.'

The next morning she went with him to the station. Despite the weather having turned to rain, there remained a skim of ice on the platform. They walked with short cautious steps to the far end, where there was no one except a railwayman in an oilskin cape and bulky leather boots, about twenty yards down the track. He'd lit a brazier over the points and was standing as close to it as he could get, swaying at the waist, clapping his hands in front and behind him. Nina gripped the loose material of Thomas's gingerbread-brown overcoat. She looked hesitantly at its buttons and then up into his face, her fists in their green woollen gloves curling deeper into the cloth.

'I wish Emily were our child,' she said simply. The pink of her cheeks, heightened by the cold air, stood out against the great black shag of her new busby.

His first thought, which came bounding out of his heart and straight into his eyes, was, Yes, oh yes, a hundred times yes, and he parted his lips to speak. Then: But what does she actually mean, that she conceive my child or that I divorce Isabel? The intricacy of the proceedings, the shame, the position of Emily ... He enveloped her in his arms and nuzzled the down on the upper curve of her jaw. Vaguely watching the railwayman joggle his feet to keep warm, he said in a low voice, 'But the complications, my pet, think of what we'd have to go through. The courts, the scandal, not to mention the expense of it all ...'

'It wasn't *that* I was thinking of, only ... Well, you must use your imagination.'

The lines quivered and began to hum. The train arrived, its driver standing boldly on the outside footplate, togged up against the weather as if he were on a whaler in the Arctic.

'Every woman wants to bear the child of the man she loves. That's all, nothing to get in a panic about.' And more gaily, 'Now off you go and buy Emily her presents. Remember, Thomas, she's on the point of becoming a woman. Get her something she'd want, not something you'd like to play with yourself.'

The whistle blew; the train started to move; her face slipped away from the window. He got out the portrait of Fred, for he always carried it on his journeys. 'Would you like a brother or another sister, old chap?' For several miles he stared at it, turning Nina's words over in his mind.

The London sky was sodden, scarcely moving. Rafts of melting snow slid down the roof slates and pancaked onto the street, spattering people's legs. Gutters overflowed. The streams belching from downpipes swirled cabbage leaves, orange peel, chicken bones, scraps of newspaper and eroding plugs of dog turd over the calloused pavements. The smoke from a million coal fires hung imprisoned beneath the clouds, indistinguishable from them. In the rain were smuts that blackened everything. Umbrellas jousted dangerously. Cabmen on their boxes shouted half-hearted revolutionary slogans whenever a wealthy carriage blocked a street trying to turn or to let its passengers descend. The city had come to a wet, angry and unchristian standstill. Unhappiness was abroad in that dripping tide of humanity, and it infected Thomas also.

Every cab he saw had been spoken for and he had to walk from London Bridge to Barclay, Bevan. The distance was not so great, and he was wearing his galoshes. Nevertheless it was more than he'd bargained for, being shoved around and getting himself splashed with rubbish by the passing traffic. Before going in to see Adkins he stopped at the coffee-house to see what he could make of his accounts. What Nina had said, or what he thought she wished to say, had made him think about money.

'Spenny business, living, that is to say,' observed his neighbour, watching Thomas's pencil creep down a column of figures. There was a terrific fug in the low-ceilinged room. Everyone was jammed up against each other in the wooden booths. The heat from the cooking range and from thirty or forty bodies in wet clothes threw off a tropical steaminess.

The man, elderly, razor-nosed, and with a ragged philosopher's beard, blew reflectively on his tea. 'It'd be better for the world if money had never been thought of. A lot of harm gets caused by money. Whether one has it or whether one hasn't, it's always a mischief.'

Thomas was glad of the interruption. Accounting was a dreadful chore, an insult to the natural direction of man's intelligence. It was beyond him how a normal being could know what he might have spent in a month's time. What if he lost his heart to a painting, or a fine piece of porcelain? Or war was declared and Consols went flying? He looked despondently at his arithmetic. 'Touch and go, try as I may I can never improve on that.'

'There's many who never get as far as the touching part of it,' said the other ominously, turning an appraising eye on him. 'Hear the words of our Lord: silver and gold have I none, but such as I have—'

Swiftly Thomas left and went two doors down the alley to the bank. The hall was crowded with City gentry getting cashed up for their Christmas shopping. He had to wait. No one was talking. The marble floor was slick with the rainwater that'd been tracked in. On a day like this he should have been holed up in his studio in front of the fire. As he shuffled forward, he wondered again what he should buy Emily. Oh, but it was a tangle, the most terrible tangle, and all because Gooby wanted their land, had thought to sweeten him up with a trip for gratis and had taken Fred from him. In those fifteen seconds his family had been destroyed. Had Fred still been alive—

It was his turn. Adkins pointed out that a cheque which Thomas had written six weeks ago had yet to be presented for payment. This deepened his confusion. Should he treat the money as his or not? The fellow might have lost the cheque. Or fallen down and died, smacked his skull to fragments on the kitchen floor. To whom would the money belong then? A new set of balances, the hypothetical and the contingent, fought it out in his mind.

'Count it as a bonus,' Adkins was saying. 'Get Mrs Gage something special, that's what I'd do.'

'A bonus, eh?' He studied Adkins' face. A banker should know if anyone did, and he burst out loudly, so that everyone tried not to notice him, 'So who's been a silly chap! A fair mugglewit doan't thet man be then, bor!' to which Adkins smiled gracefully as he made up Thomas's monthly remittance.

On his way out he discovered that his umbrella had gone from the stand. He picked one from those remaining on account of its fat ash handle and gold band and hurried past the doorman into Ball Alley.

He didn't feel like walking any further, and a hansom cab was waiting, right there in Lombard Street. 'Got a customer already. Can't do that, sir, or I'll lose my ticket' – but a shilling gained the ascendant and Thomas went off to luncheon at the Belle Sauvage to see how the old place was getting on. Adkins had said he should consider the cheque as being back in his pocket: his mood improved. He said to himself, It may even be that the sun will shine. However, he continued, looking out at the sky, only a blind man would bet on it, and he decided to catch an earlier train home, the 4 p.m., despite that it stopped at Reigate and so might contain Lionel Suckling. Nina would be glad to have him home early. It hurt him – struck him suddenly in the very pit of his stomach – to recall her poignant expression of the morning, the force with which she'd pressed her childless belly against him, the yearning eyes of a woman with no certain position in society. She'd given herself to him, had compromised her reputation beyond any possibility of repair. He was her comforter, the sole haven in her lonely existence. Yes, his obligations to Nina were immeasurable. He'd return on the earlier train.

The Belle Sauvage was not as it used to be. When he came out it was raining again, with never a cab in sight. His ankles were beginning to tire and it was slowly that he battled through the crowds up Fleet Street and along the Strand to Baxters. He paused outside it, standing between the two six-stemmed gaslights that shone like huge candelabra through the dull afternoon. Packs of greedy, hot-eyed people scurried into the shop, jostling and knocking against him. Others fought them to get out, but more feebly, through being sated by spending. He could not help but notice their joyful expressions. Already, even in the middle of that melee, they were fingering their packages and peeping into bags. 'Oh, but she'll *adore* it. How clever of you to have found it, and in just the right colour too.' He wished he could reach out and steal their high spirits, their family unity. How often had he marched jubilantly to the cab rank with his arms full of knick-knacks, puzzles, candied fruit, bows and arrows and those small cardboard boxes of slingshot for Fred? How many Christmas tangerines had he bought from the two old women outside St Clements? Was he never to ride down that long slow hill to Fordwell again? Was this the bargain he'd made?

But this was getting him nowhere. Time was not on his side. He pocketed his watch and went straight to the gallery where the best Indian shawls were displayed.

'"For Emily Gage, from her adoring father . . ." – in the very finest needlework. Have it done by tomorrow. Then express it to Norwich for delivery by local carrier. Here, I'll give you the address.' He'd decided not to send a letter with it. There was too much to be said, and nothing he was capable of saying to her except in person. 'Hurry, young man, can't you write any faster? I've a train to catch.'

He swept back the brown panels of his overcoat and fished out his note-case. In its centrefold was the piece of card on which he'd jotted his accounts. He laid it on the mahogany counter, his shoulders hunched, and squinnied mistrustfully at his figurings. That loose cheque had certainly muddled things. I mean, what if Adkins was wrong about spending it? he thought. Trains, cabs, Christmas tips – yes, they were all there. He'd remembered to make provision for the turquoise ring that had been tempting him for ages. Nina'd like that, she couldn't fail to. Wasn't there something else he should have reserved for . . . ? But the rent! And the coals, gas and Annie – the sales clerk discreetly manoeuvred the bill next to his bit of card. His eyes flickered down it, to the sum at the bottom, beneath the entries for 'Carriage', and 'To Embroidery'.

'Well now . . .' He trod on the heel of a galosh and withdrew his foot. 'One moment, if you please.'

Kneeling beneath the protection of the counter, he equalised his shoe-laces and retied them assiduously. He'd been coming to all that when he'd been interrupted at his coffee: the rent, domestic expenses, restaurants, *petits cadeaux* for Nina – she wouldn't look kindly on frugality. It was that fellow trying to dun him, and then the business with the cheque that had puddled his brains. But now . . . Touch and go was no longer in it. One of his presents would have to be surrendered, the proportions of his love for Nina and Emily clarified. Was it to be the ring? He couldn't. It was too exquisite for words. But something had to move over. A month had to be survived before his next remittance . . . Calmly he surfaced, picked up his top hat, tapped it down and drew on his gloves. 'Wait. Give me half an hour. I'll pay for it then.'

Of course he'd have to tell Lutwylch. A couple of lines would do. 'Dear Leonard' (that'd please him), 'I was caught short of ten quid before Christmas and depleted the till of Roberson's, the paint people in Long Acre, by that amount. Please adjust their debt accordingly. Sincerely yours, Thos Gage.'

He stopped to straighten himself up in a shop window in Garrick Street. He'd make a joke about it, behave like a provincial trapped in the snares of a wicked city. Tell Roberson how lucky the Gages were to be doing business with a man of his stamp.

Smear him all over. But not leave until he'd got it. Lock the chap in if he turned nappy. Plunk a chair in front of the door and sit there with his arms crossed like a maharajah. Be bloody, bold and resolute. He turned the corner into Long Acre.

Thirty-three

THE RING – turquoise, the gem of happiness, turquoise to mirror the beauty of her eyes, and the setting of tiny seed-pearls as a bonus.

Covertly people stared at them, the wealthy artist dining *à deux* with the fabulous young singer, his mistress. Conversations stilled as they gorged their imaginations with the most intimate details of the relationship. The violinist tucked his instrument beneath his rolling chin, smiled upon them with seasoned eyes and struck the tune for which everybody knew her, 'My Love Will Love me in the Morning'. The waiter grasped the neck of the champagne bottle and drew it from its silvered holster.

Thomas could not restrain himself from opening the tooled leather case first. The blue, it was irresistible! That old coat of his had surely had the same idea in its youth. Shyly he advanced the box over the crisp creases of the tablecloth, past the darker blue of the little well of mustard, past the sprigs of holly and through the sultry pool of candlelight. He gave it a final tap with his fingernail, to within an inch of the silver trestle on which her lobster fork was resting. He settled his elbows astride his plate of oysters and raised his glass. 'To the moon! To us!'

But Nina was unprepared. It was in her mind that they'd exchange their Christmas gifts in private, cross-legged in front of the fire like children. She'd seen the box creeping over the table, and the hairs glinting on the back of his fingers. But the lid was raised against her, she couldn't see in, and she was engrossed with the lobster that she'd been determined to celebrate Christmas with, as she always had when she could afford it. Her hands were full, her chin was greasy, and the juices were about to run down her wrists into the ruffles of her shimmering silk blouse. She sucked a taper of coral flesh into her mouth, smacked her lips and swallowed.

'To us!' he repeated.

She had her fork poised to rootle around in the lobster's toe. She glanced up, it seemed to him with an effort, as if the lobster were the greater prize. 'Do turn it round so that I can see . . . oh, it's divine, my poppet, but not now, can't you see how messy I am? Will it disappear if it has to wait for thirty seconds?'

It irritated him that she didn't even offer to stop eating or to clean up in the fingerbowl. It had been a glance and no more, wholly insufficient when he considered the trouble he'd been to and the jibes he'd suffered from Roberson. Did she get presents like this on a regular basis? Did she have a strong-box full of them somewhere?

'Well! If that's the best you can come up with, if that's all our love means to you . . . I dare say there are other pebbles on the beach beside Nina O'Reilly.' Petulantly he waved the violinist away with his napkin and half-rose in his chair.

But by the time the savouries arrived Thomas had conceded that the moment could have been more aptly chosen, and Nina had admitted to behaving insensitively. Whatever remained of his grumpiness was dispelled around midnight by the affection of her love-making, which was helpful to his vanity and not too agile.

He always avoided any mention of the disparity between their ages for fear that she might suddenly awaken and see him for the portly old man he was. But as the cruel months tightened their grip, the fact could not be concealed. The padded socks in bed, a period of embarrassing and painful frequency, falling asleep beside the fire, a tendency to repeat anecdotes of times long past, all these were noticed and to some extent commented on by Nina. She meant no ill. Her concern was to help rather than correct him. But he took her remarks as a sign of estrangement, perhaps also of revulsion, and began to skimp on his drawing, to hurry over the little seafront happenings in case he should keep her waiting and draw displeasure on himself. Several times she asked when they were going to 'start their own Emily'. He would look out at the mist crawling in over the harsh grey sea and murmur about the hideous complications of it all, how unfair it would be on the child to have a father of his age. Yes, there were crossroads, of which this was the most sharply defined. But when, in their different ways, they had examined all the destinations on offer, it invariably became apparent that the most pleasing route was the one they were treading together. On Sundays they would exhibit their devotion in public, strolling solidly to St Peter's church amidst the aloof burghers of Brighton; Nina upright, determined, boa'd and handsome – Thomas in his silk top hat, the crook of his arm laden with her kid glove and the profounder weight of her thwarted maternity.

On St Valentine's Day he gave her a heart-shaped wreath so immense that it had to be trundled along the street on a set of wheels by the florist's two young sons. In the evening she played to him as he unwrapped her present, a painted wooden pigeon that bowed and cooed when it was wound up. With it was a card –

> Oh little bird, go to my love
> (acting the part of a carrier dove)
> and tell him that I wish to know
> if loving me he did bestow
> a flow'r garden on Nina O.

At the beginning of March the weather took a turn for the better. Skifters of dust blew across the fields and farmers rubbed their hands at the prospect of an early drilling. Thrushes sang from treetops. Rooks lost their winter surliness and began to repair their nests. Thomas perked up. The crocuses and the nodding white hats of his snowdrops were a wonderful piece of cheeriness every time he walked out of the door. Miss Mimms scolded him for them, saying, 'What happens if you leave and my new tenants hate flowers, as some people do? Who's going to pay for digging them up, you or me?' He took her firmly by the elbow – perhaps too firmly, for she yelped a little – and led her back inside. 'It's worth the chance, Miss M. Romance! Think of it, romance at my age!' Then he went singing to his studio, 'And a partridge in a pear tree,' and busied himself with Daedalus, slashing the canvas with colour even though the old man was obviously heading for trouble.

May, however, was a disappointment to him. For the first time he knew the southern air for what it was, fat and listless; and the provincialism of the short, mean, white-toothed waves, which were ever before him, stabbed him in the eye. Moreover, as the season approached, there began to be too many people in town, too many and of the wrong sort, speaking nothing but the language of railway stocks and the four per cents.

The 17th was Emily's birthday. He wrote to her, surreptitiously. What started as an awkward salutation took wing. Page after page he covered, spraying his tall, generous hand across the paper as the thunder of remorse, guilt and conflicting love overwhelmed him. He asked her advice: 'She wants me to give her a child and already calls the poor thing "our own Emily". What should I do? What dare I say to her, that you alone can be my Emily?' But later he crossed it out, savagely, with curt ripping strokes, and when the letter was posted, knew the agony of disloyalty.

His spirits went into a deeper decline. He yearned for the emptiness of Norfolk, to be living with Nina and Emily beneath its endless sprawling sky, and to see again how tiny the moon could be, like a pellet flicked into the huge bulk of the night. The landscape that he'd known since birth became endowed with magical qualities. The high church towers knuckled in flint, the loitering rivers; the brown sails of the inland water traffic gliding through meadows; asparagus, none juicier; the butterscotch leaves of the poplars bursting from their buds; the rollingness of trees and fields; and the light that was so stark and lucent, straight from God's eye, as if the air had been thinned with turpentine and all that was noisome expunged. He chose to remember nothing of the cold, of the hardness of the water and the fighting winds from Russia, only that which was magnificent to him – Fred, Emily, home and the sense of potency, of an elevation of the soul, that came from overlooking the curve of the world.

'Just a little upsy-downsy, that's all,' he admitted, and when Nina started to cry and said it would be better for them both if she released him, 'But I always feel like this in spring. Do you think it's something to do with having survived winter?' She had dressed to go out and was sitting on the edge of the bed, having brought him a second cup of tea. He soothed her hands, dwelling on the turquoise ring. 'Don't say things like that, my pet, don't ever say such a thing again. I'd be nobody without you. I'll be up and about soon enough, you just see.'

A week later he was awakened from his Sunday nap by cheers and the unmistakable thumpa-thump of a marching band. Summer had been declared and here, to honour the occasion, was the resplendent Bandmaster of the Royal Artillery, whiskered and martial, seven foot tall in his scarlet-plumed busby, swaggering down the Esplanade at the head of a blue-coated column of trumpets and cornets, trombones and drummers, oompapa and pageantry. He leaned out of the window, beside himself with excitement. 'Bravo! Bravo! That's the spirit, men,' he shouted and hurriedly pinning on his Waterloo medal, dashed out of the house and fell in behind them, throwing his chest forward and keeping excellent time for a man of his years, one hundred and ten paces a minute. The sun shone, the crowd clapped him. And when the band reached the end of the Esplanade, they did as he'd thought very likely: drained the saliva from their instruments, left the youngest members to guard them, and sauntered over to The Fishermen's Arms to drink beer. In no time at all he was in there amongst them, showing off his medal and sitting down to a comradely chinwag.

Every Sunday that summer the band climbed onto two horse-drawn wagons and came into town to play, for as long, in fact, as they were in their camp on the Downs. Soon Thomas had been enrolled as an honorary artilleryman. If he re-lived the Battle of Waterloo once, he did it a hundred times. The story about Charlie Bedingfield's head bowling down the slope with its moustaches still twitching and his tongue popping in and out as though (he embellished) he were a child slavering over a plate of ice-cream, was invariably the high point of the afternoon. Nostalgia blossomed in Thomas's heart. 'By Jove, those were the days, I'm telling you! None of this namby-pamby railway style of getting around, we marched every inch of the road and were the better men for it . . . you should have seen the Frogs scamper . . . The Duke, you ask, old Nosey? Magnificent. Like an eagle. Man in a million. Hey, fellows, this round's on me. What do you say, shall we drink to him, old blood-and-guts?'

The Bandmaster was his favourite to sketch, especially when he could be prevailed upon to wear his uniform from pre-reform days. Its splendour eclipsed even the sun, Thomas would tell him.

But he'd done them all by the time the regiment returned to London.

In August he and Nina were invited by Galley to join a party the theatre's owners were getting up for the highlight of the season, the three-day race meeting. By now they had ceased to worry about bumping into Lionel Suckling. 'Be hanged with all that,' Thomas said. 'If we're fit to be asked to a thing like this, who cares about Lionel?' So that they could be equally proud of each other, they went out and had new clothes made for the occasion. For him Nina chose a light-brown suit with curly black frogging on the pocket flaps; for herself a dress as close to turquoise as she could get, with a pale lemon jacket (double-lined in case a sea-mist made it chilly) and hat and parasol to match. The dress was a trifle snug round her bottom, but it was too late to have it altered and in any case Thomas said there was nothing to be ashamed of. 'On the contrary,' he laughed, admiringly, as she climbed into their hired landau.

The picnics and wines, the gay conversations, the sparkling sea, the races (which included a dead-heat) and the boisterous crowds, set their emotions alight. The fact of being treated, with only barely perceptible reservations, as man and wife aroused them in a way that was both novel and intense. And there was more. While the horses were being saddled up for the last race of the meeting, Nina was taken to one side by Galley. Thomas watched jealously as she waddled away in her tight dress; spied on the confabulation which took place beside the flaking bole of a plane tree – her attentive lemon hat, the movement of his gloved hands, the invisible passage of question and answer. Then she was returning, a smile on her the size of a meringue. She laced her fingers behind his neck and drew him down until her mouth was at his ear – it had concerned a new contract. 'My poppet! O my lucky, lucky poppet!' They took leave of their hosts with shameless alacrity and bolted for home where they made love as if responsible for the Creation.

It was three weeks later, on the very day – September 14th, 1852 – that Thomas was renewing the lease with Miss Mimms that the blow fell.

He was drinking tea with her in her apartment on the top floor. Quick footsteps sounded on the stairs, Nina's. She rushed in without knocking, her face paler than he'd ever seen it. A telegraph had been received at the Town Hall. Not five minutes ago she'd heard the news. She'd run every inch of the way back. The Duke of Wellington had suddenly been taken ill and had died, at 3.15 p.m., at Walmer Castle. His doctors had been away in Scotland, shooting grouse. Only a few of his family had been with him. The fits had commenced in the early hours of the morning. It had been the fourth that had killed him, she said, and fell into a chair.

Miss Mimms made a fresh pot of tea. 'There'll be people who say it's the end of an era, but I say there's always another one round the corner. Now, Mr Gage, where had we got to? Weren't we speaking about the rise in the price of coal? Or was it the water rate?'

He stared at her, horrified. How could she, at such a moment? Was she without any feelings at all? He ripped the notes from his wallet; threw them down on the table; emptied his trouser-pockets; shook the linings under her nose. 'Here, take it then, take everything I have. Dear God almighty, this was the man who saved our skins and you want to talk about the price of coal? Have you forgotten what Napoleon stood for? Does the word liberty mean nothing to you? Or that men died like beetles under his boot to save you and me and Nina? Do you know what stood between him and slavery?' He was getting confused by the torrent of his thoughts, could see nothing but the Duke lying stiff on his bed and that great fang of nose pointing to the heavens. 'Do you know? Well let me tell you, Miss landlady Mimms, he was the only man with any real balls in the whole of Europe, and not just ordinary balls' – he gesticulated wildly, oblivious to everything except the death of old Nosey, who'd seen him safely through that ferocious day – 'I mean balls the size of cows' bladders, things you could float yourself across a river on, balls of iron, the sort of balls you need to beat a monster like that. He was a god to me.' Then everything about him collapsed. He covered his ears with his hands and shook his head. 'I really don't feel very well.'

It was true. Last night he'd gone down to the wine-cellar to fetch Nina her half of Riesling, walked straight into the stone lintel and given his skull the most awful wallop. He'd thought little of it but now, a day later, it had suddenly started to hurt him dreadfully. And Arthur, Duke of Wellington had died. It *was* the end of an era, whatever the repulsive ingrate might say. He stumbled from the room and went to bed, crying from the pain.

Thirty-four

WALTER HAD deserted him. To survey the Harwich line for the chaps at the Eastern Railway Company, he'd said, his face as honest as the ace of trumps, but shifting from one foot to the other so that he, Mr Gooby, had decided he was quitting from an attack of scruples. It hadn't surprised him. Blood would out. Walter's class were all the same. Too dainty by half when it came to the axe-work, though they'd break your hand off if they saw so much as the corner of a bank-note sticking out. He didn't care. Sir Hector was in too deep to back out now. 'Goodbye, Walter,' he'd said. 'You'll make a girl a fine husband one day.'

Thomas Gage had vanished to heavens knew where and not been heard of since. In pursuit of that singer, so the gossip went. On hearing this Gooby had cocked an eyebrow and made a note to himself: a downy young gusset is not bought cheaply by a man of Thomas's age. His absence was annoying but not crucial. For it was Isabel with whom the power lay, the wronged woman as Leonard now referred to her.

And she was proving more pig-headed than he would have believed possible. The period of mourning, the family's lonely Christmas without the boy, the nasty wet weather when her arthritis would be bad – through all these he had stayed away. He'd been a model of decorum, always solicitous, never trying to force the issue. Naturally the visits that he made to Fordwell didn't carry quite the same tone without Walter. He knew, he could feel it the moment he entered the house, that he was at a disadvantage socially. But wasn't money the thing? Was she really so wealthy that she needed no more? He didn't believe it. At the end of each meeting he'd put his hands on his knees, cupping the bone, look her in the eye and say (the two of them alone in the room where Fred had died), 'So that's your last word on the subject, is it?' and she'd say, 'Not for any sum in the world. Thomas wouldn't countenance your railway, and nor shall I.' Her prim expression could be so infuriating that he sometimes wanted to rattle her by the ears and shout, 'Don't you realise he's run off with a common trollop, that the pair of them will cost you a fortune before they're through?' But he merely smiled, told himself he'd get there in the end, and by discovering an interest in her Black Minorcans, prepared the ground for his next visit.

However, all this was taking time. What if John Suckling wanted his money back? What if Sir Hector's buyer lost interest? Or railway shares took another bloody nose and the bears got loose and went around saying, 'Railways – just a fad, old boy. I'd sell at best if I was in your shoes.' How patient could he afford to be?

He bought a pair of Indian clubs, kept to his rooms in Thorpe Road, and as he exercised in singlet and calf-length drawers, pummelled his brains for the means by which the Gages were to be detached from the ownership of Fordwell, and double quick at that.

'He's dead! Dead! Gone to his Maker! "A most dolorous telegraph has been received by the Mayor. At 3.15 yesterday afternoon . . ." Mercy me, it's too awful, I can't get on top of it at all – I've got to share the news, it's so perfectly ghastly.' His landlady wandered out of the door in the direction of the servants' quarters, the black-edged newspaper agitating as she continued to read aloud. '"In a solitary, sparsely furnished turret chamber that hadn't seen a lick of paint for years" – how *could* they do that to him . . . ?'

Gooby murmured 'fifty' and stood the clubs on the table. He called after her, 'Who? Who's died?'

'The Duke, who else? Old Arthur – girls, are you in there?'

He started to towel his face. So Wellington was dead. But what was it she'd said about paint? And it was then, while his eyes were shut and the fabric was rough against his cheeks, that this single word entered his mind, which a second before had been occupied by nothing except the cost of the bottle of Waterloo port he'd once given Thomas. It rolled leisurely round his brain-pan. Of a sudden it dropped with a chink into its socket, and as it did so, an old idea came forward in new and sparkling raiment. He recognised its provenance immediately. What was extraordinary to him as he stood there stock-still, every thought arrested save this one, was that he'd actually been there at the start of it, that with his own eyes he'd seen the opera glasses falling onto the stage, Thomas rushing out of his box, and the confusion over the second lot of flowers. And now the act was complete. Fred Gage had died. The Duke had died. Life continued as wilfully as ever, and on account of what had happened on that gala night he, Julius Gooby, would prevail. No ifs and buts. The Gages would have no option but to capitulate or come to the end of their means. It was as clear as day to a rational man.

He slung the towel round his neck and sauntered off to wash. While he was changing into his business clothes, it occurred to him that Thomas was the worst kind of fool. At this, the most critical moment in his life, he had chosen to run off with a singer. Did he have no sense of proportion? There were less destructive ways of dealing with man's eternal problem. Why risk bringing the house down round his ears for the sake of a fling with Nina (her name came back to him), for the pleasure of parting a gusset that must, by the laws of the soft anatomy, be identical to every other gusset in existence? There were plenty to be had in Norwich. He could have shown Thomas just the place, on the smarter side of Fye Bridge – expensive but clean, which was the main thing. Why go to all the bother of chasing a woman, why extend himself? It must be for love, he supposed, grunting as he speared his cravat with a mother-of-pearl pin. Love, for God's sake, when such a business as this was at stake. Then Thomas was indeed a fool and no one should feel sorry for him.

Leaning forward he picked at his teeth. He shook out his lapels and looked at himself sideways in the pier-glass.

His plan was despicable, he made no bones about it. He wished, because he thought he should at least make the gesture of wishing, that it could be otherwise. He had nothing against the Gages or against Nina, who must of necessity be involved. Thomas was a harmless relic from the age of squires and Isabel (he went down the passage, towards the narrow hallway where his hat rested on the shelf) – well, he didn't understand her. She was probably a well-meaning soul. People talked respectfully of her charitable work. But how could any woman behave like that when her husband had run off? It was beyond him. Life wasn't long enough to work it out. Anyway they were ripe, Thomas and Isabel, and sooner or later someone would take advantage of them. First come, first served. He brushed his hat on his sleeve, checked the latch-key was in his pocket, and departed to call upon Leonard Lutwylch.

The breeze was from the south and the yeasty smell of the brewery quite strong as he crossed Foundry Bridge. That there were orchards to be savoured on both sides of Rose Lane did not concern him. He walked quickly, a neat, muscled, brooding figure. The Gages were the past. It was the turn of him and his like to be the rulers. Everywhere factories were being built. New centres of wealth and power were rising. Town would oust country. The common man would get the vote. The railway cause would conquer the land. Long life and prosperity to all, that was the cry these days. About time too, he said to himself. But he modified his opinion as he got caught up in the jostle of London Street and through pale sardonic eyes observed the goitred beggars, and the deformities and vacuous expressions of all those – every tenth person, he estimated – whose parents had married too closely within the family. Prosperity for all was clearly a nonsense. For some, for the ablest, that was how it had to be. What was a rising man to tread upon if there was an insufficiency of fools in the world?

He entered the Market Place and paused, the Guildhall in front of him. Take the Gages, for example—

Oh but it was truly despicable what he had in mind. Would Thomas's ghost come down and haunt him for this deed? The man could be ruined if he didn't wake up and pay attention. It might kill him off. He was such a weak fellow within himself. And his boy, that poor innocent butchered soul, would his ghost appear too?

He grounded his cane and leaned upon the knob, ivory with silver piqué. But why be sentimental about them? It wasn't he who'd caused Fred's death. The coroner had listed all the parties at fault, the boy, the dog, the stationmaster, the engineering works, even the clouds of steam that had obscured the intention of the engine-driver, and concluded it was an Act of God. Nevertheless Fred had died in agony. Was it *right* that his parents should be punished further? No sooner had he thought this than he baulked at the word. These questions of right and wrong, these higher subtleties, were not for him to decide. Getting along in life was enough by itself. Or was it? He lowered his chin and rubbed a shaving itch against the back of his hand.

Suddenly the cathedral bells opened up behind him, a raucous jumble of biffs and bongs as the ringers practised their changes. The noise occupied the air completely. It rose, thumped the clouds and fell back, and he thought: I bought the boy his ticket. Perhaps I was a little responsible. No more than that, a fraction only, repeating always the word perhaps. And in the same easily flowing breath, Therefore I would sleep better if the burden of the Gages' downfall could be shifted onto the shoulders of another.

He looked at the Guildhall clock. In ten minutes the lawyer would be sipping his morning coffee. Leonard would ask him if he'd heard about the Duke, wondering meanwhile what had brought him there, whether Isabel had altered her mind. Blandly, though maybe tapping the edge of the desk for emphasis, he'd tell Leonard matters were desperate; that he could forget about selling his fields to the North Norfolk unless he could come up with a new plan to dispossess the Gages. Was the price Leonard would receive for his ground large enough to stimulate inventiveness? He thought so. Joan had quite fallen out of love with their villa. She wanted to move back into town; could talk of little else but the parties she'd have when they bought that ancient house in the Upper Close. Leonard might shout and roar but in the end he'd do what the lady wanted. Therefore the bait should be sufficient.

But did Leonard have the gumption to assemble these intricate pieces and thus arrive at the same answer as he had? Did he have it in him to be, how should he say, contemptible and unflinching all in one? The Gages had been Leonard's clients for a long time, and the old man, her father, before that. Was there anything other than habit that bound them to each other?

He took a turn down Dove Lane while he considered it. He remembered how regularly Leonard complained that Isabel was as tight as a miser. So there it was. The purse, the purse, it all swung on that. Therefore he'd inveigle Leonard into a new negotiation.

He would concede an increased payment for his fields – fight like the devil of course and surrender with ill grace. Then Leonard would be catched alright. After which he had only to be set running on the right lines, prompted here and there, and the job would be done. Perhaps Leonard had already thought of it but hadn't dared say. In any event he would gasp at the enormity of what Leonard was proposing, call it perfidy on the grand scale and decline to have anything whatsoever to do with it. Leonard would retort, 'Well, you think of a better way, then,' and thus the responsibility would cease to be his. For however one looked at it, only one way now remained to get the Gages out, and Leonard would have thought of it, all by himself.

The blue stable doors of Lutwylch & Lutwylch were in front of him. He stopped in the archway to adjust his neck-cloth. Then he clattered the lion's head knocker and entered without waiting.

His friends had felt sorrow rather than surprise when Thomas disappeared in pursuit of Nina. They believed him too rooted a fellow to make a go of it outside Norfolk, and feared he would come to grief. 'If only that boy of his hadn't died. Threw him off balance, wouldn't you say?' men said over luncheon in the Club. His ladies remained silent and kept their fingers crossed for him.

Isabel was of more lasting interest to everyone. To have lost a son and a husband within the space of two months and yet have remained, so far as anyone could tell, unmarked by either event, aroused universal curiosity.

All of her visitors – most of whom were female – were entertained to tea and Mrs Macbride's cakes in the fatal room. Nothing had changed: the furniture, the gloomy curtains, the dull brown colours, the little rustling fire like a hen's nose. So much was it as it always had been that Isabel's guests would instinctively examine the carpet for bloodstains and only look away, guiltily, when she spoke to them. They felt they were being asked to believe that Fred hadn't got back from school yet, that Thomas was out painting somewhere in the garden, that nothing unusual had happened.

Gooby was not alone in being unable to understand her. Sympathy there was, but it was difficult to convey this with complete and mutual satisfaction to so reticent a woman. Yet there was no shortage of people willing to brave the horrible room and the small talk round the tea-table. Some, like Gooby, wanted to shake her until she rattled. Those somnolent eyes! Her placidity! 'A cow knows more about emotion,' they'd say to their husbands afterwards. Others were driven wild by her piousness. All were agreed that if she said once more, 'To err is human, to forgive divine,' as lugubriously as if she were the Holy Ghost, they'd strangle her. However there was a morbid fascination about the scene that no one could resist: Isabel – the table – the carpet – would Thomas suddenly appear in the doorway, travel-stained and penitent? So when the weather was bad or there was nothing more exciting to do, a steady trickle of one-horse gigs arrived at Fordwell.

It was only to her closest friends like Dolly Baunt that Isabel was able to open her heart. She had displeased God. He had taken Fred from her as punishment. She had failed Thomas in his great moment of need. And she'd withheld from him that which a woman should not. This, however, she only intimated, backing into the recesses of her wing chair so that her face lay in shadow.

The hint was enough for Dolly. 'Whatever can you mean? Where does "should" come into it?' she declared stoutly. 'That's no crime. I know any number of women who can't bear to be touched by their husbands. Not only can they not bear it, but they say as much and lock their doors at night. Pull yourself together now, Isabel. You're in danger of becoming an old misery.'

'But Thomas is different. Women prey on him so.'

'Indeed he is. He's gone off with a singer, my girl, that's how he's different.'

'To err—'

'Rubbish! Pure stuff and rubbish! Just because Mr Pope felt sorry for himself one morning, it doesn't mean you have to copy him. Try saying, "Damn your eyes, Thomas," and you'll feel the better for it.'

Dolly Baunt, big, bushy and forthright – flat feet, strong in the nose – accepted a third cup of tea and returned to the charge. 'The lady in question, what of her? Are you going to tell me she captured him by accident? Whoops, like knocking over a glass of water? Is that what you mean by human erring?'

'Of course not, she took advantage of him,' Isabel said indignantly.

'There you are. So let's have no more of Mr Pope's nonsense. Time to look the facts in the face.'

'But my dear, we *are* at the facts. Thomas is the man he is. Already I've forgiven him. When he comes home, nothing will have changed, you'll see for yourself. It's the way we've arranged our lives.' She rose and walked over to draw the curtains. She halted beside the oak table and of a sudden laughed, closer to that than a giggle, a sound so unexpected that Dolly, who had swiftly seized the last slice of cake, choked and blew a spray of crumbs over the pug. Venus sneezed, and turning Isabel said, 'It's his last adventure. He's getting quite old, you know. In fact I feel almost sorry for him.'

'After behaving as he has? You can't! Really, Isabel, you are the most trying woman I know.'

'He's had several adventures since we got married. I can always tell. Mrs Farrant was the last before that – before Nina.' She pulled the curtains to and stood with her back to them, fluffing at her skirt. 'I never thought I'd be able to say her name. But now – do you believe that I could actually forgive her too?' Her face had softened and was full of a staunch beauty.

'So it's back to Saint Isabel, is it?' sniffed Dolly.

'All these people who haven't spoken to me for years, I know why they've come here. But they don't understand, how can they? I could forgive Nina because one day my Thomas will get tired of her and leave. His adventure – that's how he sees it, I promise you – will be over and he'll come quickly home, dust at his heels.'

'And you'll take him back?'

'What else? One must be constant to one's faith.'

'Well, Isabel, there aren't many women like you left in England these days. I trust you're not deluding yourself.'

'He'll come. His daughter is here and his home and all we've built together. And I am here. Does it surprise you that I should rate affection more powerful than love? But it is so, and Thomas will return to it. He cannot abide unsteadiness in his life. That Nina, do you suppose she has anything to give him except for . . . ? Enough! I don't believe I've had such an intimate conversation with anyone apart from Thomas. Ever!'

She pulled a chair up to the table. Dolly got her travelling piquet cards out of her bag and began to go through the rules again. Isabel was still learning. Her face settled back into its normal mould as she concentrated.

Thirty-five

ALL OVER Norfolk flags were flying at half-mast for the Duke. Sam Buzzerd got drunk and was insolent to Isabel. The next day, as she, Harriet and Emily were stitching the crepe for their mourning bands, they had a discussion about whether he should be sacked.

'It's all very well us talking about it, but it's really only your father who has the authority,' Isabel eventually said to Emily.

'How do you mean? If he's not here, surely it's we who must act in his place.'

'I mean the force of character, dear. Sam would just laugh at me if I told him to leave.'

'But we can't go on like this. He gets ruder and ruder every day. What he said to you was hateful. It's almost as if he owns the place. Soon it'll be him giving us the orders.' Emily was wearing a nice printed cotton dress, thin for the time of year. Her body was beginning to ripen and her face growing more and more like Thomas's: not beautiful, but full of expression and always accessible. She made Harriet lean forward and took her blue woollen pullover off the back of her sister's chair.

'Father and Sam fought side by side, remember,' Harriet said. 'Even if he was here – we all know how easily Father gets diddled by a good story. Sam'd think of something.' She'd become bolder. The month she'd spent with her friend in Norwich listening to what everyone had to say about Thomas had quite opened her eyes.

'I'm afraid he'll take it badly, the Duke dying alone in that drab attic,' Isabel said.

'But Papa *hated* being a soldier,' Emily protested.

'True, but to have fought at such a battle, under a man like the Duke of Wellington – to have been *there*, on *that* day – I know it means the earth to Thomas. Of course he'd never want to do it again, but as a man gets to a certain stage in his life and starts to look back instead of forward, well, it's there, like a milepost, something to be proud to have done. He treasures that medal of his, though you'll never get him to say as much.'

'So when's he coming home, that's what I want to know. He ought to be here now dealing with Sam. He's the one who's responsible for us.' Emily looked sternly at her mother.

'I expect we'll hear from him any day now,' Isabel said briskly. Thomas's long silence hadn't changed her opinion one whit. In fact the Duke's death had made her more confident than ever. He'd be terribly shaken up. A silly young thing like Nina wouldn't know the half of how to comfort him. 'A shout and there he'll be on the doorstep as large as life. Isn't that so?' she said to Mrs Macbride who had just come in to talk about the laundry. But she and the girls had heard it too often before and were silent. Isabel continued, 'Or a message boy will ride out from the Telegraph Company and we'll find Thomas wants to be met off the train. That's how it'll be. A pull on the bell-rope – a little brown face at the door – a little brown envelope in his mitten – and abra-cadabra!' She clapped her hands and gazed humorously around.

'We'd be the first folks hereabouts to get one of those things,' Mrs Macbride said.

'My friend Dolly Baunt knows someone who had one,' Isabel said. 'It was handed in at London at five minutes past nine and the boy delivered it just as she was about to pour the vicar his midday sherry. The stopper was in her hand when the knock sounded.'

'What did it say?' asked Emily.

'Oh Emily dear, must you always know every tiny detail of everything? Dolly didn't tell me. It was probably a private matter.'

'It's a wonder how they do it,' Mrs Macbride said. 'Tappings through the air, it makes you ask yourself what else they're up to.'

'Not through the air, down the wires you see beside the railway,' Emily said loftily.

They rose to go into lunch. The workings of the Electric Telegraph Company being of no interest to any of them except Emily, they talked instead about the medical nature of Dolly's 'worm', as they referred to her appetite. A gradual relaxation of the rules of conversation was another change in the house since Thomas's departure. As a result they found they were discussing everything much more seriously. Dolly's appetite seemed a perfectly proper subject for mealtime.

Sam was now rarely sober. In the middle of October Leonard Lutwylch sent a note round saying it was time they got together to discuss family matters. Isabel decided to take him aside and request that *he* dismiss Sam for them. This was approved wholeheartedly by Emily and Harriet, who promptly arranged to take a basket of provisions up to old Mrs Peach so as to be out of the way. They had no wish to be around if Sam stormed into the house and there was a shouting match. Mr Lutwylch was being paid to do the dirty work and do it he must, man to man – but they'd rather be somewhere else at the time.

They drank a jigger of Mrs Peach's cowslip wine while she griddled scones for them. They heard everything there was to hear about Jammy's career (he was hopeful of being promoted to Guard, business was that quick), and returned to Fordwell as it was growing dark. Both of them were tiddly in a girlish sort of way, which embarrassed Harriet, seeing as how Sam was to be sacked for the very same thing. Emily said there was all the difference between brandy and cowslip wine: Harriet shouldn't be so delicate. They approached the house through the garden to avoid any possibility of a chance meeting with Sam. There were no lights on that side of the ground floor, only in their mother's bedroom, which surprised them.

She was lying there, eyes wide open, hands flat upon her stomach, still wearing her black bootees, which were splayed out stark against the counterpane. They halted in the doorway and looked in utter disbelief at the jutting boots, at their mother resting in the afternoon. It was all so contrary to every instruction they'd received as children.

'Mother!' exclaimed Harriet.

She looked despairingly at the girls, then rolled her eyes away, towards the heavy wardrobe against the far wall, showing them the red, angry curve of one eyeball.

'Mother, what's wrong? Is it because of what Sam said to you?'

She emitted a long, shuddering 'ooh,' and was silent. Harriet ran

downstairs for a vinegar compress. Emily went and sat on the edge
of the bed.

'Was it so very awful? Say something, please, Mama.'

Isabel turned back, a tear running down her cheek. She dug her
elbows into the pillow and hoisted herself up. 'Leonard—'

'What about him? Wouldn't he do it?'

'Mr Gooby was with him. Leonard never told me he'd be
coming as well. He'd said it was to be just a family discussion, I
thought about your father being away and how it might affect us
. . . The two of them, immediately opposite me, and my Thomas
nowhere in sight. I was alone, an old woman with no one to help
her. They were *ruthless*, like animals fighting for a bone.'

'But what did they want? Was it the railway again?'

'Leonard did the talking but I saw at once it was Mr Gooby
who was behind it all. He sat there so smugly, his shrewish little
eyes not blinking once.'

'So it *was* the railway. But you've told them "No" a hundred
times. And Papa said the same, I can remember him saying it
downstairs, over tea.'

'They want to put it through our garden and across the bridge.
Leonard said they'd take down the old one and build something
much larger, in iron. They're going to do it whether we like it or
not. He said, would I agree to sell, yes or no.'

'And did you?'

Harriet returned with the compress and bathed Isabel's brow
and cheeks and behind her ears. She began to speak more firmly. 'I
said, "No, not unless Thomas wishes it." And Leonard laughed at
me, right into my face, and said, "We all know *he's* not coming
back in a hurry. Yours is the signature that counts, my dear."'

'He had the nerve to call you that?' Emily said.

'But they can't force you to sell, can they?' Harriet said.

'Leonard said he'd brought the papers for me to sign. I said,
What about my father's jointure, what about the safeguards –
meaning we both had to sign if ever we decided to sell. "Don't you
worry about that, it's all been dealt with by the courts," he said.
Mr Gooby got the pen from the desk. Of course there was no ink
in the well, hasn't been for years as I do all my business in the
small room. "There'll be some somewhere," he said and then, in
the doorway, "Tell her, Leonard, tell her what'll happen if she

doesn't." It was horrible, horrible beyond words. After all these years, and going on holiday with him . . . I can't bear it. They'd ruin us without a moment's pity, not a shred of decency between them.'

'But did you sign?' broke out Emily and Harriet at the same time, hating the idea of having to leave their home.

'"Never!" I said to Leonard, and I told them to go away. But they're desperate to get the bridge from us. All they can think of is how to make money. I'm so afraid. They'll do it, I know they will. They're capable of anything, those two. If only Thomas were here,' and she thumped the pillows with her fists.

'But what exactly can they do if you don't sign?' Emily said. 'They can't break the law, so what else is there?'

Isabel's white face stared at the ceiling. She said slowly, 'Leonard said they'd destroy my paint business, starting with the London trade and going on until I saw reason. It was my father who made him. I trusted him, I sent my friends to him—' She covered her face and began to sob, huge racking gulps. Then she rolled onto her side and opened her arms. 'Oh, my children, my children,' and they clung to each other as they had when Fred died.

Their first thought was to rid themselves of Leonard, 'that evil, evil man'. They decided to confide in Tobias Rouch. In his opinion they'd find no one local prepared to stand up to Lutwylch, and would have to take everything to a London lawyer. He gave Isabel a name, a cousin of his wife, and arranged by telegraph a meeting in a week's time. 'A whole week?' Isabel said. But nothing could be done sooner.

Her face was lively with hope when she got off the train. (Harriet and Emily had plucked up the courage to take the gig out by themselves when they went to meet her.)

'Flagrant abuse of his powers, that's what Mr Bancroft said about Leonard and the paintworks – instantly, without hesitation. "How quickly can you stop him?" I asked. "He may be up to his devilry even as we speak." He said he'd put a junior to work on the papers first thing in the morning. "A fortnight, then?" I said. But he only smiled. I should have been stronger with him but I was so grateful that he even consented to see me . . . my goodness, it's so exhausting getting around London, I think I'll go straight up to bed when we get home. We can talk about it tomorrow.'

They were having their council of war the next morning when, by one of those accidents that govern everything of consequence, news of Thomas arrived, albeit indirectly. They were so deep in the business of Leonard that they heard nothing until Mrs Macbride called through that Jem Paston, one of the Norwich carriers, was outside with a package for Mr Gage. Simultaneously there was a tap on the window pane and there was Jem himself, and looking in at them over his shoulder, as gaunt as a camel's, the head of his ugly piebald mare.

'What did I say?' cried Isabel. The four of them trooped through the hall and out onto the terrace. 'A picture, that's for sure. Harriet, look sharp now and find a pair of pliers. I expect he's starting to get his things together for coming home.'

Paston and Mrs Macbride carried the wooden-boxed case up the steps. The day being fine, they unpacked it on the spot and propped it against the stone bench. 'It's not his best,' Emily said doubtfully. 'I think he must have gone back to Daedalus, look, there he is with his plans laid out on the table. But what all these shadows can be – and the skull in the corner, and the rats, and that lout grinning behind his hand. I don't know, I don't know at all. It seems an unhappy picture to me.'

'Firewood!' shouted Jem Paston as he drove off. 'Warm my bum on it at Christmas, that's what I'd do with a thing like that.'

'Don't be so impertinent. Anyway, what do you know about pictures?' Mrs Macbride called back loyally.

'I do agree with you, Em, it is rather an odd composition,' Isabel said.

'Passing strange I'd call it,' Mrs Macbride said, hands on hips, moving her head one way and then the other as though trying to decide which was the top and which the bottom of the picture. 'What ever can be up with Mr Gage to be wandering round with that sort of nonsense in his head? If he was mine, I'd get him back home, never mind how.' She looked challengingly at the family and began to gather up the bits of packing, making small muttering noises like a pot on the hob. An envelope slipped out onto the terrace. She glanced at the address and without straightening held it up for Emily, who was the nearest. 'Master's in Brighton, that's where he's got to.' She went into the house, arms burdened.

Isabel wanted it but Emily jumped onto the bench and held it out of her reach. 'Brighton! Ugh!' She tore it open. Her face, which a moment earlier had been so full of joy, clouded over as she read the official copperplate writing. 'Oh poor Father, they don't want it. A Mr Jeffreys at the Academy says the judges don't assemble until next spring and in the meantime he ventures to return Daedalus since he scarcely thinks it apt for consideration in its present state.' She stepped down and let Isabel take the letter from her. 'The beasts! How do they know Mr Wheaton won't buy it?'

'Every cloud has a silver lining. At least we know where he is now,' Isabel said calmly, though it was far from how she felt. She started to read it for herself.

'I suppose Brighton was where Father sent the picture from,' Harriet said, 'and Mr Jeffreys gave the wrong orders to his carrier.'

'But what luck for us!' cried Emily. 'Kind, helpful Mr Jeffreys! Where is it again – Adelaide Crescent, we'll be able to find that easily enough. When shall we leave, Mama? I say tomorrow. Father'll knock the stuffing out of Mr Lutwylch. And Mr Gooby too. How I *hate* that name!'

Flushing, Isabel said, 'I really don't think we can appear at his house just like that.'

'So how are we to do it? We've got to get him back, got to.'

'Let's try sending him a telegraph, like Mr Rouch did,' Harriet suggested. 'And if that doesn't bring him home, we must write to him, all of us together.'

Mrs Macbride returned with a broom and dustpan and brush. They helped her sweep the terrace clean and afterwards agreed to drive into town to the Telegraph Company that afternoon. Lutwylch, Gooby, the railway, they should make everything clear, Emily said, even if the whole of Norwich got to hear about it. But Isabel, who remembered very well her discomfiture when her father's disgrace became public property, insisted they keep the telegraph as short as possible. Moreover, she was worried about its cost.

It was said: it was done, before any more time was lost. That night Emily had a brainwave. Thomas would be bound to travel up to town for the Duke's funeral. If the telegraph had no effect, they'd go and fetch him home bodily from London. Now that they had his address, they could write to him with a rendez-vous, perhaps a number of them at different times in case the crowds made things difficult. What good fortune that Mr Jeffreys had made that mistake! She couldn't wait to see her father. His letters had filled her with worry. He'd soon start painting in his old way once they had him back at Fordwell, out of harm's way. She covered several pages in her mind with rich, loving phrases. On reaching the end, she found herself wishing also to convey some sense of rebuke. She made no pretence of understanding the force that had borne him away so abruptly. Nevertheless, she thought something should be said, on behalf of her mother. 'Now I'm going to be your little bossy-boots . . .' No sooner had the words taken shape than she fell asleep.

In the morning they carried Daedalus into Thomas's painting-room, as it were the first instalment of his return. Their spirits were recovering. They knew where he was; the telegraph had been sent; the new lawyer had all the documents; they were getting a grip on the rudder. They discussed how the paint business should be run when Leonard was dismissed. 'But we mustn't let Thomas near it. He'd be a disaster, a complete disaster! Small enterprises only for Thomas from now on,' Isabel said.

Thirty-six

THE FUNERAL was to be on a colossal scale. In October Thomas went to London to do his banking. At the same time he would enquire if the Waterloo men were to have a place of their own in the parade.

His interview with the equerry was unsatisfactory, despite showing him his medal. A lieutenant, did he say? He was sorry. A final decision had yet to be taken. He knew it was getting late in the day, but there it was. A rumour was doing the rounds that only colonels and higher ranks were to receive specific instructions.

'Then I shall pay my respects to the old bugger in my own way,' Thomas said, and took a cab across town to Barclay, Bevan & Co.

Finding Adkins without custom and thinking he appeared out of sorts, Thomas spread himself over the counter in a conversational manner. 'You look as though you could do with a good holiday,' he said. 'Don't have anything to do with Brighton though, far too many people. Go home to Norfolk and get some of our honest air into your lungs. Norfolk, dear heavens, that's where we should all be.' A saucier thought coming to him, he checked there was no one behind him and lowered his voice. 'Or you could try a first-class strumpet. Quite the thing for a fellow who's not getting his oats as per the tariff, eh!' and his eyes disappeared between a forest of crinkles as he considered Adkins, who was the least forward man he knew, slinking into a brothel. 'No offence taken, I hope,' he added swiftly on seeing the chaste cheeks colour and the shocked eyes, 'none meant, I assure you. You just look a little peaky. At least you can't have a headache as bad as mine. Comes and goes but when it comes it's like a damned great hammer against my skull. Been free of it this last week, so here's to hoping . . . Everything alright otherwise? . . . Now,' – he rapped the counter, not despotically, more like someone with lunch and a pint of claret on his mind – 'serve it up then. It seems I've acquired some expensive tastes of late. Thrifty to fifty, spend to the end, there's a motto for you. Had it from a fellow years ago, an extraordinarily fine fellow. Apt, wouldn't you say?'

He gazed round the banking hall, at the columns of brown and red scagliola, all a-squiggle, at the ponderous cornices, the clerks at their ledgers, the quiet orderliness of everything. His fingers pattered on the counter. A gentleman of the officer type was reading the bank's copy of *The Times* in a leather armchair. After he'd got his money, he'd do the same. Then he'd have lunch and drop by the Academy to ask the Secretary what he thought of Daedalus. Give him a friendly rocket for not having sent him a receipt. What was his name? Jefferson? Jackson?

The voice seemed distant, as if Adkins was speaking from the far side of a thick belt of trees. 'Mr Gage? You're not listening, Mr Gage. I said no monies have been received for you this month.'

He turned negligently towards the anxious, owlish face. 'No money? That's a bore. Sub me till it arrives, will you? Say a hundred to keep the wolf from the door.'

Behind him *The Times* crackled. 'Daylight robbery, that's what I call it,' the officer muttered, slapping the paper down and stamping out.

'Make it a hundred and twenty if you can,' Thomas said over the edge of his shoulder, watching a man enter with his three marriageable daughters, each with a parasol and one with a tippet of Russian fox round her neck, like his autumn present to Nina.

'Please, sir, it's not easy to say this—' Adkins was off his stool and almost crawling over the counter in his attempt to be discreet.

'Eh? Have I overdone it? A hundred too much, is it?'

'Sir, telegraphs have been exchanged between this office and Mr Gurney. His people say funds have ceased to be available to your name. They speak of a family business as having encountered some difficulties in its trade.'

'Just as I said, a holiday is what you need. No funds, my fanny. You've got the wrong man. Thomas Gage, 1 Adelaide Crescent—'

'You don't understand, sir. There is no money for you. The money has been stopped in Norwich.'

'No money? How do you expect me to live without any money? Do I look like the sort of chap who can live on bread and water?'

'I don't know, Mr Gage. I believe there are people who live like that but I can't say how it's done.'

'I'm speechless. That I should be treated like a common defaulter after all these years with Mr Gurney – fetch me a director. I'll put him right quickly enough.'

Adkins smoothed a black sleeve across his brow. What a tit-bit for the wife! And she always telling him his job was so boring! First he says I should take a prostitute for the night, next thing *I* have to tell *him* he's halfway to Carey Street. Well! He thumped the bell harder than was needed and though only one person was waiting, fairly bellowed 'Next please!' at the same time as the manager was attempting to chivvy Thomas into his office.

'Only a moment, my dear sir . . . a matter of a cheque recently presented for payment . . . some regrettable shortage of funds . . . a discussion . . .'

Thomas had heard enough. He was benumbed by what Adkins had said, which seemed to him to be a thickening of a modern and quite terrifying hostility. He had felt it dealing with Gooby, among the Brighton shopkeepers, moving around London, and now, unscabbarded, in the action of this bank clerk. People had become sharper. In the old days, when cash was scarce everywhere, life had been a struggle that was common to all. The inevitability of hardship had bred tolerance and a stoical sort of humour. Even the poorest had had a nobility about them. But now that anyone could make a million on the Exchange there was only greed to be found, and fear and jealousy.

He perceived in all this a threat to him personally. The words 'cheque' and 'recently presented' could only be interpreted in the same light, as the next lunge at him by this spiteful epoch.

Showing the whites of his eyes, he was past the doorman, round the corner and three streets away before he slackened his pace. The sanctuary of the milling lunch-time crowd beckoned him. He buried himself in their midst, shuffled with them to he cared not where, and endlessly sifted through the coins in his pockets, weighing and gauging yet all the while frightened of disappointment were he to stop and count them. Soon his palms were slippery with sweat. Two farthings got stuck between his fingers and he called on them to mate and have issue. At the bottom, always at the bottom among the lint, was a heavy and important coin. Be a full fat guinea, he pleaded, and his dry lips repeated the incantation many times as the hubbub of the throng, of the street curs and the shouting cabmen, and the malevolence of the hazy, crouching sun pressed in on him, squeezing his soul like dough in a vice.

No money. He'd never had no money before. Shortages, yes – who hadn't? – but always he'd known there was money in the offing. Perhaps beyond his reach for the moment yet attainable at some point, in the manner of a shopkeeper's card hanging from its nail with the promise to return after lunch. And now there was nothing. The why of it didn't enter his mind. He could concentrate only on the fact of nothingness, on the annihilation of zero. It was as if someone had suddenly said, 'You can't wear clothes any more.' What would one do? What was it possible to do? How long could he survive? The whole thing was unbeginnable. Nina, the presents she so adored, the warmth of her body, their love larger than a continent, than the seven seas entwined – what was he to say to her? Never mentioning the rent and Miss Mimms—

Dear God, and coals and food and visits to the doctor – he closed his face and marched on blindly. Without warning – not a drum-beat – oh, but that was craven of someone, the meanest form of stabbing. What had Adkins meant? How was it possible that Isabel's business had gone down?

He was shivering, his skin grey and loose. Grapes of sweat were bowling down his nose. Panic clawed at his throat. He saw the debtors' prison in front of him, the gates swing open, Emily's pathetic face at the grille, chains, stone-breaking and the final moments, coughing on a bed of damp straw. An hour ago wealth and ease – and now nothing.

He passed two beggar women on their stools, trays of lardy cakes and meat pies on their squat raddled knees. He turned in his tracks and looked down at them, at the bluebottles crawling over the congealing gravy. How did one get one's nerve up to do that sort of thing?

'Only a penny for a gentleman like yourself. Take pity on a woman's starving children – baked no more'n ten minutes back – feel the warmth in 'em – oh sir, please . . .'

A penny each! A miserable copper! Nina's turquoise ring had cost him twenty pounds. Nearly 5,000 pies – how long would it take to find that number of customers? How many pies could one sell an hour? Did people eat throughout the day? What if one had to go off and have a piss, or it rained? He realised that he was thinking small, as Emily did, and this had a calming effect on him. Yes, that was it, he had to be practical; apply himself to the problem in a soldierly way, determine the fixed points and construct a plan around them, step by step.

An inventory, that was the place to start. Lutwylch had been fond of preaching about the importance of a regular inventory to prevent thieving: oils, barrels, canisters, the raw materials of richness. He fingered his change again. He could sink no lower than what he had in his pocket.

So: he'd left home with thirty shillings, plus or minus. Ten shillings and sixpence had gone on the first-class fare to London, fourpence on a newspaper, eightpence and one and fourpence on hansom cabs (but what had he tipped them?), and sixpence on morning coffee with a vanilla cake coated in hot chocolate sauce. He'd had his shoes polished – a penny; and his whiskers trimmed – another sixpence. Total expenditure – thirteen shillings and eleven-pence; residue – sixteen shillings and a penny.

The crowd had thinned. He found he was in the vicinity of St Paul's and laid a course for its dome, having the idea he would rest there a while and get the feel of the place in his bones for when the Duke was buried.

But never mind the Duke for now. What was important was that he had sixteen shillings certain and Miss Mimms was due her rent in a week. Very well, they would move into cheaper lodgings. Retrieve his deposit and improve the position by ten pounds. Then what? And Nina? Would she do the laundry, cook and make the bed? He tried to capture the scene and knew it instantly for a failure. Not Nina doing chores in a mob-cap, sweeping the stairs on her hands and knees. He could never ask it of her, not of a woman who'd given him so much.

He picked an alley to take him from Gresham Street to St Paul's.

It was shabby and the buildings decrepit, not the sort of place he would normally have cared to venture. But the washing slung from one side to the other was a picture, and his spirit desperate for colour. The blues and reds struck his eye, filling him with the memory of a flag the Russians had flaunted in Paris after Waterloo. Back and forth they'd swept it, carelessly, drunkenly, amid peals of childish laughter. An officer riding up to remonstrate, they'd netted him for the sheer fun of it. Horse rearing, the officer's cocked hat rising beneath the flag like the egg-cup in a pie – happy chaos! Happy distant days! So up the alley he went and halted in a derelict doorway to count his coins. He picked out the lint. Be methodical now, Thomas. What you see is the exchequer.

It was neither better nor worse than he'd reckoned. The status quo, or as you were – sixteen shillings and some copper. First things first: he had to get back to Brighton. He pulled out his Bradshaw. Five and fourpence was the cheapest fare, in an open truck, cheek by jowl with the workers, a hard bench and rain and smuts for two long hours. What was he to say to her, ragged as a tramp and stinking of railway filth? Was she the sort of woman to say, 'Here, help yourself, I've got plenty for us both'? Better not to risk it. Better to have a plan; look bold; carry it off in the grand manner.

However, he had no idea for the moment what this might be. He stood his cane against the wall, raised his hat and re-settled it towards the back of his head, at an angle. Something would come if he gave it a chance. He took out his note-case. There was never a harm in hoping.

But whatever was he thinking of! He'd paint! Rigorously and with discipline, in the commercial style, quick, dainty sketches of lovers on the pier. A handful of brush strokes and charge them a pound. Or run up some views to sell to the souvenir shops. In the winter there'd be stormscapes – fishing boats in danger, tumbling masts and green water, marvellous acts of heroism. All he'd need was a canvas-bottomed stool, a luncheon box and a bottle of lemonade pop. He could do them standing on his head, knock 'em out by the dozen—

Or how about becoming Nina's agent? Kick Pauntley out and do the job himself? There'd be tricks to it. Every business had its ins and outs. It'd take him a week or two to learn the ropes. Of course Nina would have to be won over; she could be bullet-nosed where money was concerned. A cautious entangling manoeuvre, then. Not a blessed word about Adkins, shortages or survival. He'd have to raise enough wind, here in London, to make everything appear normal. Then he'd get to work on her. But where was the money to be had? He pulled at his nose. Well now, what about tapping his old friend Roberson for a start?

The voice at the bottom of the steps was thick with fatigue. 'Waiting for the daughter, are you? Can't say as how I recognise you, there are so many of 'em.'

'Pausing only,' Thomas said, standing to one side to let him into the house. 'On my way to Long Acre.'

The man – a porter perhaps, grimy, beaten by the world, his leather shoulder pads very shiny – trudged up the steps. He glanced at Thomas's note-case. 'Looking for something, were you?' They were standing very close. The points of his waistcoat were curled like stale bread. He smelt much the same as Jammy had some mornings, like chicken stock on the simmer. A couple of slatterns were airing themselves at the door opposite, grinning. 'Early shift. Ten hours for just pence. It'd make you spit if you had any spit left in you. How's your eyes? Need any help looking into the fancy thing of yours?'

'Empty,' Thomas said, and holding out his note-case, he parted every fold to show it was so. 'Not a farthing.'

'You too?'

'Me too. But I have hopes of replenishment. How far do you reckon to Long Acre? An hour?'

'Depends how big your bloody feet are . . . eh, mister, wait a tick, she'd do it cheap, five bob on the dresser. The change in your pocket, that sort of thing. Have her like a doggy if it pleases you. All one to the likes of Lizzie. Sixpence extra to belt her a few. Eh? Penny a crack. But no more'n six or she starts singing. Nice white skin, you'd like her . . .' The leering face, the teeth and the breath, closed in on Thomas, who retreated.

The man started menacingly down the steps after him, but it was only to fetch a hod of coal from the basement. Thomas walked hastily up the alley between silent stares, slapping his note-case against his wrist to show anyone was welcome to it.

Now he was in a hurry. It was imperative he catch Roberson

before he closed for the day. He splashed out a shilling on a cab, which got him as far as Lincoln's Inn Fields, and puffed the rest of the way at a shambling trot. Of course Adkins had only been saying what he'd been told to say. It was Isabel who'd cut him off, no one else could have had a sufficient motive.

The door was ajar and he hurtled in, red-faced, breathless, and boiling with pent-up indignation. 'She's no right to do this to me. One third of the business is mine and one third of the profits, to spend as I wish. Who does she think she is? You can't conceive how humiliated I've been today. That fellow at the bank – I tell you, I was stamped on as if I were a pauper. I've been worrying myself to death ever since. Thank God I've found you in.'

Roberson laid down his spectacles, put his hands behind his head and began to rock his chair. In short, not rising to his feet, which Thomas, in the stew that he was, thought nothing of – took as an invitation to make himself comfortable. He flopped into the chair opposite with a loud exhalation of relief.

'Well, well, talk of the devil,' Roberson said, fixing Thomas in the eye. 'Damn me if it's not the great Mr Gage I have before me, proprietor of one third of the miracle daub, Meredith's Grey. He's a little hot around the chops, a little dusty, a little put upon, and doubtless hoping that when I've filled his purse again I'll give him a soothing cup of tea. Well I never did, Mr Gage himself.'

'At last, a bit of civility. May I put my feet up for a few minutes while I get my wind back? I practically ran the last half mile. I can't describe to you how it felt – perhaps you'd be ill, or out with clients. The people one has to deal with nowadays – hyenas! Rip and claw, anything to shove another man down.'

'No you may not!' shouted Roberson. His chair falling forward, he catapulted himself out of it. In four strides he was around the desk and had Thomas by the lapels, was hauling him up and shaking him until his cheeks bounced. 'Not now, not ever! Get this into your lugs, Mr Fine and Mighty. Item one: I get the contract for the job at Spencer House. Item two: they ask for Meredith's Grey throughout. Item three: what do I get from your factory? Piss. The whole bloody consignment, nothing but piss. Runs down the walls like watery shit. Piss and shit! "So very sorry," I say to my lord Spencer, "I'll sort it in a jiffy." "Sorry be buggered," says he. "I wiped my arse on your contract this morning." Gone! A thousand pounds up his arse! A thousand, do you hear? The finest contract in my life. I could have bought myself two houses—'

'But—'

'So what do I do? I telegraph your man and say, what are you doing up there? Do you want to destroy me? No answer. I write to him, sign myself your respectful and obedient servant, which I am not and never will be. Not a murmur . . . You're finished. No one'll take Meredith's Grey after this, I'll see to it personally, so help me I will.'

Thomas sat down. The afternoon was closing in. It was a long walk back to the station.

'Finished! Bust! Done for!'

Slowly Thomas turned his sad and noble face towards the other. 'I have a woman to go home to who is not my wife. The paint was nothing to do with me, I swear it. So please, a tenner on account . . . A fiver, then, cock.'

'Not a penny! Never again will I give so much as a farthing to the Gages. Never! It's monstrous the way you've treated me. Get out. Go and do your crying somewhere else, you fat fool.'

Thomas stumbled into the October dusk. The door was slammed and bolted behind him.

Cloud covered the stars. Beneath its scudding cloak the train raced to Nina. Gouts of flame and fiery necklaces of sparks volleyed into the night. The stoker shovelled, his face contorted and grotesque, like a painting of the devil against the scarlet mouth of the furnace. The driver pulled the lanyard at every crossing. The whistle shrieked. Ghostly sheep scattered and grew faint. In the glowing carriages merchants slept or read newspapers; ladies fretted about the evening meal; and children played at cat's cradle, swayed exaggeratedly at the bends, and stored away for dreamtime the sound of ticketty-tack, ticketty-tack and the exciting crackle and shudder as they sped through sets of points.

In the last of the open wagons sat Thomas. Believing he'd seen Lionel Suckling on the platform, he'd skulked in the shadows until the last moment; found the snuggest benches already filled; had to sit with his face to the engine. His coat was buttoned to the throat, his hands wrapped in his armpits. Upside down on his lap, like a silk-lined bucket, was his top hat, anchored to his cold thighs by a parcel of ironware lent to him for the duration by a kindly fellow-traveller. The acrid brown smoke swarmed through his hair and coated it with soot. He huddled against his neighbours for warmth, envying them their makeshift tarpaulins.

Eyes like slits, his forehead stinging, frozen within and without, he fled the appalling day.

Thirty-seven

THE WINDOWS were dark and the curtains undrawn. He hurried up the path, fumbling for the key. The hallway was colder than a tomb. He lit the gas. 'Nina?' He went into the drawing-room and spoke her name again – louder, sharper, with alarm. But there was no carry to the sound, for the air was dead, already mortifying into the mustiness of an empty apartment. The piano lid was closed, there was no music on the stand, no impress on the cushions of her favourite chair, no scent, no presence, not the tiniest echo of her. Even as he stood there, he could feel the dust settling and mould starting to grow. The lies he'd prepared to account for his appearance, the scheme to usurp Pauntley, the pleas hoarded in reserve, all disintegrated beneath the weight of the sudden knowledge that the household gods had departed and Nina with them.

He placed Fred's picture on the mantel-shelf – his boy, the hope of the family. Bracing his hands against the hateful green valance, he looked down on the miniature with bloodshot eyes. He picked it up, scrutinised every lineament and kissed it. The bedroom door was open. He walked in.

The bare rails and shelves of her wardrobe gaped at him. Shoe-boxes, ointment jars, her silver hair-brushes, the lucky mascot she kept propped against the mirror, everything had been swept away. Not even a handkerchief had been overlooked in her ruthlessness. She had erased herself totally, as if she'd never entered his life, as if he'd dreamed her up. All that remained was the leather case he'd bought for her riding hat, in the centre of the sofa at the foot of their bed. He thought – but it was difficult for him to be clear what he was thinking. How silly to have forgotten it, how unlike her, its cost, that it could do with a dressing of saddle soap – all these entered his mind without alighting.

The double set of pillows mocked him. He trailed a finger along the window ledge. The blinds were down. He parted the laths and stared out at the sea.

There was a noise behind him: the creak of door hinges, the shuffle of bedroom slippers, Miss Mimms' dry cough.

'Go away, creepy-crawly,' he said, not turning.

The sullen beat of the waves reached him. He wondered how cold the water would be. Was she out there, with her trunks and the turquoise ring, blue eyes laughing, on the paddle-steamer to France? Was she steadying the bead on a fresh victim? How long had she been planning this? But why today? How could she have known?

He extinguished the gaslight and lay on the bed in his filthy clothes. After a while he got up, washed his hands and face, removed his shoes, and put Fred on the pillow beside him, where for a year he had awakened to watch Nina's face fill and grow smooth. His feet ached, and within his skull the dreadful pain had started afresh. He pulled the quilt up to his chin and lay there unmoving, eyes wide open, afraid and insuperably alone.

Thirty-eight

PARALLEL TO her corner window on the top floor stood Miss Mimms' prize chair, which she had had with the dwarf palms as a legacy from the late Captain Vincent, mariner of the eastern seas. Its legs were thick, black and crudely carved. The upholstering she had bought locally, clumsy repeats of a moated pagoda, bamboo fronds and a white-robed Chinese man being carried, smiling, in a litter. Suspended from the crown of the woodwork was a small oblong cushion in pink velveteen on which had been stitched, 'Be Thou My Sunbeam'. On this she would rest her scanty hair as she admired the sunsets or kept watch on the street below.

Beside the chair, on a low round table, was a slim pair of lady's folding binoculars.

From this vantage point Miss Mimms had observed the comings and goings of her tenants. She'd watched Thomas marching behind the band of the Royal Artillery, and the joint expeditions depart to go riding, painting, picnicking on the beach, and to church. She had apprised herself of the fact that on the third Monday of each month he went to London, related these trips to the payment of rent, and drawn the correct conclusion.

On the morning in question Thomas had walked out as usual at 8.10 a.m. About two hours afterwards – she couldn't be exact, but she was sipping her coffee so it must have been about 10 – a singular event had occurred: the arrival of a messenger boy from the Telegraph Company. She knew who it was from the satchel alone, which she saw bouncing against his hip long before she could make out the gold lettering on his cap. The telegraph was accepted (she heard Nina bang the door shut). She took the cat onto her lap and waited. Fifteen minutes later Nina rushed out and ran down the street as if chased by bees; hatless, arms and legs flying in all directions. Towards lunch-time the carrier drew up with his wagon. Miss Mimms scrutinised every trunk that left the house through her binoculars. At 2 o'clock – and this, she told everyone, she was absolutely certain of – a hansom cab trotted up. Nina, wearing a fur-trimmed cloak and a Leghorn bonnet with a grey lining, came out with an overnight case. The driver offered to take the case. She refused him. There were no backward glances, no sighs, no last-minute checking of pockets. She removed her bonnet and clambered in. The cab door opened a crack; an errant corner of the cloak was whisked inside; the door was slammed so violently that the vehicle rocked on its wheels, and they drove away in the direction of the railway station.

First Miss Mimms looked in her rent book. Easier in her mind, she then consulted her Bradshaw. It was as she supposed: London by teatime. Putting two and two together, she murmured, 'Addioo happiness, old Mr Gage.' She went downstairs, let herself in with the pass-key and began to check for dilapidations and pilfering.

By mid-afternoon, at the very time Thomas was making his way to 99, Long Acre to see Mr Roberson, the news was hopping round Brighton. Mrs Gage's telegraph, left by Nina beneath the leather hat box – the odour of blackmail – Mr Gage's impending ruin – the flight of the Pearl. So there had been a wife, after all! It was as fruity a bit of gossip as anyone could have hoped for out of the high season.

Thomas was popular in town. Therefore, when Annie woke him with a breakfast tray at around eleven, it was sympathy that he saw in her eyes.

After he'd dressed, he gave notice to Miss Mimms. She came downstairs and showed him Isabel's telegraph. 'Lying on the settee under the case, hidden away as if she was ashamed of what she'd done. As well she might be, opening what wasn't hers to open. Bad news is it, Mr Gage?' He sent her away and read it swiftly. Isabel had been trying to economise. Or the sense had been altered somewhere along the way. The bit about the money was clear enough; he'd discovered that for himself. But what exactly was it that Gooby had done to put Isabel in such a state? Could it really be important when set against the fact that Nina had left him?

Annie came in to say goodbye. He put the telegraph in his pocket.

In the afternoon he cleaned off his paintbrushes and packed up the easel. He went through his clothes, throwing to one side those he could sell. In the band of his church-going hat he discovered a pound note, money for the collection plate. He remembered the ten pounds he'd given Miss Mimms as a deposit against break-ages.

He sat down to make a list of his assets. The pen being in his hand, he wrote to Jeffrey at the Academy asking for news about his Daedalus picture. 'P.S. I am growing shameless. I very much need to dispose of same for cash.'

It was sympathy too that he met at the theatre when out of habit and lostness, he drifted along there later. Stooped and unshaven, in the faded blue coat of his father, he slunk in and took a seat in a darkened wing of the hall.

The orchestra was rehearsing with Nina's stand-in. Wearily the leader said: 'Imagine it. The place is full. You get the cue, so how do you make your entrance? With a swirl, for God's sake. Don't creep onto the stage like a raindrop sliding down the window. Pretend you're enjoying it. Let's get this bit right at least.' Whack! went the cymbals, the resounding exclamation that had always introduced Nina.

He should have stayed put. This was too close to the bone. The poor girl, she simply didn't have what Nina had, that greediness to own the audience, to be where the tunes were. He thought about leaving. But it was cosy in the theatre, he wouldn't have to spend money on heating, and he felt himself to be among friends. Moreover – he went so far as to undo his top coat-button – there were matters attendant upon Isabel's telegraph that had started knocking afresh at his mind. How had Isabel known his address? Was that the reason that Nina had cleared out, because she was afraid of his wife turning up on the doorstep? And this business about Gooby . . . He tasted the word and found it bitter.

A hand descended on his shoulder. Galley had seen Thomas through the spy-hole and come to cheer him up.

'I'm like a dead man,' Thomas replied. 'She took everything

down to the last pin. Cheated? I don't know yet. If you emptied me out, you'd find nothing. Hollow, that's what I've become . . . Angry? You're the one who should be angry. It was you she worked for.'

'Not a bit of it! Didn't you notice how the gate was falling? Same songs, same jokes, same voice. Get her to try something new? Impossible! Too successful too soon, the usual story. I told the owners they shouldn't renew, but of course they knew best. And money! You never saw such a woman for money,' to which Thomas nodded.

Galley had intended to say nothing whatsoever about the money side of it, which to his mind was a far more serious loss than the woman. To disguise the remark, he budged Thomas down one and slipped into the seat he'd vacated. 'She was a bitch. A blind man could have seen it coming—' There he went again. It was deuced awkward to hit on the right words. He looked out of the tip of his eye at Thomas. Perhaps the old boy hadn't heard. But what a performance, getting to pole a saucy young thing like Nina! He must have some specialised knowledge, tricks that only a woman could see signalled. He was about to continue when Thomas said, 'You're right, blinded by love.' He turned away from the stage and faced Galley directly. 'But Nina was never a bitch, just practical. She gave me more happiness than I've had from any other woman.' He looked down at his fingers and said in a tired voice, 'Life is sad, that's the fact of it.'

'What'll you do now?' asked Galley.

'I haven't thought. Go back, I suppose.'

'To Norfolk?'

'Probably. I'll need to get on my feet, put some money together somehow.'

Suddenly Galley stood up and shouted: 'Throw your voice around. Imagine they're all deaf out there. Don't warble, *sing*, woman . . . Sorry, Thomas. She'll be alright when she hits her stride. Tell you what . . . ' He called down, 'Break for tea, everyone. Start again in fifteen minutes . . . Go and have a word with the boys. They won't laugh at you. They feel about Nina the same as I do. Davie Pyment there, on the French horn, he and his wife'll give you lodgings until you're fit again. For farthings, I wouldn't be surprised. They were talking about it earlier. Off you go – women, eh! Worse than locusts. Lucky if you get left with the stalk.'

He watched Thomas shamble down to the orchestra pit. He could swear he'd had a couple of inches chopped off him overnight. It was pitiable really, when you thought about it, what a grabber like Nina could do, even to a fellow as intelligent as Thomas. As swack as anything he'd been when he arrived and now he was smashed to pieces, like one of the broken barrels that one found on the beach. What a capsizing for a man his age. He went off to see about the wages.

Apart from the noise of Pyment practising, guffaw-like rumbles that made his head throb, Thomas was comfortable enough in his new lodgings. The cooking was homely, his room dry and he had it to himself.

Thirty pounds was the sum he settled on, enough to buy Isabel and the girls a present each and return with dignity. Third class from Brighton to Norwich was eighteen shillings and a halfpenny – call it a pound to keep things simple. Plus a tip-top cab out to Fordwell; he very much wanted to arrive looking the part. Add a night in London for the Duke's funeral. Add something for the Pyments, a little thank-you present . . . To be set in the balance: the ten pounds deposit he'd retrieved from Miss Mimms, and the pound from under his hat-band. Anyway, thirty pounds net was what he'd fixed his sights on.

He went out to work with his heavy wooden painting-chest strapped to his back and the easel lengthways across the top of it. He learned to ignore the unkind remarks about pedlars that came his way. 'Thirty pounds' he would say to himself, gritting his teeth and scanning the seafront for custom.

It was cold on the pier. The wind whipped at his forehead and set up an additional pain in his skull. When it became too violent, he retreated to the toll-house and allowed its custodian, Harry Lomax, to pour him a nip.

Trade was hard to find. He began to brood about Nina and Fred. Little by little his misfortunes turned into wrongs.

A cold sore developed below one lip. Shaving days were reduced from four to two a week. He skimped around the sore, whereby the tufts of stubble made it more conspicuous than ever. He blew his nose with his fingers to avoid the cost of laundry, the only charge the Pyments would agree to. He trained himself to approach people obsequiously, to say things like, 'A memento of your day in Brighton, madam?' or 'Now, my dear, your children look *so* angelic.' But his tone rarely hit the mark, and the sore and his food-stained coat also told against him.

Lomax, who'd taken it upon himself to see Thomas came to no harm, said he shouldn't wear those woollen gloves since it gave people the notion that his brushwork would be clumsy; that he should be more persistent; wear a clean coat; work in crayons, and a dozen more pieces of advice. When the pier was deserted, which was increasingly the case as the autumn weather roared in from the Atlantic, they were joined in the toll-house by Jack Shepherd, the lank, nimble-witted fellow who made his way by cutting silhouettes for people on the spot. The flames babbled in the dumpy iron stove, the brandy circulated, the windows steamed up.

'For a florin I give 'em a full length in two shakes of a monkey's pizzle,' Jack said. 'Whereas you want to keep 'em standing around for half an hour and then charge 'em a quid for the privilege. Wrong price, wrong merchandise. It's not art they're after, not this sort of trade.'

Paint was what he understood, not pencil-flicking, Thomas replied. And surely someone who'd been hung at the Academy was worth a quid?

'Not the point, Tom, not the point at all. If you'd got yourself hung at Tyburn and come back to life, hallelujah and three rousing cheers, you'd be fame itself. But this type of mutton couldn't give a pinch of shit for the Academy. I'm telling you, it's down you must take your style.'

'Be sensible, Tom,' said Lomax, wiping a port-hole in the fugged-up window with the back of his mitten, 'do some outside views like you once said. Fancy things for the better class of folk. Other roads I don't know how you're to come to thirty quid. Maybe in the summertime you could work your passage, but not now you won't. Not a cat's chance. Look outside.' He pointed at the pier and the three towers stretching into the sea. 'Not a soul to be seen anywhere.'

This time Thomas paid heed. Sometimes he painted listening to Lomax's yarns in the toll-house. At others, when the weather allowed him, he did picturesque water-colours of the Esplanade, the Pavilion and the bustling side streets. To his surprise he managed to sell almost everything he did to a bric-à-brac shop. His reserves mounted. By Guy Fawkes Day he had a clear surplus of twenty-one pounds in cash, which he squirrelled away among the rags in his painting-chest.

Yet he felt neither elation nor relief. His head pained him day and night, at times horribly. The gloss was going off him fast. He feared he was becoming impotent, and shrank from the company of women. He declined Galley's invitations to the theatre, and spoke only to Lomax and the Pyments. Existence was ceasing to be attractive: the old terms were no longer available, and the new held nothing for him. He was certain that if he could get it out and examine it, he would find that his heart had become smaller and was growing bald, in the sense that the pallor of its skin would now be completely visible. He gazed constantly at the miniature of Fred, and in so doing arrived at the opinion that he alone, among all the people on the universe, had been singled out for injustice on such a savage scale. Life had humbugged him; fitted him out as a loving, generous father and then put him to the sword. To excuse it on the grounds that it was innately sad now struck him as absurd. Sadness was in the very nature of the animal. It was its onslaughts of out-and-out cruelty that could sink a man. The name Gooby returned to haunt him.

He was in his bedroom one evening, touching up the day's work. Isabel's telegraph was in his inside coat pocket, crinkling whenever he moved. He spread it on the easel, smoothed out the creases and peered at the pencilled capitals, now starting to fade. What could Isabel have meant, that it was Gooby who'd caused the blow-up? Had he wronged her, then? Had it been Gooby's work all along that had lost him Nina? Gooby. The word flew up at him. He painted a scarlet ring round it. In the kitchen below, he could hear Mrs Pyment's knife busy at the chopping board. He smeared a fingertip of Friar's Balsam on his cold sore and went downstairs.

Pyment was at the theatre. Mrs Pyment was slicing onions for her winter pickle. He sat down at the end of the table.

The way she leant on the knife, the swift passage of the blade, the ice-sharp point winking in the candlelight, the sound as it severed the pungent flesh, the seeping juices, all these became of interest to him. He ignored what she said and stared in silence at the tumbling rings, dabbing at the sore with his tongue.

She gathered them into a heap and was about to start the cross-cut when he said, 'Do another one,' so commandingly and with such urgency that she looked twice at him. 'It's just that I like the smell of onions,' he said more congenially, so she went on making pickle until the little wooden cuckoo-clock on the mantel struck eight when she declared enough was enough. She washed her hands and got out the cribbage board for their usual best of three. But his fingers trembled so violently, in fact shook as if he had a fever, that he was incapable of fitting the pegs in their holes, and she had to do it for him. There was something unnatural in his eyes that scared her. After only one game she said she was tired and went to her bedroom, dropping the bar in its socket behind her. That night she wondered to Mr Pyment whether Thomas might not have a bottle of laudanum in his room. 'He had ever such a queer face on him,' she said. 'Sort of like a gargoyle. You know?'

Pyment told him over breakfast that a proposal was afoot to commission him to paint the orchestra. 'Could be a fiver in it for you,' he said, after studying Thomas carefully and deciding Mrs Pyment had been seeing things. He finished his cup of tea and turned his attention to the sheet music on his lap. Thomas went upstairs to count the money in his paint-chest. A fiver would be near enough. He took the day off.

After reading the advertisements in his Bradshaw, he chose Major Culverwell's 'Private and Commercial Boarding House' in Arundel Street and wrote to the Major reserving a room for the night before the Duke's funeral. He was, he said, an old Waterloo man himself and if by chance this entitled him to a modest reduction of the tariff of three and sixpence, no one would be more grateful *at this moment of national distress* than his hapless servant, Thos Gage.

He took the letter to the Post Office. At the bank he exchanged his accumulation of coins for notes so as to lend him the appearance of prosperity. He treated himself to a lunch of pork chops with fried onions, sprouts, boiled potatoes and a glass of brown beer. Afterwards he bought a knife that was identical to Mrs Pyment's.

'Going to give the wife a hand, then?' remarked the man. 'Usually it's around marmalade time I get husbands coming in. Still, takes all sorts.'

Yes, said Thomas, he was going to give Isabel a hand. She'd been too long doing everything by herself.

From there he went to the theatre to discover from Galley what was involved in the commission. It was for a large commemorative picture of the orchestra in full swing. What was crucial, Galley said, was that their wives should also like it. He would be responsible for the identity key with which it would be framed. It was to be hung in the entrance hall in perpetuity.

'We're getting you on your feet again, aren't we, Tom?' he said, thumping him between the shoulder blades. 'What does that make it now? You must be getting close to the thirty mark.'

'Twenty-eight,' Thomas said. He accepted the job and started for home, turning west on the Esplanade and passing Adelaide Crescent.

Miss Mimms had collected the mail for the house after her mid-morning cup of coffee. Isabel's handwriting was still giving her trouble. She had three letters of hers now, each more frenzied than the last. It was as good as a novel, all these goings-on up there in Norfolk; and the touching confidences of Emily and Harriet – always on a separate sheet and thank goodness, wonderfully legible – were enough to wreck a heart. As Thomas walked beneath her, she was standing at the window, trying to remember where'd she put her magnifying glass. He had no hat on – she fancied his hair had sprung a lot more grey recently – and was talking to himself, making rapid darting movements with one hand, like a fish swimming upstream. She reached down for her binoculars and kept her eyes tight on him until he was out of sight. Then she found the glass, which had been on her writing-desk all the time, and settled down for the afternoon to decipher the latest instalment from Fordwell House, seven folds of Isabel's distraught writing.

A week later Thomas started his paints home by carrier and travelled to London. Fred's picture and his medal were in the pocket of his coat, which Mrs Pyment had spent the previous day sponging. Though he'd told her of the Duke's order that the two parts of the decoration were never to be separated, she'd untacked the crimson and blue ribbon and sewn it on the breast of his coat. 'The wideawake men'll be out in force so you keep that medal of yours tucked away safe. I don't want to be reading in the newspaper about the mischief a nice old gentleman got himself into,' she said, squaring him up and wishing he hadn't had to sell all his good clothes. She'd quite got over her earlier suspicions. He'd done such a good likeness of Mr Pyment playing his horn. There wasn't a thing wrong with him that wouldn't be cleared up by a long rest in his own house.

Thirty-nine

IT WAS evening when Thomas reached Arundel Street. He took against Culverwell immediately. The sleekness of the man, his fidgets, his lack of pepper – a bogus Major, he decided. So limp a sword hand could never have cut more than a wedding cake. A proper soldier wouldn't finger another man's battle honour. It'd be a smile of recognition, at the most a salute, as between comrades in arms. And he was all over him from the word go, which Thomas found offensive.

Nevertheless, he wasn't going to have to share a bed, which was a stroke of luck, the city being as full as it was. He unpacked the canvas rucksack that Pyment had given him, hung his coat on the hook behind the door, and lay down with Fred's picture on the table beside him. Rouch's saw, the backwards-forwards cut, the stink of ether, the pit. 'Old fellow, you should have been here with me. It was a very great wrong that was done you.' His lips moved, nothing else. The lines in his face had deepened since Nina had left him. His eyes had sunk and their beauty flown. As he lay on the edge of the candle shadow listening to a man pacing heavily in the room above, they glittered like lacquer, and their whites had a yellowish tinge. 'Gooby, I shall kill you.' He touched the knife beneath his pillow.

He counted his change and went downstairs in his shirtsleeves to ask Culverwell for a second bucket of coal.

More guests had arrived, military men all of them. They were sat drinking brandy and water around the fire in the Major's snug. Out of politeness, Thomas introduced himself while he waited for Culverwell. The conversation turned to the details of the funeral procession. Then Culverwell bustled in with a copy of the printed programme and began talking nineteen to the dozen as he fiddled around, picking the officers' hats and gloves off one table and setting them down on another. Seizing the poker, he began to enumerate the extraordinary vintages in his cellar. The Waterloo port, the 1815, 'the most famous grapes in history – ah! Saintly! Exquisite!' at which he flared his nostrils and executed a little skip of ecstasy. Then he was off again on a different tack, so that Thomas had no opportunity to ask for his coal.

'Oh, do go away and leave us, Culverwell, this is a funeral, not a circus,' one of the officers said before very long.

'Mr Gage here is a Waterloo man,' Culverwell said, untroubled. 'I was coming to that. It's not every day – well, should I air the port in his honour? That's the question of the minute, slacken the cork or not. Only two bottles left at the last count. What do you say, good good?'

Their heads turned as one to inspect Thomas, who was sitting quietly in his shirt and braces looking through the programme. 'I see the 33rd is coming down from Glasgow,' he said with diffidence, not wishing to see a bottle of the 1815 on his bill in the morning.

'The Duke's Own, most appropriate. Fine men, as they always have been. Who's their Colonel now, does it say? McLaren was the last name I had.'

For some reason, Thomas thought to do with his headaches, he was having difficulty keeping print in focus. The extremities of sentences would slip out of his vision, leaving him with only the words in the middle. It was all swirling too much for him, and he handed the programme to his neighbour.

'No, it doesn't give any names . . . The advance party to leave Horse Guards at eight, six battalions to line the road. The show proper to commence with the band of the second battalion of the Rifle Brigade. They'll be playing the Dead March from *Saul*. Handel?'

'Playing it the whole way to St Paul's? My goodness.'

'The Frogs sending anyone?'

'Over the page . . . The envoys of Spain, Russia, Prussia, Portugal, Holland and Hanover. No mention of our friends.'

'Typical. Still sulking. No sense of fair play.'

'And they had their chance, by God! Nip and tuck, I'll say – yes, what is it, Culverwell? Of course we'll have the 1815, both bottles. Now off you go and leave us to our stories.' He shooed the Major out of the room. Turning to Thomas, who had started up with an anxious look on his face, he said, 'Don't worry, Gage, we'll deal with the commercial side of the victualling. What we want to hear is – how did it feel? What was it like afterwards? On a Sunday, too! That's what I call church parade with a difference. Eh! Eh! Come on, let's settle in and put our feet up.' He called through the doorway, 'Major Culverwell, sir! A brandy for Mr Gage, at the double!'

Thomas was warm, and his dinner coming to him gratis. He was more than ready to let himself be rocked in the snug, rosy cradle of the long ago past where nothing could hurt him. No railways, no scrabbling for money, none of life's mutilation, just the featherbed of memory. He looked at the eager faces around him. These were men! Not sharpers like Gooby, but men you could trust to be alone with the silver; decent and dutiful men who understood the business of fighting. Proud! Steadfast! Honourable! Slowly at first, but then like grapeshot, the words flowed from him. The preliminaries, the manoeuvring for position on the fields of Ligny and Quatre Bras; the lightning, the doom-claps of thunder and the torrents of rain the night before the battle; the suspense of waiting until Napoleon showed his hand—

'I tell you, there was a hollow in my stomach that nothing could have filled. It was like a whirlpool. You could have poured in umpteen breakfasts, umpteen gallons of brandy and had nothing to show for it. They'd just have spun round and round and vanished into that tiny hole – wherever whirlpools go. Hours we stood around for that morning. And then – I don't need to tell you gentlemen how a man's belly flinches when it sees the sun glinting on half a mile of bayonets. A yard of steel inside me, it thinks, and before the thought is half done with, its brain has gone straight to the Bible and all that strong language about bowels. One can be as brave as a lion in action, but that first sight of bayonets is always a sinker.'

'Don't I know what you mean! The bigger the belly, the more it wants to run away and hide,' said an officer, looking tenderly at the creases in his waistcoat.

'You're right, Gage, it's the waiting that's the worst,' said

282

another. 'I pace around and try to remember how the stars look at different times of the year. If I had to stand rooted there like my men, I'd be a total mess.'

'That's exactly it!' Thomas cried. 'A mess! Believe you me, I was dripping from every crack by the time Boney made his mind up. And it was no better when their cavalry started at us.' He told them about the hare that had jumped out of a patch of long grass and been sabred by a dragoon; how a bullet had ricocheted off the hilt of Colonel Mayhew's sword and lodged in the muscular part of his chest. 'And the smoke and the racket, and the screams of the wounded horses thrashing around just yards away, bellies torn open, guts spilling out – oh yes, that was hell on earth the first time they attacked. But you know what, it got easier as the day wore on and still we were there, for all that they charged us and bombarded the line. It began to seem normal, as if we did it every day.

'At last Blücher arrived with his Prussians – God knows where we'd have been without them. The Frenchies saw the game was up – they broke. Mayhew got the order to advance. "Slowly now, boys," he shouted, "a bit at a time, we've got until Christmas" – which was a ridiculous thing to say, soldiers being as they are. You'll have read that we gave a mighty cheer as we went for them. It wasn't like that. It was a growl. We were like an immense breaker that's been gathering its strength for miles out there in the ocean. It rears up, it bares its teeth – and God help anyone in its way. Discipline? It went out of the door the instant we left our squares. We became butchers, hacking and chopping at all the defeated sausage-meat around us. I was no better than the rest of them. Gentlemen, I went berserk . . .'

He was astonished to hear himself say it. The memory of that terrible nightfall had swum up from nowhere. The shattered horses, the stench of human gore, scavengers already plucking the corpses, the remorseless, insatiable brutality of the victors. His voice tailed off, and his mind retreated to the fire waiting in his room and to Fred, whom he'd never once found the courage to tell how he'd been consumed by rage and had slain a wounded, thirst-crazed soldier merely because the man had had the effrontery to raise his arm and cry out for help; how he'd spotted the arm and in his lust for blood had run over and stabbed him repeatedly through the eyeball.

'I can't go on. It's over and done with. Let the dead sleep in peace.' He got up from the sofa and left, covering his eyes and so not seeing the step at the door, on which he stumbled. The officers watched him silently, reliving their own nightmares.

The morning of the funeral was bitterly cold, spits of rain on an east wind. When Thomas came down, the officers were milling around in the hallway, asking if anyone had been outside and whether it was a two-vest day.

Culverwell walked in from the street and was told to shut the door damned quickly. 'Brrr!' he said, 'cold enough to make a lawyer keep his hands in his own pockets, ha ha – breakfast, gentlemen, before the fray? Fried eggs, kedgeree, kidneys, what's it to be, or shall I just call for a dish of each? Eggs for everyone, then? Good good, this way if you please.'

Thomas was restless. As he'd lain waiting for sleep, he'd decided that the next two days would be the largest he'd ever lived through. His farewell to the Duke – the train home – the meeting with Isabel whom he'd wronged, and with Emily whom he loved. Then tomorrow he'd take his head to Rouch, and if Rouch said it was the end of him, he'd go round the corner to Thorpe Road and kill Gooby, not furtively but leaning into the stroke with all his weight, for the deed would be just and he'd have nothing to lose.

He breakfasted by himself, crouching over his plate and eating small because his head ached. His eyes continually darted towards the door, as if expecting the appearance of someone vital. He had no idea whom it might be. He knew only that matters were not far off boiling and anything might happen. From time to time he made covert thrusts with the table knife, imagining how it would be with Gooby sagging on the blade.

The officers finished and rose in unison. As they passed him, one said, 'Why don't you come and join us, Gage? We've hired a room in Piccadilly – food and drink, a fire ready and waiting, all paid for in advance – why not? You'd be more than welcome. It'd be a privilege to have the company of a Waterloo man.'

But Thomas declined, mumbling about wanting to walk the course and see everything for himself.

Yes, he was restless, but the greater truth was that he was afraid to leave Culverwell's boarding house. He felt safe. It suited him to be a pin in a packet, solitary and without responsibility, for he was tired in his bones and desired above all else warmth and ease. The instant he went outside, the world would have him by the throat again. Events, the captious hurly-burly of being, would sweep him along, force him to bow to their whims, and thwick-thwack their cane would fall about his shoulders. The century was against him. He'd been hit too often. He didn't think he could stand any more.

Yet there was that which had to be done tomorrow, the act of retribution.

He pushed away his food and called for a copy of *The Times*, which he read while the maids cleared up around him.

'Knock, knock.' It was Culverwell, his knuckles rapping lightly on the front-page advertisements. 'Awfully sorry to hurry you, old boy, but we need to make your room ship-shape. Ever such a crowd in tonight. There'll be some high jinks, I'll wager. Always the same after a big funeral. Leave your bag with me if it's handier for you.'

Thomas went upstairs and packed. Suddenly he felt queasy. He tried to vomit, but nothing came of it. Culverwell was waiting for him in the hallway with his bill.

'I say, you look dreadful, hope you don't mind me saying so. That pain still bothering you, is it? Have a swig of poppy juice, here' – his glossy black head disappeared as he bent to open a cupboard in his desk – 'just the job – how to drive care away, pain and despair away, with tinct. opii or better to say, Mother Bailey's Quieting Syrup. I believe I'll prescribe a couple of grains extra to give it body – here we are, good good . . .'

But Thomas had gone, awkwardly, having forgotten the knack of closing a door behind a rucksack. The mention of laudanum had been a sufficient propellant.

Forty

THE WIND was strung like a bow. He turned up his collar, showing the strong, unweathered blue of the original material, the colour of fashion sixty years past, before progress got out of control. The straps of his rucksack were disfiguring the lines of his coat; he plumped out his ribbon to restore it to prominence and walked up to the Strand. The air rushed at him, a tang of the steppes in it that reminded him of home. He began to feel more resolute.

But what people there were! The Major had spoken of a million and more and how they'd be packed like blades of grass all the way from Horse Guards to the top of Constitution Hill, past Apsley House and down Piccadilly to Charing Cross and St Paul's. He could believe it. They were hanging from trees, from balconies, out of shop windows. On every rooftop was a frieze of bullet-round heads, black against the galloping clouds. Fragile edifices like race-course stands had sprung up along the streets. On them the wealthy were roosting in furs and toppers, while in the passageways beneath enterprising lads scampered back and forth ransoming dropped gloves and handkerchiefs. Baxters had stripped out all the interior fittings and were doing a roaring trade in cakes and spiced drinks. In whichever direction he looked the crowd was ten to a dozen deep, sombre and respectful, for once not chaffing the soldiers, who lined the route at intervals of six yards. Even the boys on their fathers' shoulders were wearing mourning bands.

He halted, and again sniffed the air. Nelson had been buried on a keen blue January day, but this was the proper class of weather for a funeral, dark and joyless. He looked around for a vantage point.

Beside him a man began to scramble up a pile of bricks and builders' refuse. Turning he saw the decoration on Thomas's chest and handed him up. Together they stamped themselves a level platform.

'A right champion! The country will never look on the likes of him again,' Percy said. 'One of those faces – a single glance and you knew the stuff he was made of. He'd take no truck from any fellow. A nobleman through and through – a right champion lad.'

Thomas, who had observed the Duke at close quarters and seen for himself that he had a thin, obstinate, philistine head and the strongly sloping skull of someone fond of getting his own way, said, 'Yes, old Nosey was every inch a nobleman.'

'That ribbon you've got, so you were there when us wapped the Frenchies? Oh man, that must have been champion afterwards, when thee got t' boots off.'

'But not during the battle it wasn't,' Thomas said mildly as the white plumes of his friends in the Royal Artillery band came nodding down the Strand towards them.

Hard on their heels were the guns, their iron-shod wheels rumbling over the cobblestones. Then it was the turn of the cavalry, and for a moment it seemed to Thomas that fear scurried through the crowd as the champing horses and tall stern men of the 17th Lancers filled the street from side to side. Were they imagining what he'd witnessed for himself all those years ago?

'Wouldn't like to have one of those through my guts,' said his companion, and Thomas, putting away his vision of sabres swinging at the charge and seeing things as they were, rows of sedate and upright lances from which fluttered the gay bannerols of the Duke's coat of arms, said with a professional air, 'Looks worse than it is, Percy. Completely impractical, as a matter of fact. How do you shake the chap off the end once you've got him? A bayonet's much easier.' He made a jab with his knife hand. 'Much easier.'

Light Dragoons, Hussars, the Scots Greys in their busbies and double chinstraps, they clopped jingling past and satisfied every-one, especially those who couldn't give a hang about the Duke but wanted to be able to tell their grandchildren about the gleaming cuirasses and the pageant of bold-coloured warriors they'd once seen in London town. Turbaned regiments from India; the official deputations; the goatish face of Benjamin Disraeli smirking at his carriage window ('clever mister flashy, old moneybags the Chancellor,' said Percy, with obvious admiration on all counts); the Prime Minister, Lord Derby, whom no one recognised; Prince Albert; the Marquis of Anglesey ('Hey, Tom, wasn't he the fellow who had a leg shot off at Waterloo? Bang and it was gone, just like that? Strewth!'); the band of the Grenadiers and at last, at about a quarter to twelve, the cadaver.

'Hats off!' The command rippled down the street as the towering golden catafalque, embossed with lions' heads, figures of Victory and a magnificent rearing dolphin, rolled past behind eight black-plumed horses. On its summit lay the coffin, unhappily small.

'Amen,' said Percy, head bowed, hat clasped against his chest. And in a sideways hiss, 'Keep your elbows clamped, Tom, this is when the pickpockets'll try and rush us.'

By common accord the two men waited until the mourners' carriages, the Duke's horse – saddled and bridled, his boots reversed in the stirrups – and the Queen had passed. Then they set off for St Paul's as best they could among such a crowd.

'How do they do that trick with the boots, Tom? How is it they don't drop out of the stirrups? A spot of glue under the heel? String? Oh, and didn't the Queen look like a plump little pigeon! Breeds well enough, that's for sure. However, in my experience that can lead to trouble,' and as they walked down Fleet Street, not too far behind the bier, Percy began to tell him about his loft of racing pigeons.

They passed the Belle Sauvage. Thomas pointed across the street to it. 'That's where I used to board the coach for home,' he said.

'Ay, those were some days. Never went on one myself. Never rich enough. But the railways now . . . What happened, I reckon, was that God called down and said, "If you lot swear to behave yourselves in future, I'll give you trains, 'cos you'll find they're cheaper for the common man." We should be saying "Thank you" to him every day of our lives.'

'I had money then,' Thomas said. 'And a son, and happiness.'

'Ah, a tumble, was it? I was wondering . . . Here, Tom, you look none too sparky. Shall us have a sit-down for a while?'

But under the huge black-curtained arch at Temple Bar and up Ludgate Hill they went, the pair of them, for Thomas was determined to see it through to the end.

The concourse in front of the cathedral was packed with a far greater multitude than they'd met so far, and they had to wrestle their way among them to get a view. A whippety man with a fiery face, a bowler and a red handkerchief round his throat, took exception to the knock he got from Thomas's rucksack. 'What's all this barging for? Since when does a couple of bloody nobodies get to have the front seats?' Percy said he'd wallop his breakfast clean out of his gob if he wouldn't let them through, and twisting the man's handkerchief knot up to his ear-hole, dragged his face to within inches of Thomas's ribbon. 'My friend fought with the Duke, so you hold your tongue, fellow.' A few yards on it became impossible to proceed further.

An hour of quiet amusement followed as first the funeral men and then engineers and locksmiths endeavoured to release the coffin from its gilded throne. The rain had gone and a mean-spirited sun broken through. There was no impatience, just a wry and most human enjoyment of the Duke's predicament.

'He only had to cough and Boney trembled.'

'"Tell the right to wheel," he'd order and ten thousand men would wheel, on the dot!'

'And now he's come to this, jiggered by a twopenny padlock.'

'Well, well, it just goes to show we're all the same when the trumpet sounds . . .'

At last it was done. The great bell tolled, hats came off, the crowd fell silent, and the saviour of Europe, preceded by his Field-Marshal's baton on a cushion of imperial purple with four gently swinging tassels, was borne up the steps and disappeared into darkness. The doors closed.

'I loved that man,' Thomas said. 'A brute but I loved him.'

'Right champion lad,' agreed Percy, which he muttered at least twice more as they shouldered their way out of the crowd. On the edge, when at last they had space, he turned to Thomas and said, 'Poor buggers, having to wait in a cold church for an hour with the doors wide open and the wind whistling round their ankles.

Who'd be famous! Let's see if we can get a bite to eat somewhere.'

It was well into the afternoon when they parted, Thomas on foot to Shoreditch Station, Percy on foot to stay with his brother across the river.

'Now, Tom, you're to jump on the omnibus if you feel poorly, d'ye hear? There's no fun to be had in being a dead hero. And here's some more advice. There's summat sitting on your mind like a wet pancake and it's not doing you a blasted bit of good. I can hear it ticking away. D'ye know summat else? It feels like I've known you a hundred years though it's only been a piece of a day. We'll never meet again, so that's why I'm speaking like this. Whatever's happened to you in the past, it's done with. No point in brooding, chopping the same old sticks morning and night. Gone's gone and it's only fools don't know it. What was it the Duke said? Up and at 'em, that's it. So up and at 'em, Tom. Get yourself home and have a good plain woman love you. Love, nothing to beat it in the whole wide world. Goodbye!'

Tears came to Thomas's eyes as he mingled with the throng heading for Shoreditch. He'd been vain and selfish, considered himself wronged, and sought revenge for an act that had been committed by God alone. Nina had made a gull of him and all the while he lay with her, his family were struggling with ruin. 'Life is a jest, and all things show it.' He'd thought so too, at one time. But he'd erred, and so had Mr Gay. Yes, he said with a strange exhilaration, I have erred and now I shall go home and end my days meekly, as a grizzled patriarch, grandfather of the village.

The shops were all closed. Even the flower-sellers were absent from their usual pitches. Never mind, I myself will be the gift that I bring my darlings, he thought exultantly, and still smiling, freed from his bitterness by those few words from a stranger, he walked defenceless into the pandemonium of the station.

'Excursions only! Excursions only!' The officials were snatching tickets out of people's hands and scrutinising them fiercely. 'Yes, madam, platform on your left – on the road with you, Bob, come back tomorrow – excursions only! – normal running in the morning – don't blame me, blame his bloody nibs for dying – excursions, excursions, ticket-holders only!'

Thomas halted at the rope, weary but at the same time light-headed, everything within him resolved and glowing. He unshouldered his rucksack and swung it to the ground. He gazed benevolently upon the travellers being marshalled into queues, unable to hear exactly what the shouting concerned and in any case certain it wasn't intended for him.

What a to-do! What a broth of insanity! Now, how best should he tackle it—

The toothy sweating face, red as a lobster beneath the jutting peak of the cap, seemed to hurl itself at him. 'Ticket! Ticket!'

'Goodness, you made me jump ... steady on, don't panic.' Specks, tiny black specks like spiders, were weaving through his vision. Nevertheless he spoke calmly. 'No one's going to harm you. Of course I wasn't thinking of travelling without a ticket.'

'You deaf or something? Excursions only. The Duke's bloody funeral. Normal running tomorrow.'

'Surely not for everyone ... Tomorrow's no good to me. It's today that matters, I promised it myself. You've no idea ... Oh come, do I look like a cheat? You've only to point out the nearest ticket office and I'll do the rest. In fact I think I'll travel first class. I pray indulgence, if you would be so civil.'

'Indulgence! Fiddlesticks to your fancy words, nobby. You come back tomorrow like all the others. No ticket, no train.'

'People will have changed their minds. Met up with friends, decided to spend the night in town. You know what people are like. There's bound to be empty seats. Don't be daft.'

'Daft am I? Maybe I am and maybe I'm not. Stand here long enough and you'll discover which. Like till the morning.'

Thomas pointed to his ribbon. The desire to get home was raging within him. 'Know what this is? I wouldn't want to be in your boots when the newspapers get to hear you've turned a Waterloo man off the train. Your job won't be worth cinders.'

'Doesn't mean diddley-swot to me. Could be a piece out of my old woman's garter-strap for all I care. Now shove off. Tomorrow – don't you understand your own language?'

At that moment Thomas saw Jammy striding towards the barrier, cap set very proper on his head, his uniform spick and span, a furled green flag in his hand.

'Jammy Peach!' But this was the luck he needed. He'd get there, by God he would; come waltzing out of the dark and surprise them at their dinner. His face puckered into a thousand creases as he picked up the rucksack. 'Over here, Jammy!'

It was his same old back-house boy. He was a little fatter through the waist, but the simple, anxious expression was unaltered. The hair was still cropped up the back of his neck, and the small-pox blisters as marked as ever.

'Oh, Jammy, what a relief! How're you doing? Everything going well for you? Married yet?'

Jammy measured him up, distant at first, then – 'Can it be . . . ? Bless my soul if it isn't Mr Gage!'

'You mean you didn't recognise me?'

'It's just that you've changed . . . I wasn't expecting . . . well, I never did! But not now sir,' – he glanced at the station clock – 'my train's got steam up and I can't wait.'

'To Norwich? Then frank me through, Jammy, for old times' sake. Tell this fellow I'm not a villain trying to get a ride for nothing. Here, young man, Mr Peach and I are friends from way way back. He'll speak for me.'

Again Jammy looked up at the clock. 'Tomorrow, Mr Tom. I'll be on the seven o'clock. We can have a good chat then.' His earnest eyes begged for release.

'For the love of God, an open truck'll do, I beg it of you, Jammy. The family are desperate for me. Home! I'm coming home at last, don't you see?'

Now the stationmaster was marching towards them, and Jammy had seen him, was hastily unrolling his flag. 'Can't, sir, or he'll have my liver out. Old times aren't what they used to be – don't go getting me mixed up inside. Tomorrow, seven o'clock, platform three.' He gave Thomas a sorrowful look and set off at a stumpy run.

'Wait!' Thomas ducked beneath the rope. But it caught on his rucksack, and he had never been nimble.

Rough hands pushed him away. 'Try that once more and I'll call a copper.'

Of a sudden it seemed he had the weight of the ocean on his back. Somewhere in his skull a screw was being tightened, thread by thread, inexorably. Shoulders sagging, the colour draining from his cheeks, eyes dull with pain, he watched Jammy slow to a trot.

A last knot of passengers made a rush for the train; a swirl of dark clothing, without detail except for a man with a winish complexion, about half a length in front, who was shouting, 'Norwich? Is this the Norwich train?'

A porter finished strapping a tarpaulin over the cases. He jumped down from the roof. 'Hurry up there, ladies and gents, over an hour before the next one,' he urged, flinging open a door and making a scooping movement with his arm, like a farmer getting sheep into a pen. The engine-driver was hanging out of his cab, one foot swinging in mid-air, looking back down the train. Jammy was balanced on the running-board. His eyes went from his watch to the overhead clock, to the porters resting on their barrows, to the dwindling file of passengers as they scrambled aboard.

He raised his flag. 'Stand well clear!' He gripped the whistle between his teeth.

'Hurry, miss, hurry. Pick them skirts up now.' The porter jiggled the door handle impatiently.

Still holding the folds of her coat, so that its hem was level with the top of her boots, she paused on the step to thank him. Her dark cowl turned. For an instant, as she looked down at the porter, everything about her was visible to Thomas. That nose, that mouth, those truthful eyes, the spritely, wayward beauty of her face . . . His heart, like an old and faithful hound who heaves himself off his bed on hearing the cry of a distant horn, made a last gargantuan effort. It surged upwards, gorged his veins with love and illumined his entire countenance. 'Em!' he shouted, 'Emily Gage!'

Jammy blew his whistle, two long blasts, and dropped the flag.

Her head snapped back. She looked around, her brown eyes searching. He went up on tiptoes, waving his arms. 'Tomorrow!' he shouted. The porter shoved her in and slammed the door. A succession of blustery snorts rose from the funnel. Salvos of smoke peppered the vault of the huge roof. The wheels began to turn. The red tail lamp glided away into the gloom of the November dusk.

'Hello! Missed the train, did you?' Culverwell was standing at his desk in the hallway, preening his moustaches with the middle joint of his forefinger as he directed his patrons to their rooms.

'Number six this time, General. First floor, turn right. Billy will take your bags up for you. Have you dined? Good good. Breakfast from the usual hour . . . Now, what *are* we to do with you, Mr Gage? I warned you, don't say I didn't.'

'Excursions only, they said.' He thought of telling the Major how he'd seen Emily, but he wanted a bed more, and to keep the memory of that moment to himself.

'If it isn't one thing it's another. But it's a long lane that never turns, that's how I console myself when my plans get in a stew.' Delicately Culverwell traced with his fingernail a path between the slabs of his pomaded hair. 'Still, here we are, and for a hero nothing is impossible today. Would you object to sharing a bed?'

'Anything will do,' Thomas said humbly.

'The company is not what you would choose if you had your own way. You should know that in advance. Perhaps you would wish to camp on a sofa down here? I could shave a few pennies off the price.'

'Very rowdy are they?'

'Some and some. Young bucks – but a point always comes when they get bored with their cards and go out to seek other pleasures. You know how it is at that age. Have a son of your own, do you? Little monkeys, aren't they just . . .' Culverwell chattered on as he looked through his keys. 'Steal the clothes off your back, milk you for money, run up debts as if they were ladders, oh, sons, Mr Gage! Good good, here we are, number seventeen, right at the top. The noise'll guide you there . . . Billy, take Mr Gage's bag and tell one of those whelps he's got to share.'

'May I – Mother Bailey, might a man in some discomfort ask you for a tot?'

'A couple of grains, fifty drops, say?'

'Make it a hundred.'

'Coming up right away. Red as a bishop's nose. Guarantee of a perfect slumber.'

The stairs became narrower and darker, the carpet more threadbare. There was no handrail. Every step was a mountain to be climbed. At last he was there, under the eaves. The boy Billy was holding the door for him. 'Bed on the left, sir. Good luck.' Impulsively, because the bed that was now yards away was the most precious thing in the world, Thomas dug all the remaining change out of his pocket and poured it into Billy's hand. He squeezed past him, lowered his head and went in.

In the centre of the table a candle shone its drab yellow light over wine-glasses and scattered coins. The air was putrid with cigar smoke and coal fumes. On the bare planks beside the chair of each of the three card-players was an open bottle of wine. Coats off, cravats awry, young faces flushed by heat and the temper of luck – he took it in at a glance, and went across to the bed on which Billy had set his rucksack.

'Good Lord, look what's turned up. Is it an apparition I see? The ancient mariner in person? Your deal, get a move on with it.'

Thomas removed his shoes, thinking to himself, Fresh socks for the homecoming. He took out his knife and the picture of Fred, pushed the rucksack off the pillow and lay down.

'Hey, make sure you're the other way round by the time I get in. Last man to arrive gets the arse end, that's the rule. What's the knife for, Methuselah?'

'Tomorrow I was going to kill a man called Gooby.'

'What, were? A viler name I never did hear. Death to all Goobys is what I say. Hell's teeth, Boot, why do you always deal me twos and piddling threes? You're a crook, do you know that? Care for a splash of red, Mr Thingamebob?'

Boot, was it really possible? There'd been a man called Dog Jennings, dead for many a long year now. But who'd want to go through life being called Boot? He must have misheard. Everything was unravelling at the seams. It was probably Bute, another of those bottle-nosed Scotsmen on the make.

He held Fred in front of his face. What had happened to that tiny portrait of himself he'd painted into the corner? Gone? In such a twinkling? 'Rubbishy paints, sack the fellow,' he tried to say but the words refused to obey him. Paralysis had seized the muscles at the base of his tongue, and nothing came out save a choking gurgle. He wrapped his arms round his head, clamped his eyes shut and bolted them. He'd never experienced such agony before. The fluids sluicing his brain had become petrified. Someone was inside his skull attempting to break it apart with a mattock, a prisoner whom he'd wrongfully confined and who was now flattening the walls with colossal swinging blows. Perhaps it was a cricket ball striking the cranium, the Brighton doctor had offered. Only a cellar lintel, he'd said, because the lady was thirsty and I hurried and in love. Was this his reward? Was Nina to kill him a second time? Was it true what they said about one's portrait fading in the last moments?

But he had things to do. Emily – Isabel – and a gig of canary yellow, like Tobias Rouch's, to carry him home down the long slow road to Fordwell. Count the chimney pots, test Emily on the window-panes—

A hand was rocking his shoulder. A monstrous, pulverising din enveloped him. 'You alright, Methuselah?'

Water, he heard water booming into an empty cistern, and tiny bubbling splashes as frogs jumped in. Why should they do that? Had there been a drought in Norfolk? The sound of the water grew solid as it reached the lip, and ceased. He reached behind him; gripped the bedposts; waited for the hammer to strike the nail.

'No snivelling, Papa.' The voice was like gossamer, as silvery as the powder on a moth's wings.

His tired brown eyes sprang open, marvellously wide and round. 'I'm sorry, old fellow. It'll be a fearful nuisance getting me down those stairs. You were as light as a pinch of hay,' he said with absolute clarity.

The hammer fell; the explosion rang out. He arched his back violently. A shiver travelled upwards through his stomach and chest, imparting a ripple to his coat. Millions of small, oval, pearl-grey leaves flowed through a sky that was transparent and without boundaries. He reached up, as if to pull them towards him. Several times his fingers clenched and opened. He groaned deeply; his arm slackened and fell, over the side of the bed, knuckles on the floor, palm upturned.

The card-players gathered round him.

'Anyone know who he is?'

'Some old soldier. Wonder if Culverwell had the money off him first.'

'What was the name of that chap he was going to kill? He'd have fetched the kinks out of the hangman's rope, that's for certain.'

'Gooby.'

They returned to the table. 'First one-eyed jack goes down and tells Culverwell. Agreed?' The youth they called Boot dealt with deliberation, manoeuvring the cards round the candle and the glasses, looking at the corner of each before he turned it.

Thomas was sure he was smiling. The leaves were beginning to settle, noiselessly, like flakes of ash, upon a plain of loose brown soil. In the centre, a diminutive black figure, stood a pug trying to catch them. He heard the contemptuous snap of its jaws. Someone laughed, not coarsely but with true merriment. Others joined in, out of his sight, he thought from a glade behind him. He looked cautiously over his shoulder. The air slid from between his pores as it had from the flounces of Bella Cartwright's ball-gown.